AF559717

Tareekh Pe Justice

Tareekh Pe Justice

Reforms for India's District Courts

Prashant Reddy T.
Chitrakshi Jain

SIMON &
SCHUSTER

London · New York · Sydney · Toronto · New Delhi

First published in India by Simon & Schuster India, 2025

1 3 5 7 9 10 8 6 4 2

Simon & Schuster India
818, Indraprakash Building,
21, Barakhamba Road,
New Delhi 110001.

www.simonandschuster.co.in

Hardcover ISBN: 978-81-982003-0-3
eBook ISBN: 978-81-982003-6-5

Typeset in India by SÜRYA, New Delhi
Printed and bound in India by Replika Press Pvt. Ltd.

For Vaishnavi & Laasya

—Prashant Reddy Thikkavarapu

For my parents, Anjuli and Pavan

—Chitrakshi Jain

Contents

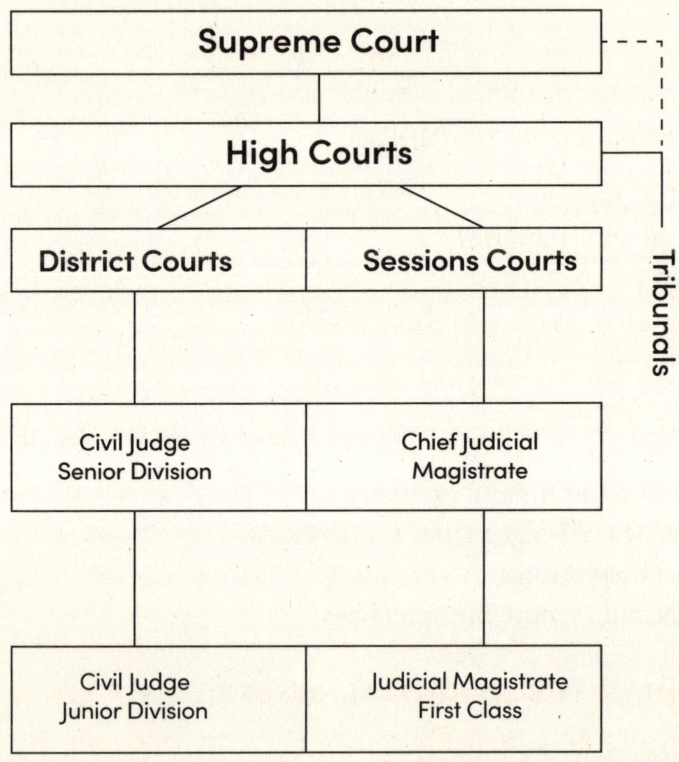
Judicial Architecture
Supreme Court
High Courts
District Courts
Sessions Courts
Tribunals
Civil Judge
Senior Division
Chief Judicial
Magistrate
Civil Judge
Junior Division
Judicial Magistrate
First Class

Introduction

One of the most iconic movie dialogues that captures the essence of public frustration with the Indian justice system is from the Hindi movie *Damini*, where Sunny Deol, playing the role of an angry young lawyer faced with yet another adjournment, screams out in rage at the judge: '*Tareekh pe tareekh, tareekh pe tareekh milti gayi*, My Lord, *par insaaf nahi mila*!'[1]

Loosely translated into English, the dialogue means, 'We have received only adjournments from this court, but we have never received justice.' Of course, the Hindi version carries a certain 'zing' that gets lost in translation.

The dialogue has even made its way into official records, with judges and policymakers referencing it to explain their frustration with the workings of Indian courts. In 2018, the authors of the Economic Survey, the government's key pre-budget publication on the state of the economy, fell back on Deol's famous rant while moaning about how delays in the justice system were frustrating enforcement of contracts and negatively affecting economic growth.[2] As recently as 2022, a High Court judge who was obviously resigned to the adjournment culture in his courtroom noted in his order: 'Today learned counsel for the respondent is absent, so again a "tareekh". The fate of this case is "Tareekh Pe Tareekh". So, another "tareekh" is given.'[3] Even former Chief Justice of India D. Y. Chandrachud has referenced the iconic dialogue in open court to warn a lawyer seeking an adjournment against converting the Supreme Court into a 'tareekh pe tareekh' court.[4] In each of these official utterances, there is a sense of resignation towards the culture of adjournments that has consumed Indian courts.

There is a very real human cost to this 'tareekh pe tareekh' culture which takes many forms at the level of district courts: the undertrial prisoner who languishes in jail awaiting trial, the young protester who must spend days to get bail, the mother who is unable to get maintenance for herself or her child after walking out of an abusive marriage, the worker who has been wrongfully terminated from employment, the businessperson who faces losses due to delays in enforcing a contract and, of course, the farmer who has to fight the state in court for years in order to get fair compensation for farmland that the government has acquired. Each of these failures is a blemish on the promise of justice, liberty and equality made in the Preamble to the Constitution.

Seven years before the movie *Damini* indicted the Indian justice system, the Government of India had rather brazenly denounced the Indian judiciary before an American court. The backdrop to this episode was the Bhopal gas tragedy in 1984. Two years later, the Government of India sued Union Carbide Corporation (UCC) before a federal district court in the United States for the deaths caused by the leak of a poisonous gas from its storage facility in Bhopal. The leak killed an estimated 3,787 Indian citizens and injured another 5,58,125 citizens.[5] It remains the world's worst industrial disaster.

At the time, in an attempt to get the case thrown out from the American legal system, UCC invoked the doctrine of *forum non conveniens*. UCC's simple argument was that it would be more convenient for an Indian court to hear the case since the tragedy had occurred in India and all the evidence and witnesses were located in the country. In rebuttal, the Government of India made the stunning argument that the Indian judiciary, burdened by its colonial legacy, was not up to the task of delivering justice in a complicated case like the Bhopal gas tragedy! The task of defending the Indian justice system fell upon UCC! The following was the reporting in the *New York Times* about the arguments in the case:

> India's lawyers insisted that Indians could not get justice in their country. They cited court inefficiencies, fees and other obstacles, called the legal structure obsolete and procedures for gathering

> evidence inadequate. It was left to Carbide to defend India's law while promising the judge that it would cooperate in providing evidence and abiding by Indian judgments.[6]

The subsequent judgment of the American district court summarized the arguments of the Indian government in the following words:

> . . . plaintiffs, including the Union of India, have argued that the courts of India are not up to the task of conducting the Bhopal litigation. These assert that the Indian judiciary has yet to reach full maturity due to the restraints placed upon it by British colonial rulers who shaped the Indian legal system to meet their own ends. Plaintiffs allege that the Indian justice system has not yet cast off the burden of colonialism to meet the emerging needs of a democratic people.[7]

It was perhaps unprecedented in the history of the world for the government of a sovereign country to argue, before a foreign court, that its own judicial system was incapable of delivering justice with the same efficiency as a foreign judicial system. Yet, this is exactly the legal strategy adopted by the Government of India almost four decades after independence from the British.

To help establish the problems with the Indian judiciary, the Government of India engaged Prof. Marc Galanter as an expert witness to testify on the state of the Indian legal system. A professor at the University of Wisconsin Law School, Galanter is a celebrated scholar on the Indian legal system. In his testimony before the American court, Galanter explained the many problems afflicting the Indian judiciary. These included an alleged shortage of judges, poor infrastructure and a number of observations on a staggering backlog of cases. His testimony was backed by observations from the reports of the Law Commission of India and judgments from Indian courts.[8] It was left to the expert witnesses of Union Carbide, including the legendary Indian lawyer Nani Palkhivala, to defend the Indian judiciary and its capability to hear a case as complex as the Bhopal gas tragedy.[9]

Judge Keenan of the United States District Court for the Southern District of New York, who was the presiding judge, was unconvinced with the arguments of the Government of India and concluded, in a judgment delivered in 1986, that Indian 'courts have the proven capacity to mete out fair and equal justice' and that he 'defers to the adequacy and ability of the courts of India'.[10] The Government of India lost that case and eventually had to go back to the Indian judicial system where the case was settled under a cloud of controversy.

Not all foreign judges have been as deferential to the capabilities of the Indian judiciary as Judge Keenan. There have been several cases in both the United Kingdom and the United States where courts have come to the opposite conclusion and deemed Indian courts incapable of rendering timely justice. The Law Commission of India has documented these cases in its 188th report published in 2004, while stoutly defending the Indian judicial system and claiming that 'there can be no general presumption of delays in all types of cases in India'.[11] In addition, an international arbitral tribunal, in 2010, concluded that the inability of the Supreme Court of India to decide a case pending before it for over nine years was a breach of an obligation owed by India, under a bilateral investment treaty, to provide investors with an 'effective means of asserting claims and enforcing rights'.[12] As a result, the Indian government had to pay the Australian investor who had sued it a sum of $4.7 million.

Simply put, the Indian judiciary's 'tareekh pe tareekh' syndrome is not just a national tragedy that is the subject matter for angry dialogues by fictional lawyers, despondent judges and policymakers, but also an international embarrassment for the country with direct consequences for the Indian economy.

The typical response of the Indian judiciary to complaints about delays has been to point a finger at the Union and state governments, accusing them of not appointing enough judges and failing to provide sufficient funding. The Indian judiciary has been incredibly successful in pushing the 'resource crunch' narrative to explain its extraordinary inefficiency. This narrative has been built through a combination of actions by the Supreme Court of India, the Law Commission of India, which is generally headed by a retired judge of the Supreme Court, and the All India Judges Association (AIJA), a professional body of judges who staff the district judiciary, which is the first point of contact for most litigants.

Since the year 1989, AIJA has been filing petitions in public interest (known as public interest litigation or PIL) before the Supreme Court of India demanding better working conditions for its members. This includes better pay, accommodation, vehicles for transportation of judges, an increase in retirement age, etc.[13] The Supreme Court, in an unbridled display of judicial activism, has indulged AIJA's demands, ordering the Union and state governments to comply with them. This, despite constitutional propriety requiring the court to defer to elected legislatures on any decision regarding the expenditure of public money. In these judgments, the Supreme Court has also gone to the extent of prescribing specific formulae to calculate the number of judges required by district judiciary and has also altered the qualification requirements for the district judiciary, despite the Constitution vesting these powers in states and the High Courts.[14]

To be fair to the Union and state governments in India, not only have they nearly tripled the strength of judges at the level of the district judiciary from 7,675 to 25,511 (approximately 5,000 posts remain vacant) between the years 1987 and 2023, they have also poured in money for building judicial infrastructure and digitization programmes exclusively for the district judiciary.[15] Since the year 1993–94, approximately Rs 10,000 crore has been allocated by Parliament for the building of courtrooms and residences for judges of the district judiciary.[16] Since states have to contribute their funds to this scheme, the actual figure is much higher. The Central Sector Scheme for the e-courts project for the digitization of the courts has released Rs 2,308 crore since 2007.[17] The XIII Finance Commission allocated an additional amount of Rs 5,000 crore specifically for the judiciary.[18] These are significant amounts allocated by Parliament in addition to the annual spending by states on salaries, maintenance, etc. for the district judiciary. Clearly, the political class has responded to the call for greater spending on the district judiciary. In addition, the Government of India, through Parliament, has created new judicial fora, like consumer courts and Debts Recovery Tribunals, which have diverted significant volumes of complex litigation away from the district courts, considerably reducing stress on the district judiciary.

Yet, none of these additional resources, in terms of more judges and more money, appear to have made a discernible difference to the mountain of cases and horrifying delays at the level of the district judiciary. As per the most recent figures available on the National Judicial Data Grid (NJDG), there are approximately 1 crore cases (presuming that the figures are accurate) that have been pending for more than five years before the district judiciary. The cumulative pendency before the district judiciary is approximately 5 crore cases. The human stories behind these frightening statistics are painfully recounted in a steady stream of reporting by the press. These include stunning delays faced by innocent citizens who have been jailed for years before being acquitted by the courts. It appears that despite all the additional judges and funding provided to the district judiciary over the last few decades, India is no closer to solving the problem of judicial delays.

It may be time to confront the prospect that perhaps a lack of resources was never the main reason for the mind-boggling delays faced by litigants at the level of the district judiciary. Perhaps the Supreme Court and the rest of the pundits have misdiagnosed the issue by focusing on an alleged shortage of judges at the level of the district judiciary. Perhaps the problem lies elsewhere.

In this book, our attempt is to go beyond the usual scapegoat of 'resource crunch' and offer alternate explanations for the delays at the level of the district judiciary.

We focus on the district judiciary, which consists of three tiers of judges: Civil Judge (Junior Division), Civil Judge (Senior Division) and District Judge, who is senior to the former two categories. These judges can also hear criminal cases when designated as Judicial Magistrate of First Class, Chief Judicial Magistrate and Sessions Judge. In many states, these judges will hear both civil and criminal cases and will be known by both titles. These judges are the first point of contact for most litigants in India, be it bail, criminal prosecutions, contractual disputes, compensation for accidents, protective orders for women facing domestic violence, divorce cases, injunctions against demolitions of houses by the government, etc. This is the layer of the justice system that has an immediate impact on the daily lives of Indians.

Our attempt at reframing the debate on reforming the district judiciary has five themes.

The first aims at shifting the primary focus of the debate away from the 'resource crunch' argument to the rarely discussed issue of *how states and High Courts appoint, transfer, evaluate, discipline and remove judges of the district judiciary*. Many of these practices date back to colonial times, when the district judiciary was modelled on the lines of the civil bureaucracy. Our working hypothesis is that the district judiciary basically lacks the 'decisional independence' to deliver fearless and decisive justice. This is because they are constantly worrying about reprisals in the form of disciplinary inquiries by High Courts. Add to this fear, bizarre transfer policies and a rickety performance assessment system, and it quickly becomes clear that the system incentivizes judges to avoid hearing risky and complex cases. In our opinion, these are the issues at the core of the astonishing judicial delays at the level of the district judiciary.

The second is to *fix accountability* of the Supreme Court and High Courts for their acts of omission, opacity and activism that have contributed in substantial part to the poor administration of the district judiciary. From discontinuing the publication of judicial statistics to adopting faulty methodologies to calculate the adequate number of judges to operating in extreme opacity to negotiating budgetary demands with governments at the gunpoint of contempt notices, the higher judiciary has contributed generously to the woeful state of the district judiciary. In particular, we highlight the opacity of the High Courts which control the administration of the district judiciary and the dangers of approaching complex problems of judicial administration through the route of judicial activism. Court-room policymaking by the High Courts and the Supreme Court is an affront to the constitutional scheme of separation of powers. It also excludes experts and citizens from exercising their democratic right to participate in policymaking.

The third theme deals with the *structural reforms* required to create a more efficient, powerful and accessible district judiciary. This is a discussion that includes not just the seemingly mundane issue of how the judiciary manages the small army of bureaucrats working behind the scenes to serve summons, manage dockets, take dictation from the judge, etc. but also the very interesting question of whether India needs a separate Union judiciary in addition to the state judiciaries, as is the case in the United States, which also has a federal system of administration where powers are distributed between the federal and state governments. After all, the Indian Constitution expressly allows for such a scheme and there are considerable advantages of imitating the American system. Inherent in this discussion is the question of improving access to justice by devolving key judicial powers from the High Courts to the district judiciary. It is important to discuss these issues because the present structure of the Indian judiciary was devised by the British more than 170 years ago and has remained unchanged since.

The fourth theme is to reiterate the *importance of procedural law,* which, along with 'resource crunch', has been the primary target of judicial reforms since Independence. For example, it is common to hear demands for limits on the number of adjournments granted by any judge in a single case, but an existing procedural clause limiting adjournments has already failed spectacularly. On the other hand, there is the seeming popularity of PILs, which offer the illusion of swift, definitive justice by completely ignoring procedural laws. Encoded in the debate over procedural law are differing visions of 'rule of law'. Strict procedural law recognizes the reality that even judges must be restrained from abusing their power and that fair procedural rules ensure equal treatment of all litigants. A more cynical view will condemn procedural laws for making litigation more complicated, expensive and inaccessible for the common person. These cynics also argue for giving judges a wider latitude, unrestrained by procedural encumbrances, to do justice as they see fit. This is an issue that eludes simplistic arguments but has divided proponents of judicial reform in the country.

The fifth theme is about *bringing back the participation of people in the justice system*. With the abolishment of juries, the Indian courtroom has completely eliminated the participation of people in the justice system. The move to eliminate juries was spearheaded by legal elites who were contemptuous of the ability of ordinary citizens to participate in the justice system. Not only has the abolition of juries robbed India of a crucial opportunity to educate the citizenry about the workings and realities of the justice system, but it has also reduced the justice system to a system controlled entirely by judges and lawyers. This alienation of citizens from the justice system has likely contributed to the steady erosion of its legitimacy in the eyes of the common citizen. It may be an opportune time to bring back the participation of people in the courtroom, if it helps restore some faith in the Indian legal system.

Over twelve chapters, these five themes intersect in different ways as we explore workable paths to reforming India's district judiciary.

PART ONE

About the Judges

The focus of Part I of this book is on the most ignored persons within the Indian legal system—the judges of the district judiciary who decide the fate of millions of litigants. In particular, we examine the disciplinary rules regulating the conduct of these judges and the performance assessment policies which may be contributing to, if not incentivizing, delays.

As we will establish over the course of the next few chapters, these judges are subject to an opaque disciplinary mechanism that can result in unfair punishment for alleged legal errors in their judgments, despite no allegations of corruption. Even in cases of alleged corruption, the disciplinary proceedings conducted by High Courts against the district judiciary are opaque and often unfair. We argue in the first three chapters that the disciplinary measures put in place by High Courts to ostensibly hold the district judiciary accountable have most likely created an atmosphere of 'fear' amongst these judges. As a result, these judges are likely 'fearful' of handling cases perceived to be 'risky' from a disciplinary standpoint. This risk-averse behaviour then, possibly, leads to judges avoiding 'risky' cases or, worse, 'risky' remedies, such as the grant of bail in cases involving serious crimes.

Two additional aspects that facilitate, if not encourage, this practice of avoiding risky or complex cases, are the transfer policies that shift judges across a state or city and the performance assessment system put in place to review the disposal rates of individual judges. Together, these policies have created the perfect incentive for judges to pick and choose cases that help them meet targets used to evaluate their performance, while avoiding risky or complex cases, until they are transferred to a different court complex where the same cycle restarts. As a result, the 'risky' and complex cases, which also tend to be time-consuming, are likely to fall behind in the queue, while the easier and less risky cases get resolved.

The last chapter in this part deals with the practice of appointing young and inexperienced lawyers as judges to the first tier of the district judiciary, which is the office of the Civil Judge (Junior Division) and Judicial

Magistrate First Class. The system currently in place to select these judges dates back to the 19th century when India was still ruled by the British. This issue deserves urgent attention, as no amount of judicial independence or increased funding for the district judiciary will suffice if India continues to select the wrong candidates for these critical judicial offices.

1

Fearful Judges

In November 2022, shortly after being appointed as the head of the Supreme Court, Chief Justice of India (CJI) D. Y. Chandrachud, in a public speech discussing the reluctance of the district judiciary in granting bail to undertrial prisoners, remarked, 'Judges at the grassroots are reluctant to grant bail not because they do not understand crime, but there is sense of fear of being targeted for granting bail in heinous cases.'[1]

This talking point has been reiterated by other judges of the higher judiciary, but they too have been cryptic and have steered clear of explaining who is 'targeting' judges for performing routine judicial functions like granting bail.[2] After all, the judiciary in India is insulated from the government. In particular, Article 235 of the Constitution has vested 'control' of the district judiciary with the judges of High Courts.

The Constituent Assembly gave High Courts this power over the district judiciary after a specific demand, in a memorandum submitted by the Conference of Judges consisting of judges who staffed the erstwhile Federal Court and High Courts.[3] The demand for such control was justified by the Conference of Judges on the grounds that the district judiciary could be influenced by state governments if the latter had the power to influence transfers, postings, promotions, etc. of the district judiciary. In response, the Constituent Assembly inserted Article 235 into the Constitution.[4] This Article clearly spells out that High Courts will have the power to control transfers and promotions of the district judiciary. Further, the Supreme Court has interpreted the phrase 'control' in Article 235 to mean that High Courts would have the last word on investigating and disciplining judges of the district judiciary.[5]

As a result, state governments practically have no say in any disciplinary action taken against the district judiciary by the High Courts. They are bound by the decisions of the High Courts and merely issue the necessary orders in the name of the governor. This arrangement means that the district judiciary is effectively insulated from the state governments. So, if not the state governments, whom are the judges of the district judiciary in 'fear of', as hinted by CJI Chandrachud?

In our opinion, the 'fear' within the judges of the district judiciary is the possibility of having to face disciplinary action at the hands of High Court judges, who may be of the opinion that a judgment is erroneous. These disciplinary actions take place despite there being no allegation of corruption or other forms of misconduct by the judge. Simply put, judges of the district judiciary have calculated that in order to avoid the possibility of disciplinary action for granting bail, it is better to deny bail. This problem, which extends beyond bail petitions to other categories of cases, appears to be unique to the district judiciary in India, with no parallels in countries with legal systems similar to that of India.

In countries like the United Kingdom and the United States, judges have qualified immunity against complaints about their judgments, unless backed by allegations of corruption or misconduct, such as allegations of bias by the judge. For example, the Judicial Conduct Rules, 2023 in the UK specifically require the Judicial Conduct Investigations Office to dismiss any complaints about judicial decisions or judicial case management unless it raises a question of misconduct.[6] Similarly, in the US, rules framed under the Judicial Conduct and Disability Act make it clear that federal judges will not be investigated for any 'allegation that calls into question the correctness of a judge's ruling, including a failure to recuse'.[7] However, if the decision is alleged to be the result of an improper motive, such as bribes, racial bias or other improper conduct such as derogatory comments, an investigation can follow against the judge, but even then, that investigation will not get into the legal reasoning in the judgment. Similarly, most states in the US also provide for similar immunities to judges of the state judiciaries.[8] The underlying logic of providing such immunity is that judges can differ on their interpretation of the law and if at all there is an erroneous judgment, the appellate courts will correct it if an appeal is filed challenging it.

The lack of similar immunity in India for judges of the district judiciary has led to a situation where they have been subject to disciplinary inquiries by High Courts for alleged flaws in their judgments. These inquiries have been instituted against individual judges on grounds that they have been too liberal in granting bail, too lenient in sentencing the guilty, for acquitting persons accused of serious crimes, for being liberal in granting compensation in cases of land acquisition and for granting temporary injunctions against the government without prior notice. These are not hypotheticals but actual cases where judges of the district judiciary have been subject to disciplinary inquiries despite no allegation of misconduct, such as corruption.

These inquiries were initiated solely because some person within a High Court, quite often a judge or a registrar, was of the opinion that a particular judgment was flawed. The following extract of a judgment rendered by Justice Atul Sreedharan of the Madhya Pradesh High Court has explained the role of the Registrar-Vigilance in the High Court, who is usually a district judge on a temporary posting with the High Court and oversees complaints of corruption against the district judiciary[9]:

> The combined effect of some members of the bar and disgruntled litigants, ever ready to complain against judges by anonymous communication coupled at times with an overzealous District Judge (Vigilance and Inspection), out to prove the worth of his existence, whose overbearing presence and attitude of selectively examining the orders passed by the Judges of the District Judiciary relating to anticipatory bail, regular bail and acquittals (especially in those cases relating to heinous offences or cases which acquire prominence in

> the print, electronic and social media), has a demoralising effect on the Judges of the District Judiciary for whom such action is the proverbial sword of Damocles, perpetually hanging over their heads, always threatening to drop.
>
> The office of the District Judge (Vigilance and Training) continues to have a debilitating effect on independence and individuality of the judges of the District Judiciary. The post is a surplus appendage, akin to a vestigial organ in the body of the Judiciary in the State of Madhya Pradesh.
>
> Sometimes, the post can be occupied by an individual who to prove his preeminent importance to the High Court, as a conduit of information, can assess the orders of the Judges and comment upon the same being passed with a dishonest motive only because in his or her opinion, the order is bad in law. This demotivates the Judges of the District Judiciary, especially in criminal cases from doing justice and may convict in the absence or inadequacy of evidence and dismiss bail applications even in cases in which were fit to be granted bail.

The above extract is a rare instance where a judge of a High Court has broken the judicial 'omerta' to broach a topic that even judges of the Supreme Court have only hinted at in their public speeches. While the Registrar-Vigilance is clearly one of the key players, as mentioned in this judgment, it should be clarified that the decision-making powers in most states is actually in the hands of High Court judges. The Registrar-Vigilance at most can get the ball rolling to initiate a disciplinary inquiry against judges of the district judiciary but the actual inquiry itself is either conducted or supervised by High Court judges. There is little that the Registrar-Vigilance can do without the nod of judges of the High Court and much of the scathing criticism of the Registrar-Vigilance quoted earlier should be read as an implicit indictment of High Court judges.

These disciplinary inquires, conducted by administrative committees of judges of the High Court, conclude with recommendations of punishments, which necessarily have to be endorsed by the full court, which consists of all judges of the High Court. These punishments range from the dismissal of judges of the district judiciary from the judicial service to the docking of their pay or increments or pension (in case of retired judges). A milder form of punishment is an 'adverse' entry in the Annual Confidential Report (ACR), which is a performance assessment report prepared for every judge of the district judiciary. An adverse entry can have either an immediate fallout for judges, affecting their career progression, or long-term consequences in the form of compulsory retirement, as discussed later.

These various forms of punishment that can be inflicted on the district judiciary, despite there being no allegations of bribery or other misconduct, is likely the cause of 'fear' amongst these judges. Such pervasive insecurity effectively means that the district judiciary in India lacks adequate 'decisional independence', which is a core component of judicial independence. This issue does not get any attention in the press or academia, unlike the constant spotlight on the perceived and actual threats to the Supreme Court and High Courts from the government, especially when headed by powerful prime ministers who have won resounding electoral mandates. These threats to the higher judiciary were well understood by the framers of the Constitution of India, who guaranteed these judges security of tenure in office by allowing for their impeachment through a procedurally complex process, only on the limited grounds of 'proven misbehaviour' or 'incapacity'.

The Constitution, however, does not give similar protections to judges of the district judiciary. In fact, as mentioned earlier, it is entirely silent on any protections for the district judiciary since it was presumed that placing them under the control of High Courts would automatically protect their independence. While this arrangement may help in protecting the district judiciary from retribution by state governments, it has done little to protect the district judiciary from High Courts. Ideally, state legislatures should have put in place a transparent and fair disciplinary framework for High Courts to exercise disciplinary power over the district judiciary. That never happened.

Instead, the district judiciary have been subject to the same disciplinary framework that applies to the bureaucracy of the state government, except for the fact that it is the High Court, and not the state government, which administers the disciplinary proceedings. For example, in Uttar Pradesh, judges of the district judiciary have historically been disciplined and removed from office under the UP Government Servants Conduct Rules, 1956 which also apply to the bureaucracy of the state government. Similarly in Karnataka, the relevant rules under which the district judiciary are disciplined are the Karnataka Civil Services (Classification, Control and Appeal) Rules, 1957 which also apply to the bureaucracy of the state government. In the state of Delhi, the district judiciary are subject to the All India Services (Conduct) Rules, 1968 which also apply to the Indian Administrative Service (IAS) and the Indian Police Service (IPS). Even the states which have separate rules for the district judiciary tend to model such rules on the disciplinary rules for the bureaucracy.

The problem with this arrangement is that the job of a judge is very different from that of a bureaucrat. A judge of the district judiciary is responsible for adjudicating disputes between the state and citizens or between citizens themselves. In almost every case, a judge necessarily has to rule against at least one litigant. The prospect of unhappy litigants and their lawyers filing complaints against a judge who passed an unfavourable order is very high. Given this reality, it does not make sense to subject judges to the exact same standards of conduct as the bureaucracy.

The problem is further exacerbated by the fact that the standards of conduct laid down in these disciplinary rules are remarkably vague and include requirements such as maintaining a 'devotion to duty'. It is these ambiguous standards that have been invoked by High Courts to initiate inquiries against judges of the district judiciary for allegedly erroneous judgments, despite no evidence of corruption or other forms of misconduct.

Since this entire disciplinary mechanism against the district judiciary operates behind a veil of secrecy, the inquiry reports are not publicly available, even under the RTI Act. The only source of public information on these disciplinary inquiries against the district judiciary are the judgments delivered by High Courts and the Supreme Court when judges of the district judiciary challenge findings of misconduct and punishments meted out to them. Unlike the secretive disciplinary proceedings, legal challenges filed before High Courts and Supreme Court are public proceedings and hence the judgments are publicly available. What follows next is a narration of disciplinary inquiries, as recounted in these judgments.

Investigation of judges administering the criminal justice system

The most worrying instances are those where judges of the district judiciary have been subjected to disciplinary inquiries for their judgments in criminal prosecutions. These include instances where judges have been hauled up for granting bail, acquitting citizens in criminal prosecutions and awarding lenient sentences where the accused were found guilty. A few illustrative examples are discussed below.

The first case on the list is of District Judge J. K. Verma of the Madhya Pradesh Higher Judicial Service. The Madhya Pradesh High Court initiated an inquiry against him for allegedly granting bail improperly in thirty cases without applying his mind and without recording proper reasons. The inquiry officer found no evidence of corruption but did criticize the manner in which the judge had granted bail in these cases. The disciplinary committee of the High Court concluded that the judge was reckless in granting bail and on the basis of its recommendation, the judge was dismissed from his job by the state government on 30 January 1999.[10]

When Judge Verma sought a judicial review of the decision before the High Court, a bench of two judges dismissed his petition in a detailed judgment dated 15 July 2011, which was delivered twelve years after he first approached the court. The court reasoned as follows[11]:

> Even though there may be no direct evidence to show corrupt or improper motive, but the question is as to whether a judicial officer having more than 20 years of service can be let off merely because the material on record does not directly establish corrupt motive. If a judicial officer acts in the matter of granting bail or deals with a criminal case improperly in an isolated case or one or two cases, the benefit can be granted to the judicial officer, but when within

> a short span of time, in more than 22 cases, consistently it is seen that the judicial officer has acted in a manner which cannot be approved of in any manner whatsoever, the inference of improper motive and extraneous consideration can always be drawn.

In simple English, the Madhya Pradesh High Court concluded that it was okay to draw an 'inference of improper motive and extraneous consideration' against judges of the district judiciary if they were 'reckless' in granting bail, despite there being no evidence of corruption against the judge. The Supreme Court declined to hear an appeal filed by Judge Verma.[12]

The second case is of District Judge Krishna Prasad Verma from Bihar. The Patna High Court initiated a disciplinary inquiry levelling two charges against Judge Verma. The first charge accused Judge Verma of granting bail to a particular accused after the High Court had rejected a bail petition by the same accused. It should be noted that the law does not bar district judges from granting bail if the High Court has rejected previous bail petitions. The second charge against Judge Verma is reproduced as follows[13]:

> You, Sri Krishna Prasad Verma while functioning as Additional District and Sessions Judge, Chapra with an intent to acquit Raju Mistry, the main accused in N.D.P.S. Case No.15/2000 arising out of Revealganj P.S. Case No.137/2000 (G.R. No.1569 of 2000) registered under sections 22, 23 and 24 of the Narcotic Drugs and Psychotropic Substances Act, 1985 closed the proceeding in great haste resulting in acquittal of Raju Mistry, who was charged of driving a Jeep bearing No.W.B.C.4049 carrying 90 Kg. Charas, without exhausting all coercive methods to record the statement of the Investigating Officer of the case as there is no proof on the record to show that the non-bailable warrant issued against the said Investigating Officer was ever served on him. The aforesaid act of yours is indicative of some extraneous considerations which tantamounts to gross judicial impropriety, judicial indiscipline, lack of integrity, gross misconduct and an act of unbecoming of a Judicial Officer.

This was an astonishing charge because the investigating officer failed to show up in court on eighteen different occasions to testify before the judge. The public prosecutor had informed the judge in writing that he was unable to produce the officer before the court![14] Despite no evidence or allegations of corruption against Judge Verma, disciplinary proceedings were initiated against the judge.

The Patna High Court's disciplinary inquiry found against Judge Verma on both charges. The High Court punished him by withholding most of his pay during his period of suspension and also held him back from being considered for any promotions for three years.[15] It took Judge Verma a legal battle spanning ten years, including eight years before the Supreme Court, before he was exonerated of all charges in a judgment dated 26 September 2019.[16] In its judgment, the Supreme Court cautioned High Courts against initiating disciplinary proceedings over allegedly erroneous judgments unless there were 'clear-cut allegations of misconduct, extraneous influences, gratification of any kind, etc.'. Not only High Courts, but other judges of the Supreme Court have routinely ignored this cautionary advice.

In another instance, the Patna High Court punished a retired judge by docking his entire pension on the grounds that he granted bail improperly. Once again there was no allegation of corruption against the judge in this case. [17] The retired judge had to fight a legal battle for eight long years before the Patna High Court set aside the punishment and restored his pension.

A third example, this time from Gujarat, is the case of Chief Judicial Magistrate R. R. Parekh, who was the subject of two disciplinary inquiries that began in the years 2000 and 2001. Both inquiries pertained to lenient sentences given by Judge Parekh after finding the accused guilty and also one charge of improperly transferring cases to himself. The relevant portion of the one publicly available charge, accusing Judge Parekh of ignoring the minimum sentencing provisions applicable to the offence of smuggling silver, is reproduced below[18]:

> Thus, the manner and mode in which you awarded the sentence in Cri. Case Nos.675/94 & 1293/95, clearly show that the accused

> had managed with you for showing favour in awarding sentence and accordingly, you awarded the punishment fixing the term of sentence in such a way that the accused need not have to remain in custody for any longer period and thereby:
> (a) You are guilty of indulging in Corrupt-practice.
> (b) You are guilty of dereliction in discharging your judicial functions.
> (c) You acted in a manner unbecoming of a Judicial Officer.
> These acts of yours, would amount to acts of grave misconduct and tantamount to conduct unbecoming of a Judicial Officer, violating the provisions contained in Rule 3 of the Gujarat Civil Services (Conduct) Rules, 1971.

The second inquiry pertained to lenient fines imposed by Judge Parekh in prosecutions under the Factories Act and for improperly transferring pending prosecutions under the Food Adulteration Act to himself.[19]

In both of the disciplinary inquiries, the inquiry officer concluded that there was no evidence of any corruption or conduct unbecoming of a judge and that any legal errors could be rectified via an appeal to a higher court.[20] As for the transfer of cases, the inquiry officer noted in the final report that Judge Parekh explained that his only motive for requesting cases to be transferred was to meet certain targets that judges have for disposing cases.[21] On a separate note, it is worth mentioning that it is common for the district judiciary to ignore minimum sentencing provisions in the law, especially for economic offences.

The recommendations of the inquiry officer were considered by two disciplinary committees consisting of judges of the Gujarat High Court. The first disciplinary committee consisting of two judges agreed with the recommendation of the inquiry officer to exonerate Judge Parekh.[22] However, after a disagreement at the meeting of the full court, a new disciplinary committee was set up to examine the issue. The second disciplinary committee came to a different conclusion and recommended Judge Parekh's dismissal. It stated in the pertinent part[23]:

> . . . even if it is accepted, for the sake of argument, that there was no oblique motive or corrupt practice, even then it would reflect on his functioning as a judicial officer after so much of experience and it would be sheer negligence or recklessness in discharge of his duties which would lead to an inference about the proof of charges regarding dereliction of duty and also having acted in a manner unbecoming of a judicial officer.

The disciplinary committee's recommendation was accepted by the full court and Judge Parekh was dismissed from the judicial service.[24] His petitions challenging the legality of his removal were dismissed by the Gujarat High Court and the Supreme Court.[25] By the time the Supreme Court passed its judgment on 12 July 2016, it had been sixteen years since the first of the two inquiries had been initiated against Judge Parekh.

While the above examples are from Madhya Pradesh, Bihar and Gujarat, we also came across cases from other states where judges have been charged or punished for granting bail and acquitting persons, despite no allegations of corruption or misconduct against them. We did not come across a single case where a judge was subjected to disciplinary inquiries for improperly denying bail or handing out excessive punishments in a manner that hampered the liberty of a citizen.

Judges punished in civil cases over the grant of generous compensation and injunctions against government

In addition to the above examples which pertain to judges being punished for their judgments in criminal cases, we also found cases where judges were punished for their judgments in civil cases, despite no allegations of corruption being made against them. In particular, cases of land acquisition, where district judges have to decide compensation payable by the government for private lands that it has acquired, appear to easily attract such disciplinary inquiries.

Reproduced below is one of the two similar charges framed by the Allahabad High Court in a disciplinary proceeding against District

Judge Sadhna Chaudhary in Uttar Pradesh, where she had increased the compensation payable by the government for the acquired land[26]:

> Charge No.1 That you on 10.02.2003 while posted as IInd Additional District Judge Ghaziabad decided Land Acquisition Reference No.193/1996 Lile Singh Vs. State of U.P. and 35 Agra Development Authority v. State of UP, 2004 All LJ 1853. others illegally and against all judicial norms and propriety awarding to the claimants solatium, additional amount and interest over and above the rate at which two other claimants had entered into compromise which was inclusive of such other benefits at an enhanced rate of Rs.265/ per sq. yard as against Rs.74.40 determined by the S.L.A.O. for land area 276 Bighas 12 Biswas and 15 Biswansi, unduly awarded an additional amount of Rs.47,73,39,903.86 which leads to an inference that you were actuated by extraneous considerations and you thereby failed to maintain absolute integrity and complete devotion to duty and you thus committed misconduct within the meaning of Rule 3 of UP Govt. Servants Conduct rules 1956.

As can be seen, the charge does not actually accuse the judge of receiving a bribe in exchange for increasing the compensation payable. In fact, there was no complaint by the government that had to pay up the higher compensation. Rather, the charge against the judge was that the increase in compensation that she ordered led to 'an inference' that she was influenced by 'extraneous considerations'.[27] This led the inquiry to conclude that she failed to 'maintain absolute integrity and complete devotion to duty', resulting in misconduct. The inquiry led to her dismissal from the judicial service.

Judge Chaudhary had to fight a legal battle for sixteen years, including fourteen years before the Allahabad High Court and another two years before the Supreme Court, in order to have her dismissal set aside by the highest court in the land. This when the Allahabad High Court, on appeal, actually increased compensation in one of the two cases for which she was charged in the inquiry.[28] In its judgment dated 6 March 2020, a clearly unhappy Supreme Court remarked that the honesty and integrity of judges could not be questioned merely because they were liberal in granting bail or awarding compensation in civil cases.[29]

However, merely two years later, when retired District Judge Muzaffar Husain from Uttar Pradesh approached the Supreme Court with facts identical to Judge Chaudhary's case, the court declined to set aside the finding of the disciplinary committee or the punishment of reduction of his pension by 70 per cent. The inquiry against Judge Husain had charged him with improperly increasing the compensation in twelve different cases of land acquisition. Like in Judge Chaudhary's case, there was no allegation that he had received any bribes or other consideration to increase the compensation. The Allahabad High Court took twelve years to decide Judge Husain's petition challenging the reduction of his pension, ultimately ruling against him. On appeal, the Supreme Court took another three years, delivering its judgment on 6 May 2022 upholding the punishment meted out to Judge Husain.[30] Quite incredibly, the bench that heard Judge Husain's case failed to express any reasons for treating his case differently from that of Judge Chaudhary's case despite being made aware of the latter case.

We noticed similar disciplinary inquiries initiated by the Andhra Pradesh High Court and Karnataka High Court against judges for increasing compensation in land acquisition cases.[31]

Apart from land acquisition cases, some High Courts have initiated inquiries against the district judiciary over allegations that they improperly granted temporary injunctions, i.e. judicial orders that impose a temporary restraint on certain activities until the trial can be conducted and evidence parsed. In one such case, the Karnataka High Court charged a civil judge with failure 'to maintain absolute integrity and devotion to duty' because he granted a temporary injunction against the government without first providing it with a mandatory period of notice, as required by the law. It is not uncommon for judges to ignore the mandatory notice period in such cases, especially while granting emergency injunctions. Importantly, there was no allegation of corruption against the judge for granting this particular injunction.

The disciplinary committee constituted by the High Court found against the judge on this and several other charges levelled against him, resulting in his dismissal from the judicial service. Upon challenging his dismissal before the High Court, he was exonerated by the Karnataka High Court and the Supreme Court on this particular charge but was still dismissed on other charges. The legal battle that spanned ten years ended in the judgment of the Supreme Court on 11 April 2023.[32]

In another instance, the Karnataka High Court framed the following charge against a Civil Judge (Junior Division) for allegedly improperly granting injunctions, despite no evidence of corruption[33]:

> That during the year 1998-99, you created factions amongst the advocates and granted temporary injunctions to the members of the Bar and imposed less fines and entertained these advocates who supported your causes, in your Chambers and refused the relief to other advocates and thereby caused discrimination amongst the entire members of the Bar with the prejudiced mind and thereby did an act unbecoming of a Judicial Officer which amounts to misconduct within the meaning of Rule 3(i)(iii) of the Karnataka Civil Services (Conduct) Rules, 1966.

There are examples from other states, too, of the district judiciary being charged with misconduct for the manner in which they granted or vacated interim injunctions in civil cases.[34]

The burden of Annual Confidential Reports and compulsory retirement orders

While disciplinary inquiries are required for the imposition of any penalty under the disciplinary rules, a relatively simpler method to punish judges is for the judges' supervising authority to enter adverse remarks in the Annual Confidential Reports (ACR) of the judges of the district judiciary. The ACR is a method of performance assessment for each judge. For the principal district judges, it is typically the judges of the High Court who make entries in the ACR while it is the district judges who can make such entries for the lower ranks of the district judiciary such as the civil judge or judicial magistrate.

The criteria in the ACRs for which a judge is to be evaluated are worryingly vague and include subjective assessments about the judge's integrity, knowledge of law, quality of judgments, devotion to duty and relationship with the bar. Technically, any adverse entries are to be supported by evidence and communicated to the judge for his response before being finalized in the ACR. This does not always happen.

The question now is whether allegedly erroneous judgments should be the basis of adverse entries in the ACR of a judge. There is at least one judgment of the Supreme Court where the court suggested that instead of punishing judges for supposedly erroneous judgments via the disciplinary rules, the High Court should simply enter adverse entries into the ACRs.[35]

But adverse entries in the ACRs can have adverse effects on a judge's career. For instance, an adverse entry may reduce opportunities for promotions. As a result, judges will sometimes file legal challenges before the High Court contesting the 'adverse entries'.

An illustrative example in this regard is the case of District Judge Musharaff Hussain in Uttar Pradesh. On 2 July 2005, an adverse entry was entered in his ACR with regard to his integrity and his ability to be fair and impartial in dealing with members of the public. The reason was that his supervising judge was of the opinion that in one particular case that had been decided by Judge Hussain, he had 'disbelieved the testimony of injured wife and brother of deceased on whimsical grounds, and acquitted the accused'.[36] Due to the adverse entry, the judge claimed that he was being superseded for promotions. After a lengthy litigation that spanned six years, a Division Bench of the Allahabad High Court concluded in a judgment dated 26 August 2014 that there was no basis for the adverse entry and set it aside.

The more serious consequences of an adverse entry in the ACR for judges is the spectre of 'compulsory retirement'. The way this works is that judges are subjected to a performance review at certain milestone ages, which can result in a premature and forced retirement of the judge from the judicial service, albeit with some retirement benefits. In some states, this can take place at 50, 55 and 58 years. Since the retirement age is generally 60 years in most states, a judge forced to compulsorily retire can lose up to ten years in service. These decisions on 'compulsory retirement', which are taken by administrative committees consisting of judges of High Courts, do consider adverse entries in the ACRs. There is at least one judgment of the Supreme Court declaring that 'even if there is a solitary remark of lack and breach of integrity, that may be sufficient for a Judicial Officer to be compulsory retired'.[37] Given these implications, adverse entries into the ACR may have the same 'chilling' effect on the decisional independence of the district judiciary as a disciplinary inquiry.

Creating fearless judges by giving them immunity for their judgments

In the history of the independent Indian republic, there has been only one instance of an impeachment motion being moved in Parliament against a judge of the High Court for something that he had written in his judgment.[38] In virtually every other case of egregiously flawed judgments of the Supreme Court and High Courts, there has never been a motion for impeachment in Parliament. This includes a judgment of the Supreme Court diluting the Scheduled Castes and Scheduled Tribes (Prevention of Atrocities) Act, 1989, which triggered violence and deaths of protesters, before the Supreme Court itself recalled its own judgment.[39] The restraint shown by the political class in Parliament in acting against judges of the Supreme Court for this flawed judgment is an implicit recognition that there can be a difference of opinion regarding the interpretation of the law and that judges should not be punished for one particular interpretation, even if it is flawed.

In contrast, as recounted in this chapter, there is plenty of anecdotal evidence to suggest that the judges of the district judiciary are regularly penalized by judges of the High Courts for allegedly erroneous judgments, either through disciplinary inquiries or through adverse entries in their ACRs. It is very likely that the repeated punishment of judges in several states for being liberal in granting bail has had a chilling effect on the district judiciary, leading to a marked increase in rejection of bail petitions, as noted by former Chief Justice D. Y. Chandrachud and others. While the crisis with bail petitions has received some degree of national attention because of litigants flooding the Supreme Court and High Courts with bail petitions, we suspect that the fear of disciplinary inquiries has a deeper impact on other types of cases heard by the district judiciary. This fear likely also contributes to delays, as judges avoid hearing 'risky' cases for fear of punishment in the form of disciplinary inquiries.

In our opinion, the only way to protect the decisional independence of the district judiciary is to provide them with ironclad immunity from any disciplinary action, be it in the form of an inquiry or an entry into the ACR, for any errors in their judgments. Judicial errors are best corrected by the appeals court. Judges should be subject to disciplinary inquiries only when there are credible allegations of misconduct, such as bribery. Guaranteeing the district judiciary such immunity for their judgments will improve the quality of justice dispensed by them while also significantly improving their efficiency, leading to quicker disposal of cases.

2

Kafkaesque Inquiries

In the history of independent India, there have been only seven occasions where attempts were made to impeach judges of the Supreme Court and the High Courts.[1] The allegations against the judges were of misbehaviour, ranging from corruption to financial mismanagement to sexual harassment to improper statements against marginalized communities. Of these seven judges, only two judges resigned, one after an inquiry committee was set up and the second after the Rajya Sabha voted to impeach him.[2] The rest continued to serve on the bench; one even got elevated to the Supreme Court.

The odds are clearly stacked in favour of judges of the High Courts and Supreme Court, as should be the case, since it is these protections that guarantee judicial independence. Judges who are aware that the legal procedure for removing them from office is fair, rigorous and transparent are more likely to dispense justice without fear or favour. This was exactly the logic for the Constitution and the Judges Inquiry Act, 1968 creating a procedurally complex and transparent mechanism to inquire into allegations of misbehaviour against judges of the Supreme Court and High Courts.

Regrettably, the same protections against unfair inquiries have not been offered to judges of the district judiciary, who are the first point of contact for a majority of litigants in the country. It is upon the district judiciary that the duty falls, not just to adjudicate private disputes between citizens but also to protect citizens from the worst excesses of the Indian state, be it arbitrary arrests or the threat of demolition of homes. Despite this onerous responsibility and the contentious nature of their office, which tends to attract a steady stream of complaints from upset litigants and angry lawyers, these judges unlike their counterparts in the higher judiciary are not offered any special protections.

It is difficult to source accurate statistics on the frequency with which the disciplinary mechanism is invoked against the district judiciary because the High Courts do not proactively release such data. This is unlike in the UK, where the Judicial Conduct Investigations Office publishes such statistics in its Annual Report, categorizing the complaints to indicate the main grievances raised.[3] Since such data is publicly unavailable in India, we filed requests for information with some of the High Courts, asking them for the number of disciplinary inquiries that were conducted against the district judiciary in their states between the years 2018 and 2023. While the Rajasthan High Court refused to give us the information on the grounds that it was 'secret and confidential', some of the other High Courts were more forthcoming in their replies. Cumulatively, the Bombay High Court (30), Punjab & Haryana High Court (49), Gujarat High Court (19), Patna High Court (51) and the Allahabad High Court (49) have initiated a total of 198 disciplinary inquiries against judges of the district judiciary in these years.[4] To reiterate, merely five High Courts have initiated 198 disciplinary inquires against judges in a five-year period! Even if we were to account for the larger size of the district judiciary, these are significant numbers when compared to the mere seven impeachment motions in the last 75 years against judges of the High Courts and the Supreme Court. A further caveat to these numbers is that they do not account for probationary judges or judges who are compulsorily retired without the requirement to conduct any disciplinary inquiries.

So, what explains these trends? Are judges of the district judiciary inherently more corrupt or incompetent or immoral and hence more prone to allegations of misconduct than judges of the High Courts and Supreme Court? We think not. Instead, the answer, we suspect, lies in the capricious enforcement of the existing disciplinary mechanisms put in place by High Courts to investigate allegations of misconduct, especially corruption, against the district judiciary. A survey of the legal community published in 2022 by Professor Shivaraj Huchhanavar, the only Indian academic to study this issue, reported that a majority of the respondents believed that the disciplinary mechanism for the district judiciary could be misused 'at the instance of judges and officials in the High Courts'. They also agreed that the disciplinary mechanism was insufficient to protect the district judiciary from false and vexatious complaints.[5] In the professor's words, the results of his survey 'strongly indict the mechanisms for undermining the individual and internal independence of lower court judges'.[6]

These are serious allegations to make against a disciplinary system controlled by judges of the High Courts, but some of these allegations can be corroborated by judgments of the Supreme Court and High Courts. Take, for example, the case of District Judge R. C. Sood in Rajasthan who was subject to two disciplinary inquiries by the Rajasthan High Court regarding an administrative error made in an advertisement for recruitments and allegations of corruption by unverified sources. Both inquiries were nixed by the Supreme Court after passing scathing comments against the Rajasthan High Court. In the first judgment, delivered on 22 November 1994, the Supreme Court described the disciplinary inquiry as 'wholly arbitrary, unwarranted' and 'unsustainable'.[7] The Supreme Court also made the following remark about the conduct of the High Court:

> At a time when fairness and non-arbitrariness are the essential requirement of every administrative State action, it is more so for any administrative act of the Judges. It is necessary that members of the subordinate judiciary get no occasion to think otherwise. We are afraid, this incident appears to shake this faith. We do hope it is an inadvertent exception.

In the second judgment delivered on 13 May 1998, a different bench of the Supreme Court concluded that the Rajasthan High Court was retaliating by initiating a second inquiry against Judge Sood. Pertinently, the bench concluded as follows[8]:

> It is evident that there was a deliberate design to bring to a premature end the judicial career of the petitioner, whose name,

> at that time, was being actively considered for elevation as High Court Judge . . . Apparently stung by the judgment dated 22nd November, 1994 of this Court it retaliated by launching a fresh set of charges against the petitioner clearly with a view to ruin his judicial career. We have no doubt that the action taken by the court was not bona fide and amounts to victimisation. This is certainly not expected from a judicial forum, least of all the High Court, which is expected to discharge its administrative duties as fairly and objectively as it is required to discharge its judicial functions.

These are damning statements made by the Supreme Court against the judges of a High Court. There are other examples where judges of a High Court have been critical of their own colleagues for conducting unfair disciplinary inquiries against the district judiciary. In one such instance from the Gujarat High Court, its Chief Justice wrote in a judgment, 'Judges are at times poor judges of Judges, especially in judicial administration . . .'.[9] This comment was made in the aftermath of a particularly unfair disciplinary inquiry that led to the dismissal of a district judge. These statements by sitting judges, in their judgments, provide some corroborative evidence to the concerns flagged by Huchhanavar's survey.

Clearly, judges of High Courts, like other human beings, are capable of errors and prejudice. The mere fact that they are in control of the disciplinary mechanism for the district judiciary is no guarantee of justice. This is a problem because the workings of this disciplinary mechanism have direct ramifications for the decisional independence of the district judiciary, which is well recognized as a core component of judicial independence. Judges who are worried about being subject to unfair disciplinary mechanisms are also likely to adopt a more risk-averse behaviour, meaning that they will likely avoid deciding cases or granting remedies that are considered risky. For example, granting bail appears to be a magnet for disciplinary inquiries against judges in many states, which may explain why judges in those states are increasingly reluctant to grant bail. Such risk-averse behaviour may also contribute substantially to delays, as judges avoid adjudicating 'risky' cases by simply adjourning them for a later date. Safeguarding the decisional independence of the district judiciary should therefore be at the front and centre of any conversation on reforms aimed at improving the quality of justice delivered by the district judiciary.

So where exactly do the flaws lie in the disciplinary mechanism? To begin with, it must be understood that neither Parliament nor the state legislatures have enacted laws laying down specific procedures governing the conduct of disciplinary inquiries into complaints against the district judiciary. At most, Article 235 of the Constitution states that the district judiciary shall be under the control of the High Courts. In the absence of any specific rules, the High Courts have simply followed the procedures and standards of conduct laid down in the disciplinary rules for the bureaucracy of the state government. The only difference is that the inquiry is conducted entirely by the High Courts, whose decision is then binding on the state governments.

In its current form, the disciplinary mechanism for the district judiciary is a four-step process.

The first step is the screening of complaints by the High Courts in order to decide whether a disciplinary inquiry is to be initiated against a judge of the district judiciary.

Once a decision is taken to act on a complaint, the second stage of the process involving the actual inquiry is initiated. For this purpose, the High Court must appoint a 'presenting officer' to present the charges and also an 'inquiry officer' to hear the evidence and arguments on the charges as well as the defence of the judge who is the subject of the inquiry. The inquiry officer then presents a final report to the High Court on whether the charges stand proven. The inquiry officer tends to be another judge of the district judiciary, although, on occasion, judges of the High Court have been appointed as the inquiry officer.

The submission of the inquiry report triggers the third stage, where the disciplinary committee consisting of two or more judges of the High Court first affords an opportunity to the judge under investigation to defend herself against the findings of the inquiry officer before making recommendations regarding guilt and punishment, if any, to the full court consisting of all judges of the High Court. These disciplinary committees are not bound by the findings in the inquiry report and there have been cases where the findings and recommendations of the inquiry report have been completely ignored by disciplinary committees.

The fourth and final stage is the decision of the full court, which either accepts or rejects the recommendations of the disciplinary committee. The decision taken by the full court is considered binding on the state government, which issues an order in the name of the Governor implementing the decision of the full court.

At first glance, the four-step process may appear to be rigorous, but that is clearly not the case in practice. In order to understand the workings of the system, we reviewed a hundred judgments of High Courts and the Supreme Court, where judges have sought judicial review of disciplinary actions against them. From our research it is apparent that there are serious issues with how the system works in practice. What follows is a narration of select cases to illustrate how the disciplinary system fails the district judiciary at different stages of the process.

The triggers for disciplinary inquiries

The most crucial aspect of any disciplinary process against judges is the threshold for triggering it into action. For example, in the case of judges of the High Courts or the Supreme Court, the Judges Inquiry Act, 1968 requires the motion for impeachment to be supported by either a hundred members of the Lok Sabha or fifty members of the Rajya Sabha. The Speaker or Chairperson may then choose to admit the notice and constitute the inquiry committee to conduct an investigation into the allegations made in the notice. Of the seven motions for impeachment moved so far under this law, only four proceeded to the stage of an inquiry committee being constituted. Moreover, the entire process is conducted in the public eye and the motion for impeachment is a public record accessible by any person.

In contrast, the procedure followed by individual High Courts to screen complaints against judges of the district judiciary is not publicly available. The few High Courts with which we filed requests under the Right to Information Act asking for copies of rules or resolutions laying down the process to screen complaints and initiate inquiries either refused to provide the information on the grounds that it was confidential or directed us to guidelines from the Chief Justice of India who was alarmed by the number of anonymous complaints being filed against the district judiciary.[10] These guidelines merely require that the complaint should be accompanied by an affidavit and that its 'authenticity . . . should be duly ascertained' and that 'further steps . . . should be taken only after satisfaction of the competent authority designated by the Chief Justice of the High Court'.

In most High Courts, the 'competent authority' appears to be the Registrar-Vigilance, who is generally a district judge who is temporarily posted to the High Court. More often than not, the Registrar-Vigilance conducts a 'discreet' preliminary inquiry to probe the veracity of the allegations before making a recommendation to the High Court on whether an inquiry must be initiated. It is not clear as to how these preliminary inquiries are conducted by the Registrar-Vigilance, given their lack of skills and resources to conduct the type of investigations required to corroborate allegations of corruption. Given these powers, it is not surprising that the Registrar-Vigilance is a controversial figure who has attracted criticism from even judges of High Courts in their judgments. The following is an extract of a judgment by Justice Atul Sreedharan of the Madhya Pradesh High Court, criticizing the role of the Registrar-Vigilance[11]:

> The office of the District Judge (Vigilance and Training) continues to have a debilitating effect on independence and individuality of the judges of the District Judiciary. The post is a surplus appendage, akin to a vestigial organ in the body of the Judiciary in the State of Madhya Pradesh. The post is occupied by a Judge, senior enough to occupy the post of the District Judge. His duties involve calling at random, the judgements and orders passed by the Judges of the District Judiciary and examine them for quality and integrity. A position of immense power and influence over the Judges . . . An adverse report from the District Judge (Vigilance and Inspection) can be sufficient to initiate an enquiry by this Court against the Judge in question.

The second part of the process, which remains a mystery to us, is the number of judges of the High Court who have to agree with the recommendation of the Registrar-Vigilance to initiate an inquiry. If this power lies solely with the Chief Justice of the High Court, as we suspect is the case in most High Courts, it is deeply worrying because the Chief Justice is always a judge from another High Court and generally knows little about the workings or politics within the state. In effect, this could mean that the Registrar-Vigilance is the final word on initiating disciplinary inquiries against judges of the district judiciary. This is far too awesome a power to vest in the hands of a single person and is a recipe for creating distrust in the entire system, especially when the process is so opaque.

In an ideal world we would not have to make these calculated guesses about the procedure followed by the High Courts while screening complaints against the district judiciary. Ideally, the High Courts should be transparent about this process, with all information being made publicly available.

Apart from the lack of transparency and clarity in the screening process of complaints, the absence of any time-bound procedures to act on complaints is deeply problematic. There have been instances where complaints have been kept pending, only to be revived after several years to initiate disciplinary inquiries against the judge in question.[12] In one case, two vague complaints of misconduct against a judge filed in 2014 were suddenly activated two years later when his order in a high-profile case came under criticism from the Madras High Court.[13] If complaints can be kept hanging over the heads of the district judiciary, judges are going to be vulnerable to undue pressure from either the Registrar-Vigilance or the judges of the High Courts.

The flawed evidentiary standards adopted by disciplinary committees

The second deeply problematic aspect of the disciplinary proceedings is the evidentiary standard used to hold judges guilty of misconduct, often resulting in their dismissals.

The most problematic cases are the ones involving allegations of corruption against judges. These cases typically involve accounts of litigants claiming to have been approached by a 'middleman' on behalf of the judge to negotiate a bribe for a favourable judgment. Alternatively, litigants often rely on rumours to claim that the judge has been bribed by the opposing litigants. While judicial corruption cannot be ruled out, it is also possible that some litigants making such complaints are looking for an excuse to get their cases transferred to another judge or to simply retaliate against a judge who has ruled against them.

Common sense and the principles of fair justice would dictate that in the case of allegations of a middleman soliciting bribes on behalf of a judge, a criminal investigation be conducted to establish the identity of the middleman and his links with the judge—before any disciplinary inquiry is conducted. Similarly, if the allegation is that the judge received bribes directly from a litigant, the inquiring authority should be required to collect some evidence to establish a *quid pro quo* or a money trail. Regrettably, the quality of evidence in most disciplinary inquiries examining allegations of corruption against the district judiciary is laughable.

Take, for example, the case of District Judge K. Ganesan of the Madras High Court, who was suspended on 16 September 2014 and then dismissed from the judicial service on 24 April 2017 after complaints that he received bribes in exchange for granting bail to a person accused of sexually assaulting and murdering a minor girl.[14]

Judge Ganesan had granted bail only after the investigation was completed by the police and a chargesheet was filed against the accused. Further, in this case, Judge Ganesan imposed on the accused the requirement to mark his presence at the police station twice a day while out on bail. The grant of bail, especially after the chargesheet has been filed, is a common practice since the assumption is that the accused can no longer interfere with the investigation. The allegation of corruption in this case was made by the deceased girl's father, who allegedly heard from others in the locality that the accused had told people about bribing the judge for the grant of bail. In the language of the law, this was hearsay evidence and would not be admissible in a regular court of law since such evidence is inherently unreliable.

Clearly, this was a complaint that should not even have proceeded to the stage of a disciplinary inquiry because there was no reliable evidence of a bribe being paid to the judge. But disciplinary inquiries against the district judiciary are not governed by any formal rules of evidence. As a result, not only did the disciplinary inquiry take place, the judge was also dismissed from the judicial service, as a result of the inquiry. This, despite the girl's father being unable to provide any evidence, apart from second-hand rumours, about the alleged bribe paid to the judge.

When Judge Ganesan approached the Madras High Court seeking judicial review of the order dismissing him, the High Court declined to set aside the dismissal order despite agreeing that there was no 'direct evidence' that the judge had received any illegal gratification. The High Court reasoned that 'finding/procuring a (sic) direct evidence is a Herculean task, since the "Beneficiary of Bribe" will seldom come forward to depose about the tainted transaction (sic)'.[15] As an alternative, the High Court also tried, rather unconvincingly, to conclude that bail had been granted in exchange for bribes because the order granting it allegedly contained errors. But mere errors in the order, without any evidence of bribes being paid, does not logically lead to a finding of bribery. The Supreme Court declined to admit an appeal against the judgment of the High Court.[16]

A second example is the case of Civil Judge (Senior Division) A. N. Pattan who was dismissed from the judicial service on the recommendation of the Karnataka High Court on charges of corruption on 1 October 2012.[17] The main charge against Judge Pattan was that he had demanded bribes from a litigant through a middleman. The evidence against the judge was a sworn affidavit of a litigant who claimed to have been contacted by a middleman demanding a bribe on behalf of Judge Pattan and the allegation that he met the judge in the middleman's car. The second piece of evidence was the testimony of lawyers from the local bar association who alleged that the judge was corrupt. This was hearsay evidence. The final piece of evidence was a report by the police officer in the court's vigilance department who claimed to have confirmed the complainant's allegation about the judge being in the 'habit' of visiting properties litigated before him 'through some agents and litigants' before delivering judgments in their favour. It is not clear whether the inspector had personally witnessed the judge's visits or whether he had 'heard' about this from other people. In any event, the disciplinary committee of the High Court, along with the full court, found this evidence sufficient to recommend Judge Pattan's dismissal from the judicial service.

When the judge sought judicial review before the Karnataka High Court, a single-judge bench set aside the order dismissing Judge Pattan on the grounds that the allegations were very vague and the evidence unreliable.[18] On the main charge of demanding a bribe through a middleman, the bench pointed out that the alleged middleman and the complainant's lawyer who told him about the middleman were not examined by the inquiry officer. Further, the complainant had waited a year after the supposed demand to file a complaint and had not mentioned the date on which the alleged meeting took place. Amongst other findings, the judge also pointed out that the allegations by the lawyers were hearsay and that the police officer had not provided the case numbers of the properties that the judge had allegedly visited.[19]

However, the Registrar of the Karnataka High Court filed an appeal, which was heard by a division bench of two judges of the Karnataka High Court, who took another five years to dispose of the case. In a judgment delivered on 23 March 2022, this bench overruled the single judge on a technical issue, i.e. evidence assessed by the disciplinary committee could not have been reassessed by the single judge, since the scope of judicial review (unlike an appeal) of disciplinary decisions is limited to procedural review, i.e. whether proper procedure has been followed by the disciplinary authority.[20] The Supreme Court declined to admit an appeal filed by Judge Pattan and so he lost this decade-long legal battle to get back his job.[21]

The third example in this category is the case of District Judge K. S. Raju in Kerala. He was dismissed from the judicial service in 2007 on the recommendation of the Kerala High Court after a disciplinary committee found against the judge on a range of charges. The main charge was that he had solicited bribes from litigants while officiating over the Motor Accidents Claims Tribunal, which decides compensation in cases of motor vehicle accidents. The allegation of corruption against Judge Raju was that a person by the name of Radhakrishnan acted as his 'agent' by approaching various litigants on his behalf, asking for bribes in exchange for favourable orders.

When the dismissed judge sought judicial review of the decision to remove him from office, his lawyer argued before a single-judge bench of the Kerala High Court that there was no evidence establishing the identity of the alleged 'middleman' Radhakrishnan and also no evidence establishing that he was acting on behalf of District Judge Raju.[22] Unfortunately for Judge Raju, the single judge sidestepped this key evidentiary question on the ground that the court could not re-examine evidentiary findings by the disciplinary inquiry while hearing a petition for judicial review.

As a result, we cannot confirm if the issues with the evidence raised by Judge Raju's lawyer were valid. The Kerala High Court refused to give us a copy of the inquiry report, but if these allegations were indeed true, the entire disciplinary inquiry should have collapsed.[23] An appeal filed by Judge Raju against this decision in 2016 is yet to be decided by the Kerala High Court, eight years later.[24]

A fourth example is of Judge Syed Hasan from Uttar Pradesh. The Allahabad High Court had demoted Judge Syed Hasan from the rank of district judge to the rank of civil judge on 17 January 2006, after a disciplinary inquiry found against him in a complaint of bribery.[25] The complaint, filed by the brother of a murder victim, alleged that Judge Hasan received bribes to grant bail to the person accused of the crime. The charge framed in the disciplinary inquiry accused him of granting bail for 'extraneous considerations'. The final inquiry report rejected, as hearsay, the oral evidence offered by the court staff, alleging that bribes were paid through middlemen to Judge Hasan. However, the same inquiry report concluded that the judge was guilty of granting bail for 'extraneous consideration' because of alleged flaws in his legal reasoning. The disciplinary committee and full court agreed with the finding and recommended that the judge be punished with a demotion from the rank of Additional District & Sessions Judge to the lower rank of Civil Judge (Senior Division).[26]

When Judge Hasan sought judicial review of this order, a division bench of the Allahabad High Court ruled in his favour on 6 November 2012. In this judgment delivered six years after Judge Hasan first filed the petition, the court reasoned that the inquiry officer had reached the wrong conclusion since there was no evidence of Judge Hasan receiving any bribes in exchange for granting bail. In the words of the court[27]:

> The passing of the order after taking bribe is clearly a misconduct for which an officer can be punished, but what is the extraneous consideration on the basis of which the learned Enquiry Judge found the charge proved, has not been spelled in the inquiry report. The grant of second bail substantially on the ground on which the first bail application was rejected, cannot itself be an extraneous consideration unless such extraneous consideration is spelled.

As a result, the High Court set aside the punishment meted out to Judge Hasan, restoring him to his original rank within the judicial service.

A fifth case, this one from the Gujarat High Court, is of District Judge S. J. Pathak, who was suspended in 1999 on charges of corruption and eventually dismissed from service in 2006.[28] The High Court had initiated two disciplinary inquiries against him, on the charge of granting bail in exchange for bribes and on the charge of receiving a bribe to acquit, in the year 1994, a person accused of evading sales tax. The inquiry officer returned a finding that there was no evidence of corruption in either case. At most, the inquiry officer concluded, Judge Pathak did not follow established principles of law while granting bail. Despite this finding, two of the three disciplinary committees set up in this case, quite extraordinarily, recommended Judge Pathak's dismissal. The first and third disciplinary committees had the same two judges. After much disagreement at the meetings of the full court, Judge Pathak was eventually dismissed.

When Judge Pathak sought judicial review of the order removing him from service, a division bench of the Gujarat High Court, headed by the Chief Justice, set aside the dismissal order. As noted in his judgment, one of the three disciplinary committees made a finding that 'the Inquiry Officer has observed that the department has not led any evidence much less cogent evidence to substantiate the charges of corruption'.[29] The same committee also noted that most of the allegations were 'on the basis of the loose talks in the bar regarding doubtful integrity of the judicial officers. . . . [and] that none of the witnesses has made any specific allegations against the delinquent (sic.)'.[30] Simply put, Judge Pathak was the victim of gossip and rumours. He ultimately got back his job in 2009, with 50 per cent backpay for the ten years of employment that he had lost.

In each of the five cases above, across five different High Courts, the evidence of corruption against the judge in question was hearsay, which would have been inadmissible in regular judicial proceedings governed by the Evidence Act due to the inherent unreliability of such evidence. Due to the lack of clear-cut evidentiary rules, these five judges had to endure significant setbacks to their careers. The larger, immeasurable fallout of these cases is the chilling effect on the colleagues of these judges, making them more averse to hearing cases they deem 'risky' from the perspective of attracting patently unfair disciplinary inquiries.

The opacity of disciplinary committees and full courts

As mentioned earlier, the key decision-making powers during the disciplinary process are exercised by administrative committees, consisting of judges of the High Court, as well as the full court, consisting of all judges of the High Court.

The problem, however, is that except for the orders of dismissal by the state government, which reveal no details about the inquiry, none of the other records are publicly available. This includes the complaints that led to the disciplinary inquiry, the reports of the inquiry officer, the testimonies before the inquiry officer, the reports of the disciplinary committees and the minutes of the meetings of the full court that make the recommendations to the state government.

The lack of transparency makes it difficult to assess the fairness of the process and also opens the door to abuse of power. This is unlike the impeachment process of judges of the High Courts and Supreme Court, where the inquiry report and the defence of the judge in Parliament, as well as the parliamentary deliberations preceding the impeachment vote are broadcast live on television. Similarly, in the US and the UK, the Committee on Judicial Conduct & Disability and the Judicial Conduct Investigations Office, respectively, publish the outcomes of complaints against judges on their websites for anybody to read.[31] Such transparency is key to building public confidence in disciplinary mechanisms meant to hold judges accountable.

Apart from the lack of transparency, the procedure followed by High Courts while considering the report of the inquiry officer is also unclear and appears to lack finality. For example, on the point of disciplinary committees, some High Courts, like the Gujarat High Court, have constituted multiple such committees one after another due to disagreements within the meetings of the full court over the findings of the first disciplinary committee. In Judge Pathak's case, discussed earlier, the Gujarat High Court set up not one but three disciplinary committees. After the first committee submitted its report recommending Judge Pathak's dismissal, the report was placed in the 'committee room' for 48 hours, during which period one of the judges of the High Court requested that it be discussed in a meeting of the full court. At this meeting, there were disagreements between the judges and hence it was decided to set up a second disciplinary committee consisting of two different judges of the High Court. This committee returned with a contrary finding, declaring that none of the charges against Judge Pathak were proved. This report was taken up again at a meeting of the full court and after disagreements in this meeting, a third disciplinary committee was set up. This committee had the same judges as the first disciplinary committee and they repeated their finding of guilt and recommendation to dismiss Judge Pathak. This is hardly a credible process, as admitted by the Gujarat High Court in its judgment setting aside the dismissal of Judge Pathak. In its judgment, the High Court concluded that the manner in which these disciplinary committees were instituted indicated a 'non-application of mind as well as legal and factual bias'.[32] This was a strong indictment by the High Court of its own processes.

The other problem, identifiable from publicly available judgments, is the manner in which the meetings of the full court are conducted. One would expect that a full court would consist of all the judges of the High Court actually meeting in a room and casting their vote on whether to accept or reject the recommendations of the administrative committee. But this is not always the case. For example, as mentioned earlier, in the Gujarat High Court, the practice at one point was to place the recommendations of the disciplinary committee in the 'committee room' for 48 hours. Unless a judge of the High Court specifically requested that the matter be discussed in a meeting of the full court, the report was deemed accepted after this period. This procedure came under criticism from judges of the Gujarat High Court, one of whom publicly expressed his disapproval in a judgment. The judge stated:

> I find that no safeguards are being taken in this High Court and no other Judge except two Judges who are the members of the Disciplinary Committee applies their mind to the facts and circumstances of the case on administrative side for recommending imposition of major penalty.[33]

There is also the question of the quality of deliberations within the full court meetings that consider the report of the disciplinary committee. The observations of the Chief Justice of the Gujarat High Court reproduced below are a surprisingly candid description of the quality of the full court meetings in that court:

> Chamber Meeting in which all the Judges of the High Court are expected to participate is a serious meeting, where important decisions touching the administration of the entire judiciary is taken. Larger the Committee, lesser the application of mind, which is a hard reality, but members of quorum are free to express their views, but at times too much of views and opinions takes the House from the real issue and leads to unchartered areas just like the present case. If serious thought was bestowed on the issue in the Chamber meeting held on 6.5.2003, then the High Court would not have entrusted the enquiry to the Committee which had already prejudged the issue, which we have already found

> was a serious legal infirmity. We are sure that the Chamber would be more watchful and circumspect when such issue comes up for deliberations before it in future and would not be carried away by personal views or predilection.[34]

It is rare for judges to be as self-reflective as those of the Gujarat High Court. We suspect that full court meetings in other High Courts have similar problems. This is evident from some of the examples discussed in this chapter, where judges of the district judiciary have been penalized on the basis of laughable evidence. That the minutes of the meetings of the full courts are not public records, opens the door for brazen abuse of power and further undermines the legitimacy of the process.

No independent appellate process

The last and fatal flaw with the entire disciplinary process is that judges of the district judiciary who are punished by High Courts at the end of disciplinary proceedings have no right to appeal the decision. At most, these judges can file a petition before the High Court seeking judicial review. However, these petitions, heard in open courtrooms and resulting in publicly available judgments of the High Court, are hardly an effective remedy for three reasons.

First, the scope of judicial review is generally limited to a procedural review, i.e. ascertaining whether principles of natural justice were followed during the conduct of the inquiry. For example, if a judge has not been given the right to be heard or there was bias in the proceedings, the court can intervene to ensure that the judge is given a fair hearing. In these proceedings, High Courts will typically not get into questions of evidence or the reasoning of the disciplinary committee or the proportionality of the punishment. The bar for intervention in such review petitions is quite high. Only in cases where the reasoning or punishment is so unreasonable that no reasonable person could have come to similar conclusions will the court intervene. As can be seen from some of the cases cited earlier, High Courts can be extremely deferential to the disciplinary process, even when the inquiry officer and disciplinary mechanism rely on laughable evidence of bribery.

The second reason why judicial review is rendered ineffective is because the petition has to necessarily be filed before the same High Court that punished the judge. This usually means that the judges of the High Court who hear the petition for judicial review challenging the disciplinary process may have participated in the decision of the full court. This is hardly an appropriate or credible mechanism. The judicial review process can get even more complicated in High Courts where the disciplinary committee is staffed by the senior-most judges, while the petitions for judicial review are heard by the junior judges of the High Courts. This puts the junior judges in the awkward position of ruling against the manner in which their senior colleagues have conducted disciplinary inquiries.

The third problem is the fact that High Courts rarely ever treat petitions for judicial review against disciplinary action with the urgency required. It is not uncommon for judges who have been punished by the High Courts to litigate their cases for years together. For example, Judge Pattan's case took ten years to resolve before the Karnataka High Court. Judge Raju's case was pending for eight years before the single judge of the Kerala High Court and the appeal against the order of the single judge before the division bench has been pending for another eight years and is yet to be decided. Judge Hasan's case took six years to be decided by the Allahabad High Court.

There are other cases, such as that of Judge Sadhna Chaudhary who fought a legal battle over a period of sixteen years before being reinstated in service.[35] There is also the case of Judge T. C. Tanwar who had to litigate for fifteen years before the Punjab & Haryana High Court against his dismissal from service.[36] Similarly, there is the case of Judge Ramesh Prasad Tihaiya who litigated for fourteen years before the Madhya Pradesh High Court, challenging the punishment imposed on him after disciplinary proceedings.[37] From Karnataka, there is also the example of Judge Narasimha Prasad who litigated for fourteen years before the Karnataka High Court and the Supreme Court, challenging his dismissal from service.[38] From Gujarat, there is the example of Judge R. K. Divyeshwar who fought a legal battle over twenty-one years before the Gujarat High Court after he was dismissed from service on the grounds of misconduct.[39] Lastly from Bihar, there are the cases of Judge Krishna Prasad Verma and Judge Neelam Sinha who litigated for ten years and eight years, respectively, against minor penalties imposed on them by the Patna High Court.[40] Such extraordinary delays are bound to be demoralizing for judges of the district judiciary who are looking for some legal recourse against a clearly flawed disciplinary mechanism.

More worryingly, the lack of a robust, timely and independent appellate process has meant that there has been no independent oversight of the manner in which High Courts have conducted disciplinary inquiries and hence there has been little self-correction by the courts.

The road to reform

It is rather ironical that judges of the district judiciary tasked with dispensing justice on a daily basis are not guaranteed an independent, transparent and timely disciplinary process with adequate procedural and evidentiary safeguards. The lack of such safeguards is particularly striking in light of the robust safeguards put in place by the Judges Inquiry Act, 1968 for the judges of the High Courts and Supreme Court.

As we have demonstrated with examples, the existing disciplinary process is open to abuse and, more often than not, relies upon gossip and innuendo to punish judges of the district judiciary. It is also inefficient in the time that it takes for complaints to travel through the system. Apart from such a system being inefficient and unjust to both complainants and the judges of the district judiciary, we should really worry about the effect of such a rickety system on the decisional independence and morale of the district judiciary. These factors likely have a direct impact on the willingness of judges to grant bail or adjudicate cases they perceive as 'risky'. This may be contributing to a flood of petitions before the High Courts and Supreme Court by litigants who are unable to get bail from the district judiciary.

There are two routes to reform.

A short-term reform that can be achieved relatively quickly is for the High Courts to make the entire process transparent. This would require High Courts to publish the reports of the disciplinary committees, the evidence led before the committee, the minutes of the meetings of the full court, along with voting patterns of judges on the recommendations of the disciplinary committees. High Courts should also release aggregate statistics annually on the number of complaints received, the type of complaints, and the action taken on the complaints by the High Courts. Until the veil of secrecy is dropped and the High Courts make public the decision-making process, there is little opportunity to hold judges of the High Court accountable for their role in the disciplinary process.

The virtues of ensuring transparency, in the context of open courts, was best outlined by English philosopher Jeremy Bentham in the following quote, often repeated by Indian judges in their judgments:

> In the darkness of secrecy, sinister interest and evil in every shape have full swing. Only in proportion as publicity has place can any of the checks applicable to judicial injustice operate. Where there is no publicity there is no justice. Publicity is the very soul of justice. It is the keenest spur to exertion and the surest of all guards against improbity. It keeps the judge himself while trying under trial.[41]

While the above quotation is in the context of proceedings in court, the Indian judiciary has also advocated for more transparency in the workings of the state. Over the last few decades, the Supreme Court has repeatedly waxed eloquent on the virtues of transparency and open government, going as far as to elevate the right to information to the status of a fundamental right.

We are, however, unlikely to see any such transparency within the judiciary because while the judiciary has been vocal on advocating for transparency in government, it has been hostile to the idea of subjecting itself to external scrutiny. This can be discerned from the fact that the Supreme Court took almost a decade to decide whether its Chief Justice was covered by the RTI Act.[42] There are other more brazen examples of how several High Courts have subverted the RTI Act by creating exclusions for certain categories of records they hold, doing so in a manner that is clearly not legal. Even with inquiry reports prepared in the course of disciplinary proceedings against judges of the district judiciary, most High Courts do not share copies of these reports under the RTI Act, citing privacy or other grounds in their own RTI Rules. There is no defensible logic for such denials, especially when inquiry reports under the Judges Inquiry Act, 1968 against judges of High Courts and Supreme Court are made publicly available on the Parliament website. In our opinion, there is little likelihood of High Courts volunteering more transparency in the manner in which disciplinary proceedings are conducted against the district judiciary.

As a long-term constitutional reform, Parliament should aim to create a permanent, full-time commission, separate from the High Courts, with its own staff to screen complaints, conduct investigations, inquiries and recommend punishments for the judges of the district judiciary. It is vital that the powers to nominate persons to this commission be distributed between different power centres and not placed under the complete control of the High Courts. For example, if there is to be a six-member commission in every state, the High Court should be allowed to nominate only two members, while the remaining four members should be nominated by a combination of the President of India, the Governor of the State, the Leader of Opposition or the Chief Justice of India. This is to ensure that there is some external oversight over the functioning of the judges in each state. Further, the law should lay down well-defined and transparent procedures for the commission to carry out its duties.

Building a political consensus for such reforms will be challenging given that this issue has not entered public conversation. In our view, this is the issue that should be at the front and centre of any discussion on reforming the district judiciary. Once the district judiciary is assured of a fair and transparent disciplinary process there will be less reluctance on their part to grant bail and adjudicate cases they perceive to be risky.

3

Fired without Cause

On 22 June 2017, Additional Sessions Judge Ajay Dinode, a designated 'special judge' presiding over the trials of sensitive criminal prosecutions under the Prevention of Money Laundering Act, was summarily dismissed from the judicial service by the state government on the recommendations of the Bombay High Court. Having been appointed as a judge only in 2014, Judge Dinode was still a 'probationary judge' and was not entitled to either a hearing or reasons for his dismissal from service.[1] All new judges to the district judiciary, across the country, are subject to a minimum probationary period of two years before they are 'confirmed' in service based on the recommendations of administrative committees consisting of judges of the High Court, allowing them to serve until the age of retirement.

Judge Dinode challenged the legality of his dismissal from service before the Bombay High Court on the grounds that he was not provided an opportunity to be heard by the judges of the High Court who made the decision to dismiss him from service. However, as is usually the case with 'probationary judges', his petition was dismissed by the Bombay High Court on the grounds that probationary judges had no right to be heard before being dismissed from service.[2] The Supreme Court refused to grant leave to appeal.[3] Simply put, the decision to terminate his services was a lawful exercise of power by the High Court, whose recommendation was the basis of the government order dismissing the probationary judge.

The outcome in Judge Dinode's case was not surprising since

the very concept of 'probation' in employment law is meant to give employers a window to assess the performance, competence and suitability of a new employee after she begins employment. During this period of probation, employees are generally not provided the regular protections of employment law and can be terminated from a job without any notice or reasons or severance pay. In the context of public employment in India, almost all 'service rules' for the civil service, including the judicial service, provide for a probationary period of at least two years (which is often extended at the pleasure of the High Court). During this period, most public servants can be dismissed from their job without the government having to conduct a disciplinary hearing or providing a cause for their dismissal.

The question that deserves closer examination is whether the concept of 'probation' should apply to judges at all. This is an important question to ask for two reasons. The first reason is that a judge, unlike other 'employees' in the private or public sector, is expected to take decisions that directly impact the lives of other persons from the very first day she assumes office. In the case of a judge, these decisions pertain to the life, liberty and property of citizens. In effect this means that the system is 'experimenting' on litigants in order to collect the information necessary to make a decision on the competence of a 'probationary judge' and whether they should be given permanent tenure in service until retirement. Given the implications for litigants, one would hope that the competence and suitability of a judge has been vetted appropriately before her appointment to a judicial office. This is clearly not the case in India and litigants are unwitting guinea pigs on whose lives High Courts are experimenting with probationary judges.

The second reason is that 'security of tenure' for judges is considered to be one of the essential prerequisites for guaranteeing judicial independence.[4] This means that a judge should either have tenure until a specified retirement age or for the term of office specified under the law.[5] Can a probationary judge be expected to decide cases freely if she can be dismissed from the judicial service without being provided any reason or hearing? We think not. A probationary judge worried about losing her job during the probationary period is unlikely to deliver fearless and decisive justice. Instead, such a judge is likely to take the most risk-averse route, which could be disastrous, especially in cases involving the liberty of litigants.

There is a second category of judges who, like probationary judges, have no right to be heard before being dismissed from the judicial service. These are the judges who can be dismissed via the route of 'compulsory retirement' after they reach certain milestone ages. For example, in Gujarat, the judges of the district judiciary can be considered for 'compulsory retirement' as they cross the milestone ages of 50, 55 and 58 years.[6] These judges are not new appointees and generally have at least a decade in service, if not more. The High Courts are not required to conduct any disciplinary hearings in these cases or provide reasons to them in writing.[7] The decision is taken by committees of judges of High Courts based on their perception of the judge's performance. These official orders compulsorily retiring judges generally state that the judge is being dismissed in the larger 'public interest' and no specific reasons are provided for the dismissal. Usually, these judges will receive some retirement benefits.

Over the last two decades, High Courts have increasingly used the route of compulsory retirement to dismiss judges of the district judiciary from the judicial services. For example, in the year 2016, the Gujarat High Court 'compulsorily retired' eighteen judges on the grounds that their performance was below par.[8] While High Courts do not proactively release statistics on the number of judges of the district judiciary being compulsorily retired, we do know from newspaper reports that just five High Courts compulsorily retired ninety-four judges of the district judiciary, between the years 2009 and 2024, in mass firings.[9] This statistic does not include instances that did not make it to the newspapers.

So why are judges fired in such a brazenly unfair manner? A bit of history may help explain the problem.

The origins of 'compulsory retirement' can be traced to norms laid down in 19th-century British India for the civil services which were aimed at getting rid of bureaucrats who were unable to secure promotions to higher posts within the civil service. A report of the Public Service Commission on the colonial civil service in India, published in the year 1888, had this to say about compulsory retirement in the civil services[10]:

> No officer, who is declared unfit for promotion in due course, should be retained in its ranks. The efficiency of the Provincial Service is scarcely of less importance, and the Commission accordingly recommends, as a general rule, that officers of the Imperial and Provincial Services, if declared ineligible for promotion, should, after a certain period of service, be liable to be compulsorily retired on reduced pensions calculated with reference to their period of effective service.

A similar system exists in many private sector organizations, where it is called an 'up or out promotion system'. Under this system, if an employee fails to qualify for a promotion at a certain level, they are asked to leave the organization.

In the case of the judiciary, it appears that compulsory retirement without cause was introduced relatively recently, at the urging of the Supreme Court, without completely comprehending the effects of the policy. This policy is the result of litigation, during the mid-1990s, by the All India Judges Association (AIJA), which represents the district judiciary and advocates for an improvement of their employment conditions. Amongst other demands, the AIJA had asked for raising the retirement age of the district judiciary from 58 years to 60 years. The court asked state governments to raise the retirement age, with the rider that the extension of two years should be contingent 'on the basis of the judicial officers' past record of service, character rolls, quality of judgments and other relevant matters'. The court then proceeded to instruct High Courts to compulsory retire judges who failed to pass such an assessment.[11]

In that same judgment, the Supreme Court had asked the government to set up a commission to study conditions of employment of the district judiciary. The commission, set up in 1996, was headed by a former judge of the court, Justice K. Jagannatha Shetty, and is generally referred to as the Shetty Commission. The Commission recommended a review of the performances of all judges of the district judiciary at the ages of 50 years, 55 years and 58 years. In pertinent part, it urged High Courts to 'weed out in public interest' those judges of the district judiciary who were considered to be 'deadwood'.[12] There was not a whisper in the report on the impact of such a 'compulsory retirement' process on the decisional independence of those judges in the district judiciary in the age bracket of 50 to 58 years.

In both these scenarios, be it the dismissal of a probationary judge or 'compulsory retirement' of judges who reached milestone ages, the decision-making process by High Courts is guided significantly by an assessment of the Annual Confidential Reports (ACRs) prepared by the supervising judge. Much of the criteria in the ACR is subjective and reflects only the views of the supervising judge. For example, the supervising judge has to provide his assessment about the integrity, knowledge, quality of judgments and the relationship of the judge with the bar and the staff. The disposal rates of the judge, as measured by the unit system, are also reflected in the ACR. In essence, ACRs are an evaluation of the judge's competence on an annual basis but are not the sole guiding factor. The quality of judgments written by the judge, allegations made against the judge, pending disciplinary proceedings and her track record on the administrative side are also reviewed by the administrative committee of judges of High Courts, which makes the final recommendation to the Full Court, which then makes a binding recommendation to the state government. In the case of both, probationary judges and judges being compulsorily retired, the assessment is essentially of the competence of the judge to continue serving in office.

Since there is no requirement for High Courts to provide specific reasons for dismissing probationary judges or compulsorily retiring judges of the district judiciary, there is little transparency in how these decisions are being made by the High Courts. Given the opacity baked into the process, it is entirely possible that High Courts use these avenues to dismiss judges against whom they have suspicions of impropriety but lack evidence to conduct proper disciplinary proceedings.

Since judges who have been dismissed from office in this manner are not provided reasons for their dismissal, they find it very difficult to challenge the legality of their dismissal before the High Courts. They do not have a right to appeal against their dismissals. They only have a right to seek 'judicial review' before the very same High Courts that have made the decision to dismiss them. A petition for judicial review, unlike an appeal, is generally limited to an assessment of whether the administrative committee of judges of the High Court have followed the basic principles of natural justice. There is little scope for the High Court conducting judicial review in these cases to get into the reasoning underlying the decision to dismiss judges, especially since none of these orders contain any reasoning explaining the cause for the dismissal. It is not surprising, then, that a majority of these petitions seeking judicial review of the dismissal of probationary judges and the 'compulsory retirement' of judges above 50 years fail before the High Courts. By way of illustration, of the 50 judgments of the Supreme Court and High Courts that we reviewed, where probationary judges of the district judiciary had challenged their dismissal from the judicial services, they won only in 10 cases. A narration of a few of these judgments may help explain just how unfair the entire process is towards the district judiciary.

The challenges faced by probationary judges

In order to understand the travails of probationary judges, we picked four judgments from different High Courts to illustrate the manner in which the process worked.

The first case, and one that is particularly egregious, is that of Judge Jayshree Chamanlal Buddhbhatti of the Gujarat Judicial Service. She was a probationary Principal Civil Judge & Judicial Magistrate First Class at Kodinar, Gujarat, when her services were terminated by the state government on the recommendations of the Gujarat High Court in 2007.

The official notification stated:

> The Hon'ble High Court, on the strength of material on record relating to period of probation of Miss J. C. Buddhbhatti, Civil Judge and

> JMFC, has found that her performance is not good and satisfactory and that she is not suitable for the post she holds and therefore recommended to terminate her probation period immediately and she should not be continued to officiate for long term.[13]

When Judge Buddhbhatti filed a petition for judicial review before the Gujarat High Court, it came to light that her former supervising judge, now appointed as Registrar-Vigilance at the High Court, had carried out a preliminary inquiry into Judge Buddhbhatti's conduct regarding her relationship with a judge based in Rajasthan (whose wife's death by suicide was then attributed, by gossip mongers, to the alleged relationship between the two judges, despite no evidence to support the allegation), her relationship with some politicians and her conduct with the bar and staff.[14] This inquiry, which concluded without providing the judge an opportunity to respond to allegations against her, found against the judge on all three counts.

Since no reasons are required to be provided for the dismissal of a probationary judge, it is not clear as to the extent to which this inquiry report formed the basis of the decision of the High Court to dismiss the judge from judicial service. The dismissal order, reproduced above, followed the standard template for such orders by citing a general assessment of competence as a ground for her dismissal. Legally speaking, Judge Buddhbhatti had a weak case and the High Court would have been well within its rights to dismiss her petition challenging her dismissal.

Luckily for Judge Buddhbhatti, the bench of the Gujarat High Court that heard her petition surmised that the inquiry report had contributed to the decision of the High Court to terminate her services (despite no reference to it in the dismissal order) and that she was not provided an opportunity to defend herself. The judgment also painted a sorry picture of the manner in which Judge Buddhbhatti was harassed by a primarily male establishment of judges, lawyers and court-staff. The judgment stated, in pertinent part, the following[15]:

> Considering the number of ladies who are now joining the profession, it is about time that we come out of the archaic narrow minded mentality whereby any sort of friendship between male and

> female colleagues is frowned upon and viewed with suspicion, as otherwise it would be difficult for ladies to discharge their duties independently and fearlessly. It is not uncommon for a colleague to consult another colleague or discuss issues in connection with one's work. Merely because in the present case, one colleague is a male and the other is a female is no reason to suspect anything more. The report of the Registrar (Vigilance) to say the least, projects a very distorted version before the High Court.

The High Court also accused the supervising judge of 'adding fuel to the fire by taking sides with the staff against the petitioner and making unwarranted remarks in her Annual Confidential Reports.'[16] As a result, the court, in its judgment dated 15 May 2009 set aside the order terminating her service and restored Judge Buddhbhatti to the judicial service with full back-wages.

Astonishingly, the registrar of the Gujarat High Court filed an appeal before the Supreme Court against the judgment of the Gujarat High Court, only to lose once again.[17] The Supreme Court, in a judgment dated 22 October 2013, six years after Judge Buddhbhatti's dismissal, doled out the following advice to High Courts:

> We would like to take this opportunity to emphasise that the High Courts must see to it that the hostile work environment for junior judicial officers, particularly the lady officers, is eliminated. This is necessary to encourage the young officers to put in good judicial work without fear or favour. We are constrained to say that in the present case the High Court administration has clearly failed in this behalf.

The happy ending in this case had to do more with judicial conscience than the law because technically, the termination order made no reference to the inquiry and instead read like any other order terminating the services of a probationary judge. A more deferential bench may have simply dismissed Judge Buddhbhatti's petition on the grounds that the inquiry was inconsequential since it was not mentioned in the dismissal order. Judicial conscience, not the law, saved this judge's career.

The second case is of Judge Gurunath Dinkar Mane of the Maharashtra Judicial Service who was appointed as Civil Judge, Junior Division before being dismissed during the period of his probation on 17 May 2012 on the recommendation of the High Court. As is generally the case with the dismissal of probationary judges, Judge Mane was not provided with any specific reasons but merely informed that he was not found suitable for the judicial service by the High Court.[18]

When Judge Mane sought more information about his service record under the Right to Information Act, he discovered that a discreet inquiry had been conducted into his behaviour by the High Court after receiving a complaint from the administration of the judicial academy (where new judges attend a briefing training program) that Judge Mane was found to be drinking alcohol on the premises of the academy. As per Judge Mane, the inquiry was conducted without providing him with an opportunity to present a defence. He also claimed that the administration of the Judicial Academy was retaliating against him for complaining about the quality of food. However, when Judge Mane filed a petition seeking judicial review of the decision to dismiss him during the probationary period, the Bombay High Court, in a judgment delivered on 23 September 2016, declined to set aside the order on the grounds that the inquiry was part of a broader exercise to assess his performance during the probationary period and not a disciplinary inquiry into a complaint of misconduct. In the latter case, the judge would have a right to be heard. The Supreme Court declined to grant leave to appeal against this judgment of the Bombay High Court.[19]

The third case is of District Judge Abhay Jain who was dismissed during the probationary period by the Rajasthan High Court in 2016, three years after he joined the judicial service. Prior to his dismissal, the Rajasthan High Court had initiated a disciplinary inquiry against Judge Jain on the grounds that he had improperly granted bail to a public servant charged with corruption. During the pendency of the disciplinary inquiry, the High Court recommended to the state government that Judge Jain be dismissed from the judicial service and an order to that effect was issued. This was not a dismissal resulting from a disciplinary inquiry and since the dismissal of probationary judges is not required to be backed by reasons, it is impossible to assess whether the pending disciplinary inquiry actually featured in the decision-making process of the administrative committee assessing the performance of probationary judges.

When Judge Jain challenged his dismissal before the Rajasthan High Court, his petition was dismissed, as is the most common outcome for petitions filed by probationary judges.[20] In pertinent part, the High Court concluded that the pending disciplinary inquiry 'was not the foundation' of the dismissal and that Judge Jain's dismissal from the judicial service was based on an assessment of his entire service record.[21] Since the allegation of 'misconduct' was not the basis of the judge's dismissal, the court concluded that the judge had no right to be heard before being dismissed.[22]

Luckily for Judge Jain, when he filed an appeal before the Supreme Court, it agreed to hear his case and ruled in his favour in a judgment delivered on 15 March 2022, i.e. six years after he lost his job.[23] The bench of the Supreme Court which heard his case surmised that Judge Jain was dismissed by way of punishment for granting bail in the corruption case and due to some adverse entries in his ACR, without being provided an opportunity to defend himself. This was an extraordinary outcome since the Rajasthan High Court had categorically stated in its judgment that the allegation of misconduct was not the reason for Judge Jain's dismissal. Yet, the Supreme Court was convinced that the disciplinary inquiry featured in the decision-making process since one of the judges on the disciplinary committee investigating Judge Jain had also been made part of the administrative committee assessing the performance of probationary judges.[24] The Supreme Court also noted other procedural improprieties on part of the Rajasthan High Court, such as not informing Judge Jain of the adverse entries against him in his ACR.[25] The Supreme Court went even further to conclude that the disciplinary inquiry against him was unwarranted since he had followed the law while granting bail in the case that was the subject of the disciplinary inquiry.[26] This was an extraordinary case where the Supreme Court went to great lengths to reinstate Judge Jain and should be viewed as an exception to the general rule.

The last case is of District Judge Rajeev Kumar of Jharkhand who was dismissed by the Government of Jharkhand on 11 March 2006 on the recommendation of the Jharkhand High Court, during his probationary period. As is the case with dismissals during the probationary period, the judge was not given an opportunity to be heard by the High Court before it made the recommendation to the government to dismiss him. On receiving the order dismissing him, Judge Kumar filed a petition before the High Court seeking judicial review of his dismissal. He alleged that the High Court had carried out a preliminary inquiry into one of his orders granting bail to an extremist and had not provided him with a chance to defend himself before discharging him from judicial service. The Registrar General of the High Court rebutted this charge by claiming that the preliminary inquiry was not about a single judgment but instead meant to assess the judge's entire record in service in order to make the decision on whether to dismiss or confirm him in the judicial service. The High Court dismissed Judge Kumar's petition on the grounds that as long as the inquiry was not a disciplinary inquiry into misconduct but merely a preliminary inquiry meant to assess the judge's suitability for judicial service, there was no requirement for him to be given an opportunity to be heard.[27]

As can be seen from the above four examples, probationary judges face precarious odds because the entire process leading to their dismissals, which takes place within the High Court, is frightfully opaque and manifestly unfair. Presumably, such uncertainty and lack of transparency have a chilling effect on the decisional independence of probationary judges, making them exceptionally risk-averse until they receive the order confirming their tenure in service. Given that probationary periods often extend beyond two years, the risk-averse attitude of a probationary judge can continue for more than two years. For judges eventually confirmed, the uncertainty experienced early in their career is likely to adversely affect their confidence throughout the course of their judicial career.

The impossible battle for judges who are compulsorily retired

The story is no better when it comes to the compulsory retirement of judges, many of whom may have decades of experience. As mentioned earlier, this exercise of reviewing a judge's service record is carried out when the judge turns 50, 55 and 58 years old. The administrative committees consisting of judges of the High Court are only required to review the judge's service record before deciding on whether the judge is fit to continue in service. There is no requirement to interview the judge or investigate her conduct before the retirement order is issued.

The key input in the process is the ACR of the judge. The supervising judge has to provide his assessment in the ACR, which includes parameters such as integrity, knowledge, quality of judgments and relationship with the bar, amongst other criteria. In addition to the ACR, complaints received against the judge and pending disciplinary charges against the judge also form part of the assessment leading to a decision to compulsorily retire a judge.

The problem with making the ACR the central basis of the decision to compulsorily retire judges is threefold.

The first problem is that the entire grading process in the ACR is remarkably subjective, vesting enormous power in the hands of the supervising judge. This is not ideal for a post as powerful as that of a judge since it makes them vulnerable to pressure from the supervising authority.

Second, it is not uncommon for rumours and innuendo to make their way into the ACR, especially when it comes to the assessment of a judge's 'integrity', which is one of the criteria required to be assessed by the supervising judge. Illustratively, the following is an example from a judgment explaining how a judge received a poor assessment on the count of integrity[28]:

> In Inspection Report for the same year, the District & Sessions Judge, Delhi, reported that he did not enjoy good reputation for honesty among lawyers and general public and that he was in the habit of drinking and gambling almost daily. In the Inspection Report dated 7.12.1985 for the year 1984-85, the concerned

> Hon'ble Inspecting Judge had observed that his reputation was under cloud although no specific instance of corruption had come to his notice, but watch was called for . . .

As can be seen in the above extract, there is no specific evidence cited in support of the allegation that made its way into the ACR as an adverse entry. Much of it appears to be rumour and innuendo. The Supreme Court has ruled that it is absolutely legal for a supervising judge to enter an adverse entry of 'doubtful integrity' in the ACR based on verbal complaints that were never investigated or subjected to a disciplinary inquiry, where the judge is provided with an opportunity to defend herself against the allegations. Lest this appears to be an exaggeration, the following is an extract of a judgment of the Supreme Court backing this practice of relying on vague allegations in ACRs for judges of the district judiciary[29]:

> The reputation of being corrupt would gather thick and unchaseable clouds around the conduct of an officer and gain notoriety much faster than the smoke. Sometimes there may not be concrete or material evidence to make it part of the record. It would, therefore, be impracticable for the reporting officer or the competent controlling officer writing the confidential report to give specific instances of shortfalls, supported by evidence . . .
>
> When even verbal repeated complaints are received against a judicial officer or on enquiries, discreet or otherwise, the general impression created in the minds of those making inquiries or the Full Court is that concerned judicial officer does not carry good reputation, such discreet inquiry and or verbal repeated complaints would constitute material on the basis of which ACR indicating that the integrity of the officer is doubtful can be recorded.

Simply put, the Supreme Court has extended its blessing to the practice of entering adverse entries in a judge's ACR solely on the basis of the rumour mill without any requirement for substantial evidence.

The third problem with relying on ACRs is that adverse entries are often not communicated to the judge being evaluated, thereby depriving the judge of the opportunity to invoke the administrative mechanism that allows them to seek a review of adverse entries. These uncommunicated adverse entries can then be considered by the High Court when making assessments about whether to compulsorily retire a judge. In the Supreme Court's own words[30]:

> Opportunity of hearing is not necessary before adverse remarks because adverse remarks by themselves do not constitute a penalty. However, when the order of compulsory retirement is passed, the authority concerned has to take into consideration the whole service record of the officer concerned which would include non-communicated adverse remarks also. Thus it is settled by several reported decisions of this Court that un-communicated adverse remarks can be taken into consideration while deciding the question whether an official should be made to retire compulsorily or not.

These rather serious issues in how ACRs are prepared can work to the detriment of judges in the district judiciary. The following narration of cases where judges were compulsorily retired, should illustrate the impossible legal battles they faced in court while trying to challenge the legality of the orders compulsorily retiring them from the judicial service.

The first case involves the compulsory retirement of three district judges from the Delhi Higher Judicial Service. One judge had served for five years, while the second judge had served twenty-two years and the third judge had served twenty-eight years. Sometime in 2001, all three were compulsory retired on the recommendation of an administrative committee consisting of judges of the Delhi High Court. All three judges challenged the orders and their case went all the way to the Supreme Court.[31]

Since High Courts are not required to provide any reasons justifying the compulsory retirement orders, the only viable legal strategy for these three judges was to poke holes in the manner in which their ACRs had been dealt with by the High Court because it is the ACRs that form the basis of the decision to compulsorily retire them. These judges argued that the adverse entries were entered into their ACRs without being communicated to them. In the case of one judge, his representations contesting the adverse entries were decided after the Screening Committee had already made its decision to compulsorily retire him. For another judge, the supervising judge had completed the ACRs for three years in one shot, instead of doing it at the end of every year, as required by regulations. Despite the haphazard way in which the ACRs were managed by the supervising judges, neither the Delhi High Court nor the Supreme Court agreed to set aside the compulsory retirement orders, after a legal battle which lasted ten years and ended on 12 September 2011.[32]

A second example is from the Orissa High Court, where a judge was compulsorily retired on 23 August 2012 after serving fifteen years in the state's judicial service.[33] As is the case with all compulsory retirement orders, the judge was not provided with any reasons for his dismissal. This judge had been subjected to two disciplinary inquiries into the manner in which he had passed certain judicial orders. The first inquiry had ended with a warning from the High Court. The second inquiry was still pending when the order of compulsory retirement was issued by the High Court. In his ACRs, the judge had received a 'good' rating for three years and 'average' ratings for the remaining years.

So, what was the basis of the High Court's decision to compulsorily retire the judge? Well, technically, nobody knows since there are no reasons provided in the order retiring the judge. However, the judgment of the High Court, deciding the petition for judicial review and presumably written by judges who participated in the full court meeting confirming the recommendation to compulsorily retire the judge, reveals that the basis of the retirement order was the 'ratings of performance in the CCRs [Confidential Character Rolls], the nature of allegations, charges in the pending disciplinary proceeding against him, the report of the review committee, his performance on judicial as well as administrative side, his reputation as such during entire service period'.[34] This is revealing since it shows that disciplinary inquiries that were still in progress and vague notions of reputation are being factored into the decision-making process while deciding to compulsorily retire judges.

As can be seen from the examples provided above, the manner in which High Courts take the decision to compulsorily retire judges is hardly the model of transparency or fairness.

The fact that judges staffing the district judiciary worry about how they can be compulsorily retired is evident from the fact that they have challenged the constitutionality of the practice on at least two occasions in two states.

In the first instance, a bench of three judges of the Andhra Pradesh High Court, on 23 July 2008, struck down as unconstitutional certain provisions of the Andhra Pradesh Public Employment (Regulation of Age of Superannuation) Act, 1984 that allowed for the compulsory retirement of judicial officers at the age of 50 or 55 years. This provision was incorporated into the state law based on the recommendations of the Shetty Commission, to compulsory retire judges at the ages of 50 years, 55 years and 58 years, if their performance was not up to the mark.

In its lengthy judgment striking down the provision allowing for the compulsory retirement of judges of the district judiciary, the Andhra Pradesh High Court noted that no other class of public servants were subject to such a mechanism of mandatory review for compulsory retirement. More pertinently, it noted that the very concept of compulsory retirement would 'certainly damage independence of judiciary' by impeding the ability of judges to 'function without fear'.[35] In other words, the High Court was concerned about the impact of compulsory retirement on the decisional independence of the judges and the fact that the judges, subject to such a mechanism, would be vulnerable to the influence of those who could wield this power over them.

An appeal against this judgment filed before the Supreme Court was pending for almost a decade. Finally, a bench of two judges of the Supreme Court, in a rather flippant order of merely forty-five words, set aside the well-reasoned judgment of the Andhra Pradesh High Court. The Supreme Court did not bother to engage with the High Court's concerns regarding the implications of such compulsory retirement orders on the ability of judicial officers to 'function without fear'.[36]

As a result of this order by the Supreme Court, a second challenge that had been pending against a similar rule in Gujarat since 2016 was dismissed by the Gujarat High Court in 2024.[37] Since 2009, the Gujarat High Court has compulsorily retired forty-three judges—no other High Court comes close to this frequency, per reporting in the press.

Should competence be a basis for dismissing judges?

As is evident by now, the dismissal of probationary judges and compulsory retirement of judges are essentially based on assessments of the judges' competence to hold judicial office. However, it is important to ask whether competence should be a factor in dismissing judges from their jobs, given the possible consequences for the independence and efficiency of the district judiciary.

It should be noted that there is a line of academic opinion that advocates against 'competence' being a ground for dismissal of judges. As one academic put it, excluding incompetence as a ground to discipline judges is 'an inevitable price which society has to pay for maintaining the independence of judges . . . it would be difficult to draw the line, if judges were to be removed for incompetence, [as] this standard could be used as a pretext for removing from office judges who were perfectly competent but for some reason or another do not enjoy the support of those who control the machinery of removal . . . .'[38]

The better way to handle the issue of competence of judges, as explained by other academics, is 'by the selection of competent individuals to take judicial office, ongoing education regimes and the appeal process'.[39] Simply put, it is better to ensure that only competent judges are selected in the first place, instead of removing judges of the district judiciary on the grounds that they are not suited to be judges after they have served for several years and rendered judgments in potentially hundreds of cases. Such assessments of competence vest immense power in the hands of those wielding it, opening the door to abuse and extraneous influence over the judges being subject to such assessments.

It may also be pertinent to mention that the Constitution of India allows the removal of judges of High Courts and the Supreme Court only on the grounds of 'proven misbehaviour' or 'incapacity' (generally when a judge has a physical or other ailment impairing their ability to discharge the functions of a judicial office).[40] The Constitution does not provide for removal of the judges of the higher judiciary based on assessments of their competence. This is unlike some other post-colonial countries like Ghana, Kenya, Malawi, Pakistan, South Africa and Uganda, which allow for judges of higher judiciary to be removed on the grounds of competence.[41] If India does not follow the 'competence' standard for the higher judiciary, it is worth questioning why judges of the district judiciary in India are removed on the grounds of competence and that too in such an opaque manner without any reasons or a hearing.

The more worrying aspect of an approach that relies on competence to assess judges is that it is likely to compromise the decisional independence of probationary judges and those judges who are nearing the milestone ages when they are up for a mandatory review that could lead to compulsory retirement. We suspect that these two categories of judges, in a bid to ensure the security of their jobs, will try their best to avoid hearing cases perceived to be risky, or worse, they may refuse to grant certain risky remedies to litigants (such as bail in high-profile cases), for fear of how their conduct may be perceived during the assessment process. Such trepidation amongst these two categories of judges is possibly contributing in significant measure to judicial delays in India. This factor alone is a significant reason to eliminate the concept of probation for newly appointed judges and compulsory retirement for older judges.

Nevertheless, if competence continues to be one of the criteria for dismissal of these two categories of judges, it is absolutely necessary to replace the ACR system with a more well-rounded performance assessment system that involves multiple stakeholders and which is not controlled entirely by one supervising judge, as is currently the case. An ideal performance assessment system for judges should include feedback from colleagues on the bench, lawyers from the bar, the litigants and court staff. Such an approach would help provide the High Courts with a more holistic view of the performance of judges. Further, any decision based on performance assessment reports leading to the removal of these judges should be preceded by providing the judge in question with an opportunity to be heard on specific charges of incompetence. Any decision to remove the judge should be backed by a reasoned decision, with the right to appeal. These measures will hopefully provide an assurance to the district judiciary that they will not suffer arbitrary dismissals from the judicial service. Most importantly, if judges are going to be dismissed on grounds of competence, it should be incumbent on the High Courts ordering such dismissals to institute mechanisms to review judgments passed by these judges. It would be incongruous for the High Courts to dismiss these judges on grounds of competence and then remain silent on the judgments passed by these judges, especially in cases where the life, liberty and property of litigants is implicated.

4

The Curse of the Revolving Docket

In January 1986, Bombay witnessed the shocking deaths of fourteen patients at J. J. Hospital due to adulterated medicine. That scandal led to a commission of inquiry chaired by a sitting judge of the High Court, the resignation of the state health minister and the criminal prosecution of the manufacturer of the adulterated medicine. Thirty-six years later, in 2022, after a similar scandal in a foreign country involving medicine allegedly manufactured in India, a curious reporter followed up on the prosecution of those accused of the deaths at J. J. Hospital. Astonishingly, she discovered that the trial had yet to begin, thirty-six years after the incident.[1]

Tracing the journey of the case through the legal system, the reporter noted that one of the likely reasons for the delay was the frequent transfer of the judges assigned to the case. During its pendency, this case had reportedly travelled through the dockets of approximately a dozen judges! As a result, it is impossible to blame any single judge for the delay. In this anecdote of revolving dockets of judges lies the most mundane, yet important, cause of judicial delays in India: the transfer policies within the district judiciary.

Transfers of judges within the district judiciary are a routine administrative practice in India, as is the case within the civil services staffing the bureaucracy of the government. Except, with the district judiciary, the transfer policy can work at two levels. Apart from being transferred every few years between districts, judges can also be rotated through different portfolios (could be civil or criminal cases or specific types of cases) every few months within the same district. For example, in Uttar Pradesh, a judge posted to Unnao district for three years functioned as a civil judge for eight months, a judicial magistrate for thirteen months and again as a civil judge for eleven months before being transferred to Agra district.[2] This is very common in Uttar Pradesh. Commenting on the frequency of transfers, the Allahabad High Court noted in 1997 that as per a study, a judge 'within a period of two and half years' posting in a district was shunted nine times. His average period of posting in one court at a time came to a hundred days which is too short a period to rotate even once the pending cases in that court'.[3] Simply put, the system is organized in such a manner that it is impossible for a single judge to hear a case from start to finish.

As also explained by the Allahabad High Court, one of the factors aggravating the general transfer policy is the policy of assigning judges to courtrooms within the same district based on the 'seniority' of judges, i.e. the judge who entered the judicial service first is the 'senior'. For example, the senior-most judge will be the District Judge, while other judges of the same rank who are junior will preside over the courts in the same district as the 1st Additional District Judge or 2nd Additional District Judge, as per the *inter se* seniority. However, if there is a vacancy in the district and the new judge posted to the district is 'senior' to the District Judge, the existing District Judge will have to move to the court of the 1st Additional District Judge and the existing 1st Additional District Judge will move to the court of the 2nd Additional District Judge.[4] The Allahabad High Court concluded that such transfers had 'a serious telling repercussion on the disposal of the pending cases, particularly the old ones' since it would often become 'difficult to pinpoint the responsibility' for the continued pendency of an old case. Further, the High Court pointed out that even if a new judge 'familiarises himself with the pendency of the old cases and chalks out a phased programme to decide them, he is shifted to another court' as part of the routine transfer policy, as per which judges are generally transferred every three years.[5]

Left unsaid in the above judgment is the reason for some cases maturing into the category of 'old cases'. The most likely reason, we suspect, is that these old cases are either 'risky' cases that may attract disciplinary inquiries or, equally likely, these are complex cases that require the presiding judge to oversee a trial consisting of several witnesses and wade through voluminous evidentiary records. The reluctance of the district judiciary to hear complicated cases has been the worst-kept secret within the judiciary for at least a hundred years now. Back in 1925, the Rankin Committee on Civil Justice set up by the colonial government to study the problem of delays within the Indian judiciary had linked the delay of complicated cases to constant transfers. In pertinent part, the Committee had this to say about the problem[6]:

> The existence of a mass of arrears takes the heart out of a presiding officer. He can hardly be expected to take a strong interest in preliminaries, when he knows that the hearing of the evidence and the decision will not be by him but by his successor after his transfer. So long as such arrears exist, there is a temptation, to which many presiding officers succumb, to hold back the heavier contested suits and devote attention to the lighter ones. The out-turn of decisions in contested suits is thus maintained somewhere near the figure of institutions, while the really difficult work is pushed into the back-ground.

In contrast to the above mildly-worded report on the reluctance of judges to hear 'heavily contested' suits, i.e. complex cases, there are sharply-worded circulars published by the Allahabad High Court berating the district judiciary for avoiding complicated cases on their docket. For example, a circular published in 1932 by the Allahabad High Court had this to say about the tendency of judges within the district judiciary to delay hearing the more complicated cases until an additional court was created, at which point they would transfer the complicated cases to the new court[7]:

> There is a tendency in subordinate courts to postpone complicated cases and to take up the disposal of such cases as are short or convenient and when an additional court is created such old and complicated cases are often transferred to it in order to give relief

> to the permanent court. The Presiding Officers of such additional courts are generally less experienced than those of permanent courts, and such an arrangement is not satisfactory, and is disapproved by the High Court.

A similar circular was issued by the High Court in 1962, berating the tendency of the district judiciary to avoid hearing complicated cases:

> In order to avoid accumulation of old cases the tendency of leaving such cases as are of complicated nature involving lengthy arguments, recalcitrant witnesses, voluminous documents and intricate law points and taking up only such cases as are short and convenient for heavy disposal should be deprecated.[8]

We suspect that the rest of the country faces a similar problem when it comes to complex cases. This trend may be one of the reasons why 26 per cent of the cases on the docket of the district judiciary have been pending for over five years, per the National Judicial Data Grid.

One reason for the judiciary's reluctance to hear complicated cases is likely the normal human tendency to avoid complex tasks. There is, however, a second reason that contributes to the problem and that is the performance assessment system put in place to evaluate the judges of the district judiciary. In its current form, this measures the work done by every judge of the district judiciary per a 'unit system'. Basically, every judge earns a certain predetermined number of 'units' for each judicial task (e.g., examination or cross-examination of witnesses) that they complete. Additionally, they are expected to dispose of a minimum number of cases to secure a rating of 'good' in their Annual Confidential Report (ACR). Judges with a higher administrative workload are given lower targets.

For example, in Delhi, as per the 'unit norms' laid down by the Delhi High Court, a sessions judge has to earn three hundred units in order to get a rating of 'good' in her ACR, provided she also disposes a minimum of nine contested cases per quarter.

The unit weightage for each case is determined by a number of different factors, including whether it was contested by the opposing parties. In some states, the number of years for which it was pending (older cases get more weightage) also contributes to the units earned. In addition, the judge also gets units for other judicial tasks. For example, for the task of presiding over the examination of a material witness in a trial under the Prevention of Corruption Act, the judge will be awarded three units. For disposing of a criminal appeal, a judge will be awarded three units, while disposing of a criminal appeal older than five years will be awarded four units.[9] A similar system exists across India to evaluate the performance of the district judiciary, although the weightage of the units may differ.

The rating in a judge's ACR will then influence not just decisions on the judge's promotion to a higher office but will also feed into any decision by the High Courts to compulsorily retire the judge before they reach the mandatory retirement age of 60 years, as explained in the previous chapter. Judges who believe they have received an unfair rating in an ACR have in the past sued the High Court by filing writ petitions, seeking a correction of the rating. As a result, ACRs are a serious business within the district judiciary.

This assessment system, combined with the practice of transfers, creates perverse incentives for the district judiciary to delay hearing complex or risky cases. Knowing very well that their posting at a location is for only two or three years and that they need a minimum number of units in order to get a 'good' rating in the ACR, the average judge is incentivized to pick and choose the simpler cases in order to meet the targets required for a good rating. The unpredictability of both the inter-district and intra-district (where the judge's portfolio is changed within the same district) transfer system provides a second incentive for the judge to pick the simplest cases with the highest probability of being disposed of before the docket revolves once again. This is not to say that the complex cases are completely ignored. Since units are awarded for different tasks, a judge may still conduct the examination or cross-examination of witnesses in a complex case to earn some units but is likely to delay the more complicated aspects of such cases, such as framing of charges or deciding interim motions or hearing final arguments. In no circumstance will a judge have an incentive to spend a majority of her time on a complex trial from start to finish since that could lead to missing the target of minimum cases that must be disposed of to attain a good rating. As a result, complex cases will likely go to the end of the queue, slowly transforming into 'old cases'. Once the judge is transferred to a different court, a new cycle of delays will start at both the new courtroom as well as the old one.

Since the ACRs of judges are not publicly accessible documents, it will be difficult to prove the above hypothesis unless the judiciary releases anonymized versions of the ACRs for the benefit of an academic evaluation. However, it should be noted that the gaming of such statistical evaluation mechanisms is inevitable and will result in unintended consequences. As British economist Charles Goodhart put it, 'When a measure becomes a target, it ceases to be a good measure.' Other commentators have similarly warned the Indian judiciary of this risk when using quantitative evaluation measures for assessing judicial performance.[10]

As is obvious by now, the general human tendency to avoid complex or risky work, combined with the unit-based performance evaluation and the system of revolving dockets due to the transfer policy, creates strong incentives for the district judiciary to delay the hearing of these cases for as long as possible. The root of the problem, in our opinion, is the revolving docket. If this practice were to end and judges were aware that a complex case is going to remain on their permanent docket till they retire from the bench, they will alter the manner in which they approach such a case, provided, of course, that the 'unit' system of performance evaluation is also reconsidered.

Despite the deeply disruptive effect of transfers on judicial efficiency, the issue receives almost no public attention in India. There appears to be only one article by American academic Robert Moog, published in 1992, where he took a critical look at transfers.[11] In this article, Moog picked up the thread from the Rankin report on the link between judicial transfers and delays and further expanded on it, based on his study of district courts in Uttar Pradesh. He described the effects of transfers as follows[12]:

> Besides disrupting many of the cases pending in these courts by displacing the presiding officer responsible for each one, such a

> system does little to promote an interest in the efficient disposal of cases or a commitment to a particular caseload. The realization that within the foreseeable future most or all of their cases will be left behind encourages a wait-and-see attitude.

Further, as explained by Moog, since judges are the only temporary players in a courtroom where both the staff and the advocates are permanent players, it is the judge who will have to adapt to the informal practices in the court rather than reform prevailing inefficient practices. A judge who does try to reform such practices may face pushback or boycotts or complaints from the local bar associations, which are generally well-organized. Since these complaints can trigger disciplinary action against the judge by the High Courts, there is little incentive for the average judge to try and reform existing inefficient practices in the courtroom.[13]

Since transfers of judges appear to be the cause for much disruption in the Indian judicial system, it is important to try and understand why the system of transfers was put in place for the district judiciary. Except, as we learnt the hard way, tracing the history of this practice is quite difficult. We know for certain that the practice of transfers was widely prevalent within the district judiciary during the colonial rule, because the Rankin report complained about the problems created by transfers.[14] It is, however, difficult to identify the exact reason for its introduction. It is very likely that this transfer policy for the district judiciary was simply borrowed from existing policies that applied to the civil service who staffed the bureaucracy of the provinces. After all, the district judiciary during colonial rule was modelled on the lines of the provincial civil services.

It is evident from official reports of the British government from that era, such as the Royal Commission on Decentralisation, published in 1909, that transfers within the civil services was deeply disruptive to daily governance and caused a great deal of inefficiency.

The Commission's report attributed the practice of transfers within the bureaucracy staffing the civil service to five 'principal causes'. At the top of the list was the need for European bureaucrats to be given leave on a 'liberal scale' in order to visit their families back in Europe.

The vacancies caused by their visits to Europe had to be filled by transferring serving bureaucrats. Other reasons included the need to balance the differing workload in different districts, seniority in officiating appointments, the necessity of selecting bureaucrats for 'employment at the headquarters' or 'special duty' and finally, personal requests from bureaucrats for transfers.[15] Despite past attempts by Lord Curzon at reforming the practice, the report complained that transfers were 'still far too numerous', and 'that the evils attendant upon the constant moving of district officers have not been adequately recognised in the Provincial Secretariats'.[16]

Despite its many inefficiencies, the policy of regular transfers in both the civil services and judicial services continued after India attained independence from the British. Many of the High Courts have made the transfer policies applicable to the district judiciary publicly available on their websites, but none of these policies lay out the rationale for transferring judges at the frequency of three years or less. Rather, these policies only lay out the mechanics of the process, such as the schedule of transfers and concessions that can be made in special circumstances. At most, the transfer policy laid down by the Delhi High Court does state that one aim of the policy shall be 'an endeavour to give exposure of work of all possible jurisdictions so as to build capacity of each judicial officer', but it does not explain why it is necessary to transfer judges every two to three years to achieve this aim in a city-state like Delhi where litigation patterns across all thirteen court complexes are very similar.[17] Even presuming that this is the rationale for transfers in the larger states with widely varying litigation patterns between urban and rural areas, it is worth asking whether the disruption caused by transfers is worth the benefit of a judge with wider judicial experience.

Unlike India, there are countries like Kenya, which is also a former colony of the British, but has a well-defined transfer policy for judges. The Kenyan policy clearly states the aim of transfers from the perspective of judges as well as litigants. With regard to judges, the policy states that it aims to provide 'an equal opportunity to experience the benefits and challenges of serving in different areas' and 'an equal opportunity to gain equal exposure and experience'. From the perspective of the litigant, the policy categorically states that all litigants deserve to be served by the best judges and hence transfers will not be employed as a disciplinary tool to punish judges. Similarly, the policy states that the aim of transfers is also to ensure the impartiality of judges, who may develop a familiarity 'with the community in the area including lawyers, litigants, police, prosecutors and other members of the public' if posted for a long period of time at the same court.

There is some speculation in academic literature that India transfers judges of the district judiciary for the same reason, i.e. to ensure the impartiality of judges by ensuring they do not get too familiar with lawyers or litigants in one district.[18] However, the official policies of the few High Courts that we reviewed make no mention of ensuring impartiality as an objective of the transfer policy. In any event, there is little logic or empirical evidence to support the argument that a judge is likely to become more partial to particular lawyers or litigants if they are stationed at a particular district for a long time. A judge susceptible to displaying favoritism towards specific lawyers at a posting over three years is fundamentally unsuited to be a judge. On the contrary, one could also argue that a judge who has some familiarity and experience in the courtroom will find it easier to spot the dilatory tactics of lawyers of the local bar association. Further, if there were any valid rationale or logic to this assumption of impartiality guiding transfers, it should be applied even to judges of the High Court. Currently, judges of the High Court generally spend their entire careers at the same High Court in the same city. At most, these judges will be rotated through different rosters, i.e. they will sit in different courtrooms within the same High Court building, hearing different types of cases. But it is the same lawyers from the High Court who appear before them in these different courtrooms.

So, to briefly answer the question about whether there is any rationale for the mandatory transfer policies imposed on the district judiciary, we plead ignorance. Our best guess is that this policy of mandatory transfers for the district judiciary appears to be a remnant from colonial times when the judicial services were styled on the lines of the bureaucracy and drew a number of its judges from the bureaucracy. The practice likely continued post-Independence as an administrative ritual, without adequate attention being paid to its impact on delays.

Given the lack of any thought given to the continuation of these transfer policies, it is hardly surprising that the High Courts have weaponized transfers as a punitive measure in a number of cases, including when a judge used 'inappropriate language' in a judgment and when a judge sexually harassed a survivor of sexual violence.[19] This practice of transfers as punishment ignores the obvious ethical issues with imposing an incompetent or corrupt judge on a new set of litigants.

Equally problematic is the fact that High Courts routinely use transfers to deal with complaints of bar associations locked in confrontations with judges of the district judiciary. Even the Supreme Court has noted this practice in disapproving terms, calling it 'a disturbing trend nowadays that Judicial Officers are made scapegoats and penalized whether by inconvenient transfers or otherwise, whenever there are agitations/demonstrations against the Judicial Officers whether by Advocates or others . . .'.[20] The obvious consequence of such punitive transfers, as argued by Moog, is that judges have no incentive to reform inefficient administrative practices at the level of district courts. Knowing that the transfer policy can be used as a disciplinary tool without any due process also means that powerful elements within the High Courts can misuse transfers to impinge on the decisional independence of the district judiciary by leaning on individual judges to rule in a particular manner.

These numerous administrative inefficiencies are compounded by the disruption of the family lives of judges, especially the schooling of their children, every few years. Given these disruptions, it is not uncommon for the judges of the district judiciary to lobby the judges of the High Courts for their choice of posting, since it is the High Court that controls the transfers. The lobbying can get so intense that High Courts have had to put out notices instructing the district judiciary to stop visiting judges of the High Courts at their residences in order to lobby for a posting of their choice.[21] There is at least one reported instance of a Union Minister lobbying a High Court on behalf of a recently appointed judge who was requesting a particular posting. The High Court ended up dismissing the judge in question.[22] Such lobbying also opens the door for powerful elements within the High Courts to harass the district judiciary. There is at least one known instance of a married female district judge accusing a judge of a High Court of orchestrating her transfer to a remote district because she turned down his overtures.[23]

An interesting historical anecdote in this context is that the power to transfer judges of the subordinate judiciary was shifted to the High Courts from the provincial governments in 1935 specifically because of concerns that the power over determining transfers of judicial officers gave ministers of the provincial government too much control over the subordinate judiciary.[24] When the new Constitution was being drafted after Independence, the Conference of the Judges of the Federal Court and the Chief Justices of High Courts held in March 1948 demanded that the new Constitution continue to vest the power of transfers with the High Courts. The Drafting Committee and the Constituent Assembly consented to this demand in the form of Article 235.[25] This arrangement may have insulated the district judiciary from the influence of the state government and its ministers but may very well have opened the district judiciary to a new kind of pressure from elements within the High Court.

Can India put an end to the revolving docket?

It is difficult to identify one good reason to continue with the present system of transfers and revolving dockets within the district judiciary. We suspect that the only reason that judges continue to be transferred is because the practice is a hangover from colonial times. The common argument that judges are likely to become partial to particular lawyers or litigants if they are posted at one location for a long period is not convincing and is in any event not mentioned in any of the transfer policies. The other argument that supporters of transfer policies are likely to make is that judges gain more experience when rotated through different districts in a state. But as mentioned earlier, the only relevant question is whether the disruption caused by transfers is justified by this possible gain in experience by judges of a wider variety of cases. In our opinion, the gain in experience through transfers is only a marginal benefit when compared to the massive disruption and lack of accountability caused by transfers.

If the policy of transfers is revoked, the concept of revolving dockets will also likely end and be replaced with a permanent docketing system, increasing the probability that a case is with the same judge from its institution to disposal. This will result in far greater efficiency and better outcomes compared to the present system, where a single case can easily revolve through the dockets of two or three different judges, with each judge presiding over a different part of the case before it is disposed. Not only will a permanent docketing system give the judge a sense of predictability over the expected workload but also make it easier to hold judges accountable for cases getting unreasonably delayed. The permanent posting of a judge in a particular district will also change the power dynamics between the bar, the court staff and the judge in favour of the latter, who will have more of an incentive to put in motion long-term reforms.

Despite the obvious advantages of extinguishing the practice of transfers within the district judiciary, it will be a politically contentious reform measure. If High Courts were to abolish transfer policies and announce that all judges would continue in their present postings till the end of their careers, it is highly likely that the bar will protest, perhaps even go on strike. Local bar associations that are stuck with strict and uncompromising judges will protest the loudest. The only way then to extinguish transfer policies in this environment is to stagger reforms. For example, the period between transfers should be increased gradually from three years to five years.

It is unlikely that such reforms will be executed by the judges of High Courts since it would require them to surrender their own power over the judges of the district judiciary. Any permanent solution to the transfer policy will have to come from the legislature. A law that ensures that new appointees to the judicial service serve in the same court for the duration of their careers, until retirement, may be the only way to end the practice of a revolving docket.

5

Too Young to Judge

India today is a land of coaching institutes, including for the examinations conducted in every state to select judges for the judicial services that staff the district judiciary. For some time now, there has been a direct pipeline from the coaching institutes in coaching hubs like Rajender Nagar, New Delhi to courtrooms in Patiala House, Tis Hazari and other court complexes across the country. These coaching institutes help prepare candidates for the judicial service examinations and interviews conducted by the High Courts or the public service commissions in different states.

When the results of these examinations are declared, these coaching institutes inevitably advertise their 'victories' on their websites to attract future candidates. These advertisements, especially for the subordinate judiciary, which comprises judicial magistrates and civil judges, usually feature the photographs of cherubic-looking youngsters who are barely out of law school. For example, in the year 2019, a young man who was just 21 years old cleared the qualifying examination and interview to be appointed to the subordinate judiciary in the state of Rajasthan, mere months after completing his law degree.[1] This gentleman is hardly an exception to the rule. In Madhya Pradesh, of the 1,079 civil judges-cum-judicial magistrates staffing the first two tiers of the district judiciary in 2024, a total of 248 judges were under 26 years of age at the time they were appointed as judges.[2]

Once selected and having gone through a short training programme, new appointees, most of whom lack any experience practising as lawyers, serve as a probationary Judicial Magistrate of First Class (FC) or a Civil Judge (Junior Division) (JD). The probationary period generally extends for two years, but is usually extended, after which a decision is taken to 'confirm' or 'discharge from service' the probationary judge. It is within the probationary period that the High Court can assess the performance of the probationary judge and make the decision for 'confirming' the judge for a permanent position within the judiciary.

In essence, the Indian state is experimenting on litigants to determine whether a new appointee has the skills and competence to hold judicial office. From an ethical perspective, such an approach is deeply problematic since, during the probationary period, a judicial magistrate or civil judge could have easily decided hundreds of cases that have profound implications for litigants. Apart from the system of appeals that exists for all cases, there is no other system to review the judgments passed by probationary judges subsequently dismissed during the period of probation.

This is a worrying state of affairs because the Judicial Magistrate (FC) and Civil Judge (JD) are both very powerful judicial offices. For example, under the Code of Criminal Procedure, the Judicial Magistrate (FC) is the first line of defence of civil liberties. As per Article 22 of the Constitution, the police are required to produce every person that it arrests before a judicial magistrate within twenty-four hours. Most of these persons will be produced before the Judicial Magistrate (FC). It is the judicial magistrate who decides whether to remand the person to police custody or release them on bail. Similarly, when a criminal complaint is filed directly with the criminal courts requesting investigation into a particular offence like criminal defamation or copyright infringement or sedition or substandard drugs, it is the judicial magistrate who is required to examine the complaint and make the decision to set into motion the wheels of the criminal justice system.

The Judicial Magistrate (FC) is also responsible for trying several serious offences under the law. While the sentencing power of the Judicial Magistrate (FC) is limited to three years' imprisonment, if the magistrate thinks that the offence demands a longer prison term as permissible in the law, a sentencing recommendation can be referred to the Sessions Court for confirmation.[3] For some of these offences, the punishment prescribed in the law can extend to ten years (such as robbery) or fourteen years (in the case of lurking house trespass in the night).

Similarly, the office of the Civil Judge (JD) has wide jurisdiction to hear civil disputes. Their jurisdiction is generally determined by the valuation of the lawsuit. For example, in the state of Telangana, the Telangana Civil Courts Act, 1972 requires the Civil Judge (JD) to hear cases valued at less than Rs 20 lakh. All suits valued above Rs 20 lakh will be heard by the more experienced Civil Judge (Senior Division) and district judge. To illustrate with an example, a person dwelling in a slum or *basti* and facing the possibility of their home being demolished by the municipal corporation will have to approach the Civil Judge (JD) for an emergency temporary injunction against the demolition. Similarly, a civil judge of this rank will also have to adjudicate contractual disputes and lawsuits for recovery of monies within the range of Rs 20 lakh.

As should be obvious from the above illustrations, the judicial offices of the Judicial Magistrates (FC) and Civil Judges (JD) are of immediate importance to the common citizen. Yet, the present system of appointments ensures that most appointees to these judicial offices are in their twenties with little to no experience of practising law at the bar and only limited life experience outside of a law school or university. It is worth asking whether these young judges have the legal skills and emotional maturity to dispense justice that impacts the lives of Indian citizens in profound ways.

The Bar Council of India (BCI) addressed this issue in a scathing press release published in January 2021 where it described the current crop of appointees to the office of judicial magistrates and civil judges in the following, rather unflattering language[4]:

> Judicial Officers not having practical experience at the Bar are mostly found to be incapable and inept in handling matters. Most of such officers are found impolite and impractical in their behaviour with the Members of the Bar and Litigants. They have lack of

> understanding of the aspirations and expectations of Advocates and Litigants in the matter of proper and decent behaviour.
>
> The inexperience at the Bar is one of the primary and major reasons for delays in the disposal of cases in the subordinate judiciary. Trained and experienced judicial officers can comprehend and dispose of matters at a much faster pace, thereby leading to efficient administration of justice.

These statements were made in the context of a pending case before the Supreme Court regarding the length of mandatory practice requirements at the Bar as a prerequisite for lawyers being appointed to the offices of judicial magistrate or civil judge. The BCI was in favour of bringing back the practice requirement of three years as a solution to the problems outlined above in its press release. The BCI is not alone in its criticism of the current crop of judges staffing these important judicial offices. The Uttarakhand High Court has voiced similar criticism, stating[5]:

> Fresh Law Graduates, with no exposure to the Court environment are not steeped into the culture, etiquette, temper and conduct of the Court proceedings. This leads to complaints of misbehaviour and ill treatment of advocates and litigants by such new Officers. Many of the freshly recruited officers enter the Court precincts only after appointment. Moreover, judging is a serious task and requires some maturity of thinking and experience of life.

Given these criticisms, there is a need for a broader relook at appointment practices and not just the practice requirement at the Bar. To this end, we focus on four issues pertaining to the appointment of lawyers to the offices of Judicial Magistrate (FC) and Civil Judge (JD): qualifying age, practice requirements at the Bar, written examinations as a mode of selection and the practice of having 'probationary judges'.

Qualifying ages for judges—why are so many in their twenties?

When it comes to public office in India, of any kind, not just the judiciary, age is not just a number but a crucial qualifying criterion. Not all adults over the age of 18 years are qualified to hold all public offices in India. For example, the Constitution mandates 25 years as the minimum age to be elected to the Lok Sabha while the minimum age to be elected to the Rajya Sabha is 30 years.[6] Similarly, the Constitution requires that a citizen be at least 35 years old in order to qualify for the post of President of India.[7]

Even more interesting is how age plays out in the appointment of judges to the High Courts and district judiciary. To qualify as a judge of any High Court, the Constitution requires that a lawyer has at least ten years of experience at the bar.[8] It is silent on a minimum age requirement, although it does mention a retirement age of 62 years. Theoretically this means that any lawyer aged approximately 33 to 35 years should have enough experience to be appointed to the bench. However, in reality, it is very rare for lawyers under the age of 45 years to be appointed as a judge of the High Court and this age requirement had reportedly been agreed on by the judiciary and government during the course of negotiations on the method of appointing judges to the High Courts.[9]

Similarly, although the Constitution requires that a lawyer have a minimum of seven years of experience at the bar to be considered for appointment as a District Judge, which most candidates can complete by the time they turn 30 years, most states have mandated 35 years as the minimum qualifying age for this office.[10] The average age of actual appointment in most states is higher than 35 years. For example, in Madhya Pradesh, the average age of the 610 district judges staffing its district courts in 2024, at the time of appointment to the post, was 44 years.[11] In Karnataka, the average age of 537 district judges in the state was 50 years at the time of their appointment.[12]

The fact that the age of potential candidates for judicial office is being given preference, over and above the practice requirements laid down in the Constitution of India, is not surprising. Across cultures and nations, the task of adjudicating legal disputes has always been vested in the older members of a society or the 'village elders' because it is presumed that their life experience has given them a certain degree of wisdom that is necessary to deliver justice. Life has a way of imparting experiences that cannot be learnt in a classroom. Routine life experiences after graduating from university can profoundly mould the personality of a young adult by diluting the arrogance of youth. Take, for example, the experience of finding a house to rent in urban India, where property owners regularly discriminate against possible tenants on the basis of their religion, occupation, caste, gender, marital status and dietary habits. For most upper-caste young Indians who are Hindu males and generally at the top of the societal ladder, 'house hunting' is most likely the first time they experience discrimination. Similarly, other experiences of young adulthood such as searching for employment, navigating a demanding workplace, getting married, convincing reluctant parents for an inter-caste or inter-religious marriage and managing a household are all crucial experiences that mould the personalities of young adults, imparting to them some worldly wisdom.

These life experiences, which cannot be taught in the classroom, can be critical in giving young people a degree of emotional maturity. Such emotional maturity is not merely a virtue but an essential requirement in judges who dispense justice to citizens.

Aside from emotional maturity, it should also be remembered that India is a deeply hierarchical society, wherein age matters in societal relations. The younger the judge, the tougher it is going to be for them to exercise control over their courtrooms, typically staffed by older court staff or older lawyers at the bar. An inefficient courtroom contributes to delays.

Also instructive is the fact that other countries ensure the appointment of older candidates to all tiers of the judicial system, not just the highest tier. This includes the US and the UK, both of which have legal systems very similar to that of India. In the US, for the office of the Magistrate Judge in the federal judiciary, despite the law laying down a practice requirement of only five years, the average experience at the bar of new appointees in 2021 was 23 years and their average age at appointment was 50 years.[13] The American Magistrate Judge has only a fraction of power of the Judicial Magistrate (FC) in India and can try only petty offences (punishable with only one year of imprisonment) committed on federal lands, issue bail, warrants and handle pre-trial motions in civil and criminal cases.

In the UK, the district judges who staff the county courts and magistrate courts are the first tier of professional, salaried judges and are required by law to have mandatorily practised law for a period of five years. However, the applicants for judicial positions requiring five years of practice (which includes district judges) in the year 2022-23 had an average experience of between 17 years and 19.5 years.[14] Also, 74 per cent of the new appointees for the post of district judge in that year were older than 50 years of age.[15]

There is no system in India for releasing the age profiles of the district judiciary in a similar format. However, we were able to use publicly available data in some states to calculate the average age at which judges were appointed to the first tier of the district judiciary as Civil Judges (JD) or Judicial Magistrates (FC) in Madhya Pradesh, Assam and Uttar Pradesh (based on data from five districts).

In Madhya Pradesh, the average age of judges currently in the district judiciary, across all ranks, at the time of their appointment was merely 29.68 years.[16] In fact, it appears that the average age has fallen from 31 years for judges appointed in 2000, to 28 years for judges appointed in 2023 to the post of Judicial Magistrate (FC) and Civil Judge (JD). In Assam, the average age at which the current crop of serving judges were appointed to the judicial services was 31.5 years. The average age of the appointment in Assam to this office reduced from 32.8 years to 31.1 years over time.[17]

For Uttar Pradesh, we collected age-related data for approximately 200 judges across five districts. The average age at time of appointment for these judges was 30 years. The average age of judges, in fact, reduced from 32.86 years for appointments prior to the year 2010, to 29.49 years for judges appointed post 2010. Simply put, the average age of new appointees is dropping. It is very likely that this trend of increasingly younger judges being appointed to the judicial services is repeating itself in other states within India.

One reason these judges are getting appointed at such young ages is because most states, in their qualifying rules, prescribe an outer age limit of 32 years (Delhi Judicial Services) to 35 years (Uttar Pradesh Judicial Services) for those applying for the office of civil judge or judicial magistrate.[18] As a result, the older and more experienced candidates cannot even apply for these offices. Such upper age limits for judicial offices are rather strange. Age limits make sense for jobs requiring physical fitness. For example, soldiers need to be in a certain state of physical fitness and it makes sense to have an upper age limit of 30 years. But it is difficult to comprehend the rationale for an upper age limit of 32 years or 35 years for the office of judicial magistrates and civil judges. Lifting these upper age limits would open the door for experienced lawyers to apply for the offices of civil judges and judicial magistrates.

The question we must ask in this context is why exactly does India bar more experienced lawyers from applying for the office of Judicial Magistrates (FC) or Civil Judges (JD)? The same question can be asked for the office of the district judge, where the upper age limit in most states to apply for this position is 45 years?

The most likely answer is that these age limits are a continuation of 19th-century colonial policies which structured the judicial services on the lines of the bureaucratic services. There does not appear to be any sense in continuing with these age limits. Lifting these limits will open the door to a larger pool of older and more experienced lawyers to apply for these very important judicial offices. Older, more experienced lawyers will certainly make for better judges and, in all likelihood, improve the quality as well as speed of justice.

Mandatory practice requirements at the Bar: can lawyers be trained in the classroom to be effective judges?

The second qualifying criteria for judicial office, which intersects with age, is the mandatory requirement for lawyers to have practised a minimum number of years at the bar. This requirement exists in order to ensure that potential candidates have gained practical experience of legal advocacy in the courtroom. They need to have a working knowledge of how the courtroom operates in order to be effective judges. More importantly, they need to know how the law works in practice. In most common law countries, such a practice requirement at the bar is compulsory for lawyers seeking judicial appointment. This has not always been true in India. While the Constitution mandates a minimum practice requirement of seven years for district judges and ten years for judges of the High Courts and Supreme Court, it does not specify any qualifications for the office of Judicial Magistrates (FC) or Civil Judges (JD). As per the Constitution, the state governments can decide these qualifications in consultation with the High Courts.

Historically most Indian states have prescribed a requirement of at least three years, if not five, at the bar for all lawyers seeking to apply for the post of Judicial Magistrate (FC) and Civil Judge (JD). This requirement of a minimum of three years' practice goes back to the 19th century. The Report of the Public Service Commission, 1886 referenced a similar requirement in the Presidency of Bombay and Province of Bengal for civil judges.[19] The Rankin Committee Report published in 1925 also references the existence of a practice requirement for appointment to the provincial judicial services in most provinces, while also noting that such a requirement was no guarantee of the candidate having picked up any useful legal experience.[20]

After Independence in 1947, the issue of practice requirement has been examined, to different degrees, in at least four different reports of the Law Commission—the 14th report (1958) by the First Law Commission and the 116th, 117th and 118th reports prepared by the Eleventh Law Commission in the 1980s. The common thread running through these reports is the acknowledgment that the practice requirement of three years at the bar was insufficient to prepare young lawyers for a career on the bench as judges. The logical response to such a finding should have been to advocate for an increase in the practice requirement for lawyers seeking appointment to the judicial service. However, this logical recommendation was never made by the Law Commission. Instead, the 11th Law Commission under retired Justice D. A. Desai, in its 117th report, recommended abolishing the practice requirements completely and, instead, selecting fresh graduates with no experience through an examination and training them in judicial academies. In its words: 'If training is imparted to an impressionable mind, not contaminated by some of the prevailing undesirable practices in vogue in the present-day Bar, amongst others by judges who have mastered the art of rendering justice, the same can be acquired.'[21]

The Supreme Court also weighed in on the debate regarding practice requirements on two occasions, coming to completely opposing conclusions. In 1993, while hearing a PIL filed by the All India Judges' Association (AIJA), which is an association of judges staffing the district judiciary, the court remarked that the experiment by some states to do away with the mandatory practice requirement was a failure. The court justified the practice requirement on the following grounds[22]:

> Considering the fact that from the first day of his assuming office, the judge has to decide, among others, question of life, liberty, property and reputation of the litigants, to induct graduates fresh from the Universities to occupy seats of such vital powers is neither prudent nor desirable. Neither knowledge derived from books nor pre-service training can be an adequate substitute for the first-hand experience of the working of the court system and the administration of justice begotten through legal practice. The practice involves much more than mere advocacy as lawyers has to interact with several components of the administration of justice. Unless the judicial officer is familiar with the working of the said components, his education and equipment as a judge is likely to remain incomplete.

These were wise words from the Supreme Court, which then proceeded to 'direct' all states to ensure a mandatory practice requirement of three years at the bar for all lawyers seeking to qualify for the office of Judicial Magistrate (FC) and Civil Judge (JD). Eight years later, in 2002, a different bench of the Supreme Court, in yet another PIL filed by the AIJA, came to the exact opposite conclusion, ordering states to undo the mandatory practice requirements at the bar, suggesting that a career in the judicial service loses its charm as legal practices flourish and that it is best to catch the talent young.[23] The court coupled this direction with a recommendation that new appointees be imparted training in a judicial academy.

Legally speaking, these directions by the Supreme Court were brazenly activist since the power to decide qualification criteria for the judicial services vests with the state governments, which generally consult the High Courts before deciding such criteria. But ignoring for a moment such judicial activism with complete disregard for the constitutional scheme, the more important question is whether a lawyer without any experience practising law at the bar can be 'trained' in a judicial academy to become a competent and compassionate judge.

From what little we know of clinical training programmes in the national law universities, it is very challenging to provide law students in law school with the advocacy skills required for a career in legal practice as lawyers. Such clinical training programmes require close monitoring and evaluation by a skilled tutor on a daily basis. Done right, such programmes require a very high student-to-faculty ratio, making them very expensive. Even in the West, where law schools have far more resources, clinical training aimed at preparing law students for the bar has proven to be so challenging to implement in reality that there have been some discussions to simply forgo clinical training in law schools and instead mandate apprenticeship programmes after graduation as a necessary requirement to qualify for the bar.[24] If it is so challenging to impart basic advocacy skills to law students in preparation for a legal career at the bar, one can only imagine the challenges of training new law graduates, with no experience at the bar, for a career on the bench as judges.

This challenge of moulding a law graduate into a judge through training in a classroom brings us to the fate of judicial academies in India. Since the Supreme Court's judgment in 2002, many states have set up judicial academies that operate under the control of High Courts. One of the many problems with most of these state judicial academies is that they do not have a permanent teaching faculty. These academies generally have one or two judges from the district judiciary serving as the director or deputy director, while the other instructors are generally guest lecturers. The Tamil Nadu Judicial Academy, which has three centres in the state of Tamil Nadu, has a sanctioned staff strength of 115 people. But not a single one of these is for teaching staff.[25] Instead, these posts comprise section officers, typists, computer operators, drivers, cooks, etc. Such a set-up, which is basically limited to providing hospitality and lodging services, may be appropriate for an academy conducting 'continuing legal education' for serving judges but it is completely inadequate to serve the purpose for moulding new law graduates into able judges. A professional training academy needs a sizeable and dedicated teaching staff who have the academic independence to develop and work with different pedagogical techniques and closely evaluate the progress of potential trainee judges. As argued by a former faculty member at the National Judicial Academy, such reform is unlikely to happen as long as the state judicial academies lack autonomy and continue to operate under the direct control of judges of the High Courts.[26]

Separate from the training in the academy, new appointees are also expected to train with judges holding court by sitting with them in the courtroom. A study of which we were a part conducted interviews with a relatively small number of young judges to find out more about how this training process works and the responses were not particularly encouraging. A common complaint was that the presiding judge was too busy to actively mentor and teach the trainee judge. For the most part, this aspect of the training seems to operate more like a clerkship for law students who provide research assistance to the judges rather than a structured programme to mould the law graduate into a judge.[27]

A third component of the training programme is supposed to be deputation to other government departments such as the revenue department, police department and forensic laboratories to understand how different arms of the state function. These deputations appear to have been reduced to one-day 'picnics', as described by a former faculty member at the National Judicial Academy, rather than a well-structured learning exercise.[28]

Given the inherent complexities of training new law graduates to become skilled judges, it may be time to give serious thought to reintroducing the mandatory practice requirement. In this regard, it should be pointed out that apart from the Bar Council of India, sixteen out of the twenty High Courts surveyed by a committee of the Supreme Court recommended that the mandatory practice requirement be reinstituted for appointment as Civil Judge (JD) and Judicial Magistrate (FC).[29] It may be time for the Supreme Court to rethink its 2002 judgment directing the states to abolish the three years' practice requirement. The court has seriously underestimated the challenges of both building good judicial academies and the inherent complexity of imparting practical skills to candidates through a training programme.

However, if a mandatory practice requirement is brought back, it is worth debating whether a requirement of three years serves the purpose or whether it is time to increase the minimum practice requirement far beyond three years. As mentioned earlier, the practice requirement of three years came about in the 19th century, when India had an abysmal life expectancy. Surely, with a life expectancy of 70 years and a steady supply of lawyers, India can increase the practice requirement to ensure that only the more experienced lawyers are appointed as civil judges and judicial magistrates.

Should written examinations be the mode of selection?

The last and final issue that deserves attention in the context of recruitment of judges for the judicial services is whether the present process of a written examination followed by an interview is the best way to select judges.

Historically, under colonial rule, judges for the civil judiciary at the subordinate level in most provinces of British India were selected through a combined system of written examinations and nominations by a selection committee of judges from the High Court. Regarding the format of the examination, the Rankin Committee report had recommended that candidates be tested on their ability to 'draft pleadings, appreciate evidence and write judgements'.[30]

By 1954, when the First Law Commission under M. C. Setalvad submitted its report on reforming judicial administration in India, at least five states were selecting judges to the subordinate judiciary through an open competitive examination combined with a *viva voce* test, while six other states followed a system of selecting these judges on the basis of interviews conducted by the Public Service Commission and judges of High Courts.[31] The Law Commission recommended that all appointments be made through the first route, i.e. a written examination followed by an interview for those who cleared it.[32] Like the Rankin Committee, the Law Commission recommended an examination format that tested the skills of candidates rather than their ability to reproduce 'rote' legal knowledge. To that end, it recommended an 'open book' examination format that allowed candidates to rely on 'bare acts' and 'law reports' to answer questions that tested their ability to apply the law to various factual scenarios posed to them in the examination.[33]

As of today, all states in India have open competitive examinations combined with an interview to select judges for all posts in the district judiciary, including for the post of district judge. There are generally two examinations. The preliminary examination, which generally has multiple choice questions, serves as a filtering mechanism for the main examination, which generally has questions that require subjective answers. There is also a language examination. The natural consequence of prescribing an entrance examination in India is the emergence of coaching institutes. In the context of the judicial services, these coaching centres can charge prospective candidates anything up to Rs 2.5 lakh for training them to crack the entrance examinations.

The problem with examinations to select judges is the format of examinations followed in most states. Our limited survey of recent examination papers for judicial services, copies of which are sold by commercial publishers, shows that most states generally end up testing the rote memory skills of candidates rather than their analytical legal reasoning skills. There are a few exceptions, like the Delhi Judicial Services Examinations that contain 'problem-style' questions that test the legal reasoning skills of the candidates, who are also provided with bare texts of the laws on which they are being tested.

The analytical skills of potential judges can be tested only if the examination is conducted in an open book format wherein candidates are allowed to access, during the course of the examination, any legal books, commentaries and manuals. There is plenty of scope for improving the current format of the judicial service examinations.

The examinations are followed by an interview of candidates who have cleared the written examinations. Since these interviews are conducted in a closed-door format and transcripts are not maintained or accessible, it is difficult to examine the efficacy of such a format. Anecdotal accounts indicate that interviews can last anywhere between five to thirty minutes and the scoring can be quite arbitrary. In states like Delhi, this largely subjective process accounts for 45 per cent of the total score. As a result, the interview process can significantly influence outcomes for candidates. It is, therefore, important for the interview process to be more transparent in order to ensure better outcomes.

Probationary period: experimenting on litigants

As of today, after the completion of the training process at the judicial academy, new judicial officers are appointed to the bench to try actual cases as either a 'probationary' judicial magistrate or civil judge for a minimum period of two years. It is important to remember that these probationary judges sit on the bench by themselves. There is no other judge sitting alongside them, guiding them along or pointing out their mistakes.

There are two mechanisms by which the actions of the probationary judge may be scrutinized. The first is if appeals are filed against the orders of the probationary judges. The second is during the annual evaluation process wherein the district judge rates the judge's performance in the Annual Confidential Report (ACR). The ACR along with judgments written by the probationary judge are evaluated by a committee of High Court judges which makes a decision to either confirm the judge who will serve until retirement at 60 years or dismiss the judge from service.

Although High Courts do not publish data in this regard, it is our calculated guess, based on anecdotal data, that most probationary judges are confirmed and only a few are dismissed.

Nevertheless, the fact of the matter is that the Indian state is experimenting on its citizens by allowing new law graduates, with no experience of advocacy at the bar and poor training in judicial academies to sit as probationary judges and hear and decide both civil and criminal cases that have serious consequences for the life, liberty and property of litigants. Since the probationary period is for a period of two years (or longer if the High Court decides to extend it), the probationary judge would have heard a fair number of cases, including requests by the police for remanding suspects to police custody and requests for bail by those detained in prison. Especially worrying is the fact that the High Courts, after dismissing probationary judges on the grounds that they are not suitable for the office, remain completely silent about the cases already decided by the dismissed judge.

The very concept of probationary judges, in our opinion, is bizarre. The High Court, as the appointing authority, should have complete confidence in the abilities of new appointees to the bench. It is absolutely unethical for High Courts to experiment on litigants with probationary judges in whose capabilities it lacks complete confidence.

How can India reform this 19th-century system of selecting judges?

As evident from the recent criticism of the BCI on the lack of professionalism of young judges, as well as the overwhelming agreement amongst the High Courts on the need for young judges to have more experience, it is vital to demand the reinstatement of a mandatory practice requirement for all new judges appointed as civil judges or judicial magistrates.

The question now is the length of the practice requirement. So far, the demand appears to be for a practice requirement of three years without questioning the rationale and sufficiency of a mere three years' practice requirement. After all, as the anecdotal data discussed earlier in the chapter demonstrates, the effective practice requirement for both district judges and judges of the High Courts is between fifteen years and twenty-five years, despite the Constitution prescribing a practice requirement of only seven years and ten years, respectively, for each post. This trend aligns with the practice in the US and the UK of appointing more experienced lawyers as judges at all tiers of the judiciary. Given this anecdotal data, it is pertinent to advocate for a practice requirement that is longer than three years for lawyers seeking appointment as civil judges and judicial magistrates.

Surely, independent India can think beyond the practice requirement of three years that was put in place more than 140 years ago. If the mandatory practice requirement of a period longer than three years is in fact reinstated, it would also make sense to reconsider the current practice of appointing judges on the basis of a written examination. If a lawyer's experience at the bar is the key consideration while appointing them as a judge, holding an examination to test the applicant's legal knowledge about obscure provisions of the law is not useful. It would make far better sense to assess the candidate's legal experience by scrutinizing their experience as a lawyer at the bar.

The simple way to do this is to require applicants to submit their applications to the appointing authority, listing their experience at the bar as lawyers, along with copies of judgments in cases where they appeared and an essay explaining their career as a lawyer. Shortlisted candidates can be called for an interview (conducted in a location open to the general public) to evaluate the candidate. The purpose of the interview should be to assess whether the candidate has the temperament and personality for judicial office. The entire point of selecting judges on the basis of their experience practising as lawyers before the courts is to shift the focus of the appointment process from 'legal knowledge' to 'legal experience'. An examination, in this context, is a pointless exercise that is time-consuming for all parties involved in the process.

An anecdote worth mentioning here is that Justice H. R. Khanna, famous for his dissenting opinion in the most important case during the Emergency—*ADM Jabalpur* v. *Shivkant Shukla*—was selected as a district judge not because he cracked a judicial service examination, but on the basis of an application he made in response to a public call for applications from the High Court and an interview by the High Court.[34]

The one possible downside of reinstating a mandatory practice requirement and doing away with a written examination is that it may affect the entry of women and marginalized communities into the judicial services. This is because women and marginalized communities often lack the social capital to build legal practices or even join the chambers of senior advocates in order to acquire the practice experience required to qualify for appointment as judges. Such an outcome would be a tragedy given the surging number of women who have been appointed to the subordinate judiciary over the last two decades in the absence of any practice requirement.[35] This trend of an increasing number of female judges is likely reflective of the fact that more women are graduating from law schools and that women generally outperform men in competitive examinations in India. The increasing numbers of female judges are particularly encouraging, given the generally distressingly poor participation of women in the Indian workforce.

One way to avoid a situation where women and marginalized communities are sidelined is to continue the system of reserved quotas in the judicial service, which already exists in many states for women, Scheduled Castes and Scheduled Tribes. In fact, it may be politically impossible to roll back these quotas. However, even if mandatory quotas are put in place, there is no obligation on the appointing authority to ensure those quotas are fulfilled, especially if they do not find suitable candidates with sufficient experience at the bar. The aim then should be to create a qualified pool of candidates by ensuring marginalized communities and women have opportunities to practise law at the bar and gain the necessary experience. One way to achieve this policy goal is to leverage the government procurement of legal services since the government is one of the largest litigants in India. The Union government and state governments can tailor their procurement of legal services to ensure that women and marginalized communities are given opportunities to accrue the necessary legal experience at the bar as soon as they graduate. This already happens to a certain extent since many states have open recruitments for the posts of assistant public prosecutors and law officers. However, very often, these posts require candidates to have a minimum experience at the bar, which then begins a vicious cycle for those who are unable to get the requisite experience. These criteria need to be overhauled to allow for the recruitment of new law graduates so that women and members of marginalized communities can become government lawyers upon graduation without any requirement for prior practice at the bar. These concerns about the participation of women and marginalized communities must be seriously factored into any serious experiments with the selection mechanism for the district judiciary, especially since diversity in the judiciary directly affects its credibility in the public eye.

Most of the reforms outlined above are not simple and are likely to face resistance. However, they are crucial to improving the quality of justice dispensed by the district judiciary and building public confidence in the justice system. More experienced judges will improve judicial efficiency and will likely reduce judicial delays. Further, if these judges come from diverse backgrounds, it will help bolster confidence in the district judiciary across all communities.

India cannot continue with the qualification criteria put in place by colonial rulers in the 19th century, especially when the system has failed to perform for over a century now. A system reboot must begin with rethinking this fundamental issue of who India is appointing to the first tier of the district judiciary.

PART TWO

Statistics, Budgets and Bureaucracies

In this part of the book, we tackle the issue of judicial administration of the district courts. While the judge sitting in the courtroom is the face of the justice system, there is a small army of bureaucrats working behind the scenes under the control of judges in order to process paperwork in the registries, recruit personnel, serve summons, provide support to the judges in the courtroom, maintain court complexes, prepare budgetary estimates and coordinate with the state government. The smooth functioning of a courtroom depends as much on the efficiency of judicial administration behind the courtroom as it does on the efficiency of the judge in the courtroom. In this context, we focus on four issues pertaining to the administration of the district judiciary.

The *first* is the seemingly simple issue of judicial statistics. Astonishingly, we discovered that High Courts used to publish more credible judicial statistics back in the 19th century than has been the case over the last five decades. Without accurate statistics on the workload of the judiciary, it becomes difficult to assess judicial efficiency or plan for future expansions of the judiciary. In this story of pervasive scarcity of accurate judicial statistics lies the deeper story of the unaccountability of the judiciary in the guise of 'judicial independence'.

The *second* issue is the seemingly simple question of the appropriate methodology to calculate the number of judges required by the district judiciary in India. One would expect this to be a relatively simple matter, but as we describe in Chapter 7, this question has been bouncing through different courtrooms of the Supreme Court and expert committees for more than a decade. The situation is a glaring example of the dangers of trying to make policy in courtrooms.

The *third* issue is the funding of the Indian judiciary. The debate on funding has traditionally focused on the underfunding of the district judiciary. To its credit, over the last two decades, the Government of India has significantly increased funding for the district judiciary, much of which has remained unspent. This has not stopped the judiciary from demanding more funding and 'financial autonomy' while making no commitments towards greater transparency or accountability. We explain why it would be a disastrous idea to give the judiciary more financial autonomy from a policy and constitutional perspective.

The *fourth* and final issue is the manner in which the district judiciary is administered. The efficiency of the district judiciary is directly proportional to the efficiency of the administrative machinery in High Courts and the bureaucracy within the district courts. Suffice it to say that neither the High Courts nor the bureaucracy within the district courts are very good at their task and they shoulder the lion's share of blame for the chaos at the level of the district judiciary. We explore the origins of the problem and offer workable suggestions for revamping the present system of judicial administration.

6

The Missing Judicial Statistics

Most conversations about the woes of the district judiciary in India are likely to begin by quoting an eye-popping statistic on the number of cases pending before this layer of the judiciary. Take, for example, a report in the *New York Times* titled 'A Lifelong Nightmare: Seeking Justice in India's Overwhelmed Courts', published in January 2024.[1] The report pegged the pendency of cases in India at an intimidating 5 crore cases. The source for this data was the National Judicial Data Grid (NJDG). This statistic appears even more daunting when one learns that the district judiciary is staffed with approximately 20,000 judges across the country. The basic arithmetic would suggest a system on the brink of collapse, or worse, a judicial system that is unsalvageable.

However, before jumping to these conclusions, it is important to question the reliability of the data on the NJDG, which collects its data from the e-courts project that has digitized all district courts in the country. There are several problems with the rollout of the e-courts project, which is also the reason that the NJDG data cannot be taken seriously. To begin with, it is important to note that the e-committee of the Supreme Court and the National Informatics Centre (NIC), both of which are responsible for the e-courts project, and the NJDG have actively disclaimed any responsibility for the accuracy of the data available on the website of the NJDG.

The original 'disclaimer' on the NJDG website informed viewers that the data is '. . . of a general nature and **cannot substitute for**

the authentic verified information, i.e., by a competent authority designated by each Court' and that 'Neither the Courts concerned nor the National Informatics Centre (NIC) nor the eCommittee is responsible for any data inaccuracy or delay in the updating of the data on this website.' The disclaimer then further twisted the knife into the earlier warnings with a third warning: 'It is reiterated that the visitors should not fully rely on the information accessed herein and must crosscheck with the concerned Court for accurate and latest information.' These are rather strange disclaimers for the e-courts project, which has consumed Rs 2,308 crore of public money since its conception in 2005.[2] In 2024, the lengthy 'disclaimer' was shortened when the NJDG website was revamped, but even this revised disclaimer very clearly reiterated that neither 'the Courts concerned nor the National Informatics Centre nor the e-Committee is responsible for any data inaccuracy or delay in the updating of the data on this website'.

These disclaimers are a reminder to take the data published by the NJDG with a pinch, if not a bucket, of salt. A simple example, based on some very rough, back-of-the-envelope arithmetic, may help illustrate the magnitude of the problem with the data. As per the NJDG, the district judiciary in the city of Delhi, consisting of approximately 805 judges, disposed of a total of 6,25,344, cases in 2023. This works out to an average disposal rate of 777 cases per judge in a single year. These are mind-boggling numbers when compared to the expected disposal rates per the performance assessment policy laid down by the Delhi High Court for the district judiciary.[3] As per this policy, a district judge presiding over a family court is expected to dispose of a minimum of forty-eight cases in a year (twelve cases per quarter), to avoid the lowest possible rating which is 'inadequate'. In contrast, a Chief Metropolitan Magistrate, who hears less complicated cases, is expected to dispose of a minimum of 120 cases a year (thirty cases per quarter) to avoid an 'inadequate' rating. If one were to believe the NJDG data, it would indicate that some judges in Delhi are six times more efficient, while others are sixteen times more efficient than expected by the performance assessment policy. Either the performance assessment policies laid down by the Delhi High Court are completely unrealistic or, more likely, the NJDG data is grossly inflated. We suspect the latter.

As with disposal data, we suspect that even the pendency data on the NJDG is not accurate because of cases being double- or triple-counted. For example, the pendency data from the NJDG website for an Additional Chief Metropolitan Magistrate in Ernakulam city, who is to hear only offences committed by legislators, lists 1,190 cases as pending. But when we examined the data closely, we noticed that 255 cases had been counted more than once.

Double counting aside, one of the main reasons for the inflated pendency and disposal figures on the NJDG, in our opinion, is the way the NJDG counts cases. In any civil or criminal case in India, there are multiple stages to the progress of the dispute before court. First, a plaint or FIR is filed containing the main allegations. Subsequently, each party to the dispute may file motions or applications before the court at different points during the lifecycle of the litigation. For example, in a civil case, after the filing of a plaint, both litigants typically file motions or applications for interim injunctions or to have the lawsuit dismissed on various grounds, prior to trial. Similarly, in criminal cases, the accused will file different motions or applications making requests for bail or discharge from the case or turning approver or exemptions from personal appearance for the accused. While in civil cases, the various motions or applications are logged as part of the same case number, in criminal cases, it appears that each motion or application filed in the same prosecution is logged as a separate case by the Case Information System (CIS) of the e-courts project and is hence also counted separately by the NJDG. What this means is that if there are three accused in a case who have been arrested, and each files their bail application, the system will log each bail application as three separate cases. If their bail applications are rejected and they refile after a few weeks, the CIS will count the new bail applications as three new cases. Similarly, if a criminal miscellaneous application is filed by the same accused seeking exemption from personal appearance before the court or to turn approver, each application will be logged and counted as a separate case. Similarly, when an accused files an appeal before the sessions court against a conviction by the judicial magistrate, the normal practice is to file an application seeking a stay on the magistrate's sentencing order until the appeal is heard. The CIS system logs each such application for stay as a case separate from the appeal. As a result, what should be one case ends up being displayed as two cases on the NJDG. This is the wrong way to count cases. Ideally all motions or applications filed as part of the same criminal prosecution should be counted as one case.

For the reasons mentioned above, it is best to ignore the NJDG data until the e-committee of the Supreme Court rethinks the manner in which cases are counted and is willing to certify the accuracy of all data displayed on the NJDG. However, there is little conversation on the various problems with the data on the NJDG and instead this flawed data regularly features not just in press coverage of the judiciary but also during Question Hour in Parliament, when ministers respond to specific questions raised by parliamentarians on the issue of case pendency.[4] It is worth questioning the reason for this state of affairs with judicial statistics. Is it because India lacks the technical capacity to collect and release accurate statistics? We doubt that this is the reason. India is a country that has boasted, since the colonial era, of a robust system of collection of all kinds of statistics. Aside from the decadal national census initiated by the British in colonial India in 1872 to collect data on the Indian population, the colonial government also collected statistics in several areas of governance ranging from agriculture to trade to prices to wages to industrial production. In fact, the British had set up specialist departments in India whose sole focus was to collect and publish statistics.[5] After independence from the British, the erstwhile Planning Commission developed a voracious appetite for high-quality statistics to help it execute the government's vision of a planned economy in India.[6] Parliament even enacted a surprisingly coercive law called the Collection of Statistics Act, 1953 that armed the Union government with sweeping powers to collect statistics. Simply put, India is a country that knows how to collect statistics.

The more likely reason for the unavailability of high-quality judicial statistics in India is a deep-rooted culture of opacity within the Indian judiciary. The allegation of opacity against the judiciary may seem surprising, given that all courtrooms are open to the public, with some courts even webcasting their proceedings on the internet. However, judicial administration, i.e. the manner in which the judiciary manages its records, finances, infrastructure and staff has always been frighteningly opaque for a democratic country that aspires to be transparent and accountable to its people. This culture of opacity has extended to the issue of judicial statistics, despite the fact that they are key to planning more efficiently for the judiciary. Additionally, the lack of credible judicial statistics makes it tougher to hold the judiciary accountable for its performance. But it is not just judicial administration that is affected by the lack of accurate judicial statistics. The lack of such statistics also hampers our understanding of how Indian society litigates its disputes before the courts and the manner in which judges are deciding these disputes. This information is also critical to understanding governance in India. For example, basic statistical information about the number of cheque-bouncing cases or commercial disputes under various laws is unavailable on the NJDG website, despite the e-courts system logging this data.

The unavailability of such basic data is in sharp contrast to the detailed crime statistics published by the National Crime Records Bureau (NCRB), which operates under the Ministry of Home Affairs, but which is limited to prosecution trends by the police across India under various legislations. Similar information about crimes prosecuted by agencies other than the police is limited while details regarding private criminal complaints, such as cheque-bouncing cases, are unavailable in NCRB reports.

There is a serious cost to the incompetence with which the NJDG has been designed and executed; the world's largest democracy is ignorant about something as basic as how its citizens are using the courts to litigate their rights and disputes. That this scarcity of judicial statistics began only after independence from the British speaks poorly of the judiciary, which used its independence as a shield to resist any form of accountability.

The deterioration of judicial statistics after Independence

Originally under colonial rule, each of the High Courts created by the British would publish an annual report containing statistical data on the judicial work done by the High Courts and all courts under their jurisdiction. For example, the Report on the Administration of Civil and Criminal Justice in the Presidency of Madras for the year 1879 published by the Madras High Court and running into 45 pages, contains a wealth of data on the functioning of the High Court as well as the civil and criminal courts functioning under it. The data included the categories of cases heard and the nature of disposals (contested/ uncontested), as well as the number of persons convicted or acquitted. As recounted in this report, the government's recommendations, from the previous year, for collecting additional categories of information were complied with by the High Court. The High Court was legally bound to respond to such requests by the government because the Letters Patent issued by the British Crown, creating each High Court during colonial rule, contained a clause requiring the High Court to comply with 'requisitions' for 'records, returns and statements' in the format prescribed by the local government. As a result, all High Courts in colonial India had a practice of publishing relatively detailed judicial statistics and responding to specific requests for information from the government.

Post Independence, in the year 1947, the role of requesting statistical information was assumed by the Ministry of Home Affairs of the Union Government. Archival records indicate that this ministry was writing to the Registrars of High Courts requesting them to provide statistical information in specific formats.[7] It is not clear till when this practice continued but academics who tracked judicial statistics have complained that the availability of such information began to dry up in the mid-1970s. Robert Moog, one of the few academics to have studied the workings of the Indian legal system, observed that judicial statistics in India were typically 'old and scattered'. With specific reference to the Allahabad High Court, he notes that it stopped publishing all statistical data after the year 1976.[8] This drought of publicly accessible judicial statistics spanned the entire judiciary, including the Supreme Court.

But what explains the scarcity of judicial statistics after India became a democratic republic? Were the High Courts not collecting statistics or were they reluctant to release statistics to the public? We suspect it is the latter because the registry of each district court necessarily has to track filings and disposal of cases for the purpose of requesting the creation of additional courts, performance assessment of judges and related administrative tasks.

We suspect that the same is true for the Supreme Court. Although it has historically not published any judicial statistics detailing its workload and disposals, we know it has always maintained detailed statistics internally because select academics have been given access to these statistics for the purpose of academic research. Writing in 1986, Dr Rajeev Dhavan, a senior advocate and an academic, speculated that the Supreme Court was reluctant to make available its statistics to academics for fear 'that a critical researcher might find more than a key under the front carpet'.[9] He complained that the 'Registry of the Supreme Court was most reluctant to allow research'. According to Dhavan, the registry 'was anxious to drape the working of the Supreme Court within a shroud of secrecy' since '[i]t was afraid that its actual working and procedure may catch the public eye'. While Dhavan does not spell it out, it should be noted that the registry of the Supreme Court functions under the control of the Chief Justice of India.

We believe that Dhavan is right to blame the lack of credible judicial statistics on the judiciary's reluctance to subject itself to scrutiny. The following narration of the manner in which judges have evaded providing even simple judicial statistics to Parliament and RTI activists substantiates our hypothesis on the culture of opacity within the judiciary when it comes to statistical information.

When judges refused parliamentary requests for judicial statistics

One of the most powerful tools of democratic accountability in a parliamentary form of governance is Question Hour, where elected ministers of government are required to respond to questions posed by other parliamentarians on matters of governance. This is serious business and while ministers do at times provide vague answers, it is rare to completely reject a question. The only institution to thumb its nose at parliamentary questions, by flat-out refusing to provide any information to the minister to enable him to reply in Parliament, is the judiciary.

One such instance from 1969 involved a question raised in the Rajya Sabha about the particulars of cases pending for more than six years in Delhi courts and reasons for the delays. The minister informed Parliament that the Delhi High Court declined to provide the information on the grounds that the exercise of collecting such information would take 'considerable time' and that the 'labour involved would be disproportionate to any benefit likely to be derived from it'.[10] This was an audacious, jaw-dropping response by the Delhi High Court to a question raised in Parliament.

Another example is from 1985, when the Supreme Court refused to share information sought by two parliamentarians during Question Hour in the Rajya Sabha, regarding the number of cases where judges of the Supreme Court had completed hearing arguments but were yet to deliver judgments. In addition, these parliamentarians specifically asked for information about the longest period for which a judgment had not been delivered after the conclusion of arguments in court and the reasons for the delay, along with remedial steps being taken to reduce such delays.[11] This question was aimed directly at one of the long-standing complaints against the Indian judiciary, which is the habit of judges simply not writing and delivering judgments for months together after oral arguments have concluded. In response to the first question, the Law Minister H. R. Bharadwaj provided the information—51 cases—but for the second and third questions, he informed Parliament that the Supreme Court declined to provide this information on the grounds that Article 121 of the Constitution forbade discussion in Parliament of the conduct of any judge in discharge of his duties except during impeachment proceedings! This was an incorrect interpretation of Article 121 since the query did not pertain to the conduct of any specific judge but the institution as a whole. The more likely reason that the Supreme Court declined to give this information was because it would have revealed some uncomfortable truths about the efficiency of its judges.

The reluctance of the judiciary in sharing statistical data came up for discussion once again in the Rajya Sabha on 2 May 2003 during a debate on judicial reforms. In the course of this wide-ranging debate, Kapil Sibal, an Opposition MP and also a lawyer of repute, raised this specific issue of the courts refusing to share basic information.[12] In his words:

> If I want to find out how many judges in this country have not delivered judgments in the last six months or eight months or one year and I want that information from the Chief Justice of a particular High Court, the Chief Justice of that High Court writes back and says, 'It is confidential information, to give this information; destroys the independence of the judiciary.'

The late Arun Jaitley, who was then the minister of law, interjected at this point to share an anecdote in support of the point being made by Sibal. In his words:

> I must share this information with the House—a question was raised either in this House or in the other House as to how many judgments have not been delivered in the High Courts for more than one year. So, factual information had to be sought to file a reply. I got a response from some of the High Courts, not all, that the Judiciary is an independent body and this shared information cannot be given for being placed in Parliament.

Both Sibal and Jaitley were also senior advocates with flourishing practices before the Supreme Court when they were not in government. Despite this meeting of minds of two of the most influential lawyers in two of the largest political parties in the country (Sibal later become the law minister in the UPA government), there was no visible attempt by either to enact legislative measures compelling the courts to share the required information. If the Letters Patent issued by the British Crown during colonial rule could impose a duty on the High Courts to comply with information requests from the government, surely a democratically elected Parliament could impose a similar duty on the judiciary.

While the Government of India did nothing to rectify the issue, the late senior advocate Fali Nariman, who was nominated by the President to the Rajya Sabha as an MP, introduced a bill called the Judicial Statistics Bill, 2004 to create a legal framework for the collection of judicial statistics from all courts in India. In an interview with *Frontline,* Nariman explained that it was necessary to create such a system because the judiciary was frequently refusing to provide the law ministry with judicial statistics, even when such data was required to answer a parliamentary question, on the grounds that it would compromise judicial independence.[13] Nariman questioned the judiciary's stand, saying:

> Judicial independence means deciding cases without being influenced by anybody. But disseminating information about how many cases get decided in the courts will not compromise judicial independence at all. This is a wrong impression that the judiciary, among all organs of the government, must remain totally secretive, and nobody must know anything that is happening in the judiciary.

In the Statement of Objects & Reasons accompanying the Judicial Statistics Bill, Nariman had explained that it was important to put in place mechanisms using information technology to collect empirical data to 'help legal scholars to better assess the performance of our judicial institutions'. The statement went on to explain how the practice of publishing annual judicial statistics was a common feature in other democracies such as the UK and the US. Towards this end, the legislation envisaged the creation of a three-tier structure to collect judicial statistics from the Supreme Court, High Courts, district judiciary and tribunals.

The bill also laid down the type of data to be collected and published in the form of 'Annual Judicial Statistics' reports along with a commentary on trends and flow of cases. The data to be collected and published included the following parameters: the legal nature of the dispute; the outcome of dispute; in case of an appeal, whether the decision of the lower court was upheld or reversed; the names of the judges who heard the case; the legislation under which the dispute was heard; the number of hours taken; adjournments granted; the lawyers who appeared for the parties; the interval between filing of cases and their hearing by the court; the date of final disposal of the case; the time taken for delivery of judgments after conclusion of hearings and other details that may be prescribed.

Despite this legislation having the potential to radically reframe the debate on judicial accountability, it died a quiet death, like most bills introduced by MPs who are not ministers.

Commodore Batra's battle for judicial statistics under the RTI Act

The enactment of the Right to Information (RTI) Act, 2005, a year after Nariman's legislative attempt, opened the door for citizens to ask the judiciary for more information about its functioning, including statistics. Except, the judiciary's attitude towards the RTI Act has remained shockingly hostile, with many High Courts making it difficult to even file a request for information.[14] There is no better example to showcase this hostility towards transparency than the case of *Commodore Lokesh Batra* v. *Registry, Supreme Court of India*.

Commodore Lokesh Batra, who transformed into a formidable transparency activist after retiring from a career in the Indian Navy, filed a request for information with the registry of the Supreme Court of India in 2009 asking it for the number of cases between the years 2007 and 2009 where judges of the Supreme Court had completed hearing arguments, but were yet to deliver a judgment. By this time, it should be noted, judges delaying the delivery of judgments after the conclusion of oral arguments had become a significant problem, as acknowledged by the Supreme Court itself. In its judgment from 2001 in the case of *Anil Rai* v. *State of Bihar*[15], the Supreme Court had remarked that 'a few Judges in some High Courts, after conclusion of the arguments, keep the files withheld with them and do not pronounce judgments for periods spread over years'. Similar allegations have been made against the Supreme Court and, as mentioned earlier, it had invoked Article 121 of the Constitution to refuse sharing information about such delays with Parliament in 1985.

The bureaucrats within the Supreme Court responsible for processing requests under the RTI Act rejected Batra's request on the grounds that such information was not maintained by the court. They claimed that in order to collect such information, they would have to examine each and every file to compile the requested information and that this was 'a nearly impossible task given the volume of cases pending in the Supreme Court'.[16] Except, the fact of the matter was that the bureaucrat handling RTI requests simply had to contact the staff of each judge and ask them to provide the information—the Supreme Court had only 31 judges at the time. The staff of each judge maintain this information since they assist the judge in managing his docket and preparing the final judgments. More importantly, it should be pointed out that the Supreme Court, in its *Anil Rai* judgment, while criticizing judges of High Courts for delaying the pronouncement of judgments for prolonged periods of time, framed specific guidelines on collecting data regarding such pendency, one of which is reproduced as follows:

> That Chief Justice of the High Courts, on their administrative side, should direct the Court Officers/Readers of the various Benches in the High Courts to furnish every month the list of cases in the matters where the judgments reserved are not pronounced within the period of that month.

Simply put, the Supreme Court had already directed the High Courts to maintain exactly the same information that Batra was asking of the Supreme Court. If the High Courts were expected by the Supreme Court to maintain such information as far back as 2001, before the digitization of court records, there was no good reason for the Supreme Court not to maintain such information, especially since its registry had been completely digitized by the time Batra filed his RTI requests.

Faced with a rejection of his request for information by the Supreme Court, Batra filed an appeal before the Central Information Commission (CIC). The CIC, which ruled in his favour three years later in 2012, concluded that 'if the Supreme Court is not maintaining such data, it should do so now in order to facilitate the citizens to learn about the status of pendency before the Supreme Court'. The CIC also pointed out that computerization of the registry of the Supreme Court had made it easy to collect such information.[17]

Instead of providing Batra with the required information within fifteen days as directed by the Commission, the registry of the Supreme Court filed a petition before the Delhi High Court requesting it to set aside the Commission's order. The registry of the Supreme Court argued before the High Court that as per the RTI Act, it was only required to provide information already on its record and that it was not under a duty to compile or collate information in response to specific queries. Justice Vibhu Bakhru of the Delhi High Court, who heard the case, shot down the arguments of the registry of the Supreme Court on the grounds that Section 4 of the RTI Act required all public authorities to maintain records in a duly catalogued and indexed manner.[18] He further pointed out that the information requested by Batra had been flagged as an important issue by the Supreme Court in the *Anil Rai* judgment. As a result, he upheld the CIC's order and ordered the registry of the Supreme Court to comply with the disclosure order.

Given that Justice Bakhru's judgment was well-reasoned and grounded in the law, the registry of the Supreme Court should have agreed to comply with his directions, but unfortunately, the registry filed yet another appeal before a division bench of the Delhi High Court consisting of two judges. That bench took another two years to hear arguments by both parties, before overruling Justice Bakhru in favour of the registry of the Supreme Court on 7 January 2016.

The division bench surprisingly ruled that there was no duty imposed under the RTI Act to 'collate the information in the manner in which it is sought by the applicant'.[19] This despite the obligation imposed by Section 4 of the RTI Act on all public authorities to maintain all their information in a duly catalogued and indexed manner.

Commodore Batra, who was obviously dissatisfied with the judgment of the division bench, filed an appeal before the Supreme Court, only for the appeal to be dismissed on 15 February 2016, with the following one line: 'The Special Leave Petition is dismissed.'[20] In other words, the Supreme Court did not even admit the appeal for a hearing. So ended Commodore Batra's seven-year-long battle to access information on the length of time the judges of the Supreme

Court were taking to deliver judgments after the completion of oral arguments.

The ferocity with which the registry of the Supreme Court litigated this case over a period of seven years to supress information that it had ordered High Courts to maintain in the *Anil Rai* case, is a suitable illustration of the opacity and hypocrisy of the court on the issue of transparency. It is this same attitude that has filtered in to the earlier referenced 'disclaimers' on the NJDG website maintained by the e-committee of the Supreme Court and the NIC.

The folly of the NJDG—data, data everywhere but not a drop of insight

The final chapter of the saga of missing judicial statistics should ideally have been written when the Government of India decided to fund the massive e-courts project to digitize the entire district judiciary, starting in 2005. The government handed over complete control of the project to the rather unimaginatively named 'e-Committee' that operated under the operational control of judges of the Supreme Court.

The 'Policy and Action Plan Document Phase I' outlining the objectives of the e-courts project and published on 1 August 2005 envisaged the creation of a National Judicial Data Grid (NJDG) that would use the data generated through the e-courts project to display statistics on pendency, filings, disposals, etc.[21] Once the NJDG was created, the action plan envisaged a scenario where courts would save enormous time spent on generating 'voluminous monthly, quarterly, half-yearly and annual statements' through manual processes, as was the practice since the 19th century.

The NJDG went live on the internet only in 2015. However, as mentioned earlier in this chapter, the information displayed on the website is not credible, as evidenced by the reluctance of the e-committee or the National Informatics Centre (which assists in executing the project) to certify the information as accurate. But lack of accuracy is only part of the problem. Even presuming that the data on the NJDG is cleaned up, the problem of useful judicial statistics will not be solved. This is because the larger problem with the NJDG is that it simply does not collect essential data points that can be used to understand the working of the judicial system. For example, one of the critical data points required to understand the workings of the judiciary is the 'judicial time' spent by judges on different categories of cases. This is different from just calculating the time period between the institution and disposal of cases. Rather, it involves measuring the cumulative time spent by a judge on a case at each hearing until it is disposed of. This is the most crucial data point since it is judicial time that is a scarce resource when it comes to the courts. Once this data on judicial time is collected, it will be possible to formulate 'standards' for the judiciary on expected timelines for disposing of different categories of cases, which can be used to identify delayed cases and also plan for the future needs of the judiciary.

The importance of this data was highlighted in Nariman's Judicial Statistics Bill back in 2004. Since then, the paucity of such data on judicial time has been pointed out even by the Law Commission in 2014.[22] Yet, this data point was never incorporated into the design of the e-courts system and continues to remain unavailable as of the year 2024. The Supreme Court's internal think-tank has admitted to the importance and lack of this data in a report published in November 2023, almost eighteen years after the e-courts project was first conceptualized and ten years after the Law Commission pointed to the paucity of this data.[23] Yet, India is nowhere close to collecting such information.

The path forward—Parliament must act

The fact that India is yet to develop a system to publish accurate and meaningful judicial statistics in the 21st century is deeply worrying. The blame for this failure falls squarely upon the judiciary and the culture of opacity cultivated at the highest levels of the institution. One way for Parliament to impose an obligation on the judiciary to publish quality judicial statistics is to enact a law requiring the High Courts to publish judicial statistics about themselves and the district judiciary functioning under their administrative control. This law should spell out the data points that need to form part of the statistics and should include parameters specified in Nariman's Judicial Statistics Bill, with a specific focus on judicial time consumed by cases. The law should also impose upon each Chief Justice of a High Court an obligation to certify the accuracy of the data in question and present a report compiling judicial statistics to the Speaker of the state legislative assembly whose tax revenues fund both the High Court and the district judiciary.

Such a law would be in line with the obligations imposed upon colonial-era High Courts by the Letters Patent issued by the British Crown. If High Courts could comply with the Letters Patent, they can surely comply with the mandate of Parliament elected by the Indian people. In order to enable the respective High Courts to publish such judicial statistics, it would only be fair to consider restructuring the e-courts project. Since its conception in 2005, it has been supervised by the e-committee of the Supreme Court. Not only was this set-up legally flawed, but it was also inefficient. This is because the Constitution, as interpreted by the Supreme Court, vests control of the district judiciary with the High Courts. The Supreme Court has no role under the Constitution to supervise the functioning of the district judiciary. Aside from this legal reason, it should also be noted that the duty of collecting statistics on the workings of the district judiciary has traditionally vested with the administrative staff of the High Courts. It is this staff that has the biggest incentive to use technology to reduce their own workload and this is the most convincing reason to decentralize the operation of the e-courts to the High Courts. The e-committee of the Supreme Court, which has a poor track record in implementing the e-courts project, should be dissolved so that the judges on the committee can focus on hearing cases pending before the Supreme Court instead of handling administrative issues pertaining to the e-courts project.

A second way to pressure the judiciary to produce better judicial statistics is for the Parliamentary Standing Committee on Law and Justice or the Public Accounts Committee, comprising elected parliamentarians, to announce a study of the e-committee and the NJDG, since it is Parliament which has funded the e-courts project. Such a process should involve inviting the judges in charge of the e-committee to depose before the Standing Committee on the decisions they have taken with regard to expenditure of public money. If these judges are reluctant to participate in this exercise of democratic accountability supervised by the people's representatives, the Supreme Court should not be allowed to control the purse strings of the e-courts project. Judges cannot seek the power to spend public funds as they wish if they are unwilling to be accountable to the people's representatives for their decisions. Such accountability regarding expenditure of public funds is a basic premise of democracy.

The urgency of the above reforms cannot be stressed upon enough. Unless India has access to accurate judicial statistics, it will be difficult to plan for the judiciary and more importantly, measure the performance of the judiciary to hold individual judges accountable for delay. As of today, the ball is in the court of the e-committee but given its track record, it is unlikely to reform without parliamentary intervention. The Union Government, however, have taken an 'ask-no-questions' approach with the e-committee, as evidenced by the fact that it has cleared an eye-popping amount of Rs 7,210 crore for the e-courts project for a four-year period starting in 2024, without imposing any mandate on the e-committee to certify the quality of data on the NJDG or auditing the performance of the e-courts project, thus far.[24]

7

How Many Judges Does India Need?

Over the last four decades, the Indian judiciary has managed to successfully build a narrative blaming judicial delays on the shortage of judges in the country. This narrative has been built through reports of the Law Commission authored by retired judges of the Supreme Court, activist judgments of the Supreme Court and the occasional public spectacle like in 2016, when the Chief Justice of India (CJI) T. S. Thakur broke into tears at a public event claiming that the judiciary was short of 70,000 judges.[1]

To provide some perspective on the figure of 70,000 judges, the sanctioned strength of judges at the level of district judiciary across all states in India, as of 2024, is approximately 25,511 judges.[2] This number is an impressive three-fold increase over the last four decades. Although accurate statistics are hard to come by, we do know that in 1987, the strength of the district judiciary was pegged at 7,675 judges.[3] By 2001, its working strength increased to 10,705 judges with an additional vacancy of around 1,500 judges.[4] Some states have expanded at a faster rate than others. For example, the total strength of the district judiciary in Delhi in 1984 was 118 judges before increasing to 385 judges in 2000 and 884 judges in 2024.[5] As a result, in forty years, the sanctioned number of judges in the district judiciary of Delhi has increased by a factor of almost six.

Clearly, the number of judges being appointed in India has been constantly increasing over the last three decades. A more than three-fold increase over a period of four decades is not an insignificant increase. It is doubtful if any other arm of the Indian state has expanded at a similar rate. For example, the sanctioned strength of the IAS cadre increased marginally from 5,334 officers in 1991 to 6,746 officers in 2021.[6] This is a minuscule increase compared to the massive increase in the number of judges working for the district judiciary. In addition to the three-fold increase in the number of judges at the level of the district judiciary, Parliament enacted special laws creating new Debts Recovery Tribunals, Company Law Tribunals and consumer courts, thereby steering complex and time-consuming litigation away from the district courts, reducing the stress on them. Yet, the pendency of cases before the district courts continues to be daunting with millions of cases reportedly pending for more than five years, as per the NJDG website.

The question then is how do we measure whether the increase in the number of judges has been sufficient to tackle the caseload in Indian courts? The answer to the above question depends on the methodology used to calculate the required number of judges and herein lies the confusion that has dogged Indian policymaking for almost four decades, starting with the 120th report of the Law Commission, published in 1987. It is the methodology in this report that formed the basis of CJI Thakur's teary-eyed speech claiming that India was short of 70,000 judges. In this report, the Law Commission, chaired at the time by retired Justice D. A. Desai, decided that population was the relevant benchmark to calculate the number of judges required in India.[7] It had borrowed this methodology from Professor Marc Galanter's affidavit filed in the Bhopal gas litigation before a US federal court.[8]

In this case, Union Carbide Corporation, whose plant in Bhopal had leaked tons of poisonous gas killing thousands and injuring tens of thousands, was trying to have a lawsuit filed by the Indian government against it before an American court dismissed on the grounds of *forum non conveniens,* i.e. Indian courts would be the more appropriate forum for deciding the case. The Government of India tried rebutting these arguments on the grounds that the Indian judiciary was not capable of handling such complex litigation.

In this context, Galanter's affidavit, in support of the Government of India, was trying to make the case that the Indian judiciary was woefully underequipped to deal with complex litigation and one of the arguments he made in this regard was the supposedly insufficient number of judges in India. To explain the alleged shortage of judges, Galanter used the population of India as the relevant benchmark. He did so by calculating the number of judges per million Indians and compared it to the ratio in countries like the US, Australia, Canada and the UK. As per his calculation, India had only 10.5 judges per million of its population while the US had 107 judges per million, Australia had 41.6 judges per million, Canada had 75.2 judges per million and the UK had 50.9 judges per million. And so, Galanter argued, India had an understaffed judiciary.[9] However, Galanter never stated in his affidavit that these countries used population as a metric to calculate the number of judges required in their countries. Rather, the ratios were outcomes of different methodologies used in each of these countries. Ignoring this aspect of Galanter's affidavit, the Law Commission proceeded to latch on to the population-based methodology to recommend that India calculate the number of judges required as per its population. In particular, it recommended that India increase the present judge-to-population ratio from 10.5 judges per million of the Indian population to at least 50 judges per million of the Indian population in a phased manner.

But was this the right methodology to calculate the number of judges required in India? The short answer is no. Population is not a good indicator of the number of judges required by a country. This is because a country that is poor is unlikely to see much litigation due to a lack of economic activity or simply because citizens lack the financial resources to litigate against each other or the government. Studies on Indian litigation patterns, too, indicate that people who live in economically prosperous states, with better provisions for health and education, are more likely to use courts for resolving their disputes.[10] If the data displayed by the NJDG is to be believed, it becomes evident how population has little correlation with litigation rates. As can be seen in the table below, the number of civil suits filed in Bihar is less than those filed in Delhi, despite Bihar having 8.72 crore citizens more than Delhi. Even criminal cases in Bihar are only 1.6 times the number of cases in Delhi, despite Bihar having six times more people.

	Population in crores	***Civil cases instituted in 2023***	***Criminal cases filed in 2023***	***Total***
Delhi	1.67	1,48,121	4,16,391	5,64,512
Bihar	10.4	1,00,512	7,03,358	8,03,870

This data shows that the population of a state does not necessarily correlate with the volume of litigation, which ultimately is what decides the number of judges required.

Perhaps for this reason, the population-to-judge ratio was never in vogue in India till the 120th report of the Law Commission borrowed it from Galanter's affidavit. We know from the 14th report of the Law Commission published back in 1958 that the number of judges required by the district judiciary was calculated on the basis of the number of cases filed and disposed in the previous year.[11] Similarly for High Courts, consecutive conferences of Chief Justices of High Courts, held in 1960, 1963, 1965 and 1967, had called for calculating the number of judges required by High Courts as per their annual disposal rates of cases.[12]

The Law Commission in its 120th report, for reasons not clear, ignored this previous methodology that was clearly prevalent through India. Despite these rather obvious flaws with the methodology proposed in the 120th report, the Supreme Court, in 2002, relied on it while hearing a public interest litigation (PIL) on judicial reforms and went to the extent of ordering the government to 'increase, in the first instance . . . Judge strength from the existing ratio of 10.5 or 13 per 10 lakhs people to 50 judges for 10 lakh people . . . within a period of five years'.[13]

There are several problems with this approach of the Supreme Court deciding a policy issue through a judicial diktat. Understanding these problems is key to understanding the manner in which the Supreme Court has muddied the conversation on judicial reforms in India.

The *first* problem is that the court simply ignores the limitations imposed by the Constitution when it comes to administering the district judiciary. For instance, as per Article 235 of the Constitution, the district judiciary in each state is under the 'control' of the High Court of the state. It is generally the High Court that makes a determination of the number of additional judges required after gathering inputs from the district judges. The High Court then forwards the proposal to the state government, which must approve it because only the state government can request the Governor to create the additional posts required via an amendment to the judicial service rules. Then the state government must request the state legislative assembly to appropriate through a vote the public funds required to pay salaries for the additional judges, their support staff, build new courtrooms and residences for the new judges. After all, it is the elected representatives in the state legislative assemblies who are accountable to their electorate for decisions regarding the expenditure of public money. Long story short, the Constitution does not give the Supreme Court the power to determine the number of judges required by the district judiciary. The court has misappropriated this power for itself with little consideration for constitutional propriety.

The *second* problem with the Supreme Court's activist approach towards deciding complex policy issues in the courtroom, via PILs, is that it is also an autocratic approach to law-making since it leaves little room for deliberation, debate and democratic participation by all stakeholders. Perhaps if these discussions had taken place in an institution meant to foster deliberative consultations with all stakeholders, someone would have pointed out that the population-based metric was devised by an American law professor to convince an American court that the Indian judiciary was understaffed and incapable of dispensing justice to the victims of the Bhopal gas tragedy.

The *third* problem with the Supreme Court's approach in this case is the lack of transparency in its reasoning. The case in which the court had ordered the states to adopt the population-based methodology was, in fact, filed by the All India Judges Association (AIJA) asking for better pay and perks for the judges staffing the district judiciary. From a reading of the judgment, it does not appear that AIJA had sought the implementation of the 120th report of the Law Commission. So, who then made the recommendation to the Supreme Court to adopt the population-based methodology? The judgment is silent on the issue. It merely notes that the issue of backlog of cases had been raised by the amicus curie and then jumps to the recommendations of the 120th report of the Law Commission. The judgment is also silent on the government's views about this methodology, which raises the question of whether the government's lawyers were even given an opportunity to rebut the proposed methodology. In most countries with competent judges, a judgment of the court will accurately reflect deliberations in the courtroom and mention the source of specific arguments. This is the bare minimum expected of judges vested with vast judicial powers.

In any event, regardless of the many problems with the population-based methodology, it has come to define the discourse on judicial reforms, with everybody from politicians to judges to academics citing it to complain about the shortage of judges as the primary reason for judicial delays.

However, the Supreme Court's judgment in the AIJA case was not the last word on the appropriate methodology to calculate the number of judges. In fact, there have been four other official reports that have studied the issue since that judgment in 2002. The judicial activism that led to these reports being written and the activist response by the Supreme Court to the recommendations of these reports reveals an astonishingly chaotic approach to judicial reforms fuelled by the predilections of individual judges of the court.

The first of these developments was a case called *Imtiyaz Ahmad v. State of Uttar Pradesh and Ors*[14]. This case had originally landed on the docket of the Supreme Court in 2010 on the issue of certain criminal cases in Uttar Pradesh that had been pending for a long time because of stay orders granted by the Allahabad High Court. This case was converted by the Supreme Court into a vehicle to probe the functioning of the High Courts and the Government of India was made party to the case to provide an explanation on steps being taken to tackle the backlog of cases in the judicial system. Amongst other responses, the government informed the court that it had asked the Law Commission to study various issues pertaining to judicial administration. In 2012, the bench hearing the case latched on to this argument and instructed the Law Commission to specifically study the issue of whether more judges were required and to submit its report in a 'sealed cover' to the court so that it could take further action on it.[15] One of the judges on that bench was CJI Thakur.

The 20th Law Commission of India, under the chairmanship of retired Chief Justice A. P. Shah, complied with this direction of the court. In its 245th report, dated 7 July 2014, the Commission studied various methodologies that could be used to calculate the number of judges required by the district judiciary. Prepared with the assistance of Indian and American academics, this report was well-researched. Pointing out the obvious flaws in calculating the number of judges as per the population, the 245th report had proposed alternative methods to calculate the number of judges required. As per this report, the ideal method for calculating the number of judges should have been based on the average time taken by judges to dispose of different types of cases.[16] The Law Commission was particularly interested in adopting a time-based formula rather than mere case institutions because it was aware of the fact that not all cases take the same amount of time to travel through the judicial system. As it pointed out, relatively simple traffic offences and cheque-bouncing cases accounted for a fair percentage of the docket of criminal courts and would not require the same judicial time as the more complex cases.[17]

The problem with trying to calculate caseloads as per this time-based methodology, as acknowledged by the Law Commission, was the unavailability of such data in India. Hence the Law Commission suggested the 'rate of disposal' method as an alternative. This method requires calculating the required number of judges on the basis of average disposal rates of different courts.[18] Illustratively, if the average disposal rate of five judges in a district was 200 cases per year, it would mean that the five judges together could dispose of only 1,000 cases in a year. Hence, if the institution rate of new cases increased to 1,200, then as per this methodology, a sixth judge would have to be appointed to deal with the additional 200 cases.

When the Law Commission submitted this report to the Supreme Court, a bench of three judges, headed by CJI Thakur, examined its recommendations on 1 May 2014 as part of the hearings in the case of *Imtiyaz Ahmad v. State of UP*. At this hearing, the judges decided that they wanted to hear the views of the state governments and High Courts on the issue. While the court was waiting for their responses, it also declared on 20 August 2014 that the recommendations of the Law Commission would be examined by the National Court Management System (NCMS), a think-tank set up by the CJI in 2012 to advise the court on measures to 'enhance timely justice' and which operated under the control of the CJI.[19] In its order, the court gave no reasons on why it was asking the NCMS to study this issue again despite the Law Commission's report being comprehensive and rigorously reasoned.

After several adjournments, the NCMS submitted a report to the Supreme Court and a bench headed by CJI Thakur took cognizance of this report on 30 March 2016 when it directed the government to prepare its response before the next hearing.[20] It was three weeks after this order that CJI Thakur broke down in tears at the public event, claiming that India was short of 70,000 judges. The CJI appears to have based his calculations on the flawed population-based methodology, despite the recently submitted NCMS report authored by Prof. Mohan Gopal not recommending population as a metric to calculate judicial strength.[21] In fact, this report by the NCMS was in agreement with the Law Commission's idea of using judicial time spent to dispose of different types of cases as the key metric in calculating the number of judges required.[22] Identifying this methodology as the 'long term' goal, the NCMS, like the Law Commission before it, called for the collection of data on the judicial time taken to dispose of different categories of cases. The only point of disagreement between the NCMS and the Law Commission was on an interim solution until such data could be collected. The NCMS disagreed with the Law Commission's proposed method of calculating the strength of judges solely as per the rate of disposal. Amongst other grounds, the NCMS argued that such a methodology would incentivise lower efficiency because by showing a lower rate of disposal, a court could get more judges appointed.[23]

As an interim solution, the NCMS proposed an alternative formula that, according to it, would factor in the efficiency of judges and not just pending cases.[24] The new formula sought to factor in the 'unit-based' system used across the country by High Courts to assess the performance of judges in the district judiciary. The manner in which the unit-based system works is simple. It awards a certain number of predetermined units to a judge for every judicial task that they complete. For example, if the judge was to dispose of a civil suit, ten units may be awarded. Similarly, for every witness examined or cross-examined in a civil suit, the judge may be awarded one unit. The judge has to earn a certain number of units and also dispose of a minimum number of cases in order to achieve a good review in the annual appraisal.

The NCMS's interim solution proposed using this unit-based system to calculate the workload of every court and calculate if a particular court had a workload above the expected norms—in which case an additional court would be created and a new judge appointed to that court. It argued for creating new courts only if the pending docket crossed 1.5 times the number of units required for a judge to get a 'very good' rating. For example, if a judge is required to achieve 200 units in order to get a 'very good' performance rating in a year, a new court (and along with it an additional judge) would be created only if his existing docket crossed 300 units of work. At this point, as per the NCMS, a courtroom can be considered to be overworked, thereby justifying an increase in the number of judges.

An obvious reason to be sceptical about this methodology is that the unit system is not linked to usage of 'judicial time'. A judge gets a fixed number of units for completing a particular judicial task regardless of the time it takes to complete that task. For example, cross-examining a key witness in a complicated lawsuit can take 120 minutes, while cross-examination of a witness deposing on a minor piece of evidence can be completed in twenty minutes. The unit-based system does not factor in this component of time, which is what makes it a poor tool to assess judicial performance. For the same reason, the unit-based system is deeply unsuited as a metric to calculate judicial strength. This is because judicial time is a finite resource that goes to the core of judicial efficiency, which, in turn, determines the number of judges required. Any system of evaluating judicial workload that does not factor in time taken for different judicial tasks will always be flawed.

Despite these obvious problems with the NCMS reports and the crying need to collect data on judicial time consumed by different categories of cases, a bench of three judges headed by CJI Thakur passed yet another order in the *Imtiyaz Ahmad* case on 2 January 2017 (two days before CJI Thakur retired) embracing the unit-based methodology proposed by the NCMS report.[25] It ordered copies of the interim report of the NCMS to be forwarded to all High Courts and state governments so that necessary decisions could be taken by state governments in consultation with High Courts to increase the number of judges within a period of three months. This was a baffling approach to the issue because in that same order the bench headed by CJI Thakur conceded that the NCMS's method was not scientific enough and that it wanted a final report from the NCMS on a more scientific method for determining the number of judges required, before 31 December 2017.[26] If this was the case, why was the court ordering states to use an interim report that would likely involve irreversible financial implications and hiring decisions? What were the states to do if the final report proposed a different methodology to calculate judges that resulted in fewer judges being required? Who would compensate the states for the wasteful expenditure and, more importantly, what were the states supposed to do with the additional judges? The Supreme Court provided no answers to these questions in its judgment ordering states to adopt the interim report of the NCMS instead of just waiting for the final report ordered by the court.

At this point, a minor diversion is warranted to explain how two months before the above order was passed by the Supreme Court, another report was released by CJI Thakur on 31 October 2016 in his administrative capacity as the head of the court (unlike the judgments which were delivered as part of his role as a judge on the bench). This report, titled 'Subordinate Courts of India: A Report on Access to Justice', was prepared by a body called the Centre for Research &

Planning (CRP) of the Supreme Court, which is a NCMS-like body created by the Supreme Court to operate as an internal think-tank.[27] The report was silent on its authorship (which is surprising for any official document) but the foreword to this report was penned by CJI Thakur, in which he wrote that the report was meant to serve as 'an eye opener for all those who are sceptical about the need for a review of the Judge strength in the Courts'. To this end, this report discussed a few different methodologies to calculate the number of judges required but refrained from recommending any specific methodology. Given the foreword and timing of this report, which was published five months after CJI Thakur's teary-eyed comments, we suspect the report was meant to be a face-saver for the Chief Justice, since claims about the shortage of 70,000 judges had been comprehensively debunked by some experts in the press.[28] Regardless of the cause of this report, it is deeply worrying from the perspective of judicial propriety that a report of anonymous authorship was being released by a Chief Justice in his administrative capacity as the head of the court when a case related to the very same issue was pending before his bench in his judicial capacity as a judge and in which role he was expected to be impartial.

But to return to the final report of the NCMS, which was to be submitted by 31 December 2017, there is a twist in the tale, since the Supreme Court had closed the case without waiting for the report. This happened in August 2017, eight months after CJI Thakur retired, when a bench of two other judges closed the case without any mention of the 'final report' of the NCMS commissioned by the preceding bench.[29] Such endings are not uncommon with PILs, which are fuelled by the passions and predilections of individual judges. Once the judge retires, the PIL is quietly retired from the docket by his former colleagues, who then follow their own passion projects. In any event, the *Imtiyaz Ahmad* case was mysteriously resurrected on the docket from its grave in the record room after the NCMS submitted to the registry of the Supreme Court its final report sometime in November 2019.[30] The report of the NCMS, which apparently ran into five volumes, has not been made public by the Supreme Court.

Until January 2024, we had no clue about the contents of the report because we were unable to access a copy, although copies were given to the Union Government and High Courts.[31] When we requested for a copy from the Supreme Court in December 2021 under the RTI Act, we were denied the information by the Public Information Officer of the Supreme Court on the grounds that we were to apply for the same by filing an application under the court's own rules for a copy of the report. This would require us to cough up money to hire a lawyer to file the application and then make the case in court for a copy to be given to us—a steep venture riddled with uncertainty for people like us who were not litigants in this case and had limited resources.[32]

We finally discovered the recommendations of this unpublished final report of the NCMS when its conclusions were discussed in the 'State of the Judiciary' report published by the CRP on the Supreme Court's website in January 2024 during the tenure of Chief Justice D. Y. Chandrachud.[33] It is clear from the 'State of the Judiciary' report that the NCMS had recommended calculating the number of judges based on the judicial time required to dispose of different types of cases.[34] In other words, the NCMS appears to have repeated, with some window dressing, the Law Commission's very sensible suggestion in its 245th report published in 2014!

The challenge with implementing this methodology, as highlighted by the Law Commission way back in 2014, was the unavailability of data on judicial time spent by the district judiciary in disposing of different types of cases. It is evident from a reading of the 'State of the Judiciary' report that the Supreme Court did not have the required data ten years later as of January 2024. The report discusses strategies to collect such data on judicial time, suggesting at one point that an online platform be created for the district judiciary to submit timesheets on time spent on different categories of cases.[35] It should be mentioned that since its inception, the entire e-courts system, including the case management software used by all district courts in India, has been under the control of the e-committee of the Supreme Court. The e-committee could have tweaked the e-courts system to collect mountains of time-related data by the year 2024, if only it had taken the Law Commission's report seriously in 2014.

Even more worrying is the disclosure in the 'State of the Judiciary' report that the final report of the NCMS committee was still under consideration by the Supreme Court in *Imtiyaz Ahmad v. State of UP*, four years after it had been submitted to the court.[36] After the untimely resurrection of the *Imtiyaz Ahmad* case post the submission of the final report of the NCMS in 2019, the Supreme Court ordered all state governments and High Courts to file replies giving their views on the final report of the NCMS. As a result, the case now had sixty-three respondents represented by sixty-nine lawyers! As is common in PILs, a senior lawyer was appointed as an *amicus curiae* to assist the court by reviewing the recommendations of the NCMS. As is also common in PILs, the scope of the hearing gradually widened to include other issues. As noted by the court in one of its orders, 'During the course of the hearing, various suggestions have come up before the Court in regard to adopting suitable modalities for attending to the infrastructural needs of the Judiciary.'[37] And so, instead of taking a call on the final report of the NCMS on methodologies to calculate the number of judges required, the court started looking into funding for judicial infrastructure. At some point it appears that the bench hearing the case lost interest in it because as per the website of the Supreme Court, it stopped listing this case for hearings after 22 November 2022 while also not disposing of it. As this book goes to print, the case has not been listed for a hearing by the Supreme Court, meaning that no final decision has been taken by the court on the final report of the NCMS. And so, like Schrodinger's cat, this PIL is both active and inactive at the same time.

If such delay and utter confusion on such a critical policy issue had taken place within the government, it would have been possible to convince a Member of Parliament to raise the issue during Question Hour and demand accountability from the government and hold the minister accountable. Such an approach is not possible with the Supreme Court since the court was never designed to be a deliberative body that could be held accountable by the electorate—which is also why it should stay away from policy issues. The inability of the press to quiz judges in press conferences further exacerbates the accountability deficit. These shortcomings of the PIL process highlight its inherently anti-democratic nature wherein the judges of the Supreme Court are unaccountable to anybody.

The fact that this critical policy issue has been dragged out by the Supreme Court via the vehicle of *Imtiyaz Ahmad v. State of UP* over a period of twelve years, sixty-eight hearings (between the years 2012 and 2022) and five reports by three different institutions without any conclusion, should serve as a reminder that judges are no more efficient than the fabled procrastinators in the Indian bureaucracy when it comes to taking policy decisions. If anything, this episode should serve as an embarrassing reminder of the unsuitability of the courts to tackle complex policy issues.

Getting the formula right

As tempting as it is to continue blaming the Supreme Court for what can only be described as a fiasco of a policy debate on calculating the number of judges required in India, a more constructive way forward is to ask either Parliament or state legislatures to enact structural reforms.

One such reform, which has also been discussed in the previous chapter, is to put in place better mechanisms to collect data and publish statistics. This could include imposing a duty on the judiciary to publish the time being taken to dispose of different categories of cases. The only way to achieve these reforms is to seriously rethink the manner in which the e-courts programme has been executed so far by the e-committee of the Supreme Court and seriously consider decentralizing the project to the level of the High Courts.

A second reform could be to replicate a legislative idea from California, which imposes upon the state judicial administration the duty to mandatorily submit a report every two years to the legislature, detailing the need for additional courts and judges .[38] The legislation even lays out the criteria to be relied upon while calculating the number of judges required for the coming years. Either Parliament or state legislatures in India could enact similar legislation imposing similar obligations on the High Courts, requiring them to mandatorily calculate the number of judges as per the time-based methodology.

In conclusion, it is necessary to acknowledge that the framing of a policy on the number of judges required by the judiciary is too important to be left to the predilections of a few Supreme Court judges with a passion for reform. Not only does the issue directly impact the efficiency of the judicial system and the rights of citizens, it also involves the expenditure of public money in a time of increasing budgetary deficits. In this backdrop, either Parliament or the state legislative assemblies need to seize control from the Supreme Court by enacting legislation that mandatorily requires High Courts to conduct periodic assessments of judicial strength in a transparent manner.

8

The Purse Strings

Often the backlogs and huge pendency before the courts in India are attributed to the lack of funding. In this resource starved narrative, the judge is a pitiable figure holding court in a rented building, overburdened with work, with little authority to improve the court's conditions. Routinely, reports describing the sorry plight of court buildings appear in the news to reinforce the claim that the judiciary is being starved of funds.[1] A litigant-centric survey carried out in 2019 painted a worrying picture of courtrooms in poorer states.[2] For example, the survey found that 15 per cent of district courts did not have toilets for women and only 40 per cent had fully functioning toilets. A far more serious problem has been the fact that the judiciary has lacked sufficient courtrooms, leading it to rent courtrooms.

The above examples are generally cited by the judiciary as examples of 'stepmotherly' treatment by the government. However, the fact of the matter is that the state of most public infrastructure in the country, including police stations and revenue offices, is equally pathetic. The district judiciary is hardly an outlier.

The more important question is whether this visible disrepair and shortage of courtrooms is necessarily a function of inadequate funding? After all, the expenditure on the judiciary has been ramped up over the last two decades. Illustratively, the Indian state has managed to provide the Chief Justice of India a luxury Mercedes Benz sedan for his official conveyance, while the Patna High Court, located in Bihar, which is one of the poorest states in the country (its per capita income is at Rs 50,745), announced a tender to purchase Apple iPhones, worth Rs 1.25 lakh each for its judges, with state taxpayer money.[3]

Luxury expenditure aside, since 2004, Parliament has dramatically increased funding from its own coffers for the district judiciary across states. A few numbers may help paint a clearer picture. For example, the Centrally Sponsored Scheme for Judicial Infrastructure, which is aimed at building courtrooms and residences for the district judiciary, has released Rs 10,500 crore of funding, out of which Rs 7,000 crore was allocated after 2014.[4] This funding is supposed to be matched by the states in a ratio of 40 per cent.[5] A second project funded entirely by Parliament is the e-courts project for which a sum of Rs 2,605 crore was allocated to the states, starting in the year 2010, to digitize the courts, with a focus on the district judiciary.[6] In addition to both these projects, Parliament also made a grant of Rs 5,000 crore on the recommendation of the Finance Commission to augment fast track courts, court managers, etc. at the level of the district judiciary.[7]

These are significant amounts, given the fact that the working strength of the district judiciary across the country is approximately 20,000 judges, with another 5,000 posts being vacant (mostly concentrated in three states). It is also worth noting that this funding from Parliament is over and above the annual funding provided by state legislatures for the salaries of judges, court staff and maintenance of the buildings. Despite such generous funding, the state of judicial infrastructure is far from impressive, as accounted earlier.

The question, therefore, is whether the real problem is a lack of funding or a failure to spend the money efficiently. The judges of the Supreme Court have claimed in public speeches that greater financial autonomy for the judiciary, which would involve giving judges more spending powers, would lead to better outcomes. However, as we argue in this chapter, the issue of funding the judiciary is a multi-layered problem that involves far more than simply increasing budgets for the judiciary or providing the judiciary with more financial autonomy. The nuances of this multi-layered problem are hopefully evident in the following discussion, which covers a range of issues, such as the levy of court fees, the entirely inappropriate judicial activism by the Supreme

Court and High Courts forcing the legislatures to divert limited public money to the judiciary, the challenges of fiscal federalism and the very real constitutional problems with granting the judiciary more financial autonomy.

Financing the judiciary—should litigants pay for the expenses of the courts?

One of the central features of the Indian justice system since the 18th century has been to make litigants pay 'court fees' to access the civil courts, with some exemptions for the indigent. This model was introduced in 1795 by the East India Company and continued by the British Crown.[8] More than 75 years after India declared independence from the British, the system of court fees continues to exist in India despite the nature of the relationship between the state and the individual transforming from one of ruler and subject to democratic state and citizen. The only difference now is that most state legislatures, consisting of elected representatives of Indian citizens, have enacted their own legislations on the levy of court fees.

The method of calculation of court fees continues to be the *ad valorem* method introduced by the British, wherein the fee payable is calculated as a percentage of the value of the dispute. To illustrate with an example, if a lawsuit is filed over a dispute related to the sale of property for Rs 10 lakh, the court fees in most states will be in the range of 1 per cent, which is Rs 10,000. Similarly, in a motor vehicle accident where a person has lost a limb and is claiming compensation of Rs 50 lakh, the claimant in some states will have to pay approximately Rs 50,000 as court fees upfront before receiving any compensation. If the defendant raises a dispute about the amount of court fee paid by the plaintiff, the judge has to frame an issue for trial and decide whether the fee paid was, in fact, adequate, failing which the judge cannot grant any of the judicial remedies sought by the plaintiff. Only the poor may be exempted from the payment of court fees.

Since Independence, there have been calls from the Law Commission to abolish court fees entirely, given the changing notions of the state's duties with regard to the justice system.[9] This line of argument has few takers within the state governments, whose finances are constantly frayed. Far from abolishing court fees, most state governments are increasing the court fees payable by litigants before the district judiciary. Some state governments are now levying court fees even on criminal cases under the Negotiable Instruments Act for the dishonouring of cheques.[10]

For a long time now, many in the legal community, including the Supreme Court, have claimed that state governments have been profiting from court fees, which is to say that the amount of revenue collected via the levy of court fees is in excess of the amount spent by the state on judicial administration. However, a study by the think-tank Daksh in 2024 suggests that the court fees collected by most states falls drastically short of the amount spent by the states on judicial administration.[11] This is not surprising because there is no concept of court fee for the criminal justice system (with the exception of cheque-bouncing cases), which consumes a fair share of judicial resources. The deficit amount, which as per the Daksh report is up to 70-80 per cent of the budget for judicial administration in the eight states that were studied, is met from the general tax pool of the state treasury.[12]

In sharp contrast to the state governments, the Union Government has got rid of the *ad valorem* system of court fees in most legislations it has introduced in Parliament since the 1980s, starting with the Consumer Protection Act, 1986 which imposes very minor fixed fees on consumers filing complaints before the consumer courts. For example, a consumer seeking compensation of Rs 15 lakh had to pay a fee of only Rs 500, which has been reduced to Rs 400 under the Consumer Protection Act, 2019. Similarly, creditors like banks suing for the recovery of thousands of crores of rupees of debt before the National Company Law Tribunal, which adjudicates insolvency petitions under the Insolvency & Bankruptcy Code (IBC), 2016, are required to pay a fixed fee of Rs 25,000.[13]

By practically doing away with *ad valorem* court fees for consumer courts and tribunals under its purview, the Union Government has adopted a remarkably progressive stand, viewing the justice delivery system as a public good.

Given the contrasting policies of the Union and states on court fees, India faces an absurd situation where financial institutions can litigate claims for thousands of crores of rupees under bankruptcy laws on the payment of a token court fee, while citizens seeking compensation for injury suffered due to an accident before the district judiciary have to pay an *ad valorem* fee.

If India is serious about ensuring equal access to the justice system, it is only fair that it does away with a system of imposing *ad valorem* court fees across the country. The administration of justice must be considered a public good and financed from the general pool of taxes, as is the case with other essential services provided by the state, be it roads or the police. A good example to draw inspiration from is the US where the federal courts charge a fixed fee of US$55 for filing a lawsuit and reasonable charges for services rendered, such as providing access to court records.[14] Surely, a country like India that proclaims to be socialist in its Constitution can move beyond a 18th-century model put in place by the British, of taxing litigants on an *ad valorem* basis in order to finance judicial administration.

Judicializing allocation of public funds under a cloud of opacity

Post Independence, the first tectonic shifts regarding the funding of the judiciary took place in the early 1990s when the All India Judges Association, a body representing the interests of the judges staffing the district judiciary, began petitioning the Supreme Court by way of PILs. In a series of judgments passed in these PILs, the Supreme Court has unilaterally ordered the Union and state governments to increase the salaries and retirement ages of the judges of the district judiciary.[15] It also ordered the state to provide housing, conveyance and additional allowances to the judges of the district judiciary.

At the time, the state and the Union governments raised rightful objections questioning the power of the court to issue such directions since decisions regarding spending of public money have always been the domain of the legislatures. As per the Constitution, appropriation bills withdrawing money from the state exchequer are required to be voted upon in state legislatures. The court simply rejected the objections raised by the lawyers for the Union and state governments without explaining the basis of its power to order such remedies. In later judgments, it continued to pass directions, which included the setting up of a National Judicial Pay Commission to provide suggestions on revising pay scales of judicial officers followed by a set of orders directing the Union and state governments to ensure the revised pay scales were enforced. The court's judgments in these cases failed to articulate the basis of its constitutional power to compel the legislature to increase funding for the judiciary. For most part, these judgments of the Supreme Court read like royal *firmans,* not reasoned orders by a court of law.

A committee set up by the Supreme Court in 2008, in another case dealing with judicial reforms and headed by a retired judge of the court, sought to legitimize these practices of the court by relying on American precedents where courts have used the 'inherent powers' doctrine to compel the state to fund the judiciary.[16] This is a poor comparison since American courts have invoked the inherent powers doctrine on rare occasions, when faced with budgetary cuts, in order to meet the basic financial requirements necessary to continue providing services previously available to litigants.[17] In contrast, the Supreme Court of India, in the AIJA cases, compelled the state legislatures to award salary hikes, additional allowances and perks like housing and vehicles to the district judiciary.

To make matters worse, the Supreme Court has displayed little tolerance for arguments by state governments on their inability to meet the court's orders to increase spending on the judiciary, given competing spending priorities. The court has simply dismissed these objections by remarking that 'it is for the States to increase the court fee or to approach the Finance Commission or the Union of India for more allocation of funds'.[18] There appears to have been little concern within the court that increased court fees would also increase the costs of litigation for the ordinary litigant on whom the burden falls of paying the court fees. It also bears noting that when states like Tamil Nadu have resorted to increasing court fees, they have faced significant pushback from both the Madras High Court and the bar.

In one instance, the Madras High Court demanded that the Revenue Secretary be present before the court if the recommendations of a court-appointed expert committee to reduce court fees for civil suits by 2-3 per cent was not given effect to by the state government.[19] When faced with such a situation, the government has no choice but to divert funding from other areas of governance towards the judiciary.

The larger problem with the Supreme Court's poorly articulated judicial activism in the AIJA cases is that it set a precedent for the High Courts to start passing broader orders forcing state legislatures to spend public funds on the judiciary without having to negotiate budgetary demands with the executive. For example, in March 2024, the Delhi High Court passed a judicial order directing the Delhi Government to sanction a proposal of Rs 387 crore of public funds for the purchase of video-conferencing equipment for the district courts of Delhi in order to permit 'hybrid hearings' wherein lawyers could argue before courts from the comfort of their offices without being physically present before the court.[20] The legislature, however, never mandated hybrid hearings as a requirement for the district judiciary. It was the High Court which mandated hybrid hearings, without taking stock of whether the facilities and budgetary resources were available. When a PIL was filed before the Delhi High Court pointing out that the district judiciary lacked the necessary equipment and that judges were holding hearings on their mobile phones, a bench of two judges went about ordering the Delhi Government to provision money for the equipment. But the sum of Rs 387 crore for this project was more than twice the total capital expenditure of Rs 151 crore allocated in the annual budget of the Government of Delhi for the infrastructural needs of the judiciary, with most of it being earmarked for the building and maintenance of courtrooms.[21] States typically do not budget for capital spending on the judiciary's digital infrastructure because the Union government funds this project under a Central Sector Scheme where the funding priorities are controlled by the e-committee of the Supreme Court. None of these complexities and realities feature in the order of the Delhi High Court instructing the government to spend a whopping Rs 387 crore on video-conferencing equipment.

Other High Courts have passed similar orders to meet sundry demands of the judiciary, with little concern about whether they were forcing the state to divert funds meant for other essential governance functions or welfare programmes. Ideally such conflicts regarding funding for the judiciary should be resolved through negotiations between the judges and the state government. Negotiating with the government on budgetary decisions is part of the judges' administrative work profile. At the end of the day, budgetary priorities to meet the competing demands of a resource-scarce society must be decided by elected representatives answerable to citizens in every election. The judiciary has been reckless in ignoring these realities.

The era of increased funding from Parliament, the fiscal federalism problem and the lack of performance audits

When the UPA government was voted into power in 2004, it began to dramatically improve funding for the judiciary by augmenting the meagre state budgets with funding from the central pool of taxes. It did so through three different routes. First, it significantly increased annual funding for an existing Centrally Sponsored Scheme (CSS) for building courtrooms and residences for the district judiciary to Rs 595.74 crore.[22] Since then, the funds released under the scheme have averaged approximately Rs 700 crore every year compared to Rs 70 crore in the previous years.[23] Second, it announced a new Central Sector Scheme worth Rs 935 crore for the digitization of the district judiciary through an e-courts project.[24] The government spent approximately Rs 1,670 crore on Phase II of the e-courts project and the scheme has been renewed for a third phase with a financial outlay of Rs 7,210 crore.[25] Third, it accepted a recommendation by the Finance Commission to allocate Rs 5,000 crore for specific reform measures targeted at the district judiciary. These are not small amounts, given that the district judiciary has a working strength of merely 20,000 judges, with approximately 5,000 vacancies.

This enormous increase in funding during the UPA years, which has been continued by the successive NDA governments, reflects a new political willingness to invest in the judiciary. Unfortunately,

India is a country where increased funding often fails to translate into change on the ground. For example, one of the problems with the Finance Commission grant was that of the Rs 5,000 crore that was allocated only Rs 2,067.93 crore was 'released' by the Union government, and of this, only Rs 1,010 crore was spent by the states.[26] However, the government has not conducted any substantial review trying to pinpoint the reasons for this low utilization. One possible reason could be that the Finance Commission had allocated the grant amount for specific reforms that were of no interest to the states. If this was the problem, it raises the question of the manner in which the Finance Commission identified specific issues that required additional funding. A simple reading of the recommendations of the XIII Finance Commission reveals a conspicuous lack of any solid evidentiary basis backing its recommendations on the subject of judicial reforms. As one academic put it, 'No evidence is presented or cited to suggest how such spending will affect the quality of the outcome' regarding the 'delivery of justice'.[27] It is also possible that grants were not released because the state government failed to meet the conditions imposed by the Finance Commission.[28] Unless the government conducts an honest and transparent performance review of such schemes, it is impossible to pinpoint precise reasons for failure.

With regard to the implementation of the CSS for judicial infrastructure, which is focused on building courtrooms and residences for the district judiciary, the project has run into the typical headwinds expected of any infrastructure project in India. This includes problems with identifying land, coordination between government departments, etc. For example, district judges, after identifying that a courtroom must be built and receiving approval from the High Court, have to rely on district-level authorities, mainly the district magistrate, for the identification of land and other revenue approvals and the Chief Engineer of the Public Works Department for estimating costs and preparing proposals for construction. After the three (the district judge, district magistrate and the chief engineer, PWD) provide the requisite information and approvals, the plan for a courtroom is sent to the High Court's relevant administrative committee and then to the finance department of the state government for approval. The PWD, after obtaining these sanctions, issues notice for tenders of construction. Plenty of things can go wrong in this process, as evident from audits of the Comptroller & Auditor General (CAG). For example, one of the CAG audits revealed that a judicial magistrate in Cuddalore, Tamil Nadu worked in a rented building unfit for occupation for six years after a courtroom was authorized to be built because the district collector refused to allot land.[29] In Uttar Pradesh, the government department responsible for construction did not survey the land before beginning construction and so the constructed courtroom would get flooded despite being new.[30] These are just some examples from many which have been uncovered by the CAG audits of the scheme.[31]

Apart from these operational issues, a well-known problem that has delayed the release of funds from the Union government is lethargy, on part of the state governments, in submitting 'utilization certificates' to the Government of India documenting expenditure for the preceding years, without which more funds cannot be released from central schemes.[32] Sometimes utilization certificates are incorrect. For example, one year, the Government of Kerala did not get the funds that it was owed because the PWD submitted incorrect utilization certificates.[33] There are no quick solutions to any of these problems, but improved transparency can make it easier to hold the responsible authorities accountable for delays. However, even the Law Ministry of the Union government, which is the relevant ministry for this project, is lacking in this regard. For example, when once asked for simple information under the RTI Act about the number of courtrooms built after the expenditure of at least Rs 8,000 crore under the CSS, the ministry was unable to provide a clear answer.[34] Since then, the Law Ministry has created an online portal that offers more information on the progress of the scheme.[35] These issues demonstrate the realities and complexities of daily administration in India, especially the problems of federalism when it comes to states and the Union government coordinating with each other to decide funding priorities and efficient expenditure of funds sanctioned by Parliament.

Should the judiciary have greater financial autonomy?

One of the demands of the judiciary, as a response to some of the aforementioned problems, has been greater 'financial autonomy', without really explaining the nature of the autonomy that it seeks. More autonomy could mean greater spending powers for the Chief Justice of the High Court. For example, in some states, the Chief Justice of the High Court is delegated financial authority of only Rs 25 lakh to spend on the needs of the court without prior sanction from the state government. Alternatively, it could mean the power to submit its budget proposal directly to the legislature, without having to go through the government.

The only concrete proposal from the judiciary articulating a vision for financial autonomy came from Chief Justice N. V. Ramana in 2022. He had sought 'complete financial autonomy' with respect to financial decisions pertaining to judicial infrastructure.[36] In particular, he proposed a National Judicial Infrastructure Authority of India (NJIAI) to be controlled by judges and with a mandate to oversee the building of judicial infrastructure. His proposal cited insufficient funds, underutilization of funds and poor planning in matters of infrastructure as reasons to ask for greater powers.[37] This proposal never proceeded because of opposition from the chief ministers.[38] But the judiciary's demand for financial autonomy is a long-standing one and is unlikely to fade away soon. In our opinion, there are three strong reasons to oppose this demand.

The *first* of these reasons is rooted in the accountability of those spending public funds, to elected representatives of the people. Such accountability for public expenditure is at the core of democratic governance across the world and takes place through a system of parliamentary questions, parliamentary committees, and audits by constitutional bodies like CAG. At the time of the drafting of the Constitution, the position of the Constituent Assembly on whether judges should be financially autonomous can be surmised from the fact that the Chiefs of the Supreme Court and the High Courts were given rule-making powers subject to the caveat that if the rules had a bearing on the states' finances, the consent of the government would be required.[39] While debating these provisions, the Constituent Assembly weighed the question of financial independence of the judiciary against the principles of financial accountability and protecting the interests of the general public. It concluded that the government was better positioned to judge the financial health of the state and make decisions about it.[40]

Similarly, in 2001, when the National Commission for Reviewing the Working of the Constitution examined the demand for greater financial autonomy for the judiciary, it faced a pushback from state governments. They made it clear that as long as the bureaucrats of the government were answerable to the Public Accounts Committees (PAC) of the state legislatures (generally chaired by the leader of the opposition) for the manner in which public funds were spent, they would oppose any substantive financial autonomy for the judiciary.[41] This is a fair point, especially since Article 121 of the Constitution forbids any discussion of the conduct of the judges of High Courts or Supreme Court in the legislature unless it is during an impeachment motion. In essence, this means that any misappropriation or inefficiency by judges cannot be debated in the state legislature, which in any case cannot impeach judges of the High Court. The only workable solution in this scenario is for the judges of the High Courts and Supreme Court to commit to appearing before the PACs in case questions are raised about the manner in which they have spent their funds. Such assurances, along with a commitment to make themselves available for questioning by vigilance and investigative agencies, in case of corruption inquiries, is the very least that must be demanded of the judiciary before conceding to demands of greater financial autonomy. After all, with greater financial autonomy comes greater financial accountability.

The *second* reason to be sceptical of the judiciary's demand is the poor handling of the e-courts project by the e-committee of the Supreme Court. Since it was conceptualized, the e-courts project has been managed entirely by the e-committee of the Supreme Court, headed by a judge of the Supreme Court. The e-committee enjoys considerable autonomy in deciding the priorities of the project, which include spending decisions. The Law Ministry still must sign off on the e-committee's proposals but there have been no publicly reported instances of the Law Ministry disagreeing with any of the demands of the e-committee. Despite this arrangement, where the court is effectively in control, the entire e-courts project remains poorly conceptualized, designed and implemented. Take, for example, the fact that the e-courts website is accessible only in the English language despite the proceedings before the district judiciary in most states being conducted in the official languages of the states. This is in sharp contrast to many government websites that cater to the common citizens in their local languages. Take, for example, the website of the Unique Identification Authority of India (UIDAI), which administers the Aadhaar number programme. The UIDAI makes its website accessible in thirteen languages, including English. Similarly, most state governments make it a point to make their websites accessible in the official language of the state. This is a basic requirement for any e-governance project that is meant to be used by citizens on a daily basis. Yet, almost two decades after the e-courts project was conceptualized, the interface of the website remains in English.

Similarly, as recounted earlier in the chapter on the paucity of judicial statistics, despite spending close to Rs 2,308 crore, the e-courts project is still not in a position to provide credible statistics. These are but two examples of startling deficiencies in a project where the judiciary had significant autonomy in designing and executing a project.

The *third* and most convincing argument against providing greater financial autonomy to the judiciary is its conduct when it comes to matters of financial transparency. The judiciary, while ostensibly endorsing transparency and even demanding it from the political class, has consistently avoided something as basic as making public the assets of judges. Further, a scrutiny of the rules framed by many High Courts under the RTI Act reveals that many of them have carved out additional exceptions over and above those provided by Parliament in the RTI Act. This is brazenly unconstitutional and if any other government department had framed similar exceptions, the High Courts would have very likely declared them illegal.[42]

The situation is no different when it comes to the judiciary's finances. For example, in March 2022, the Parliamentary Standing Committee noted in a report that the Supreme Court registry took more than two years to file replies to objections raised by the government auditor.[43] We filed an application under the RTI Act with the Supreme Court, seeking a copy of the audit report and the replies filed by the court to the objections raised in it. The Public Information Officer of the Supreme Court refused to share the requested information on the grounds that the disclosure would prejudicially affect the sovereignty and integrity of the country and cause a breach of parliamentary privileges![44] On the other hand, the government auditor, in response to a RTI application, disclosed a copy of the same report and the replies furnished by the registry.[45]

The Supreme Court is not alone in its reluctance to be transparent about its finances or decision-making process. In 2019, as part of another research project, we had filed, along with former colleagues, applications under the RTI Act for copies of audit reports of twenty-four High Courts. It was alarming to discover that fourteen High Courts refused to share their audit reports.[46] More worryingly, we discovered that for at least three High Courts, not a single audit report had been finalized for a period of five years.

This hostility towards basic demands for financial transparency extends to the minutes of the relevant administrative committees of the High Court comprising judges who are empowered to take all the decisions regarding budgets and planning for the entire state judiciary. It is fair to expect that they disclose the deliberations and considerations that inform the preparation of budgets involving the expenditure of public money. Regrettably, these administrative committees of the High Courts function with alarming opacity. For example, when a district bar association challenged the refusal of the Public Information Officer of the Bombay High Court to provide file notings of the administrative committee of the High Court approving the creation of a new district court, the Bombay High Court declared that 'withholding file notings is, in our view, entirely salutary' and 'required for the better administration of justice'.[47] The Government of

India, on the other hand, discloses all of its file notings after an initial proposal to exempt file notings attracted an intense public backlash from civil society. In a world where the government is more transparent than the judiciary, it would be a blunder of gargantuan proportions to provide any financial autonomy to the judiciary.

The path forward

The days of sparse funding for the judiciary ended two decades ago, with successive governments providing significant financial support to the judiciary. Given the political willingness to spend on upgrading judicial infrastructure, the debate must shift from lack of funding to one of transparency and accountability regarding the manner in which the increased budgets are being spent.

The judiciary must ensure meaningful transparency, consultations and evaluation mechanisms for all decisions with financial implications. Interested stakeholders should not have to make repeated requests under the RTI Act to access basic information. The judiciary should shift to a culture of proactive disclosure of all decisions with financial implications. This should extend to inviting external evaluations of projects like the e-courts, which are currently managed by judges of the Supreme Court. Similarly, audit reports and minutes of administrative committees should be proactively published by the judiciary.

We are very pessimistic about the judiciary becoming more transparent about its finances without external pressure from Parliament. At the very least, Parliament must impose a duty on the High Courts and the Supreme Court to release, on an annual basis, detailed statements about their finances, as also minutes of administrative committees that are making decisions that have financial implications. Judges cannot be allowed to wield administrative power that has financial implications for taxpaying citizens without adhering to basic norms of transparency. In this context, Parliament should never forget that the first ever impeachment motion, post-Independence, against Justice Ramaswamy was on account of his alleged financial profligacy with public funds.[48]

Further, Parliament needs to lay down a clear financial accountability framework mandating the judiciary to respond to audit objections by

CAG, with clear penalties for a failure to do so in a timely manner. Hopefully such measures will build a culture of financial accountability within the judiciary. Unless the judiciary is willing to demonstrate such financial transparency and accountability, it cannot legitimately demand greater financial autonomy for itself.

9

Reforming Court Bureaucracies

The judges of the district judiciary are the face of the justice system for most litigants. After all, it is these judges who preside over courtrooms, conducting trials, hearing arguments and delivering judgments. It is no surprise then that most public anger over delays at the level of the district courts is directed at these judges. However, the truth of the matter is that a judge is only as efficient as the massive bureaucracy working behind the scenes, supporting the administration of the courts.

This bureaucracy, whose official nomenclature is 'ministerial services', consists of bureaucrats with a wide variety of administrative roles. Those assigned to the courtroom include bench clerks, stenographers and deposition writers, without whose presence the judge cannot function. There is then a registry for every court, whose job it is to process the paperwork for new lawsuits and petitions that are filed, in order to ensure that all filings comply with the rules of the court before being taken up by the judge. The registry also has to ensure litigants have paid court fees and process fees. There is then a record room and evidence room, both of which are responsible for maintaining all records and evidence so that the same can be produced before court when required. Another function of the registry is ensuring the service of summons on defendants and witnesses, informing them that they are to present themselves before a particular judge at a particular time. This service is effected by bureaucrats called 'process servers'. In addition to the bureaucracy in the courtroom and the registry, there is the housekeeping staff which includes book binders, court keepers, *darwans*, filers, sweepers, gardeners and peons.[1]

Most of these bureaucrats in the courtroom and registry can impact the efficiency of the judge and the progress of the case. For example, there have been cases where courts have adjourned proceedings for the entire day because of the stenographer absenting himself from work.[2] The shortage of stenographers appears to be an endemic problem in some parts of the country, as evidenced by the fact that judges in states like Jharkhand have norms giving judges some leniency in the performance assessment system if they do not have stenographers as part of their staff.[3] Similarly, any delay in the service of summons upon the defendant by the process server will result in a delay in the progress of the case, since the law requires the defendant to be notified before the case can be heard. Studies in some parts of the country indicate that summons can take the better part of a year on average to be served![4] This is not a new problem. The Rankin Committee from back in 1924-1925 had identified the service of summons as one of the main sources of delay, remarking that in no part of the country 'is service effected as speedily as it should be'.[5] The committee blamed the state of affairs in process-serving on rampant corruption and lack of effective supervision. To put it simply, the efficiency and productivity of judges is deeply intertwined with the efficiency of the bureaucracy supporting the courts.

Collectively, as of December 2023, the strength of the bureaucracy staffing all district courts in India was pegged at 2,73,696 bureaucrats, of which 73,934 positions were vacant.[6] Illustratively, the district judiciary in states like Uttar Pradesh has a working strength of 18,480 bureaucrats to support 3,698 judges, Maharashtra has a working strength of 22,225 bureaucrats to support 2,190 judges and lastly, Tamil Nadu has a working strength of 21,111 bureaucrats to support 1,361 judges.[7]

Over and above this bureaucracy staffing the district courts are two layers of management located in the High Courts. At the very top are administrative committees consisting of judges of High Courts, which are responsible for taking policy decisions with regard to the district courts. This includes decisions related to recruitments, budgets, infrastructure, creating new judicial districts, etc. The second layer of management within the High Courts are the registrars, who are sandwiched between the administrative committees of the High Courts and the district courts. Prior to Independence, these registrars were drawn from the elite Indian Civil Service. Post Independence, these registrars are drawn from the judicial services. In other words, they are not professional managers but judges from the district judiciary who are deputed to the High Courts as registrars temporarily, before rotating back to the courtroom. The registrars are also responsible for coordinating with the district judiciary across the state to implement policies laid down by the administrative committees and collect any relevant information from the district judiciary for the purpose of preparing budgetary estimates and statistical statements, amongst other administrative tasks.

To the best of our knowledge, there has never been a systematic review examining the efficiency of this bureaucracy meant to support court administration. Most of the debate on reforming court administration has been focused on four disparate issues, which are the subject of this chapter. We explore these four issues and explain why these reforms possibly never translated into improved efficiency of the district courts.

The failed court managers experiment

One of the most popular ideas doing the rounds since 2010, on the subject of reforming court administration, has been of specialist court managers with degrees in business administration to assist judges in their administrative duties, much of which involves managing the bureaucracy. For example, in Bombay, the Chief Metropolitan Magistrate's court complex at Esplanade, which has seventy-five judges, has a staff strength of 919 bureaucrats in various administrative positions spread across four classes of employees.[8] These include stenographers, clerks, cashiers, typists, drivers, hawaladars, liftmen, sweepers, gardeners, peons and *chaprasis*. Managing this staff is a full-time job and it has been argued that a 'court manager' would go a long way in solving the problem. Towards this end, the 13th Finance Commission offered funding for the post of court managers in every district court.[9]

However, the problem with the 13th Finance Commission was that when, in 2010, it allocated funding of Rs 300 crore for states to hire court managers to assist judges in the administration of the courts, it did not clearly explain their role.[10] Its report mentions that the idea for court managers came from the Department of Justice (DoJ) of the Law Ministry without specifying the problem that would be resolved by creating this new post. The report merely states that the aim was to reduce the administrative workload of the judges so that they could focus on judicial tasks.

While the DoJ's memorandum to the Finance Commission on this issue was unavailable to us, it bears noting that the idea of court managers is not new. It was proposed in the 127th report of the Law Commission published in 1988. In this report, the 11th Law Commission under Chairman Justice D. A. Desai (retd) had proposed creating the post of the 'court executive' to manage the courts. In its words, the court executive was to be 'highly qualified' with 'broad managerial skills, knowledge of the structure of judicial system, familiarity with legal procedures, comprehension of computer sciences and data processing techniques and skills and personnel recruitment etc'.[11] The court executive, as per the Law Commission's vision, was to efficiently implement policies formulated by the judiciary for its internal administration.

While making these recommendations for 'court managers', the Law Commission and the Finance Commission appear to have missed the fact that back in the year 1925, the Rankin Committee on civil justice reform had discussed this very same issue, after several district judges that it interviewed had reported that an increasing administrative burden was diverting their attention from judicial work. As recounted in the Rankin Committee report, the High Courts of Bombay and Calcutta had proposed tackling this problem by creating the post of 'registrar' to handle the administrative duties of the district judges.[12] Perhaps as a result of the Rankin Committee's recommendations, most states had already created a managerial class of bureaucrats within district courts. Their designations vary across states, being called 'registrars' in some cities like Bombay or 'senior administrative officers' in other states. For example, in the Chief Metropolitan Magistrate's court in Bombay, there already exists a post called 'registrar' sandwiched between the judges and the Class III and Class IV bureaucrats, effectively making them mid-management at the district court level.

The only problem that we could identify with these registrars or senior administrative officers is that they perhaps lack specialized training in management techniques since they tend to climb the ranks through the ministerial services. In Delhi, the supervisory cadre for the ministerial services, designated as administrative officers (judicial), is recruited through promotions or through qualifying exams from amongst the assistant and clerical cadre.[13] These candidates are required to clear a written exam and have completed graduation, preferably in law, to be considered for promotion.

Given the existence of these managerial posts, the appropriate policy recommendation should have been to upgrade the qualifications required for these posts, instead of creating a new post. Instead, the Finance Commission allocated Rs 300 crore to reinvent the wheel by creating new posts of court managers. On being informed of the availability of these funds, the High Courts duly went about hiring, on a contractual basis, court managers with degrees in business administration. Except, as has been well documented since, the experiment with court managers failed.[14] This is because the bureaucrats in the ministerial services staffing administrative positions in the district courts paid no heed to the court manager. This was because the court manager lacked a permanent place in the bureaucratic hierarchy of court administration and was employed on a contractual basis. In the status-conscious and hierarchy-obsessed Indian bureaucracy, bureaucrats tend to follow the orders of only those in their superior ranks who have the power to hold them accountable. Rather than spending money on creating new posts, it would be more sensible to upgrade the qualifications required for existing managerial posts such as registrars and senior administrative officers or in the alternate provide them with better training in management skills.

The problem of vacancies and efficiency of court bureaucracy

A second issue pertaining to the court bureaucracy, which has attracted its fair share of public attention in the recent past, is vacancies.[15] As mentioned earlier, of the 2,73,696 bureaucrats meant to support the courts, 73,934 positions are vacant. The problem is not uniform across the country and is concentrated in certain states that have traditionally been poor performers even when it comes to recruiting for the bureaucracy of their state governments. It is also possible that some of these positions have been made redundant by technology and are hence vacant. For example, digitization should have made the roles of some copyists and typists redundant.

Any discussion about vacancies of court staff inevitably leads to a focus on recruitment practices across states. As things stand, there are no uniform practices across the country. Many High Courts have centralized recruitment processes for the entire state.[16] Others have a decentralized process, where district courts conduct their own hiring as per qualifications laid down by the state governments in consultation with the High Courts. The Supreme Court took up this issue of recruitment in one of its *suo motu* PILs, regarding the administration of the district courts. In that case, on 12 February 2014, it directed the High Courts to consider centralized selection of candidates, on an annual basis, for the bureaucracy meant to staff the courts under their control.[17]

However, the question is whether centralization will result in a more efficient recruitment process. There are several examples in India of centralized recruitment not always being efficient in ensuring filling up of vacancies. Many of the State Public Service Commissions, which are constitutional bodies with a mandate to conduct centralized recruitments for the state governments, do not have the greatest track record on the count of efficiency.[18] Similarly, there are significant vacancies for the Indian Administrative Service (IAS) and the Indian Army, despite recruitment for these services being centralized. At the same time, it also bears noting that decentralization of any services in India is no guarantee of greater efficiency, as there are inevitable complaints about nepotism and corruption. The best way forward is to allow states to experiment and figure out for themselves the most efficient solutions, instead of a singular national prescription. Having said that, there are a few administrative innovations taking place in some states that should be considered by High Courts.

The first innovation is from the Punjab & Haryana High Court, which has created a body called the Society for Centralized Recruitment of Staff in Subordinate Courts, which is incorporated under the Societies Act.[19] As suggested by its name, this society has a mandate to recruit staff for the district courts functioning across Punjab and Haryana. A similar model exists in the UK, called His Majesty's Courts & Tribunals Service (HMCTS), which functions under the control of the Ministry of Justice. There have been some calls to replicate this model in India.[20] This is essentially a centralized model of recruitment but one with a corporate structure separate from government, which permits some administrative flexibilities. Over time, as such bodies develop the expertise in conducting recruitment, they are likely to become more efficient, provided they are managed by professional managers and not judges of the High Courts who can only dedicate a part of their time to this complex task.

The second innovation is the outsourcing of non-essential housekeeping functions such as liftmen, gardeners, sweepers and other cleaning staff. Outsourcing has been quite common within government. Within the judiciary, there is the example of the Supreme Court, which outsources many of its functions such as security and housekeeping to different private agencies.[21] The High Courts should seriously consider outsourcing these jobs at the district court level to professional facility management organizations selected through a fair and competitive tendering process. Such a model would hopefully reduce the administrative workload on the judges of the courts since they will no longer have to oversee the recruitment and management of housekeeping personnel.

Professionalizing mid and upper management within the High Courts

As mentioned earlier, the major administrative decisions with regard to the district courts are actually taken within High Courts at two levels. While the policymaking functions within the High Courts are spread across various administrative committees consisting of judges of High Courts, there are also the registrars in the High Courts who are effectively mid-management, enforcing the policy decisions of the administrative committees. Each registrar has a different role—for example, registrar (infrastructure), registrar (recruitment), etc. There are a number of problems with this set-up.

To begin with, the registrars within the High Courts are all district judges who are posted temporarily at the High Courts for a few years before rotating back to the district courts. Apart from being temporary in a job that requires long-term institutional planning and memory, these district judges are simply not trained for managerial tasks. A report by the Supreme Court's internal think-tank, headed by Justice Dipankar Dutta, had this to say about the appointment of district judges appointed as registrars within the High Courts:

> The jobs that the registry officials perform in the High Court are clearly at variance with judicial duties and, most often, quite a few of them are found to be all at sea. With the frequent change in the members of the registry, it becomes all the more difficult for the new incumbents to get themselves accustomed with the system and to deliver according to the needs of the institution and commensurate with their capability. The service of the senior judicial officers could be better utilized in the districts rather than foisting a responsibility on them in an environment with which they are unfamiliar and in the absence of wherewithal to deal with the daily problems.[22]

The above critique sets up a strong case for the High Courts to revamp the qualification criteria for these posts, in order to ensure that the roles are staffed by trained management professionals rather than district judges, whose services are best used in the courtroom to dispense justice.

Along with revamping the role of the registrars, there is a need to reconsider the role played by the administrative committees consisting of judges of High Courts, which make crucial decisions about the budget, infrastructure, recruitment policies, etc. Given the opacity of these administrative committees (minutes of their meetings are not publicly available, even if requested for under the RTI Act) it is unclear how exactly they go about their job. The larger problem is that judges of the High Courts have a heavy workload, which includes holding court every working day and authoring judgements after regular court hours. The administrative committees are, therefore, a 'part-time' job for judges, despite the importance of the work being conducted by these committees for the entire district judiciary. Further, it is a known fact that judges are rotated frequently through different administrative committees depending on a variety of factors ranging from seniority, retirements, new appointments and transfers. This is not ideal and likely disrupts any long-term reforms and effective oversight of the few reforms that are implemented.

The obvious reform measure to solve the above problem is to create a specialized office within the judiciary or an independent agency answerable to High Courts, staffed with experts who can do the heavy lifting so as to let judges of the High Courts focus on their main job, which is to hold court and deliver judgments. The same office or agency can also absorb the role played by the registrars. It bears mentioning that many countries have such an administrative set-up for their independent judiciaries. For example, the United States Federal Judiciary has the Administrative Office of the US Courts, which operates as an internal think-tank and 'provides a broad range of legislative, legal, financial, technology, management, administrative, and program support services to federal courts'.[23] With full-time experts working on administrative issues, the quality of management will improve and the judges of the High Court will find more time to take care of their judicial work. It goes without saying that any such specialized office to manage judicial administration should continue to remain under the operational control of the High Court so as to protect judicial independence. Such organizational reforms should be accompanied with an institutional commitment to ensure more transparency and participatory decision-making.

The National Court Management System (NCMS), set up by

the Supreme Court of India, has been working as an internal think-tank of sorts, but suffers from two flaws. First, it is staffed by judges, which means that the NCMS once again performs as a part-time body. Second, the Supreme Court has no administrative authority over judges of the High Courts, as per the Constitution. The more appropriate way ahead would be for the High Courts to create such think tanks to advise their administrative committees, rather than depend on the NCMS to formulate a 'one-size-fits-all' proposal for the entire country.

Revamping the failed e-courts project

One reform that could have significantly streamlined administration of the district courts was the e-courts project. The use of technology to manage judicial records more efficiently and transparently could have transformed the efficiency of the bureaucrats responsible for administering the district courts. After all, the judicial process is mostly about the written record, be it the pleadings, evidence or the judgment. Once filed in a paper format, most registries within district courts process the documents in the paper format to ensure compliance with the rules of the court, before producing the record before the judge. When the record is not in court, it is stored in a record room before being retrieved. All documentary evidence and witness testimony are stored as paper records. The judgment, when delivered, is in paper format and if an appeal is required to be filed before the higher courts, the paper records will have to travel from the district courts to the High Courts. Much of the efficiency of the judicial system comes down to ensuring that these records are processed seamlessly, stored securely and accessible to all important stakeholders, including litigants.

Typically, any administrative system that relies on physical records and makes a bureaucrat the gatekeeper to the records opens the door to petty corruption. For example, just moving a file from the desk of one clerk to another clerk can require greasing the palms of petty bureaucrats, thereby delaying the process. A more challenging problem for litigants is the need to grease palms to access records in the custody of the court. This could be as simple as trying to procure a photocopy of the pleadings filed by the opposing litigant or orders of the judge. Alternatively, litigants could require access to certified copies in order to file appeals before higher courts or to submit to government offices. Delays in procuring certified copies can delay the filing of appeals.

In this backdrop, a well-executed digitization project can deliver significant benefits to litigants. For example, digitization of the court registries can ensure that once paper records are digitized, the digital files are seamlessly transferred between one clerk to another with timestamps, thereby ensuring accountability of each bureaucrat in the court registry. Further, if digital court records could be transmitted between the trial court and the appellate court, it would significantly cut down delays faced due to slow transfer of the physical records. Similarly, digital court records can be easily accessed by litigants without leaving them at the mercy of advocates, clerks or the bureaucrats.

In theory, it should not be difficult to execute such an e-governance project. The Government of India has executed e-governance programmes on a massive scale in the context of the Registrar of Companies (RoC), the Patent Office and Trade Marks Registry. These are government offices that manage hundreds of thousands of records and any citizen can access all the records either for free (as is the case with the Patent Office and Trade Marks Registry) or for payment of a fee (as is the case with company records) and also place orders for certified copies of documents that they require, which are then couriered to them.

Yet, almost fifteen years after the e-courts project was first launched for the district judiciary, it looks like a relic when compared to the e-governance projects of the Union government. Most of the services referenced above are not available for litigants before the district judiciary. At most, the e-courts project will let them view the date of hearing but the text of the order or the judgment may or may not be available on the website of the district court. It is not uncommon for the court staff in the district courts to make available only a summary of the daily order on the e-courts website. There is no question of digital inspection of documents or ordering certified copies from the comfort of the litigant's home, thereby increasing their dependence on lawyers.

A few district courts offer some of these services but that is because they have innovated outside the e-courts project.

The reason for these failures is that the e-courts project did not digitize the workflows within the registry of the district courts or court records as filed by litigants. This is unlike the digitization of the Supreme Court or some of the High Courts, where workflows were digitized (digital filings of pleadings began only during the pandemic), leading to far greater transparency in the functioning of the registry. The websites of the Supreme Court and High Courts are far superior to the e-courts website since they display detailed, accurate information about each case that is pending before the court, including the progress of the case through the registry and the daily orders passed by the court. Some of the High Courts also offer digital authentication systems for their orders and judgments and interlink details of intra-court appeals. These systems in the High Courts and Supreme Court, while still not as efficient as the Union government's e-governance projects, are far superior to the e-courts system used for the district judiciary.

Apart from serving the needs of the litigants, a well-designed digitization programme should have also ensured seamless coordination with other institutions such as police stations or the prisons. Delays in transmission of court orders can delay the release of citizens even after the grant of bail. A well-publicized example of such delays was the case of the superstar Shah Rukh Khan's son, whose release on bail was delayed by a night because a physical copy of the court's order was not deposited in the 'bail box' outside the Arthur Road prison in Mumbai by 5.30 p.m.

So why is it that the e-courts project has not achieved any of the above objectives when e-governance projects of the Government of India and the digitization of the High Courts and Supreme Court are demonstrably superior? We have two working theories in this regard.

The first is regarding the flawed administrative structure of the e-courts project. It was a mistake to vest responsibility for the project in the e-committee controlled by judges of the Supreme Court, despite the district courts being under the control of the High Courts, per the Constitution. If the e-courts project had been decentralized to

High Courts, it is likely to have been better designed and executed. This is because the registries of the High Courts have a far greater incentive than the e-committee of the Supreme Court to ensure the successful digitization of the district courts. It is the officials in the registry of each High Court who are responsible for overseeing the functioning of the district courts, including collecting the necessary statistical information. They also have to liaison with district courts for the transfer of records in case of appeals, etc. By ensuring the efficient digitization of the district courts, the officials within the registry of the High Courts would have reduced their own workload.

The second working theory to explain the poor execution of the e-courts project is the fact that barring one limited evaluation commissioned by the Department of Justice, the entire project has never been subject to a comprehensive review or performance audit. Implementation of the programme in certain parts of the country has been reviewed by the Comptroller & Audit General but that is not the same as a systemic review of its design and execution. As long as the project continues to be under the control of judges of the Supreme Court, it is unlikely that any governmental institutions will have the courage to seek a serious review of the project. The only body bold enough to demand such a review is possibly the Parliamentary Standing Committee on Law and Justice, which in the past has asked for a review of other institutions like the National Judicial Academy, which is also under the control of the Supreme Court.[24]

The above reasons provide a strong case to dissolve the e-committee and decentralize the entire e-courts project to the High Courts, with a focus on ensuring interoperability between the courts and the law and order machinery, such as police stations and prisons.

Enacting a law to reform judicial administration

From the first Law Commission reports in 1958 to the most recent publication by the Supreme Court on the 'State of the Judiciary',[25] there has been a recognition of the challenges in making court administration efficient. Yet, little has changed on the ground.

Going ahead, there are three options for reform.

The first involves either Parliament or state legislatures enacting a law creating a specialized agency, with a specific organizational structure, which allows for professional full-time managers to handle the administrative affairs of the district courts in each state. Keeping with the basic principles of judicial independence embodied in Article 235 of the Constitution, any such law will need to ensure that the specialized agency is under the control of the judiciary. Such a measure of reform is likely to meet with some pushback from the High Courts, most of which are extremely protective of their turf.

A second, more palatable but less impactful reform would be to enact a transparency and disclosure law requiring all High Courts to present an annual report to Parliament and the state legislatures specifically on the state of judicial administration. This should include details on the staffing of the ministerial services responsible for judicial administration and statistical details regarding their workload—for example, the number of summons served in a year, the delays in serving summons, the number of applications for certified copies received and timelines for processing them. As of today, such information is not publicly available. The hope is that regular publication of such data about the working of registries of the district courts will throw a spotlight on inefficiencies, thereby creating the necessary political and public pressure on the High Courts to ensure more efficiency in court administration. Such transparency-oriented reform measures will be difficult for the High Courts to resist on the grounds of judicial independence.

The third reform measure, as mentioned earlier, is to overhaul the execution of the e-courts project by dissolving the e-committee and decentralizing the project to the High Courts. Such a recommendation would be in line with Article 235 of the Constitution, which places the district courts under the control of the High Courts. A well-designed and efficiently executed e-courts programme could dramatically improve the efficiency of court administration.

It is vital that the country reform the bureaucracy administering the district judiciary because, as mentioned in the introduction to this chapter, a judge is only as efficient as the bureaucracy supporting her in the courtroom and the registry.

PART THREE

The Long-Term Prescription

The first two parts of this book dealt with the bare minimum of reforms required to make the district judiciary more independent and efficient. In the third and final part of the book, we propose an agenda for long-term reforms to fundamentally rethink the constitutional design of the judiciary, reintroduce juries and finally arrest the unfortunate trend towards discarding procedural and evidentiary rules. These are the most challenging reforms to execute from a political perspective, but it is worth starting a public conversation on these issues in India.

On the point of rethinking the constitutional design of the judiciary in India, we highlight that the design is simply not efficient for a country like India where governance is split between the Union government and state governments. It is typical for countries with a federal set-up like India to also have two judiciaries—one for the Union and the other for individual states. That is not the case with India, despite the Constitution providing the Union with the power to create a separate system of courts to handle litigation emerging from laws enacted by Parliament. A related problem is that High Courts are the responsibility of the Union government while the district courts are the responsibility of the states. This is inefficient in practice since the judiciary works as a single unit. For these and other reasons, we argue for a rethink of the constitutional design of the judiciary.

In the next chapter, we argue for reviving the jury system that existed for close to a century in India before being ejected by the Code of Criminal Procedure enacted in 1973. The idea of laypersons participating in the justice system is a common feature across countries. This is because juries are thought to bolster the independence of the courts while also improving the legitimacy of the courts in the public eye. Despite these and other advantages of the jury system, India abolished it. We lay out the case for bringing back laypersons into Indian courts through the institution of juries.

In the last chapter, we argue for halting the dilution of procedural and evidentiary rules meant to govern litigation in the courtroom. Since Independence, a combination of judicial populism and a poor understanding within government of the reasons fuelling judicial delays led to dilution (and in some cases ejection) of procedural and evidentiary rules. These moves have done nothing to improve the quality or speed of justice in Indian courtrooms and instead may have backfired, enabling judges to act without any restraint on their powers. We thus make the case that it is time to restore procedural and evidentiary rules to their original integrity in order to guarantee litigants predictability and equal treatment.

10

Redesigning the Judiciary

Many of the inefficiencies of the Indian judiciary can be traced to the unwieldy design put in place by the British during colonialism and continued by successive governments post Independence. This is an issue best understood with two simple illustrations.

The first concerns cheque-bouncing cases. The Negotiable Instruments Act, 1881 was amended by Parliament in 1988 to declare the dishonouring of cheques, due to the lack of funds, as a criminal offence. This created a tsunami of litigation before the criminal courts, especially in cities. The consequences have been felt by the states upon whom falls the responsibility of providing funding and administrative support to the district courts.[1] Long story short, the states had to bear the burden of the chaotic fallout caused by a decision of Parliament, despite not having a say in the matter or the deep pockets necessary to provide adequate financial support to the judiciary to handle the new litigation.

This problem can also work the other way, with the policies of the Union government being frustrated by the inability of states to plan efficiently for the district courts. For instance, through the 1980s, recently nationalized banks were facing increasing difficulties in recovery of loans from debtors by way of lawsuits filed before the district courts. This was a problem for the Union government because it owned a whole bunch of these banks and would have to recapitalize the banks that failed to recover bad debts in a timely manner. However, the district courts hearing these lawsuits were the joint responsibility of the state governments and the High Courts. Since the Union government had little influence over the workings of the district courts, it acted on a proposal from the Reserve Bank of India to create entirely new tribunals, called the Debts Recovery Tribunals (DRTs), to hear all lawsuits regarding the recovery of debt by financial institutions. The funding and staffing of the DRTs were the responsibility of the Union.[2]

The two examples discussed above illustrate only one set of issues arising from the present constitutional design of the Indian judiciary. There are several other dimensions to this issue that are best understood in the context of the historical evolution of the Indian judiciary through three phases: colonial rule by the British, the Constituent Assembly debates leading to the adoption of the Constitution of India in 1950 and finally, the 42nd amendment to the Constitution in 1976 during the declaration of Emergency by Indira Gandhi's government. The following is a narration of how these events may have contributed to the dysfunctional nature of the Indian judiciary.

The design of the colonial judiciary in British India

The present constitutional design of the Indian judiciary can be traced back to the 19th century when the British Crown took over the administration of India from the East India Company after the sepoy mutiny of 1857. Shortly after, the Crown started a project to create a new judiciary to replace the existing judicial system, which was a mix of courts created by the erstwhile Mughal empire and the East India Company.[3]

The first step of this project was the enactment of the Indian High Courts Act, 1861 by the British Parliament, giving the Crown the authority to set up High Courts in India. Pursuant to this legislation, the Crown issued legal instruments called Letters Patents, creating the High Courts in Madras, Bombay and Calcutta. By the time the British left in 1947, another four High Courts were created at Allahabad, Patna, Lahore and Nagpur. These were the highest courts in each province and staffed by judges whose appointment and dismissal was controlled by the British Crown. Appeals against decisions of these

High Courts in civil cases could be filed with the Privy Council located in London.

The second step was the enactment of laws such as the Madras Civil Courts Act, 1873 and the Bengal, Agra and Assam Civil Courts Act, 1887 creating civil courts within each province of British-India. These laws created a multi-tiered system of civil courts headed by a district judge. Other laws such as Provincial Small Cause Courts Act, 1887 and the Presidency Small Cause Courts Act, 1882 created courts to tackle minor civil disputes. The provincial governments were empowered to decide the qualification criteria and appointment process for the judges to these courts.

The third step was the enactment of the Code of Criminal Procedure, 1861 which created a system of criminal courts consisting of three tiers of magistrates and a sessions judge, with a slightly different model for metropolitan cities. The magistracy comprised serving bureaucrats in the provincial government who carried out administrative functions in addition to their judicial responsibilities.

The above judicial structure endured for most of colonial rule in India, with the only significant change being the introduction of the Federal Court via the Government of India Act, 1935 (GoI Act). This court had a mandate to adjudicate constitutional disputes regarding the interpretation of the GoI Act.[4]

The Constituent Assembly debates

In preparation of Independence, the task of writing a new Constitution for independent India was vested with the Constituent Assembly of India, or more specifically, the Drafting Committee headed by Dr B. R. Ambedkar. The Drafting Committee wrote up the first draft of the Constitution on the basis of recommendations made by various committees consisting of members of the Constituent Assembly. The Draft Constitution was then published for public consultation and subsequently debated in the Constituent Assembly before being finalized.

Within the Drafting Committee, the task of preparing the first draft fell upon constitutional advisor B. N. Rau. On the issue of constitutional design of the judiciary, Rau, in his questionnaires to the Union Constitution Committee and Provincial Constitution Committee, had posed the question of whether India required a 'separate chain of courts' to administer the laws enacted by Parliament and law enacted by the state legislatures. His questionnaire pointed out how the US had constituted separate courts that exclusively dealt with disputes arising out of federal legislation, while the states had their own courts to decide disputes arising from state legislations.[5]

This was a relevant question to ask since British India had only one system of courts that heard disputes under both central and provincial legislations. The efficient solution would have been to mirror the administrative structure of the new Indian republic by creating two separate chains of courts—one to hear disputes under state laws and the other to hear disputes under Union laws. The states and the Union should have then been made responsible for their respective judicial systems, including the appointment of judges. This would have had the effect of clearly delineating responsibilities between the Union and states, vis-a-vis the state and Union judiciaries, making it easier to hold them accountable in case they failed to provide adequate resources to the judiciary.

Instead, the new Constitution continued with the structure put in place by the British. The only significant change introduced was Article 247, which gave Parliament the power to create new courts to hear disputes arising under parliamentary laws, if it so wanted. This provision technically opened the door to 'two different chains of courts'. But this provision was optional, which meant that if Parliament did not exercise its powers under Article 247, the courts administered by the states would also have to continue adjudicating disputes arising out of parliamentary law.

A second issue, which did not get the attention it should have from the Constituent Assembly, was the planning and administering of different layers of the judiciary. This would include issues such as the number of judges, their salaries, the location of courts across the country and the power to make appointments. Till Independence, as per the GoI Act, the British Crown had all these powers *vis-à-vis* the

High Courts, while the provinces had the power when it came to the civil courts and criminal magistracy. During the drafting process, there was a proposal to transfer some of the issues pertaining to High Courts to the states. This included the determination of the salaries of High Court judges, which, until Independence, were decided by the British Crown. The proposal in the Draft Constitution to shift this power to the states faced fierce opposition from the Conference of Judges of the Federal Court and High Courts and was therefore dropped.[6]

As a result, the new Constitution of India continued with the British-era policy, except the role of the British Crown *vis-à-vis* the High Courts was substituted with that of the Union government and Parliament. The powers vested in the Union included the power to appoint judges to High Courts, determine the number of judges in each High Court, decide their salaries and service conditions, determine the physical location of High Courts and lastly, impeach judges of the High Court. The same duties with regard to the district judiciary continued to vest with the states, although several of these powers were to be exercised in consultation with the High Courts.

This set-up meant that both the Union and the states would have to work optimally and in unison with each other to ensure that the judiciary in a state worked smoothly as a single unit. This is important because dysfunction at one level can easily cause dysfunction at the other.

Given this interplay between the High Courts and the district judiciary, it may have been more appropriate to ensure that both the High Courts and district judiciary were the administrative responsibility of the same government, preferably the states. This arrangement would have sat well with the overall scheme of the Constitution, which gave the states the principal responsibility in matters of daily governance. Regrettably this debate and analysis did not take place during the process of drafting the new Constitution, resulting in a judiciary that was unwieldy by design. Despite these flaws, this set-up remained largely untouched until the year 1976.

Indira Gandhi's 42nd Amendment to the Constitution

In 1976, Parliament enacted the infamous 42nd amendment to the Constitution. This was done when most MPs from the opposition parties were locked up in jail during the Emergency declared by Indira Gandhi.

While the 42nd Amendment is most infamous for its attack on the powers of the judiciary to strike down laws, less attention is paid to the manner in which it altered the constitutional design of the judiciary. In particular, this amendment introduced the following four changes.

First, it forbade the High Courts from hearing any constitutional challenges to any legislation enacted by Parliament. All such challenges could be adjudicated only by the Supreme Court. In essence this meant that High Courts could hear only challenges against state laws.[7] A similar provision forbade the Supreme Court from hearing challenges to state laws.[8]

Second, it allowed Parliament and state legislatures to create tribunals for deciding a whole range of disputes, ranging from grievances of the bureaucracy about their employment conditions to disputes over taxation, customs, labour, land acquisition, land reform and election. Parliament was also given the power to exclude the jurisdiction of the High Courts over these tribunals by allowing litigants to approach the Supreme Court directly by way of appeal.[9] Prior to the 42nd amendment, these disputes were heard either by the High Courts or the district courts.

Third, it amended Article 312 of the Constitution to give Parliament the option to create an All India Judicial Service (AIJS) for the rank of district judges, who were otherwise appointed by the state governments. Simply put, Article 312 gave Parliament the option to centralize the appointment of district judges with the Union government, which already had powers to appoint judges to the High Courts and the Supreme Court.

Fourth, it amended the Seventh Schedule of the Constitution, which distributes legislative powers between Parliament and the state legislatures, to shift the subject of 'Administration of justice; constitution and organisation of all courts, except the Supreme Court and the High Courts' from the State List to the Concurrent List.[10] In simple English, this meant that now, both Parliament and the state legislatures could enact laws on the organization and administration of the district courts. Until this point, this power lay solely with the state legislatures. Effectively, this opened the door for Parliament to dictate to the states the manner in which they administered the district judiciary.

Of the four sweeping changes introduced by the 42nd Amendment, only the first amendment, described above, was deleted by the 44th Amendment in 1978 after the Janata Party defeated Indira Gandhi in the general election held after the Emergency was lifted. The rationale for some of these changes introduced by the 42nd amendment is not clear. In his book on the 42nd amendment, senior advocate Rajeev Dhavan traces the origin of this Emergency-era constitutional amendment to a 'strange document' which had no 'authorship'.[11] The 'cloak and dagger' drafting of the 42nd amendment makes it difficult to ascertain the thinking that went behind it. While we may not know the thinking behind this amendment, we do know that it opened the door for the Union government to play a far more important role influencing judicial administration across the country.

The consequences of an unwieldy constitutional design of the judiciary

There have been three major consequences of this unwieldy constitutional design of the judiciary in the Constitution, as amended by the 42nd amendment.

The first has been the scenario outlined in the introduction, i.e. states have had to face the brunt of litigation generated by parliamentary laws, while the Union government has been frustrated with the district judiciary, which continued to be administered by the state governments. The disputes arising out of the banking sector discussed at the beginning of the chapter are a perfect illustration of the problems with such a design of the judiciary. It is doubtful whether the Union government coordinated with or warned state governments about the effects of the criminalization of cheque bouncing, which led to a flood of criminal prosecutions in the district courts. At the same time, the increasing delays faced by the banking sector in litigating their recovery lawsuits before the district judiciary threatened their financial health since they were unable to recover bad debt. This problem was tackled by Parliament in 1993 by creating the DRTs which took over the job from the district judiciary. While the creation of the DRTs reduced the workload on the district courts, it should be remembered that DRTs are an exception to the rule, necessitated by the fact that most banks were nationalized in 1969 and the Union government would have to pay to recapitalize these banks if they failed to recover bad debt efficiently. The Union government has shown no such urgency in dealing with the explosion of cheque-bouncing prosecutions despite nudges from the Supreme Court to create additional courts under Article 247.[12]

A second consequence of the unwieldy design of the judiciary is that the success of states in adequately staffing their district judiciary has been stymied by the inability of the Union government to adequately staff the High Courts. For most of the last decade, the vacancy rate of judges across High Courts has been approximately 30 per cent. In contrast, only two states—Uttar Pradesh and Bihar—have a vacancy rate in excess of 10 per cent for the district judiciary. This has direct consequences for the administration of justice in states since efficiency of the High Courts has a direct impact on the efficiency of the district judiciary. If a High Court lacks a sufficient number of judges due to the failure of the Union government to make timely appointments, the High Court will not be able to swiftly dispose appeals or contempt petitions arising from the district courts. This can end up causing delays before the district courts. Since states have no way to force the Union to ensure vacancies are fulfilled at High Courts, they have to quietly bear the costs of delays, despite being the ones paying for the salaries and expenses of High Courts.

The third consequence of the unwieldy design of the Indian judiciary is that it leaves states at the mercy of the Union government when it comes to creating new benches of the High Courts in other cities of the same state. For example, for several decades now, Kerala has been demanding the creation of a bench of the Kerala High Court (currently located in Kochi) in the city of Thiruvananthapuram. This would basically require locating a few judges of the High Court permanently in the city and vesting in them the jurisdiction over a particular region of the state.

This seemingly simple issue of creating new benches in the High Courts has been the source of significant tensions between the Union and states. The political importance of this issue can be judged from the fact that since 1958, questions about the creation of new benches of High Courts in other cities have been raised during Question Hour in Parliament on 96 occasions in the Lok Sabha and 39 occasions in the Rajya Sabha. In addition, since Independence, at least 18 bills have been introduced in the Lok Sabha and 20 bills in the Rajya Sabha, by parliamentarians in their individual capacity, seeking the creation of additional benches of the High Court in their states. These demands have emanated from states like Kerala, Uttar Pradesh, Karnataka, Maharashtra, Assam, Gujarat, Tamil Nadu, Odisha, West Bengal and Andhra Pradesh, to mention a few.[13]

It would be difficult to find another issue concerning the judiciary that has drawn so many questions and bills from individual parliamentarians. Outside Parliament, the demands by bar associations for the creation of benches of High Courts have led to multiple strikes, both in support as also by lawyers in opposition since it would divert litigation away from the existing seats of the High Courts.[14]

Cynics generally dismiss these demands as attempts by regional bar associations to increase their earnings, since lawyers typically can charge a higher fee from clients litigating before the High Courts. However, there is no denying that there are practical reasons fuelling this demand, such as the fact that many litigants have to spend significant time and resources travelling to cities where the High Courts are located.[15]

A more profound reason that is possibly driving these agitations for more benches of the High Courts is the recognition, within both the legal community and the political class, that High Courts, unlike the district judiciary, have powers to issue writs against the government and sanction the government for contempt when it fails to comply with its orders. This makes High Courts very powerful judicial institutions in a country where the district judiciary, despite having the power to sentence a person to death or life imprisonment, cannot issue something as basic as a writ of *habeas corpus* ordering the government to free persons being held in illegal detention. The district judiciary also does not have the same contempt powers as High Courts when its orders are not complied with by the government. In addition to these powers, the judges of the High Courts also enjoy far greater security of office, which adds to the perception that they are more independent and likely to hold government accountable.

Despite these compelling reasons, demands for new benches have faced an uphill battle. Some of the opposition, in our opinion, is elitist. Take, for example, the report submitted in 1956 by the 1st Law Commission, which at the time was chaired by M. C. Setalvad, exhorting the law minister to abandon the proposal for creating benches of the High Court at the time of reorganization of the states.[16] This five-page report was driven by a sense of urgency since the reorganization of states on linguistic lines was imminent. Amongst other grounds of opposition, the Commission argued that the lawyers in the new cities where the new benches would be located would be unable to provide the judges on those benches with effective assistance. The Commission, which also included M. C. Chagla and K. N. Wanchoo as its members, had this to say about the quality of the bar outside the High Courts[17]:

> A District or Taluka Bar, however competent it may be, cannot be compared to the High Court Bar. The litigant, therefore, appearing before a Bench will have to be satisfied with less competent advocacy or will have to spend much more by getting the services of someone from the High Court Bar.

To its credit, Parliament moved past this elitist opposition to create several benches of existing High Courts in states like Uttar Pradesh, Maharashtra, Rajasthan, Tamil Nadu, Madhya Pradesh and Karnataka. Except for Uttar Pradesh and Rajasthan, which have only one bench in addition to the principal seat, the other four states have benches in two cities, apart from the principal seat. Yet, similar demands from other states to create benches of the High Courts in other locations have been languishing despite the state legislatures and state governments backing the demand and expressing their willingness to foot the additional cost.

The main opposition has come from the Union government and successive Chief Justices of High Courts. As per Section 51 of the States Reorganisation Act, 1956, which was enacted to reorganize India on linguistic lines, the President can create permanent benches of existing High Courts in other locations 'after consultation with the Governor of a new State and the Chief Justice of the High Court for that State'. The Supreme Court interpreted this provision in 2000 to give the Chief Justice of the High Court a veto over such demands. In the court's own words, 'It is out of question to decide for establishment of a bench outside the principal seat of a High Court contrary to the opinion of the Chief Justice of that High Court which has been formed after considering the views of the colleague Judges.'[18] This was a perverse interpretation of the law by the Supreme Court, delivered at the peak of the court's activist phase, when the Court was prone to disregard the primacy of legislative intent and text. This judgment has been used as convenient excuse by the Government of India to reject demands by states to create additional benches of the High Courts on the grounds that there was no consensus between the state government and High Courts.[19] As a result, proposals from the state governments of Odisha, Haryana, Kerala and Jharkhand for the creation of new benches of the High Courts in their states have been blocked by the Chief Justices of those High Courts.[20] The proposal from Kerala has been pending since 1958, when the Kerala Assembly passed a resolution urging the creation of a High Court bench in Thiruvananthapuram.

As a result, despite states being willing to improve access to justice by funding new benches, they have been stymied in their efforts by the Union government acting in conjunction with the judges of the High Courts, who are not accountable to the electorate of the state. This example provides the most compelling reason for rethinking the present judicial structure enshrined in the Constitution.

Is it time to redesign the judiciary?

Any conversation on rethinking the constitutional design of the Indian judiciary must begin with the fact that the foundations of the present system date back to the 19th century. This judicial structure did not keep pace with the evolving governance structure of British India, especially the increasing devolution of power as successive editions of the Government of India Act from 1919 to 1935 delegated more powers from the central government to the provincial legislatures.[21] Administrative prudence would have dictated creating two different judicial systems to service the laws of the different legislative systems. That never happened during British rule. The anomaly was only partly corrected by the Drafting Committee in charge of writing India's new Constitution when it inserted Article 247, giving Parliament the power to create exclusive courts to adjudicate disputes arising under Parliamentary laws. Yet, Parliament never created an exclusive judicial system to deal with disputes arising out of parliamentary legislation. The tribunals created post Emergency are only for laws that rank high on the Union government's agenda and are not a systematic, well-planned solution to the unwieldy design of the judiciary. It does not help that the tribunals themselves have faced a crisis of credibility on the count of 'judicial independence' and their poor performance.

The optimal solution to these issues is to create 'two different chains of courts' for Union and state laws, as the constitutional advisor B. N. Rau put in his questionnaires during the consultations conducted by him. This system should automatically require all disputes under state laws to be litigated before state courts and similarly all disputes arising from parliamentary legislation to be litigated before the Union courts. The forum for disputes generated by legislation enacted by Parliament with regard to subjects on the Concurrent List should be decided by it.

The hope is that the creation of two different chains of courts for Union and state laws will improve administrative efficiency with responsibility clearly delineated between the Union and state governments. Creating this new judicial structure would obviously raise questions about the place of High Courts and the tribunals vis-a-vis the Union government. In our opinion, the High Courts should be considered to be part of the state judiciary. This would mean shifting High Courts to the state list, as was originally proposed in the Draft Constitution. State legislatures should have the power to decide the number of judges per High Court and also the locations at which the High Court would be seated in a state. A natural corollary of such an arrangement would be to give the states a greater say in the appointment, disciplining and removal of judges of High Courts. This is particularly necessary to restore a balance of power between the state legislatures and High Courts in an environment of brazen judicial activism, which at times is coloured by political partisanship.

With regard to tribunals, the logical route ahead would be to wrap up the existing tribunals into the Union judiciary and to discard Articles 323A and 323B into the dustbin of history. For good measure, the amendments to Article 312 regarding the creation of the All-India Judicial Service should be thrown into the same dustbin. At the same time, a new court of appeals should be created for the Union judiciary to subsume the functions of the High Courts and hear appeals arising from the Union judiciary.

All of these outcomes would require constitutional amendments and building a consensus towards these amendments will be challenging.

11

Bringing Back Juries

In 1959, India witnessed one of its most sensational criminal trials in the case of *State of Maharashtra v. K. M. Nanavati,* which has since inspired a number of books and movies, the latest being the Hindi movie *Rustom*. The case had all the ingredients for a sensational criminal case. Nanavati, an officer of the Indian Navy, was on trial for the murder of Prem Ahuja, a man who was having an extra-marital affair with Nanavati's wife, Sylvia. There was no doubt that Nanavati had indeed shot dead Ahuja but the question that required a trial was whether the shooting amounted to murder under the law, since Nanavati claimed it was accidental and also that he had been provoked by Ahuja, which can be a mitigating factor in the law.

At the time, in certain Indian cities, criminal cases involving serious offences were tried by juries consisting of ordinary citizens. Bombay was one of those cities where jury trials still prevailed, and Nanavati's case was tried by a jury of nine residents. In a jury trial, the judge interprets the technical rules of procedure and evidence. This includes deciding the evidence that can be admitted before the jury during the course of the trial. After the trial concludes, the judge also interprets the law for the jury, giving them clear instructions on the legal test to be used while they make a determination of guilt or innocence on the basis of the evidence presented during the course of the trial.

In Nanavati's case, the jury shocked the country with an overwhelming majority verdict (8:1) of 'not guilty' on both counts, of murder and culpable homicide not amounting to murder. Nanavati was free to go home an innocent man. The jury's verdict set off a firestorm of criticism since the trial was already in public focus with tabloids like *Blitz* covering the case in a sensational manner. Eventually, the verdict was set aside by the Bombay High Court, which then proceeded to convict Nanavati for murder. On appeal, the Supreme Court upheld the verdict and sentence of life imprisonment.[1] Three years later, Nanavati was pardoned by the Governor of Maharashtra and eventually migrated to Canada with his family.

Apart from providing fodder for novels, movies and tabloids, Nanavati's case had graver implications for the criminal justice system since it provided vocal and, some would argue, elitist voices within the legal establishment the necessary ammunition to push for their long-standing demand that jury trials be abolished in India. As argued by American historian James Jaffe, it was the elites in the legal community, like Justice K. N. Wanchoo and lawyers like M. C. Setalvad, who had loudly advocated for the abolishment of jury trials, through committees and commissions that they had headed on judicial reforms.[2] Their advocacy against the continuation of the jury system, which included arguments that India lacked 'a sufficient number of the right class of people' and that Indians lacked the 'English temperament', conveyed a certain contempt for the intellectual abilities of the ordinary Indian citizen.[3] By 1973, the new Code of Criminal Procedure abolished jury trials and the participation of ordinary Indians in the criminal justice system. The ordinary Indian could now enter the courtroom only as a litigant in a civil case, an accused in a criminal case or a witness. As 'outsiders' with no opportunity to participate equally in the courtroom, the ordinary citizen has grown more and more alienated from the judicial system.

In this chapter, we argue that despite the outcome in the Nanavati case and the attacks on the jury system by elites in the legal profession, there is a strong case for bringing back the jury system in Indian trial courts.

Why juries?

Juries as an institution have existed across civilizations and cultures, starting with ancient Athens, where a jury famously convicted Socrates for corruption. American academic R. L. Lerner, who has studied the history of juries, argues that countries with juries see the institution as the surest guarantor against bias of professional judges, who, unlike juries, may be more susceptible to influence by the government or their own perceptions of class and society.[4] Judges, after all, tend to be from the elite of society and in many countries, judges can be influenced by the government.[5] Juries consisting of common persons randomly drawn from all classes of societies act as a bulwark against these biases and weaknesses of professional judges. Given these benefits of the participation of laypersons in legal decision-making, it is no surprise that close to two-thirds of the world's countries allow citizens to participate in the adjudication of crimes.[6]

In the UK, the creation of juries has been attributed to the power struggle between the monarchy and the people. Concerns over the king having control over judges and the resulting bias demonstrated by these judges in favour of the monarchy, especially in cases of treason against the king, contributed to the development of the right to a trial by a jury of peers.[7] Similarly, in the US, the right to jury trials was enshrined in the Constitution because American colonies, prior to the War of Independence, were subject to adjudication by subservient judges who could be dismissed at will by colonial governors.[8] The resulting demand for right to jury trials manifested in the form of the sixth and seventh amendments to the American Constitution.

In South Korea and Japan, the relatively recent adoption of juries, in the years 2008 and 2009 respectively, has been attributed to the crisis of legitimacy being faced by the judiciaries in both those countries, especially in cases which involve the elites of those societies.[9] Juries were introduced in the criminal justice system of both countries to bolster the legitimacy of the criminal justice system by assuring citizens that the judiciary would function in an independent manner.[10] The format is, however, different from most common law countries since in Japan, the jurors sit along with a panel of professional judges to decide cases.

The common thread in the four examples discussed above is that juries can serve as an important means to assure a society that the judiciary is independent. In our opinion, this guarantee of judicial independence continues to be the strongest reason to reintroduce jury trials in India. Arguably, the individuals who constitute a jury, like a judge, will hold their own prejudices and preferences. The safeguard, however, lies in the fact that a diverse group of jurors, who will likely serve only once every few years on a jury, cannot be influenced in the same manner as judges, who are repeat actors looking to protect their career and post-retirement sinecures.

More importantly, jurors consisting of a randomly selected group of citizens will be informed by a diverse set of life experiences compared to a single professional judge in an Indian district court. The individual bias of jurors will be moderated to a large extent by a jury consisting of persons across class and caste groups. A diverse jury comprising jurors chosen at random is, therefore, more representative and ensures that an individual does not lose her liberty in a way that is contrary to the community's sense of justice.[11]

While judicial independence and moderating bias of the judicial class appear to be the most compelling reason to support the reintroduction of the jury system, a third reason is that service on juries allows citizens to participate in the functioning of courts by *deciding* aspects of the case.[12] The vesting of decision-making power upon the jurors makes them responsible for a fellow citizen's fate. In this regard, academics often draw an analogy to voting while discussing juries. Detractors of juries and political voting share concerns about the capacity of ordinary citizens to make the right decisions. [13] Those supporting juries argue that akin to voting, elevating citizens to the role of adjudicators empowers them and nourishes an appreciation for the rule of law in general.[14] In contrast, a judge-centric model of adjudication expects nothing but deference from ordinary citizens.

A fourth reason to support the jury system is that it serves as an educational experience for the average citizens, providing them with an insight into the workings of the legal system, especially the criminal justice system. Having to sit through an entire trial with the examination and cross-examination of witnesses, especially police officers, can be a useful learning experience for jurors. The experience can serve to build both public confidence in the courts and an appreciation for personal liberties of their fellow citizens.

A fifth reason to support the jury system is that the presence of common citizens in the courtroom forces the professional class of judges and lawyers to climb down from their high perch and demystify law in a manner that is simple and accessible to the common citizen. While technical rules of evidence and procedure will still be interpreted by the judge to determine the kind of evidence that can be presented to the jury, the legal arguments determinative to the outcome of the case have to be presented by the lawyers in a language that the jury can understand. This is of utmost importance, especially in criminal cases involving the life and liberty of the defendants. The often-elitist opposition from practising lawyers against jury trials is that much of the law is incomprehensible to common jurors. The question to ask of these lawyers is how exactly do they expect common citizens to comply with the law, especially criminal law, if only lawyers with a degree in law can understand it.

Similarly, there is also a tendency to argue that juries should be limited to relatively simpler cases. However, there is mounting evidence, from countries like the US, that jurors take their obligations seriously and serving judges concur with this evidence. Several studies from the US conclude that juries, on average, reach reasoned conclusions. Some of these studies are based on a poll of trial judges and they document that even when trial judges disagreed with the jury, they never doubted the jury's ability to understand the case as a reason for their disagreement.[15]

Justice Sonia Sotomayor, a judge on the American Supreme Court, had publicly claimed that when she compared her outcomes to those of the juries as a district court judge, she often reached the same conclusions as juries.[16] Kathleen M. O'Malley, a circuit judge of the US Court of Appeals for the Federal Circuit, wrote an impassioned defence of trial by jury and argued vehemently against the 'complexity exception'.[17] She was troubled by the fact that patent cases were being used as a vehicle to launch attacks at the collective wisdom of the jury, when her anecdotal experience suggested otherwise.

The other common criticism of the jury is that jurors are amenable to being bribed. But even Alexander Hamilton, one of the drafters of the American Constitution who was cynical about the institution, agreed that the jury constituted a 'double security' since both sets of decision makers, the individual judge and the appropriate number of jurors, would have to be bribed in order to influence an outcome.[18]

Juries also offer protection against 'the corruption of disdain and cynicism'.[19] A long stint in judicial service and the overfamiliarity with the practice of law can breed cynicism in judges. The jurors, who are randomly selected, will come to the service without any preconceived notions of lawyers or litigants.

Lastly, there have been instances across jurisdictions where juries have acted as a check against harsh penal laws by simply acquitting persons prosecuted under these laws.[20] For example, the high rate of acquittals in 19th century France by juries has been attributed to an unwillingness on part of the jury to subject those accused of certain crimes—political crimes, abortion, white-collar crimes, infanticide, crimes of passion—to the harsh punishments under French criminal law at the time.[21]

Despite these strong arguments in support of the jury system, there have also been strong suspicions about the institution from many quarters, including from Mahatma Gandhi. Writing in *Young India* in 1931, he expressed the following views on juries:

> I am unconvinced of the advantages of jury trials over those by judges. In coming to a correct decision, we must not be obsessed by our unfortunate experience of the judiciary here, which in political trials has been found to be notoriously partial to the Government. At the right moment juries have been found to fail even in England. When passions are roused, juries are affected by them and give perverse verdicts. Nor need we assume that they are always on the side of leniency. I have known juries finding prisoners guilty in the face of evidence and even judge's summing up to the contrary. We must not slavishly copy all that is English. In matters where absolute impartiality, calmness and ability to sift evidence and understand human nature are required, we may not replace trained

> judges by untrained men brought together by chance. What we must aim at is an incorruptible, impartial and able judiciary right from the bottom.

Two important points should be kept in mind while reading Gandhi's critique of juries. The first is that during colonial rule, juries in India were mainly constituted of men who fell under a certain property or income bracket.[22] In effect, this also meant that the composition of juries was limited to specific castes that owned property and had certain income. Such juries, not reflecting the caste and class diversity in society, were unlikely to have inspired public confidence at the time Gandhi wrote this critique. The second point is that in his article, Gandhi actually concluded by expressing a preference for reverting to 'village panchayats', which he described as an 'ancient and noble institution' that had been degraded by the caste system and the 'evil influence' of the 'present system of government' and 'growing illiteracy of the masses'. It is not clear how panchayats would be better than juries because panchayats would consist of the same 'untrained persons' who would staff juries, without the benefit of a key safeguard in the jury system of a presiding judge who would assist the jurors by interpreting the technical rules of evidence and procedure. Despite these obvious contradictions in his views, Gandhi's displeasure for the jury system often features in discussions on the jury system in India.

Juries and lay participation in colonial India's courts

When the British began colonizing India in the 18th century, first through the East India Company and then the British Crown, they began to transplant their legal system to India. This included the institution of juries, especially in criminal trials. Different iterations of the Code of Criminal Procedure starting in the year 1861, after the Crown took over the administration of India from the East India Company, required offences triable before the High Court or Court of Sessions (generally offences punishable with more than seven years' imprisonment), to be tried by juries but it was not a guaranteed right across British India. The local government had considerable say in whether the jury system could be used within its jurisdiction. For instance, in Madras, offences against property were tried by jury; in Bombay, all sessions cases in Greater Bombay were tried by jury in the city sessions court. As of 1958, the system was not in operation in territories like Andhra Pradesh, Assam, Orissa, Kerala, Punjab, Rajasthan and Uttar Pradesh.[23] As a result, the jury system never evolved uniformly across India.

In those parts of the country where jury trials were allowed, different iterations of the Code of Criminal Procedure limited membership of the jury to males between the ages of 21 years and 60 years. The district collector was free to choose persons 'qualified from their education and character to serve as Juror . . .'.[24] The copy of this list was advertised at the office of the collector and in the courts and other conspicuous places, and revised after the collector had entertained objections raised about persons in the list. The list was revised at least once every year. Ordinarily, the jurors were summoned three days before the holding of the trial by the district courts and the names of the persons were drawn by lot in open court. However, if the juror selected by lot did not understand the language in which the evidence was given or interpreted, the judge would not allow such a person to serve on jury.

The selection criteria for jury trials conducted by High Courts were determined by individual High Courts. There is evidence to suggest that some High Courts included specific property and income requirements in the eligibility criteria for jurors, making the jury an elitist institution, with its membership open only to the cream of society.[25]

Once selected, the jury in British India had a powerful role to play per the 1861 Code. Under this Code, the role of the trial judge was limited to accepting the verdict of the jurors with at least five jurors comprising a jury. A retrial could be ordered if a proportion of majority (6/9, 5/7 and 4/5) was not attained. The 1861 Code did not provide the prosecution with the right to an appeal against acquittal and an appeal against a conviction was provided only on a question of law. This meant that if a jury acquitted a person, its decision was final. This would change very soon with the next iteration of the Code that came into effect in 1872.[26] Under the new Code, if the sessions judge disagreed with the verdict of the jury, he could send the case to the High Court with reasons for his disagreement and the High Court could pass judgment based on the evidence recorded.[27] This arrangement continued into the 1898 Code that was in force till 1973.

The fact that a judge could effectively overrule a jury verdict significantly undermined the institution of the jury. This was not the case in the US or the UK, where the jury verdict in the case of an acquittal cannot even be appealed to a higher court by the prosecution, much less referred to a higher court by the judge. The Indian jury in the sessions court was, therefore, a significantly weaker institution than its counterparts in the West. However, jury trials conducted by the High Courts were different because if a judge did not agree with the jury verdict (which had to be supported by six of the nine jurors) he had only two options: either order a retrial or record an acquittal.[28]

Notwithstanding the fact that the Indian jury was significantly weaker than its western counterpart, the institution appears to have been popular in some parts of the country where jury trials were held regularly. As per one account, in 1892, when the Government of Calcutta reduced the use of jury trial by executive order, there were local protests on the grounds that juries were one of the greatest safeguards of liberty.[29]

The idea of juries appears to have been popular enough to make its way into the Commonwealth of India Bill (National Convention, India), 1925 that had been drafted by a section of the nationalist movement. Clause 63 of this Constitution proposed that the trial of offences should 'ordinarily' be by juries.[30]

Apart from juries, the British allowed laypersons to be appointed as 'assessors' when a jury trial was not being held. The trial could be conducted by the judge along with two native 'assessors', who were often locally significant religious or political leaders. The opinion of each assessor would be given orally to the judge and be recorded in writing but the decision-making power in such cases was vested exclusively with the judge.[31]

Unlike criminal litigation, almost all civil litigation during colonial rule was adjudicated by professional judges with no provision for juries or assessors. The only exception, in some provinces like Madras and the United Provinces, was the institution of village courts. These courts, which were modelled on the lines of panchayats, handled petty disputes of small value. The courts were manned by common villagers and not trained judges to oversee the proceedings. From the Rankin Committee report, it appears that there was significant discontentment with the workings of the village courts in the United Provinces.[32]

Post-Independence debates on juries

After Independence, the debates on lay participation in criminal and civil cases, via the institutions of juries or assessors, played out quite differently from the colonial era.

The institution of juries in criminal trials came under attack in 1953 when a MP from Madras, S. V. Ramaswamy, introduced a bill in the Lok Sabha to abolish trial by jury.[33] In the debate that followed, Ramaswamy explained to the House how the bar associations of Madras had passed resolutions against the continuation of jury trials and how juries were returning perverse verdicts. He voiced the regular complaints against juries, including their alleged inability to understand intricate questions of law in grave crimes, while also casting aspersions on the integrity of juries. The opinion in the House appears to have been evenly divided with several MPs speaking in support of juries. A member of Parliament from Calcutta, N. C. Chatterjee, who was a practising lawyer, spoke in defence of juries. Drawing on his experience from the Calcutta High Court, he observed:

> You cannot condemn and say that all jurors are corrupt, that they are open to approach or that they are amenable to caste influence and so on. In my experience, in the Calcutta High Court sessions, there has been no charge of corruption against any juror. Although passions had sometimes been inflamed, they behaved with full rectitude and uprightness. Any Judge can go wrong but on the whole they have been fair. It would not be right to condemn the jury system.[34]

In any event, a vote on Ramaswamy's bill was delayed because the House voted in favour of circulating the bill to elicit public opinion.

The very next year, in 1954, the government introduced a bill to amend the Code of Criminal Procedure. This law proposed abolishing the use of assessors in criminal trials, while the institution of juries was retained in the law. In the 'statement of objects and reasons' accompanying this bill, the government merely remarked that the opinion regarding 'trial by jury' was 'divergent'. As a result, the existing provisions in the Code of 1898 regarding the jury system remained in the law and it was left to state governments whether they wanted to use juries.

Eventually, juries were completely abolished with the enactment of a new Code of Criminal Procedure in 1973, which replaced the old Code in its entirety. In the intervening years, as noted by historian Jaffe, the drive to abolish juries was led by prominent lawyers and judges of the time. For instance, immediately after Independence, the UP Judicial Reforms Committee, headed by Justice Wanchoo, was specifically asked to examine whether the system of trial with the aid of juries or assessors should be continued. After extensively consulting with district magistrates, judicial officers, legislators and 'eminent lawyers', the committee, in its 1952 report, concluded that trials in session courts should be undertaken by the judge alone and recommended that the institution of jury should be dropped from the statute books. In pertinent part, it observed:

> The general complaint is that jurymen are open to approach and do not give a fair verdict on the evidence. It seems difficult to provide for the locking up of the jury in the present conditions as it will mean a very great expense if the system is to be introduced in all the districts of the State. Besides, it would be very difficult except perhaps in a few districts to have a sufficient number of the right class of people who would be prepared to serve as jurors.[35]

Jaffe also points out that in 1956, the Bombay High Court made recommendations for the abolition of jury trials for the districts of Pune, Ahmedabad and Surat. The same High Court later recommended that juries be withdrawn from trials in Greater Bombay. Similarly, the High Court 'had advised the State Government that the jury system had outlived its utility and had recommended that it should be discontinued in Bombay too' and as a result, in 1961, jury trials were abolished here too.[36]

By 1960, eleven state governments had abrogated the trial by jury and other states were likely to follow suit, prompted by the views expressed by the 1st Law Commission.[37] These views, which were expressed in its 14th report on the reform of judicial administration, not only reiterated the previous criticisms of the institution but also advanced the claim that Indians as a people were temperamentally ill-suited to function as jurors. Regarding the workings of trial by jury in Bombay, the Commission noted, 'It was found difficult to find jurors of the right type even in the advanced districts and such jurors as were available were shown to be easily approachable and moved by extra-judicial considerations.'[38] None of these vague allegations in the Law Commission, which were clearly aimed at delegitimizing the jury as an institution, were backed by any substantial evidence. The fact that judges and lawyers led the charge against juries should not be surprising because the jury as an institution was essentially a check on the legal profession and the judiciary.

Later in that decade, in 1969, the 41st report of the Law Commission reiterated that juries were being used in a very small number of cases by the sessions courts and should be abolished altogether.[39] Four years later, the new Code of 1973 was enacted by Parliament, doing away with juries in their entirety. Given that jury trials were prevalent only in certain cities and participation in juries was not open to all Indian citizens, we suspect that there was not much opposition to the government's abolition of juries.

Surprisingly, the same stakeholders who were suspicious of jury trials were also very enthusiastic about village courts (also referred to as Nyaya Panchayats) staffed only by laypersons not trained in law and located primarily in rural India.[40] The 14th report of the Law Commission, published in 1958, is the prime example of this paradox. While attacking jury trials and making a strong recommendation for its abolition, the Law Commission was upbeat about the continuation and even expansion of village courts created during colonial rule as an attempt to decentralize the administration of justice.

These village courts evolved in different patterns across the country since they were created primarily under legislation passed by different provinces. Justice in these village courts was dispensed by elected villagers or villagers nominated by the government. Their jurisdiction was confined to small-value civil and criminal disputes that could be punished only with a monetary fine, without any powers to imprison the guilty persons. Unlike the jury system, the village courts did not have a judge presiding over proceedings, deciding questions of procedure and evidence and most importantly, interpreting the law before it was applied to the facts in dispute. The laypersons staffing the village courts were expected to understand the law and interpret it.

It is no surprise that subsequent studies published in the 1970s and '80s noted that the village courts appeared to have lost confidence amongst the common public in the states where they were active. This was evidenced by the fact that filing of cases before these village courts was on a constant decline, while the filing of cases before formal courts was increasing, indicating a litigant preference for the formal courts. Academics studying the issue have indicated that the declining filings before the village courts was attributable to the poor confidence in their ability to dispense quality justice in a timely manner.[41] Anecdotal data presented in these studies indicated that the village courts were taking as long as the regular courts to adjudicate cases.

Despite being considered a failure, the idea of village courts has occasionally reappeared in India. This is partly because the village courts were pitched during colonial rule as a revival of a system of adjudication that traditionally existed in India. This fact, however, is hotly contested by many academics who argue that village courts as an institution were never part of traditional community life in India.[42] At most, there may have been caste panchayats, also known as *khap* panchayats, in North India, which adjudicated disputes within caste groups. In the 21st century, *khap* panchayats continue to exist outside the formal legal system and are in the news mostly for the wrong reasons given their propensity to order 'honour killings' of young couples who have dared to marry outside their castes.

In its 114th report published in 1986, the Law Commission

proposed a new model of village courts (now rebranded as Gram Nyayalayas), where a professional judge would sit with two laypersons from the local villages to hear and adjudicate disputes together.[43] This model of professional judges sitting with laypersons is followed in some European countries and can be seen as a variation of the jury system followed in the UK or the US. Like many other reports of the Law Commission, this one too was ignored by the government of the day, only to make a comeback almost two decades later, in 2006, when the UPA government proposed a legislation to reintroduce village courts, modelled on the lines proposed by the Law Commission in its 114th report.

Over the next few years, an interesting tussle played out on the issue of laypersons participating in Gram Nyayalayas. The National Advisory Council (NAC), a body of civil society activists advising the UPA government, recommended that the laypersons, sitting along with the judge, be replaced with persons holding a law degree.[44] In other words, the NAC did not want any laypersons participating on the Gram Nyayalayas. The Panchayati Raj Ministry had a different view on the issue. In 2007, it released a report authored by a committee chaired by Prof. Upendra Baxi and also translated that report into a draft law.[45]

The Baxi report made a strong pitch for bringing back village courts across India as they previously existed in many parts of the country. Rebranding the village courts as Nyaya Panchayats, the Baxi report justified the idea as a means to democratize the justice system through community participation. In its conception, these Nyaya Panchayats were to consist of five laypersons directly elected by the village, with quotas for Scheduled Castes, tribes and women. Referred to as 'nyaya panchas', these laypersons were required to be 25 years of age, have 'functional literacy' and be registered voters in the area where the Nyaya Panchayat had jurisdiction. These nyaya panchas, who had no legal training, were to be assisted in their decision-making process by a trained paralegal called 'nyaya sahayak' to assist with record-keeping and providing the required legal information to the panchas. These panchayats were to have powers to impose only monetary fines for the minor civil and criminal disputes that could be decided by these courts.

The Baxi report greatly romanticized 'grassroots forms of justicing', even claiming that 'various expert committee evaluation reports', which studied previous versions of village courts in India, had found that village courts 'eminently fulfilled justice needs and expectations of the local populace.' Except, this statement was factually not true as is evident from reading Baxi's own scholarship with Galanter in 1979. The following is an extract from their scholarship:

> Indeed the recent report of the High Powered Committee on Panchayati Raj in Rajasthan recommends the abolition of the NP altogether, partly on the ground that they have 'not been able to inspire confidence'. Similarly, the Maharashtra Evaluation Committee on Panchayati Raj finds entrustment of judicial functions to NP 'on the basis of democratic elections or otherwise' both 'out of place and unworkable' and also recommends the abolition of NP.[46]

More surprisingly, the Baxi report also ignored the red flags raised in previous scholarship co-authored by Baxi and Galanter which had painted a very worrying picture of the manner in which elections had been held for Nyaya Panchayats in the past. Discussing empirical scholarship from Rajasthan, which described how the village head was able to influence elections to nyaya panchayats, the Baxi and Galanter article concluded:

> Hence these Rajasthan findings may well be replicated in other regions. When elections to NP are overtly political or perceived to be such, it is unlikely that NP will inspire the confidence of villagers let alone symbolize 'the freely expressed will of the villagers'.

Separate from this observation from 1979, the idea of elections as a method for selection of judges is very contentious in most countries. This is because of a fear that an elected judge's decisions will be influenced by the necessity of winning re-elections to judicial office.[47] Yet the Baxi report did not engage with these dangers while recommending that nyaya panchas be elected.

In any event, the Law Ministry objected to this model proposed by the Panchayati Raj Ministry, arguing that it would be unconstitutional to involve laypersons in adjudication of disputes.[48] The final version of the Gram Nyayalayas Act enacted by Parliament in 2008 ignored all three models: the one proposed in the 114th report, the NAC version and the version proposed by the Panchayati Raj Ministry. Instead, the Gram Nyayalayas that came into existence are staffed with only one professional judge and are not very different from the existing courts, except in their disregard for the procedural rights of rural litigants.[49]

Until 2015, there were occasional mentions in the press about the Panchayati Raj Ministry wanting to revive Nyaya Panchayats staffed by elected villagers, but it is safe to say that the idea of lay participation in the justice system has died a permanent death in the last decade, with the issue completely disappearing from the manifestoes of political parties.

Bringing back the citizen into the courtroom

Most of us have come across a person whose quality of life has been significantly worsened by her interactions with the legal system. A saying in Hindi-speaking regions in India captures the sentiment well: '*Kaale coat, safed coat aur khaki vardi se bhagwan bachaaye*', which loosely translates to 'May you never have to interact with the courts, doctors and the police'. Ordinary citizens in India want to avoid the legal system and law enforcement at all costs. Even non-legal academics who study courts decry the 'out-of-placeness' that being inside court premises makes one feel.[50] This is not surprising.

As things stand, citizens in India participate in the legal system chiefly in four ways. They are either accused of committing a crime or they've been victims of a crime. If it is the civil justice system, they have been sued or they want to sue another party or they appear as witnesses. Consequently, courts are populated mostly by a class of professionals which includes judges, lawyers, court staff, law enforcement personnel and clerks. Unless you are a serial litigant, it is difficult to untangle yourself from the sense of unfamiliarity that surrounds you when you enter a courtroom. Courts, despite being public institutions, are dominated by the legal profession and ordinary persons tend to find the environment hostile.

It should be emphasized here that it is not by accident that the system evokes such feelings in persons it deems 'outsiders'. Courts and legal proceedings seem mysterious to lay people because they are often designed to be the province of lawyers and judges. Bringing back juries will bring in more ordinary citizens to the courts in a capacity where they have the significant power to decide cases. These new power equations will hopefully force the courts to be more welcoming of the ordinary citizen, making the institution of the judiciary less intimidating in the public eye.

In addition, juries as institutions offer many advantages like cultivating a civic culture, enhancing respect for the rule of law and even being a check on judicial corruption. These are useful values in a country where the judiciary at all tiers is facing a crisis of legitimacy. Judges, too, as seen in the chapters before, are insecure and indecisive when it comes to deciding cases. In this context, juries can help bolster the independence of district courts and rebuild the flagging legitimacy of the judiciary. Bringing back juries, especially for criminal cases, can infuse the judiciary with much-needed legitimacy and empower both citizens and judges along the way.

The one question that we have not addressed but which requires deep deliberation before juries are revived is the question of caste bias and discrimination by a jury of citizens. After all, allegations of casteism have been made against even judges of High Courts. Two impeachment motions against judges of High Courts (which eventually failed) were on account of allegations of casteism. Judges and lawyers within the judiciary have also complained of casteism. Skewed caste profiles within the judiciary raise further questions on the role of caste.[51] In this context, juries offer hope of greater participation of marginalized castes in the justice system. The presence of Dalit jurors on a jury deciding the fate of a dominant caste accused can serve as a powerful symbol of equality. However, the question is whether the marginalized, especially Dalits and Scheduled Tribes, will have confidence in a jury of only dominant-caste jurors. The same question can be raised in the context of Muslims, especially now when polarization along religious lines is visibly on the rise. Given that Dalits, Scheduled Tribes and

Muslims are disproportionately prosecuted in India, this is not an insignificant question. Factoring in differences along the lines of caste and religion, while envisaging the jury as a fraternal institution, will be key to ensuring that juries inspire confidence in all citizens. At the end of the day, the hope of a jury system is that individual citizens can break free of their religious and caste identities to decide cases on the basis of the law and an innate sense of justice that is at the core of humanity.

12

Making Procedural and Evidentiary Rules Great Again

Since India won independence, much of the blame for judicial delays has been placed upon the procedural and evidentiary rules which have traditionally governed judicial proceedings in the country. These rules, which are laid down in laws like the Code of Civil Procedure, the Code of Criminal Procedure and the Evidence Act, spell out the manner in which civil claims and criminal prosecutions, under other laws like the Indian Penal Code or Contracts Act, are to be litigated before a court of law.

While seemingly arcane and complex, procedural and evidentiary laws are the beating heart of any justice system seeking to offer predictability and equal treatment to all litigants. These laws lay down the rules for conducting a case in court, thereby assuring litigants that their claims will be heard by a court of law in a manner that is fair to both sides of the dispute. In doing so, these laws limit the discretion of judges in conducting litigation in a courtroom. This is important since it ensures all litigants receive equal treatment in a court regardless of the judge in charge.

For civil litigation before the district judiciary, lawsuits are conducted as per the Code of Civil Procedure, 1908. This code can broadly be divided into two parts. The first part lays down some basic principles such as principles to determine the court that has jurisdiction to hear a civil claim and also more nuanced principles such as *res judicata,* which forbids re-litigation of claims that have already been adjudicated by a court. The second part of the code lays down more specific rules on the conduct of litigation. This includes the persons who need to be made opposing litigants in a lawsuit, the format of the pleadings in which a claim must be stated, the manner in which summons are to be issued to the opposing party informing them that legal proceedings have been initiated against them, the timeline for opposing parties to respond to claims made in court, etc. These detailed procedural rules are key to ensuring that proceedings in courts are conducted in a fair manner and not hijacked by a judge's personal predilections.

In the case of criminal prosecutions before the district judiciary, the relevant procedural law is the Code of Criminal Procedure. The first version of this law was enforced in India in 1861. While the Indian Penal Code and other laws lay down the definitions of specific crimes and the punishments for each crime, it is the Code of Criminal Procedure which lays down the rules for conducting prosecutions. Apart from defining the jurisdiction and hierarchy of criminal courts, it also lays down the procedure per which the police are to conduct investigations, searches and arrests. In laying down such procedures, this law basically guarantees citizens certain rights against the police. In many ways, the Code of Criminal Procedure is as important as the Constitution in guaranteeing the liberty of citizens.

Given the fact-finding nature of both civil and criminal proceedings before the district judiciary, the issue of evidence produced by litigants before the court is of pivotal importance. This is where the Evidence Act comes into play. This law, the first version of which was enacted in 1872, lays down the manner in which documentary evidence can be proved, the kind of witness testimony that can be allowed in court (for example, hearsay evidence is inadmissible as per this law), rules for cross-examination of witnesses, etc. These evidentiary rules are critical to ensuring that courts rely only on credible evidence. Without such rules, it is difficult for litigants to know exactly the kind of evidence that they can bring to court. The Evidence Act is also key to protecting civil liberties since it is this law which prohibits courts from admitting confessions made to the police, in the hope that such a prohibition would disincentivize torture by the police.

From the above description of how procedural and evidentiary laws work in courtrooms, it is hopefully evident that the Code of Civil Procedure, the Code of Criminal Procedure and the Evidence Act are indeed the beating heart of the justice system. These laws guarantee litigants certain rights against each other, against the state and most importantly, against the judge. In a world without such procedural and evidentiary rules, litigants will be left to the mercy of individual judges and their sense of justice.

Deep-rooted opposition to procedural and evidentiary rules

Since 1947, there has been opposition from several quarters to the procedural and evidentiary rules which lie at the heart of the legal system created during colonial rule. This opposition can be broadly categorized into three groups.

The first is the 'revivalist' view, which seeks to replace everything created during colonial rule, including the legal system and the rules governing it, with norms of governance from ancient India.[1] This view continues to be reiterated in India even in the 21st century. For instance, in a public speech delivered at a national meeting of Hindu nationalist lawyers in 2021, a retired Supreme Court judge, remarked, 'There can be no doubt that this colonial legal system is not suitable for the Indian population. The need of the hour is the Indianisation of the legal system.'[2] This rather dated argument has been resisted by those with a more cosmopolitan worldview of the law and the courts. For instance, the Law Commission under the leadership of retired Justice H. R. Khanna (famous for his brave dissent in the case of *ADM Jabalpur v. Shivkant Shukla* during the Emergency) cautioned against the demand to rid India of the legal system that it inherited from the British. In its 77th report published in November 1978, the Law Commission, under Khanna, reminded the country of the following basic rule of history[3]:

> No judicial system in any country is wholly immune from, and unaffected by, outside influences, nor can such outside influences be always looked upon as a bane. The laws of a country do not

> reside in a sealed book; they grow and develop. The winds of change, and the free flow of ideas, do not pass the laws idly by... even in procedural law, which was codified by the foreign rulers in this country, the basic principles of a fair and impartial trial, which were well-known to their predecessors, were adhered to.
>
> ...Such outside influences are, however, an integral part of the historical process of development of thought and institutions all over the world, and once the new concepts get assimilated, they cease to be alien in character. Viewed in this light, it seems hardly correct to say that the present judicial system is a foreign transplant on Indian soil, or that it is based on alien concepts unintelligible to our people. The people have become fully accustomed to this system during more than hundred years of its existence.

In this report, the Law Commission also pointed out that the rules of procedure and evidence introduced in India by the British were quite similar to those that existed in ancient India. In pertinent part, the Commission drew parallels to rules in the *shastras* to claim that 'the rules of procedure and evidence in ancient India were sophisticated enough' and that there was 'considerable similarity between the system then in vogue and the system now in force'.[4]

A second line of attack has come from those who believe that the complexity of the existing procedural and evidentiary rules was the primary cause of the delays plaguing the Indian judicial system. For instance, a Committee on Judicial Reforms instituted by the State of Uttar Pradesh in 1950 blamed these laws for prescribing rules 'so elaborate, technical and lengthy that the case is sometimes prolonged to an extent that . . . it becomes an endurance test' between the litigants. It continued by saying, 'This formality and elaborateness of the procedure sometimes provide virtual breeding ground for legal quibbling and hair splitting.'[5] This report concluded that the need of the hour was to simplify procedural and evidentiary rules.

A few years later, in 1954, the 1st Law Commission under the chairmanship of Attorney General M. C. Setalvad noted that it received several complaints that the procedural rules were the 'chief cause of delay' because the rules were 'cumbrous, wasteful and time-consuming'.

The Law Commission pushed back against such criticism, arguing that it would be 'a mistake to lay the entire blame for the delays in our litigation on the defects or cumbrousness of the procedure'.[6] Rather, it argued that 'delay results not from the procedure laid down by it but by reason of the non-observance of many of its important provisions particularly those intended to expedite the disposal of proceedings'. The criticism of procedural rules, according to the Law Commission, failed to take into account the multitude of other factors that contributed to delays, such as an 'inefficient and inexperienced judiciary, insufficient number of judicial officers, an incompetent and corrupt ministerial and process-serving agency . . .'.[7]

Notwithstanding this spirited defence by the Law Commission, procedural and evidentiary rules continued to feature as the prime villains in the national discourse on judicial delays long after Independence. Even in obscure reports of the Reserve Bank of India from the year 1992, on the difficulties being faced by banks in recovering debts, the 'technical rules of evidence followed by civil courts' and various provisions of the Code of Civil Procedure were identified as some of the main reasons for delays in litigation.[8]

A third line of attack on procedural and evidentiary rules came from those who argued that the rigid adherence to these rules could frustrate substantive justice to litigants. In India, this scepticism was utilized by populist judges in the Supreme Court, such as Justice P. N. Bhagwati, to justify the complete delegitimization of procedural and evidentiary rules in the guise of ensuring swift justice to the poor and oppressed. The following words of Justice Bhagwati in a landmark case capture the angst of populist judges against procedural and evidentiary rules that are meant to restrain judicial power[9]:

> . . . it must not be forgotten that procedure is but a handmaiden of justice and the cause of justice can never be allowed to be thwarted by any procedural technicalities. The Court would therefore unhesitatingly and without the slightest qualms of conscience cast aside the technical rules of procedure in the exercise of its dispensing power and treat the letter of the public minded individual as a writ petition and act upon it Today a vast revolution is taking place in

> the judicial process; the theatre of the law is fast changing and the problems of the poor are coming to the forefront. The Court has to innovate new methods and devise new strategies for the purpose of providing access to justice to large masses of people who are denied their basic human rights and to whom freedom and liberty have no meaning.

The long and short of the approach advocated by Justice Bhagwati was that judges were to be trusted with how they exercised their immense judicial power, not restrained by procedural rules. But what, then, is the difference between a monarch and a judge, if not checks on the manner in which they exercise their immense powers? On a lighter note, as with a tyrannical monarch, it is not possible to protest against the Indian judiciary since even satirical cartoons about the Supreme Court have led to cartoonists being sentenced to imprisonment on charges of contempt of court.[10]

When rhetoric against procedural and evidentiary rules translates into policy

The three critiques discussed above of procedural and evidentiary rules have manifested in three different policy avatars, starting in the 1980s, with a range of consequences for Indian litigants.

The first institution to initiate a calculated attack on procedural and evidentiary rules, in the early 1980s, was the Supreme Court of India through the device of public interest litigation (PIL), sometimes also referred to as 'social action litigation'. The invention of PILs, in the name of protecting the liberty and rights of the poor, opened the door for the decimation of procedural rules. This judicial innovation came in the backdrop of the Supreme Court being at the receiving end of severe criticism for its rulings during the Emergency. It has been argued by several academics that in a bid to regain its legitimacy as a court of justice, the court turned to populist measures such as PILs. By ignoring well-established procedural and evidentiary rules, the court utilized the device of PILs to free bonded labourers and undertrial prisoners through dramatic judgments. Allegations made by the petitioners in these PILs, claiming to have learnt of the plight of the under-trial prisoners or bonded labourers through newspaper reports or surveys, were presumed to be true by the Supreme Court and formed the basis of its sweeping orders in landmark judgments such as *Hussainara Khatoon & Ors v. Home Secretary, State of Bihar*[11] and *Bandhua Mukti Morcha v. Union of India*[12], involving the liberty of undertrials and bonded labourers.

None of these judgments or the outcomes that followed would have been possible if the court had actually followed the prevalent procedural and evidentiary rules. For example, a long-standing procedural requirement is that only persons facing a legal injury, or their relative, could approach the court for a legal remedy. However, the Supreme Court ignored this fundamental rule by letting others make a legal claim via a PIL on behalf of the general public or a group of specific persons. A second example of ignoring procedural rules is the manner in which the Supreme Court allowed anybody to send post cards or letters to the court, which would then be treated by the court as a petition. In doing so, the court ignored its own rules on the manner and format of petitions to be filed before it. These are merely two examples of how populist judges of the Supreme Court began chipping away at procedural and evidentiary rules and, in the process, expanded their own power.

As Anuj Bhuwania argues in his excellent book *Courting the People,* the judges who paved the way for the creation of PILs, like Justice Bhagwati, were in effect mimicking, in their judgments, the populist language of politicians of the time, like Indira Gandhi, who had little regard for institutional safeguards meant to check the abuse of power.[13] These judges used the failures of the legal system, such as the lack of legal aid by the state for underprivileged undertrial prisoners to justify ignoring other institutional safeguards in the law meant to check the power of judges.

A second line of attack on procedural and evidentiary rules began after the 42nd amendment to the Constitution. This amendment opened the door for Parliament to create tribunals to deal with a whole range of disputes that were traditionally handled by the district courts. Through the creation of new tribunals, the Government of India set in motion the systematic decimation of procedural and evidentiary rules. This process began in 1985 with the creation of new judicial forums like the Central Administrative Tribunal, State Administrative Tribunals, the Debts Recovery Tribunals (DRTs) created in 1993 and continued well into 2010, when the National Green Tribunal (NGT) was created for adjudicating environmental disputes.

The uniform thread running through the legislations creating these new tribunals is a specific clause stating that these tribunals 'shall not be bound by the procedure laid down by the Code of Civil Procedure, 1908 (5 of 1908), but shall be guided by the principles of natural justice'.[14] The problem with this arrangement is that the principles of natural justice are not codified but very broad principles. As a result, judges presiding over the tribunals did not have to follow the existing procedural and evidentiary rules but instead could conduct proceedings before them as per their understanding of these vague principles of natural justice. This basically meant that litigants had no specific procedural rights against the opposing litigants and could do little to restrain the presiding judge from acting as they wished.

Even with legislation like the Consumer Protection Act, 1986, which created consumer courts and is silent on the exclusion of procedural and evidentiary rules, the courts have completely excluded the applicability of the Evidence Act and sharply limited the extent to which the Code of Civil Procedure would apply to these proceedings.[15] Excluding the Evidence Act is deeply problematic given the complex technical facts that often come up before the consumer courts. These include cases of medical negligence by doctors, where the court has to parse through issues like standard of care in each branch of medicine.

A third manifestation of the disdain for procedural and evidentiary rules, which translated into concrete policy only in 2008, was the establishment of village courts to meet the demands of an accessible justice system in rural India. The idea of village courts can be traced back to colonial India, with provincial laws like the Villages Courts Act, 1888 (in the province of Madras), the United Provinces Village Panchayat Act, 1920, The Bihar & Orissa Village Administration Act of 1922, etc. setting up a system of village courts.[16] These village courts were created during colonial rule as a more flexible and affordable alternative to the formal civil and criminal courts. Additionally, these village courts were presented as a revival of ancient Indian practices of dispute resolution through village panchayats. A key feature of these village courts, which were staffed by elected villagers or citizens nominated by the local government, was the absence of the elaborate procedural and evidentiary rules that characterized litigation in the regular formal courts. Many of these village courts, also called Nyaya Panchayats in some states, continued to exist after Independence. A 1982 study that studied the workings of some Nyaya Panchayats in Uttar Pradesh reported that these village courts were not only 'inconsistent and somewhat arbitrary but also slow' and that cases could last for 'months and even years'.[17] Some critics also claimed that proceedings before these Nyaya Panchayats took as long as regular courts.[18]

For many reasons, the Nyaya Panchayats were, reportedly, not very popular. The few official and academic studies on the workings of these courts have reported that the number of cases being filed before these courts were actually reducing. This is most likely because litigants preferred litigating their claims in the formal courts with judges trained in law, lawyers and extensive procedural and evidentiary rules which safeguarded their rights.[19]

Ignoring the failures and declining popularity of village courts, the Law Commission, in 1986, while headed by a retired populist judge of the Supreme Court, published a report evangelizing the institution of village courts.[20] Rebranding these courts as Gram Nyayalayas, the Law Commission called for the revival of these village courts in a slightly different format by vesting the adjudicatory power in a bench consisting of one professional judge and two laypersons. As was the flavour of the time, this report too attacked procedural and evidentiary rules as the primary cause of delay. It recommended that the Code of Civil Procedure and Evidence Act be ignored completely for civil disputes heard by village courts. For criminal prosecutions, it recommended retaining the Code of Criminal Procedure but with regard to the Evidence Act, the Commission recommended that it 'should not apply' to criminal prosecutions. At most, it recommended that 'an attempt should be made to devise simple procedures which may stand the test' of the Constitution.[21]

The Law Commission's recommendations on Gram Nyayalayas were ignored until 2004, when the United Progressive Alliance (UPA) won the general election. The UPA revived the idea of village courts with the enactment of the Gram Nyayalayas Act, 2008 with the major difference that these courts are staffed with professional judges unlike the earlier format, where common citizens were elected or nominated to the village courts. These courts are empowered to deal with both civil disputes (under labour laws and certain categories of property disputes common in rural India) and also prosecution of certain offences under the penal code and other laws.

As with the previous experiments with villages courts, the Gram Nyayalayas Act too gives short shrift to procedural and evidentiary rules. For example, Section 30 of this law allows the Gram Nyayalayas to receive any evidence regardless of whether it is admissible under the Evidence Act. This opens the door to litigants introducing unreliable evidence, such as hearsay testimony. More worryingly, if these courts are not bound by the Evidence Act, it is open for the prosecution to rely on confessions to the police. Further, the police will be incentivized to introduce fabricated evidence, if the regular rules of evidence do not apply to proceedings before the Gram Nyayalayas.

Similarly, when it comes to procedure, the Gram Nyayalayas Act requires all criminal cases to be prosecuted per a 'summary' procedure in the Code of Criminal Procedure. Except that the Gram Nyayalayas Act does away with the safeguard in the Code which limits punishment for cases tried through the summary procedure to only three months.

As a result, the Gram Nyayalayas Act creates an inferior system of justice for rural India, since it applies only in areas designated as panchayats. This law does not apply to urban India. There is no real reason for the very same offence to be tried differently in cities and villages comprising citizens who are equal in the eyes of law. Yet, this law was passed with barely any opposition and as of today, at least 481 Gram Nyayalayas have been operationalized across sixteen states, with the law ministry actively advocating for more states to notify more Gram Nyayalayas by dangling the carrot of additional funding for implementation of this law.

Has the ejection of procedural and evidentiary rules improved quality and efficiency of the Indian legal system?

The only pertinent question to ask at this stage is whether the assault on procedural and evidentiary rules has improved the quality and speed of justice in India.

On the issue of speed, there is no evidence to indicate that the decimation of procedural and evidentiary rules across tribunals has hastened justice. Take, for example, the DRTs. Despite being exempted from the prevalent procedural and evidentiary rules, the DRTs have faced daunting delays.[22] In fact, the delays and inability of the DRTs to deliver justice threatened the financial health of Indian banks, leading to Parliament creating an entirely new bankruptcy framework in 2016 along with new tribunals to administer the new bankruptcy regime.

Similarly, litigants before the Central Administrative Tribunal, which adjudicates complaints of bureaucrats employed by the Union government regarding their employment conditions, have faced severe delays in disposing of cases.[23] A parliamentary report discovered that 16,000 cases were pending for between five to ten years and 1,350 cases were pending for more than ten years before this tribunal.[24]

The story from the consumer courts is not any different. There have been instances of cases being decided ten or thirteen years after being filed, despite speedy dispute resolution being one of the main aims of the Consumer Protection Act.[25]

Given these trends, it is safe to assume that ejecting existing procedural and evidentiary rules is unlikely to hasten litigation.

On the other hand, there is a serious downside to doing away with these rules since litigants are left entirely to the mercy of the judge. As the following two examples demonstrate, the consequences of vesting judges with untrammelled powers can be devastating for litigants and can end up eroding the legitimacy of the entire judicial process. The first example is of the NGT. The legislation creating this tribunal is very clear that the NGT is not bound by either the Code of Civil Procedure or the Evidence Act while hearing environmental disputes, many of which can be complicated.[26] Being unrestrained by any procedural laws has led to the NGT pushing the boundaries of the law to the brink of absurdity, inviting repeated reprimands from the Supreme Court. In two such cases, the Supreme Court reprimanded the NGT for delegating its judicial functions to a committee of experts that it set up, i.e. the court simply allowed persons that it selected to decide key issues being disputed by litigants before it. In pertinent part, the Supreme Court stated the following: [27]

> The NGT has in the present case abdicated its jurisdiction and entrusted judicial functions to an administrative expert committee. An expert committee may be able to assist the NGT, for instance, by carrying out a fact-finding exercise, but the adjudication has to be by the NGT. This is not a delegable function.

This judgment was the second time in two years that the Supreme Court had to intervene to stop the NGT from delegating its judicial functions to a committee of experts.[28] There have been other cases where the NGT has been similarly upbraided by the Supreme Court for 'unilateral decision making' without hearing all affected parties. In one such ruling in 2024, an exasperated Supreme Court remarked that it was imperative for the NGT 'to infuse a renewed sense of procedural integrity' in its proceedings to 'avoid the oversight of propriety'.[29] The fact of the matter, which is conveniently ignored by the Supreme Court, is that the NGT (which is always headed by a retired judge of the Supreme Court) was actually mimicking the Supreme Court's own behaviour in PIL cases. After all, it was Justice Bhagwati who, during the course of inventing PILs, had categorically stated that 'procedure is just a handmaiden of justice and the cause of justice can never be allowed to be thwarted by any procedural technicalities'.

Similarly, PILs have lost their sheen. Unlike the early PILs, which began with ignoring procedural niceties like *locus standi* (persons who can institute a case) in cases involving liberty of the poor and downtrodden, it was not too long before other judges of not just the Supreme Court but also the Delhi High Court began ignoring other procedural safeguards. This became a problem of gargantuan proportions as the focus of PILs shifted from civil liberties to governance issues where the middle class deployed PILs against the poor and downtrodden. For instance, if the court is ordering the demolition of a house on the grounds that it was an unauthorized construction, the normal rules of procedure would require the court to hear the persons residing in the house or the owner of the house before passing such orders. Yet, as Bhuwania documents in *Courting the People* the Delhi High Court routinely ordered the demolition of slums in PILs filed by Resident Welfare Associations (RWAs) of affluent colonies without hearing any of the residents of the slums.[30] In Bhuwania's words, PILs became a 'slum demolition machine' in 'a ferocious slum removal campaign' by the Delhi High Court without any consideration to the need for humane resettlement.[31]

Apart from slum-dwellers, Bhuwania documents the fate of workers of industrial units whose jobs were endangered after the courts shuttered, in response to a PIL, these units in the garb of decongesting Delhi and reducing pollution. The court's orders were a bonanza for the owners of the industrial units who stood to make money from selling the commercially viable land. The labourers, who were refused a hearing by the court, had the most to lose after the shuttering of the units since not only did they lose steady employment, they also lost the safeguards offered under the law to workers being laid off due to the winding up of an industrial unit.

A third case study presented by Bhuwania is of a PIL dealing with air pollution in Delhi, where the Supreme Court ordered all public transport and private taxis, including autorickshaws, to operate on natural gas. The owners of these private taxis and autorickshaws had to pay for the rather expensive conversion kits out of their pockets. Neither the workers who lost their jobs nor the owners of private taxis and autorickshaws were afforded a hearing by the court, despite the court's orders directly affecting these persons.[32]

The manifest injustice documented by Bhuwania in these PIL cases are a potent reminder of how procedural rules are necessary to restrain judges from harming citizens.

Restoring procedural and evidentiary rules in India

Despite the absolutely disastrous outcomes described above, procedural and evidentiary law continue to be painted as the cause for delays and alleged complexity of the judicial system. The only exception to the legislative and judicial trend of decimating procedural and evidentiary rules has been the Commercial Courts Act, 2015, which significantly tightened procedural law to govern the conduct of litigants and judges in commercial litigation. This was because of a Law Commission report in 2004, which noted with some embarrassment 'a recent spate of judgments of the US and UK Commercial Courts declaring that the Indian Court system has "collapsed" because there are delays up to twenty years or more.' A special law to govern commercial litigation was proposed as the solution. The entire focus of this legislation, quite incredibly, was on tightening procedural requirements. Simply put, this law empowered litigants by giving them new procedural rights to hold each other and the judge accountable.

The approach in the Commercial Courts Act, 2015 of tightening procedural rules has been utilized in the past when the Code of Civil Procedure was amended in 1999 to introduce a deadline of thirty days for the filing of a response by the defendant to a lawsuit, failing which the judge can proceed with the lawsuit. This amendment, which has been very successful in curbing a legal culture of procrastination and delays, is an example of the manner in which procedural law can be leveraged to improve efficiency by giving litigants and judges the means to hold the defendant accountable. Other amendments were not similarly successful. For example, the same amendment had introduced a cap of three adjournments in a case but this rule has failed to curb delays or the adjournment culture prevalent within the Indian judiciary.

These contrasting examples are a good illustration of how procedural rules can succeed or fail in bringing discipline to judicial proceedings. The answer then is not to eject procedural rules completely but instead to experiment with different procedural rules, while deleting only those rules that are problematic and contributing to delays. For example, Section 80 of the Code of Civil Procedure requires persons suing the government to do so only two months after notice has been served on the government. This is a good example of an oppressive procedural requirement introduced by a colonial government seeking to avoid accountability for its actions. Such a rule has no place in a democratic country where the courts are meant to hold government accountable for its actions. On the other hand, the existing procedure in the Code of Civil Procedure pertaining to the service of summons is well thought out, but in reality, may be failing because of a shortage of personnel to serve summons. The answer in this case is not to disregard the elaborate process laid down to ensure summons are served on the opposing litigant, but instead to improve the process by hiring enough personnel and holding them accountable for delays.

Going ahead, it would be far more prudent for policymakers to collect data on the procedural and evidentiary rules that are actually delaying legal proceedings and target those specific rules for reform, instead of ejecting all procedural and evidentiary rules. The current approach of allowing tribunals and some courts to eject codified procedural and evidentiary rules, in favour of some vague notions of principles of natural justice, allows the judges in question far too much judicial power to operate as per their personal whims. Not only is this unbridled judicial power harming litigants, it is also undermining the legitimacy of judicial institutions in the eyes of litigants, who can see judges not being consistent in their treatment of all litigants. It is important to accept that procedural and evidentiary rules guaranteeing all litigants certain rights are at the core of a fair system of justice and should not be sacrificed, by either judges or politicians, on the false promise of expedited justice.

EPILOGUE

The Democratic Cost of Failing District Courts

There is a serious cost to the continuing inability of the district judiciary to deliver timely, decisive and fair justice. The immediate impact of this failure is felt by citizens who seek justice before these courts, including undertrials denied their liberty, victims of crime, families disputing property claims, workers seeking compensation for accidents or a small businessperson seeking to enforce a contract. These are the heartbreaking stories of delayed justice that are reported in the press on a regular basis.

There are then the second-order consequences to these delays before the district courts. This includes the steady delegitimization of the rule of law in India. The first signs have been visible for some time as the general public turned a blind eye to the cold-blooded murders of suspected criminals by policemen claiming to be acting in self-defence. Worryingly, this indifference has recently turned to active public support for cold-blooded murders. For example, in 2019, after the police in Hyderabad gunned down four suspects arrested on suspicion of sexually assaulting and killing a young veterinary doctor, there were public celebrations on social media and the streets. As reported by the *New York Times*, 'So many people poured into the streets on Friday to celebrate that traffic was brought to a standstill. Firecrackers could be heard exploding across the city. People hugged and passed out sweets.'[1] Celebrities and politicians voiced their support for the killings on social media. This, despite gaping holes in the police version of the events. A subsequent inquiry ordered by the Supreme Court accused the police of gunning down the four accused in cold blood and recommended the criminal prosecution of the police personnel involved in the killings.

Since that killing, there has been an unabashed increase in public support for brazenly illegal 'revenge' by the state. The political class has sensed the shift in the wind. One chief minister of Uttar Pradesh warned the people in his state—'*thok denge*'. This loosely translates into 'knock them off' and was perceived as a veiled death threat to those accused of crime, without a formal prosecution in a court of law. What other states were doing surreptitiously in select cases to quench the public thirst for revenge became routine government policy in Uttar Pradesh. In the next six years, 183 people in Uttar Pradesh were gunned down by the police, most suspected to be in cold blood.[2] In the same period, 5,000 people in Uttar Pradesh have faced 'half-encounters' where police, claiming to act in self-defence, shot suspects in the limbs without killing them.[3] There was no public outcry. In fact, there was widespread public support for the state-sanctioned policy of cold-blooded killings and the chief minister easily won re-election.

A second strategy has emerged in the form of 'bulldozer justice', also pioneered in Uttar Pradesh. It involves using bulldozers to destroy the houses of those accused of civil or criminal wrongs without waiting for any authorization from the courts. In some instances, the bulldozers have been rolled out as retribution for those protesting against a political party due to bigoted statements made by its spokespersons. In one such case, the house of a Muslim activist was demolished after he organised protests. The police and municipal authorities claimed that his house was an illegal construction. But the activist's family, which owned the house, had lived it in for more than twenty years and were paying all the necessary taxes to the government. 'Bulldozer justice' has proven to be so popular with the Indian populace that other states have rushed to adopt it, leading to the destruction of homes of dissenters without any semblance of judicial process.

The fact that both cold-blooded killings and bulldozer justice have received widespread public support in India is a sign of a collapsing, if not already collapsed, faith in the ability of the courts to deliver timely justice. The Indian courtroom today is no longer a symbol of justice. The average citizen is more likely to turn to a local politician, *baahubali,* power-broker or the local sub-inspector of the police for swift resolution of their disputes. Muscle and the gun, not law and justice have become the order of the day in many parts of the country. Reversing this trend is no easy task but the first step to restoring the faith of citizens in the rule of law is to get the district judiciary functioning efficiently. This is easier said than done.

The biggest challenge with judicial reforms in India, as one former judge of the Supreme Court put it is that, 'Nobody wants to discuss judicial reforms.'[4] This is especially true when it comes to reforming India's district judiciary. Within the Government of India, the only institution with a mandate to look at legal reforms is the Law Commission of India. Between the years 2014 and 2024, only two of the forty-five reports published by the Law Commission tackled judicial reforms. The larger problem with the Law Commission is that the quality of its reports fluctuates wildly depending on the chairperson, who is inevitably a retired judge. Many of its reports are poorly written. Apart from the Law Commission, the law ministry has no internal think-tank looking at the issue of judicial reforms. It does have a funding programme called the 'Scheme for Action Research and Studies on Judicial Reforms', which is supposed to give grants to universities and think-tanks looking to research judicial reforms. However, since the grant-making process is controlled by a committee consisting of bureaucrats from the law ministry and often a retired judge heading the National Judicial Academy (which is controlled by the Supreme Court), there is a tendency to not fund any research proposal that may upset entrenched interests. We say this from personal experience. The only other organizations of the state conducting some research on judicial reforms are two internal think-tanks of the Supreme Court—the National Court Management System and the Centre for Research and Planning. Sitting judges are in control of both bodies and while these think-tanks have tabled some useful reports, the institutions continue to frame the issue predominantly through the lens of a resource crunch rather than in terms of improving transparency and accountability of judicial administration. To put it politely, these reports tend to be status-quoist.

Ideally the conversation on reforming the district courts should have been shaped by academia in India's leading national law universities. Unfortunately, for a variety of reasons, especially poor funding, these universities have not been able to build a credible research culture despite housing talented academics. The more worrying proposition is whether better funding will make a difference given the fact that the governing boards of most of the national law universities are populated with sitting and retired judges of High Courts and the Supreme Court. The chancellor of these universities tends to be a sitting judge of the higher judiciary. In other words, these universities tend to be the turf of judges and this raises questions about whether these universities can foster a research culture that takes a critical look at the judiciary. There is at least one instance of an academic from overseas mentioning on social media that he was invited, and then disinvited, for a talk by a leading national university after he informed them about the paper (on judicial corruption) that was going to be the subject of his talk. While the precise reasons for the cancellation are unknown, the episode raises the question of whether the faculty at these universities feel secure enough in their jobs to point out obvious problems with how the judiciary functions. It is perhaps unfair to expect academia in these national law universities to conduct research on judicial reforms if they have to worry about the consequences of their research on their career progression.

For a moment, it appeared that this research vacuum on the topic of judicial reforms would be filled by the non-governmental sector funded by private philanthropy. The sector was well-placed to fill the research gap and initiate a candid conversation on ideas of judicial reforms by asking the tough questions that could not be raised within the government or the judiciary. However, private philanthropy in India, with some exceptions, focuses on an 'impact' oriented funding model. This means that recipients of any such funding have to demonstrate how they have influenced policy if they are to receive repeat grants. One easy way to demonstrate impact, which is encouraged by private philanthropy in India, is to collaborate with the government agency or the judiciary as external 'consultants'. The problem with this consultancy model is that much like its counterpart in the private sector, it involves repackaging ideas proposed by the 'client'. This funding model greatly diminishes the possibility of any research or public conversations that may be disapproved by the 'client' or disturb the 'status quo'. The result once again is mostly a status-quoist approach. In the context of the judiciary, the consultant will generally propose reforms in line with the judiciary's existing thinking. It is rare to see a research report that challenges the existing thinking within the judiciary on the direction of reforms.

That said, there are some green shoots. As some in the world of private philanthropy have learnt, any conversation on judicial reforms is a long-term conversation with no quick fixes or immediate 'impact'. This new philanthropy is leading to the creation of new organizations in the non-governmental space that have shown much promise in contributing to a more intellectually rigorous and candid conversation on the nature of judicial reform required in India. Whether their promise translates into viable ideas for reforms remains to be seen but the more people working on judicial reforms, the greater the possibility of finding the right answers.

If civil society in India can generate a candid conversation on the nature of judicial reform required, the next challenge lies in translating the ideas into effective policy. The challenge over here is that the High Courts and Supreme Court are amongst the most powerful institutions in the country and any policy measures aimed at making them accountable for how they control the district courts will require politicians who are willing to lock horns with the judges. This is easier said than done. The higher judiciary is populated with politically savvy judges who are very protective of their turf and have appropriated for themselves immense (and unaccountable) powers in the name of judicial independence. A well-timed *suo-motu* PIL in the High Courts or the Supreme Court on a politically sensitive issue can alter public perceptions on hot-button political issues. It is highly likely that any serious attempt at judicial reform will be attacked by the higher judiciary as an attempt to infringe on judicial independence and ultimately, it is for the higher judiciary to make this legal determination. This makes the higher judiciary particularly formidable opponents for the political class, who have much to lose and little to gain by pushing through judicial reforms which they know are likely to be resisted by the judges of the Supreme Court and High Courts. It is important for academics and civil society to recognize the reality of this skewed power equation between the political class and the higher judiciary while articulating their ideas for judicial reforms. The challenge lies in framing reforms that are difficult for judges on the Supreme Court and High Courts to oppose in the court of public opinion.

One possible strategy that we think should be at the centre of future conversations on judicial reforms is to demand more transparency of the High Courts which are in charge of administering the district courts. The advantage of framing the conversation on judicial reforms in terms of transparency is that it is difficult for anybody in public office to oppose it. After all, it is the Supreme Court that has waxed eloquent about open government and also declared that the right to know is a fundamental right—it is this right that is the foundation of the Right to Information Act.

A simple legislation enacted by Parliament, requiring the High Courts to publish statistics on certain data points such as those outlined in late Fali Nariman's Judicial Statistics Bill, can be a gamechanger. Accurate judicial statistics will enable academics to understand the working of district courts across the country and tailor solutions accordingly for different parts of the country. In addition, Parliament acting in furtherance of the Supreme Court's call for 'open government' should also enact legislation requiring that all administrative and disciplinary committees of the High Courts proactively publish the transcripts of their meetings, along with their financial accounts, audit reports and an annual report laying out future plans to tackle pendency. The potential impact of such transparency measures tends to be underappreciated in India. We are, however, quite sanguine about greater transparency having a visible change in how daily judicial administration is carried out by judges of High Courts. To begin with, once judges are aware that their decision-making process regarding judicial administration is publicly available for anyone to scrutinize, they will be more careful and responsible in how they make administrative decisions. Additionally, the mere availability of more information in the public domain will lead to more public scrutiny and a more informed conversation on the workings of the judiciary, opening the door for the next generation of reforms.

The tougher reforms are the ones that require guaranteeing the decisional independence of the district judiciary, by providing them with complete immunity from being investigated for their judgments unless there is concrete evidence of misconduct by them. This is the only way to tackle the great bail crisis and prevent the travesty of justice outlined in the first chapter of this book about judges of the district judiciary being punished for alleged errors in their judgments, despite no evidence of bribery or other forms of misconduct. Judges with security of tenure in office are more likely to deliver decisive and speedy justice.

In addition to a shield of immunity, Parliament should create an exclusive commission, staffed with professionals, to receive and process complaints against the district judiciary in a transparent manner. As per information provided to us, the Bombay High Court alone received a total of 4,138 complaints against judges of the district judiciary between the years 2018 and 2022. In one year alone, it received 1,200 complaints.[5] If this is the volume of complaints being made against the district judiciary, there is a crying need to create a full-time body in every state to process such complaints in a transparent manner. The current mechanism that involves sitting judges of the High Courts and the district courts taking up the disciplinary mantle, on a part-time basis, and balancing it with their judicial tasks, is inefficient and unfair to both the judges and the public. A full-time commission, along with a clear code of conduct for the district judiciary, is vital to assure both the judges and the public that judges will be held accountable in a fair and transparent manner. In theory, this should be a politically popular reform because judges who are secure in their job are likely to deliver better justice. In reality, we anticipate ferocious opposition from most judges of the High Courts, who would be loath to surrender a key lever of power over the judges of the district judiciary.

The toughest reform from a political perspective, despite its potential to have a dramatic impact on the efficiency of the district judiciary, is our proposal to put an end to the 'revolving docket' by ending inter and intra-district transfers of judges. This reform, combined with our earlier proposal to create a commission to process complaints against the district judiciary, will give judges at this level far greater security of office, leading them to take control of their courtrooms enabling them to set the agenda for the lawyers, instead of the other way round. A permanent docket will also make it possible to hold judges accountable for delays in deciding cases. As mentioned earlier in this book, lawyers are likely to violently protest against such reform. Much of this opposition will likely be rooted in a cynical view that judges are likely to cultivate relationships with lawyers and litigants if posted for too long in one district. But as mentioned earlier, transfers are not a solution to nepotistic or corrupt judges. Selecting more competent judges is the solution to this problem and India needs to rethink the manner in which it appoints judges to the district judiciary. It needs to appoint older and more experienced lawyers as judges for the district judiciary.

Similarly, reforms aimed at turning back the clock on the relentless dilution of procedural and evidentiary norms in judicial proceedings are the need of the hour but will be a hard sell. Populist judges and academics will oppose these reforms, but it is becoming increasingly evident that the lack of procedural and evidentiary norms is contributing significantly to the erosion of judicial legitimacy since there is no uniformity in how judges are treating litigants across courtrooms. While the speed and efficiency of justice should be the primary objectives of any judicial reforms, it would be a mistake to forget that quality of justice matters as much as speed. Procedural integrity is the key to improving the quality of justice dispensed in Indian courtrooms.

It is also important to focus on improving the flagging legitimacy of the courts. The most effective way to do this is to bring back citizens into courtrooms, by resurrecting juries and giving them a say in the justice system. Certain categories of criminal cases should be mandatorily tried by juries. The Indian courtroom should not be the exclusive preserve of lawyers and judges. As was the case post-Independence, India's legal elite will push back any attempt to bring back the jury system. If nothing else, juries will act as a check on both judges and lawyers by bringing back some common sense into the courtroom. Of all the reforms we have proposed, this is the one that has virtually no chance of success.

Executing the above judicial reforms will require astute politicians with the guile and courage to outmanoeuvre wily judges who know how to defend their turf. It would be a mistake for the political class to claim that they are not going to interfere with the working of the district courts on the grounds of judicial independence. If the High Courts are unwilling or unable to tackle the crisis at the district courts and the Supreme Court is only making things worse through poorly informed judgments in pursuance of its PIL jurisdiction, the political class has a duty to intervene and force reform upon the judiciary instead of waiting for the ever-elusive 'consensus'. The Constitution permits Parliament to step in and legislate on the issue as long as judicial independence is ensured. None of our proposals impinge on judicial independence. It is imperative that Parliament begins to think about some of these reforms. At stake is the very idea of justice, equality and liberty that we the people promised ourselves in the Preamble to the Constitution of India.

Notes

Introduction

1. Dilip Shukla, *Damini,* (1993), accessed at https://www.youtube.com/watch?v=UJqCy0SY664.
2. 'Sunny Deol's famous dialogue Tarikh pe Tarikh finds way in to the Economic Survey this year', *The Indian Express,* 29 January 2018, accessed at https://indianexpress.com/article/entertainment/entertainment-others/sunny-deol-dialogue-damini-tarikh-pe-tarikh-economic-survey-5043920/.
3. *Bokaro Power Supply Co v. Jharkhand Krantikari Mazdoor Union,* WP 6187of 2017 before the High Court of Jharkhand decided on 26 September 2022, accessed at https://indiankanoon.org/doc/36833661/.
4. PTI, 'Don't want SC to become "tareekh pe tareekh" court: SC judge Chandrachud', *Deccan Herald,* 9 September 2022, accessed at https://www.deccanherald.com/national/dont-want-sc-to-become-tareekh-pe-tareekh-court-sc-judge-chandrachud-1143689.html.
5. Government of Madhya Pradesh, Bhopal Gas Tragedy Rehabilitation Department, Bhopal, accessed at https://web.archive.org/web/20120518020821/http://www.mp.gov.in/bgtrrdmp/relief.htm.
6. 'Whose Justice for Bhopal?' *New York Times,* 14 May 1986, accessed at https://www.nytimes.com/1986/05/14/opinion/whose-justice-for-bhopal.html.
7. *In Re Union Carbide Corp. Gas Plant Disaster,* 634 F. Supp. 842 (S.D.N.Y. 1986), p. 61, accessed at https://law.justia.com/cases/federal/district-courts/FSupp/634/842/1885973/.

8 Affidavit of Marc S. Galanter, *In re Union Carbide Corporation Gas Leak Disaster at Bhopal, India* in Misc. No. 21-38 85 Civ. 2696 before the United States District Court for the Southern District of New York, 5 December 1985, accessed at https://repository.law.wisc.edu/s/uwlaw/item/42560.

9 Affidavit of N. A. Palkhivala, in support of Defendant's Motion for Dismissal on Forum Non Conveniens Grounds in Misc. No. 21-38 85 Civ. 2696 before the United States District Court for the Southern District of New York, 18 December 1985, accessed at http://14.139.60.116:8080/jspui/bitstream/123456789/706/11/Affidavit%20of%20N.A.%20Palkhivala%20in%20Support%20of%20Defendant%27s.pdf.

10 *In Re Union Carbide Corp. Gas Plant Disaster,* 634 F. Supp. 842 (S.D.N.Y. 1986), p. 62, accessed at https://law.justia.com/cases/federal/district-courts/FSupp/634/842/1885973/.

11 Law Commission of India, *Proposal for Constitution of Hi-tech Fast Track Commercial Divisions in High Courts,* (188th Report 2003), p. 23, accessed at https://cdnbbsr.s3waas.gov.in/s3ca0daec69b5adc880fb464895726dbdf/uploads/2022/08/2022081069-1.pdf.

12 *White Industries Australia Limited v. The Republic of India,* 2010, accessed at https://investmentpolicy.unctad.org/investment-dispute-settlement/cases/378/white-industries-v-india.

13 *All India Judges' Association v. Union of India,* 1992 AIR 165, accessed at https://indiankanoon.org/doc/1394975/.

14 *All India Judges' Association v. Union of India* 2002 (4) SCC 247, accessed at https://indiankanoon.org/doc/125557979/.

15 Law Commission of India, *Manpower Planning in Judiciary: A Blueprint,* (120th Report 1987) p. 3; Current data on the sanctioned strength of the district judiciary can be accessed on the following link of the Department of Justice, Ministry of Law & Justice: https://dashboard.doj.gov.in/sanctiondata/sanctioned_posts.

16 Rajya Sabha, Unstarred Question No. 1391, asked by Masthan Rao Beeda to the Ministry of Law and Justice, on the subject of 'Measures to Reduce Pendency of Cases', answered on 14 December 2023, accessed at https://sansad.in/getFile/annex/262/AU1391.pdf?source=pqars.

17 Lok Sabha, Unstarred Question No. 317, asked by Kanumuru Raghu Ramakrishna Raju to the Ministry of Law and Justice on the subject of 'e-Courts Project', answered on 21 July 2023, accessed at https://sansad.in/getFile/loksabhaquestions/annex/1712/AU317.pdf?source=pqals.

18 Government of India, Ministry of Finance—*Guidelines for release and utilisation of Grant-in-aid for Improvement of Justice Delivery as recommended by Thirteenth Finance Commission,* F.No.32(30) FCD/2010, 20 September, 2010, accessed at https://dea.gov.in/sites/default/files/Guidelines%20for%20Improvement%20in%20Justice%20Delivery.pdf.

1. Fearful Judges

1 'Judges at grassroots reluctant to grant bail for fear of being targeted: CJI DY Chandrachud', *Economic Times,* 21 November 2022, accessed at https://economictimes.indiatimes.com/news/india/judges-at-grassroots-reluctant-to-grant-bail-for-fear-of-being-targeted-cji-dy-chandrachud/articleshow/95649436.cms.

2 Sharmeen Hakim, 'District Judges Should Not Be Put Under Pressure Of Being Targeted For Granting Bail: Bombay HC Chief Justice Dipankar Dutta', *Live Law,* 21 November 2022, accessed at https://www.livelaw.in/news-updates/bombay-high-court-chief-justice-dipankar-datta-k-t-memorial-lecture-214674.

3 B. Shiva Rao, *The Framing of India's Constitution: A Study,* Indian Institute of Public Administration, 1968, p. 508.

4 Ibid.

5 *The State of West Bengal v. Nripendra Nath Bagchi* AIR 1966 SC 447.

6 The Judicial Conduct Rules, 2023, Rule 23, accessed at https://www.complaints.judicialconduct.gov.uk/rulesandregulations/The_Judicial_Conduct_Rules_2023.

7 Rules for Judicial Conduct and Judicial Disability Proceedings, Rule 4, accessed at https://www.uscourts.gov/sites/default/files/judicial_conduct_and_disability_rules_effective_march_12_2019.pdf.

8 See, for example, Maryland Rules, Title 18, Chapter 100, the Code of Judicial Conduct, accessed at https://www.mdcourts.gov/cjd/rulescode.

9 *Zarina Begum v. State of Madhya Pradesh,* M.Cr.C. No. 30933 of 2020 before the Madhya Pradesh High Court decided on 13 May 2021, accessed at https://indiankanoon.org/doc/54084720/.

10 *J. K. Verma v. The State of M.P. & Anr,* W.P. No. 1344 of 1999 before the Madhya Pradesh High Court, decided on 15 July 2011, accessed at https://indiankanoon.org/doc/1739987/.

11 Ibid.

12 *J. K. Verma v. State of M.P. & Ors.* S.L.P No. 30844 of 2011 before the Supreme Court of India, dismissed on 25 November 2011.

13 *Krishna Prasad Verma v. State of Bihar,* CA No. 8950 of 2011 before the Supreme Court of India, decided on 26 September 2019, accessed at https://indiankanoon.org/doc/23604802/.

14 Ibid, para 9.

15 *Krishna Prasad Verma v. State of Bihar,* CWJC No. 3719 of 2009 before the Patna High Court, decided on 5 October 2019, p. 3.

16 Ibid.

17 *Neelam Sinha v. State of Bihar,* CWJC No. 1780 of 2015 before the Patna High Court, decided on 13 March 2023.

18 *R. R. Parekh v. High Court of Gujarat & Anr.,* S.C.A. No. 10760 of 2009 before the Gujarat High Court, decided on 23 February 2012, para 2.

19 Ibid, para 4.

20 Ibid, para 2.2.

21 Ibid, para 4.2.

22 Ibid, para 4.3.

23 Ibid, para 4.8.

24 Ibid, para 5.

25 *R. R. Parekh v. High Court of Gujarat & Anr.* C.A. No. 6116-6117 of 2016 before the Supreme Court of India, decided on 12 July 2016, accessed at https://indiankanoon.org/doc/75859516/ (The Supreme Court reduced the punishment to compulsory retirement, which entitled the judge to some retirement benefits).

26 *Sadhna Chaudhary v. State of Uttar Pradesh* C.A. No. 2077 of 2020 before the Supreme Court of India, decided on 6 March 2020, para 5, accessed at https://indiankanoon.org/doc/151990012/

27 Ibid, para 4.

28 Ibid, para 28.
29 Ibid, para 21.
30 *Muzaffar Husain v. The State Of Uttar Pradesh,* CA No. 3613 of 2022 before the Supreme Court of India, decided on 6 May 2022, accessed at https://indiankanoon.org/doc/56696175/.
31 *G. Rama Sharma v. Government Of Andhra Pradesh,* 2005 (4) ALT 98; *V.R. Katarki v. State of Karnataka And Ors.* 1991 AIR 1241.
32 *The Registrar General, High Court of Karnataka v. Narasimha Prasad,* SLP No. of 25714-17 of 2019 before the Supreme Court of India, decided on 10 April 2023, accessed at https://indiankanoon.org/doc/149540026/.
33 *Sri SB Alawandi v. State of Karnataka,* W.A. No. 4087 of 2012 before the Karnataka High Court, decided on 26 April 2013, accessed at https://indiankanoon.org/doc/197838827/.
34 *Alakh Sinha v. State of Madhya Pradesh,* Madhya Pradesh High Court 2005 (1) MPHT 124, accessed at https://indiankanoon.org/doc/30386/; *Pullavihari Y Trivedi v. State of Gujarat* S.C.A. No. 9551 of 1998 before the Gujarat High Court, decided on 14 April 2013, accessed at https://indiankanoon.org/doc/9946829/.
35 *Krishna Prasad Verma v. State of Bihar,* CA No. 8950/2011 before the Supreme Court of India, decided on 26 September 2019, accessed at https://indiankanoon.org/doc/23604802/.
36 *Musharraf Hussain v. State of UP,* W.A. No. 52433 of 2008 before the Allahabad High Court, decided on 26 August 2014, accessed at https://indiankanoon.org/doc/175754313/.
37 *High Court of Judicature for Rajasthan v. Bhanwar Lal Lamror & Ors.* CA No. 7697/2014 before the Supreme Court of India, decided on 24 August 2021, accessed at https://indiankanoon.org/doc/57360456/
38 Mahesh Langa, 'Gujarat High Court judge removes his remarks from order', *The Hindu,* 19 December 2015, accessed at https://www.thehindu.com/news/national/Gujarat-High-Court-judge-removes-his-remarks-from-order/article60286548.ece (The judge in question had made some controversial remarks about the reservation policy for marginalised communities. After the impeachment motion was moved, the judge deleted the offending paragraph and the

impeachment proceedings were halted. Later the collegium of the Supreme Court appointed this judge to the Supreme Court.)

39 'SC/ST Act verdict, the violent aftermath', *The Hindu,* 5 April 2018, accessed at https://www.thehindu.com/opinion/editorial/scst-act-verdict-the-violent-aftermath/article59780729.ece.

2. Kafkaesque Inquiries

1 'Number of Times Impeachment Proceedings Were Initiated against a SC or HC Judge—Supreme Court Observer', *Supreme Court Observer,* 9 October 2023, accessed at www.scobserver.in/journal/number-of-times-impeachment-proceedings-were-initiated-against-a-supreme-court-or-high-court-judge/ on 25 April 2024. In addition to the judges mentioned in this list, there is Justice S. K. Gangele of the Madhya Pradesh High Court, who was subject to an impeachment motion in the year 2015.

2 The judge to resign after an impeachment motion was passed by the Rajya Sabha in the year 2011 was Justice Soumitro Sen of the Calcutta High Court. The other judge against whom the inquiry committee found evidence of misconduct was Justice V. Ramaswami of the Supreme Court in the year 1993, but the motion of impeachment failed to garner the required votes in the Lok Sabha.

3 Judicial Conduct Investigations Office, 'JCIO Annual Report 22-23' (complaints.judicialconduct.gov.uk), accessed at https://www.complaints.judicialconduct.gov.uk/JCIOAnnual%20Report22-23.

4 Reply by Rajasthan High Court under the RTI Act bearing registration no. AIRHCJDR20240855/2450 dated 5 July 2024; Reply by Bombay High Court under the RTI Act bearing registration no. R.I.A. No. 142/2023 dated 16 February 2023; Reply by Punjab & Haryana High Court under the RTI Act bearing registration no. 623/PIO/HC dated 23 November 2023; Reply by Gujarat High Court under the RTI Act bearing registration no. RTI/O.W. No. 481/2024 dated 2 July 2024; Reply by Allahabad High Court under the RTI Act bearing registration no. HCALD/R/2024/60415 dated 2 July 2024; Reply by Patna High Court under the RTI Act bearing registration no. RTI I.C./610/2024 dated 14 May 2024.

5 Shivraj Huchhanavar, 'Judicial conduct regulation: Do in-house

mechanisms in India uphold judicial Independence and effectively enforce judicial accountability?', 2022, 6(3) *Indian Law Review,* p. 352-386.

6 Shivraj Huchhanavar, 'Judicial Conduct Regulation Regimes in India and the United Kingdom: A Comparative Study' (PhD Thesis, Durham University, 2023), p. 213, accessed at etheses.dur.ac.uk/15082/.

7 *R. C. Sood v. High Court of Rajasthan* 1994 Supp (3) SCC 711, accessed at https://indiankanoon.org/doc/954886/.

8 *R. C. Sood v. High Court of Rajasthan* AIR 1999 SC 707 accessed at https://indiankanoon.org/doc/351242/.

9 *S. J. Pathak Ex, Addl. Sessions Judge v. State of Gujarat & Anr.* S.C.A. No. 9993 of 2006 before the Gujarat High Court decided on 6 November 2009, accessed at https://www.casemine.com/judgement/in/56b48efa607dba348fff69d2.

10 'Verify Complaints against Subordinate Judges before Action: TS Thakur, CJI', *Economic Times,* 24 May 2016, accessed at economictimes.indiatimes.com/news/politics-and-nation/verify-complaints-against-subordinate-judges-before-action-ts-thakur-cji/articleshow/52418935.cms.

11 *Zarina Begum v. State of Madhya Pradesh* M.Cr.C. No. 30933 of 2020 before the Madhya Pradesh High Court, decided on 13 May 2021, accessed at https://indiankanoon.org/doc/54084720/; The authors are grateful to Tanish Arora who pointed to this judgment in his article 'Why is the judiciary clogged with bail matters?', *The Leaflet,* 4 February 2022, accessed at https://theleaflet.in/why-is-the-higher-judiciary-clogged-with-bail-matters/.

12 *D. Amaladoss v. The State Of Tamil Nadu* (2006) 4 MLJ 1360, accessed at https://indiankanoon.org/doc/1046400/.

13 *Mahendra Boopathi v. The High Court of Madras* W.P. No. 17230 of 2018 before the Madras High Court decided on 11 July 2019, accessed at https://indiankanoon.org/doc/156059831/.

14 *K. Ganesan* v. *The Government of Tamil Nadu & Anr.* W.P. No. 28079 of 2017 before the Madras High Court, decided on 16 July 2018, accessed at https://indiankanoon.org/doc/162364462/.

15 Ibid.

16 *K. Ganesan v. The Government of Tamil Nadu & Anr.* S.L.P. No. 30608 of 2018 before the Supreme Court of India, decided on 4 December 2018, accessed at https://api.sci.gov.in/supremecourt/2018/43168/43168_2018_Order_04-Dec-2018.pdf.

17 *A. N. Pattan v. State of Karnataka* W.P. No. 8640 of 2013 before the Karnataka High Court, decided on 29 June 2017, accessed at https://indiankanoon.org/doc/22293724/.

18 Ibid.

19 Ibid.

20 *High Court of Karnataka v. A. N. Pattan* W.A. No. 5569 of 2017 before the Karnataka High Court, decided on 23 March 2022, accessed at https://indiankanoon.org/doc/118799460/.

21 *A. N. Pattan v. High Court of Karnataka & Anr.* S.L.P. No. 017578 of 2022 before the Supreme Court of India decided on 30 September 2022, accessed at https://api.sci.gov.in/supremecourt/2022/26447/26447_2022_1_32_38814_Order_30-Sep-2022.pdf.

22 *K. S. Raju v. State of Kerala,* W.P. (C) No. 21317 of 2009 before the Kerala High Court, decided on 10 March 2015, accessed at https://indiankanoon.org/doc/103019167/.

23 Reply from the Kerala High Court under the RTI Act bearing registration no. PIO 104/2023 dated 11 March 2024.

24 *K. S. Raju v. The State of Kerala* WA. 859 of 2016, pending before the Kerala High Court as on 24 November 2024.

25 *Syed Hasan v. High Court of Judicature* Writ A. No. 8068 of 2012 before the High Court of Allahabad decided on 6 November 2012, accessed at https://indiankanoon.org/doc/96554094/.

26 Ibid.

27 Ibid.

28 *S. J. Pathak Ex, Addl. Sessions Judge v. State of Gujarat & Anr.* S.C.A. No. 9993 of 2009 before the Gujarat High Court, decided on 6 November 2009, accessed at https://www.casemine.com/judgement/in/56b48efa607dba348fff69d2.

29 Ibid., para 12.

30 Ibid.

31 See, United States Courts, Caseload Statistics Data Tables, *'U.S.*

Federal Courts Complaints and Actions Taken Under Authority of 28 U.S.C. 351-36', accessed at https://www.uscourts.gov/statistics-reports/caseload-statistics-data-tables?tn&pn=All&t=687&m%5Bvalue%5D%5Bmonth%5D=&y%5Bvalue%5D%5Byear%5D=; State of Maryland, Commission on Judicial Disabilities, '*Annual Report for Fiscal Year 2023'*, accessed at https://www.courts.state.md.us/sites/default/files/import/cjd/pdfs/annualreport23.pdf; Judicial Conduct Investigations Office, *'JCIO Annual Report 22-23'* (Complaints.judicialconduct.gov.uk), accessed at https://www.complaints.judicialconduct.gov.uk/JCIOAnnual%20Report22-23.

32 Supra n 28, (*S. J. Pathak) at* para 31.

33 *R. K. Divyeshwar v. State of Gujarat & Anr.* (1999) 1 GLR 47, accessed at https://indiankanoon.org/doc/22179/.

34 Supra n 28, (*S. J. Pathak)* at para 34.

35 *Sadhna Chaudhary v. State of Uttar Pradesh* C.A. No. 2077 of 2020 before the Supreme Court of India, decided on 6 March 2020, at para 5, accessed at https://indiankanoon.org/doc/151990012/.

36 *T. C. Tanwar v. The High Court for the States of Punjab & Haryana & Anr.* C.W.P. No. 7559 of 1998 before the High Court of Punjab & Haryana, decided on 14 August 2013, accessed at https://indiankanoon.org/doc/50443165/.

37 *Ramesh Prasad Tihaiya v. Madhya Pradesh High Court & Anr.* W.P. No. 4126 of 1997 before the High Court of Madhya Pradesh, decided on 11 January 2011, accessed at https://indiankanoon.org/doc/241947/.

38 *The Registrar General, High Court of Karnataka v. Narasimha Prasad,* SLP No. of 25714-17 of 2019 before the Supreme Court, decided on 10 April 2023, accessed at https://indiankanoon.org/doc/149540026/.

39 *R. K. Divyeshwar v. State of Gujarat & Anr.* (1999)1 GLR 47, accessed at https://indiankanoon.org/doc/22179/.

40 *Krishna Prasad Verma v. State of Bihar,* CA No. 8950/2011 before the Supreme Court of India, decided on 26 September 2019, accessed at https://indiankanoon.org/doc/23604802/; and *Neelam Sinha v. State of Bihar,* CWJC No. 1780 of 2015 before the Patna High Court, decided on 13 March, 2023.

41 Jeremy Bentham, *Constitutional Code* Vol. IX., Russell & Russell, 1962 p. 493.

42 *Central Public Information Officer of the Supreme Court of India v. Subash Chandra Agarwal* in C.A. No. 10044 of 2010 before the Supreme Court of India, decided on 13 November 2019, accessed at https://main.sci.gov.in/supremecourt/2009/36624/36624_2009_1_1502_18247_Judgement_13-Nov-2019.pdf.

3. Fired without Cause

1 Sharmeen Hakim, 'Bombay HC Asks Judge Hearing NSEL Case to Step Down', *Mumbai Mirror*, 24 June 2017 accessed at https://mumbaimirror.indiatimes.com/mumbai/cover-story/bombay-hc-asks-judge-hearing-nsel-case-to-step-down/articleshow/59292914.cms.

2 'HC Dismisses Sacked Judge's Plea Against State Government Order', *The Hindu*, 4 February 2020, accessed at https://www.thehindu.com/news/cities/mumbai/hc-dismisses-sacked-judges-plea-against-state-government-order/article30732112.ece.

3 SLP(C) No. 16089 of 2022 before Supreme Court of India.

4 Basic Principles on the Independence of the Judiciary, adopted on 6 September 1985 by the 7th United Nations Congress on the Prevention of Crime and Treatment of Offenders endorsed by UNGA Res 40/32 (29 November 1985).

5 Ibid at Rule 12.

6 Rule 21 of Gujarat State Judicial Service Rules, 2005.

7 Typically, under Article 311 of the Constitution, all persons in employment of the union or the states have a right to be heard. Both these categories—probationary judges and judges subject to compulsory retirement—fall under the exceptions to this general right to be heard.

8 Apoorva Mandhani, 'Gujarat HC Registry orders compulsory retirement for 18 Judicial Officers', *LiveLaw*, 20 July 2016, accessed at https://www.livelaw.in/gujarat-hc-registry-orders-compulsory-retirement-18-judicial-officers/.

9 'Compulsory Retirement for 12 District Court Judges', *The Times of India*, 29 April 2014, accessed at https://timesofindia.indiatimes.

com/city/bhopal/compulsory-retirement-for-12-district-court-judges/articleshow/34367293.cms>; '15 judicial officers in U.P. given compulsory retirement by HC', *The Hindu,* 19 April 2016, accessed at https://www.thehindu.com/news/national/other-states/15-judicial-officers-in-U.P.-given-compulsory-retirement-by-HC/article14245924.ece; 'Gujarat HC gives compulsory retirement to 18 underperforming judicial officers', *Hindustan Times,* 19 July 2016, accessed at https://www.hindustantimes.com/india-news/gujarat-hc-gives-compulsory-retirement-to-18-underperforming-judicial-officers/story-mhHHg3AvAmsA5HxmbiGLjN.html; Apoorva Mandhani, 'Compulsory Retirement for 12 District Judges After Jharkhand HC notes 'Dubious Conduct', *LiveLaw,* 13 August 2017, accessed at https://www.livelaw.in/compulsory-retirement-12-district-judges-jharkhand-hc-notes-dubious-conduct/; Sparsh Upadhyay, 'Gujarat Govt. notified premature retirement of 8 Judicial Officers in 2 months on High Court's Recommendation', *LiveLaw,* 8 September 2022, accessed at https://www.livelaw.in/news-updates/gujarat-govt-ordered-premature-retirement-8judicial-officers-2months-high-court-recommendation-208769; ENS, 'High Court orders premature retirement of 17 judicial officers', *The Indian Express,* 21 May 2009, accessed at https://indianexpress.com/article/cities/ahmedabad/high-court-orders-premature-retirement-of-17-judicial-officers/; TNN, 'Rajasthan HC for removal of 12 judicial officers', *The Times of India,* 23 May 2011, accessed at https://timesofindia.indiatimes.com/city/jaipur/rajasthan-hc-for-removal-of-12-judicial-officers/articleshow/8518857.cms.

10 Report of the Public Service Commission 1886-86 (1888) at p. 88, accessed at https://archive.org/details/dli.csl.35.

11 *All India Judges Association v. Union of India* AIR 1993 SC 2493, accessed at https://indiankanoon.org/doc/1977799/.

12 Report of the First National Judicial Pay Commission, November 1999, at para 4.45.

13 *Jayashree Chamanlal Buddhbhatti v. State of Gujarat* S.C.A. No. 2880 of 2008 before the Gujarat High Court decided on 15 May 2009 can be accessed at: https://indiankanoon.org/doc/27154629/.

14 Ibid.

15 Ibid.
16 Ibid.
17 *Registrar General High Court of Gujarat & Anr v. Jayshree Chamanlal Buddhbhatti* C.A. No. 9346 of 2013 before the Supreme Court of India decided on 22 October 2013, accessed at https://indiankanoon.org/doc/179750624/.
18 *Gurunath Dinkar Mane v. State of Maharashtra* W.P. No. 2733 of 2013 before the Bombay High Court, decided on 23 September 2016, accessed at https://www.casemine.com/judgement/in/5838591ebc41683ab785eb87.
19 *Gurunath Dinkar Mane v. State of Maharashtra* SLP No. 18148 of 2017 before the Supreme Court of India.
20 *Abhay Jain v. High Court of Judicature for Rajasthan & Anr.* Civil Writ Petition No. 6749 of 2016 before the Rajasthan High Court, decided on 21 October 2019, accessed at https://indiankanoon.org/doc/124371454/.
21 Ibid at para 33.
22 Ibid at para 34.
23 *Abhay Jain v. High Court of Judicature for Rajasthan & Anr.* Civil Appeal No. 2029 of 2022 before the Supreme Court of India, decided on 15 March 2022, accessed at https://indiankanoon.org/doc/155486886/.
24 Ibid at para 52.
25 Ibid at para 47.
26 Ibid at para 57.
27 *Rajeev Kumar v. State of Jharkhand & Jharkhand High Court at Ranchi* W.P.(S) No. 2529 of 2006 before the Jharkhand High Court, accessed at https://www.casemine.com/judgement/in/5ac5e5274a93261ae6b53b29.
28 *Rajendra Singh Verma v. Lt. Governor (NCT of Delhi)* (2011) 10 SCC 1 at para 19, accessed at https://indiankanoon.org/doc/901169/.
29 Ibid at para 21.
30 Ibid at para 90.
31 *Rajendra Singh Verma v. Lt. Governor (NCT of Delhi)* (2011) 10 SCC 1.
32 Ibid.

33 *Ashok Kumar Agarwala v. Registrar General of Orissa* W.P. No. 19322 of 2014 before the Orissa High Court, decided on 19 January 2022, accessed at https://indiankanoon.org/doc/27232709/.
34 Ibid at para 26.
35 *K. Veena Chary & Others v. High Court of Andhra Pradesh* W.P. Nos. 16437 & 18123 of 2007 before the Andhra Pradesh High Court decided on 23 July 2008, accessed at https://www.casemine.com/judgement/in/56b48cc8607dba348ffeeb4a/amp#hide1.
36 *High Court of Andhra Pradesh v. K. Veera Chary & Anr.* Civil Appeal No. (S) 9700-9701 of 2013 before the Supreme Court of India, decided on 23 November 2017.
37 *Jayeshkumar Krishnakant Acharya v. High Court of Gujarat & Anr.* SCA No. 20426 of 2016 before the High Court of Gujarat, decided on 27 March 2024.
38 Shimon Shetreet, *Judges on Trial: A Study of the Appointment and Accountability of the English Judiciary* North-Holland Publishing, 1976, p. 284-285 cited from Gabrielle Appleby & Suzanne Le Mire, 'Judicial Conduct: Crafting a System That Enhances Institutional Integrity', 38(1) *Melbourne University Law Review* (2014), p. 9.
39 Ibid. (Appleby & Le Mire).
40 Article 124(4) of the Constitution of India.
41 Bingham Centre for The Rule of Law, British Institute of International & Comparative Law, 'The Appointment, Tenure and Removal of Judges under Commonwealth Principles: A Compendium & Analysis of Best Practice', 2015, p. 85.

4. The Curse of the Revolving Docket

1 Tabassum Barnagarwala, 'Mumbai's JJ Hospital to the Gambia: 36 Years Apart but a Familiar Story of Deadly Toxic Drugs.' *Scroll*, 15 November 2022, accessed at https://scroll.in/article/1036860/mumbais-jj-hospital-to-the-gambia-36-years-apart-but-a-familiar-story-of-deadly-toxic-drugs.
2 Profile of the judge on the website of the Allahabad High Court: https://www.allahabadhighcourt.in/District/Officer/3218.html.
3 *Siddhartha Kumar & Ors. v. Upper Civil Judge, Senior Division & Ors*, 1998 (1) AWC 593, para 35, accessed at https://indiankanoon.org/doc/1923406/.

4 Ibid.

5 Ibid.

6 Government of India, *Civil Justice Committee Report,* (Central Publication Branch, 1925), p. 22.

7 G.L. No. 42, Chapter XII of Vol 2. Of Compilation of Circulars issued by the Allahabad High Court, p. 415, dated 3 November 1932, accessed at https://allahabadhighcourt.in/publications.html.

8 I.C.L. No. 65 dated 31 October 1962 cited from (*Siddharth Kumar*) (Supra n. 3).

9 Revised unit criteria for assessment of work done by the officers of Delhi Higher Judicial Service and Delhi Judicial Service, Memo No. 1186-1190/DHC/Gaz/G-2/Criteria/2022 of the Registrar General of High Court of Delhi dated 10 March 2022.

10 Alok Prasanna Kumar and Deepika Kinhal, 'How to Avoid the "Cobra Effect" While Incentivising Judges to Perform Better', *The Indian Express,* 20 March 2024, accessed at https://indianexpress.com/article/opinion/columns/chief-justice-of-india-super-performing-trial-court-judges-courtroom-atmosphere-indian-judiciray-9223458/.

11 Robert Moog, 'Delays in the Indian Courts: Why the Judge Don't Take Control', 16(1) *The Justice System Journal* (1992) p. 19.

12 Ibid, p. 25.

13 Ibid, p. 32.

14 Supra n. 6, (*Civil Justice Committee Report*) p. 599.

15 Royal Commission, *Decentralisation in India,* Vol. 1 (Majesty's Stationery Office, 1907) p. 223.

16 Ibid.

17 *See generally* Akanksha Jain, 'Delhi High Court Issues Transfer Policy of Judicial Officers', *LiveLaw,* 23 October 2018, accessed at https://www.livelaw.in/delhi-hc-issues-transfer-policy-of-judicial-officers/ .

18 Supra n. 11, (Moog; 1992) p. 23-34.

19 'Kerala HC Quashes Transfer of Judge Who Made 'Sexually Provocative' Dress Remark.', *The Indian Express,* 2 November 2022, accessed at https://indianexpress.com/article/india/kerala/kerala-hc-dress-remark-8244553/; Srinjoy Das, 'Tripura High Court transfers Kamalpur Civil Judge accused of sexually

harassing rape survivor', *LiveLaw,* 25 February 2024, accessed at https://www.livelaw.in/high-court/tripura-high-court/tripura-high-court-transfers-civil-judge-accused-of-sexually-assaulting-rape-survivor-250439.

20 *The Hon'ble High Court at Calcutta v. Mintu Mallick* SLP (Civil) No.24840/2019 before the Supreme Court of India, decided on 15 November 2019, accessed at https://indiankanoon.org/doc/99699119/

21 Ayesha Arvind, 'Do Not Visit High Court Judges' Residences to Request Transfers, Favours: Madras High Court Registry to Judicial Officers', *Bar and Bench,* 26 June 2023, accessed at https://www.barandbench.com/news/do-not-visit-high-court-judges-residences-to-request-transfers-seek-favours-madras-high-court-registry-tells-state-judicial-officers.

22 Basit Amin Makhdoomi, 'Tripura High Court Upholds Dismissal of Probationary Judicial Officer For Seeking Favourable Transfer by Approaching Union Minister', *LiveLaw,* 8 February 2024, accessed at https://www.livelaw.in/high-court/tripura-high-court/tripura-high-court-upholds-dismissal-of-judicial-officer-for-attempting-to-exercise-extraneous-influence-for-a-favourable-transfer-248904.

23 Dhananjay Mahapatra, 'Gwalior Additional Judge Says She Was Sexually Harassed by HC Judge, Quits', *The Times of India,* 3 August 2014, accessed at https://timesofindia.indiatimes.com/india/gwalior-additional-judge-says-she-was-sexually-harassed-by-hc-judge-quits/articleshow/39569700.cms>.

24 Article 255(3) of the Government of India Act, 1935.

25 B. Shiva Rao, *The Framing of India's Constitution,* Indian Institute of Public Administration (1968), p. 507-509.

5. Too Young to Judge

1 This chapter draws from the following study that one of us co-authored: Prashant Reddy T., Reshma Shekhar et. al., 'Schooling the Judges: The Selection and Training of Civil Judges and Judicial Magistrates', Vidhi Centre for Legal Policy, 2019. Dev Ankur Wadhawan, '21-year-old Jaipur Boy Set to Become Youngest Judge in Country', *India Today,* 21 November 2019, accessed at https://

www.indiatoday.in/india/story/21-year-old-jaipur-boy-set-to-become-youngest-judge-in-country-1621206-2019-11-21.

2 For 2024, these calculations are based on the gradation lists of judicial officers in the state published on the website of the High Court of Madhya Pradesh.

3 Section 29(2) and Section 325 of the Code of Criminal Procedure, 1973.

4 'BCI Calls Young Judicial Officers "Incapable, Inept, Impolite", Vows to Fight for 3-year-min Practice Before Judges' Exam', *Legally India,* 4 January 2021, accessed at https://www.legallyindia.com/the-bar-and-bench/bci-calls-young-judicial-officers-incapable-inept-impolite-vows-to-fight-for-3-year-minimum-practice-before-judges-exam-20210104-11863.

5 Sub-Committee of the National Court Management System, Supreme Court of India, *Human Resource Development Strategy in the District Judiciary,* (2024) p.104-105.

6 Article 84 of Constitution of India, 1950.

7 Article 58 of Constitution of India, 1950.

8 Article 217 of Constitution of India, 1950.

9 Maneesh Chhibber, 'MoP on Appointments: Govt Gets One Ok, SC Agrees to Age Criterion for HC Judges', *The Indian Express,* 26 March 2017, accessed at https://indianexpress.com/article/india/mop-on-appointments-govt-gets-one-ok-sc-agrees-to-age-criterion-for-hc-judges-collegium-4585968/.

10 *High Court of Delhi v. Devina Sharma* CA No. 2016 of 2022 before Supreme Court of India, decided on 14 March 2022, accessed at https://main.sci.gov.in/supremecourt/2022/7506/7506_2022_34_301_34198_Judgement_14-Mar-2022.pdf.

11 These calculations are based on the gradation list of district judges published on the website of the Madhya Pradesh High Court.

12 These calculations are based on the gradation list of district judges published on the website of the Karnataka High Court.

13 'Status of Magistrate Judge Positions and Appointments—Judicial' (2021), United States Courts accessed at https://www.uscourts.gov/statistics-reports/status-magistrate-judge-positions-and-appointments-judicial-business-2021.

14 Ministry of Justice, Government of the United Kingdom, *Diversity of the Judiciary: Legal Professions, New Appointments and Current Post-holders-2023 Statistics* (8 September 2023) accessed at https://www.gov.uk/government/statistics/diversity-of-the-judiciary-2023-statistics/diversity-of-the-judiciary-legal-professions-new-appointments-and-current-post-holders-2023-statistics.

15 Ibid.

16 Data collected from the gradation lists made publicly available on the website of the Madhya Pradesh High Court.

17 Data collected from the gradation lists made publicly available on the website of the Guwahati High Court.

18 Rule 14(c) of the Delhi Judicial Service Rules, 1970; Rule 10 of the Uttar Pradesh Judicial Services Rules, 2001.

19 Report of the Public Service Commission 1886-87 (The Superintendent of Government Printing India 1888), p. 33.

20 Government of India, *Civil Justice Committee Report* (Central Publication Branch 1925), p. xxv.

21 Law Commission of India, *Training of Judicial Officers,* (117th Report 1986) p. 12.

22 *All India Judges Association v. Union of India* AIR 1993 SC 2493, accessed at https://indiankanoon.org/doc/1977799/.

23 *All India Judges Association v. Union of India* AIR 2002 (4) SCC 247, accessed at https://indiankanoon.org/doc/125557979/.

24 *See generally* William T. Vukowich, 'Comment: The Lack of Practical Training in Law Schools: Criticisms, Causes and Programs for Change', 23 *Case Western Reserve Law Review* (1971) p. 142.

25 Tamil Nadu State Judicial Academy—Staff Page, accessed at https://www.tnsja.tn.gov.in/aboutus_staff.html.

26 Geeta Oberoi, 'Limitation of Induction Trainings Offered to Magistrates by State Judicial Actors in India', 4 *Athens Journal of Law* (2018) p. 302.

27 *See also* Prashant Reddy T., Reshma Shekhar et. al., 'Schooling the Judges: The Selection and Training of Civil Judges and Judicial Magistrates', Vidhi Centre for Legal Policy, (2019) p. 13.

28 *Supra* n. 26, p. 313 (Oberoi; 2018).

29 *Supra* n. 5, p. 99. (NCMS; 2024).

30 *Supra* n. 20, p. 183 (Civil Justice Committee Report; 1925).

31 Law Commission of India, *Reform of Judicial Administration,* (14th Report 1958) p. 170.

32 Ibid, p. 175.

33 Ibid, p. 176.

34 H. R. Khanna, *Neither Roses Nor Thorns,* Eastern Book Company, 2021 p. 34-35.

35 Sumathi Chandrashekaran et. al., 'Breaking Through the Old Boys' Club: The rise of women in the lower judiciary', 55(4) *Economic and Political Weekly,* 27 January 2020, accessed at https://www.epw.in/journal/2020/4/special-articles/breaking-through-old-boys%E2%80%99-club.html.

6. The Missing Judicial Statistics

1 Sameer Yasir, 'A Lifelong Nightmare: Seeking Justice in India's Overwhelmed Courts', *The New York Times,* 13 January 2024, accessed at https://www.nytimes.com/2024/01/13/world/asia/india-judicial-backlog.html.

2 Lok Sabha, Unstarred Question No. 317, 21 July 2023, Ministry of Law and Justice by Kanumuru Raghu Ramakrishna Raju, accessed at https://sansad.in/getFile/loksabhaquestions/annex/1712/AU317.pdf?source=pqals.

3 Revised unit criteria for work done by the officers of Delhi High Judicial Service and Delhi Judicial Service, Notification bearing No. 1186-1190/DHC/Gaz/G-2/Criteria/2022 dated 10 March 2022 by the Registrar General Delhi High Court.

4 Lok Sabha Q. No. 1359 asked by Dr. Vishnu Prasad M. K. to the Ministry of Law & Justice on the subject of 'Special Courts for Disposal of Cases' and answered on 9 February 2024.

5 See for example, Woolf, S. 'Statistics and the modern state' *31*(3) *Comparative Studies in Society and History* (1989), pp. 588-604.

6 Nikhil Menon, *Planning Democracy: How a Professor, an Institute, and an Idea shaped India,* Penguin Random House India, 2022.

7 For example, see Government of India, Ministry of Home Affairs, No.19/51/69-Judl.III, 25 June 1969, Letter to Chief Secretaries of all States, Re: Statistics of work done by the High Court during half

year ending 1969, accessed through Abhilekh Patal at https://www.abhilekh-patal.in/jspui/.

8 Robert Moog, Indian Litigiousness and the Litigation Explosion: Challenging the Legend, *Asian Survey,* December 1993, Vol. 33 No. 12, pp. 1137.

9 Rajeev Dhavan, *Litigation Explosion in India,* N. M. Tripathi Pvt. Ltd. 1986 p.9.

10 Rajya Sabha, Starred Question No. 769 asked by R. P. Khaitan to the Ministry of Home Affairs on the subject of 'Cases pending in Delhi courts' and answered on 24 December 1969.

11 Rajya Sabha, Question No. 1506 asked by Suresh Kalmadi and Dharam Chander to the Ministry of Law & Justice on the subject of 'Judgment of cases yet to be delivered by Supreme Court' and answered on 2 December 1985.

12 Rajya Sabha, 'Wide-ranging reforms in judiciary', Private Members' Resolution, 2 May 2003, accessed at https://rsdebate.nic.in/bitstream/123456789/93065/1/PD_198_02052003_32_p266_p313_15.pdf.

13 V. Venkatesan, 'For Judicial Transparency', Frontline, 14-27 August 2004, accessed at https://frontline.thehindu.com/the-nation/article30224257.ece.

14 Vaidehi Misra et al, 'Sunshine in the Courts, Ranking the High Courts on their Compliance with the RTI Act', 2019, Vidhi Centre for Legal Policy, accessed at https://vidhilegalpolicy.in/research/sunshine-in-the-courts-ranking-the-high-courts-on-their-compliance-with-the-rti-act/.

15 *Anil Rai v. State of Bihar* Appeal (Crl.) 389/1998 before the Supreme Court decided on 6 August 2001, accessed athttps://indiankanoon.org/doc/1517737/.

16 *Commodore Lokesh Batra v. Supreme Court of India,* File No.CIC/WB/A/2010/000320 before the Central Information Commission decided on 3 August 2011, accessed at https://indiankanoon.org/doc/1579665/.

17 Ibid.

18 *The Registrar Supreme Court of India v. Commodore Lokesh K. Batra & Ors* W.P.(C) 6634 of 2011 before the Delhi High Court, decided on 4 December 2014.

19 *The Registrar Supreme Court of India v. Commodore Lokesh K. Batra & Ors* LPA24 of 2015 & OM No. 965/2015 before the Delhi High Court decided on 7 January 2016, accessed at https://indiankanoon.org/doc/8210205/.

20 *Commodore Lokesh Batra v. The Registrar Supreme Court of India* SLP(C) No. 3978 of 2016 before the Supreme Court of India decided on 15 February 2016, accessed at https://main.sci.gov.in/jonew/courtnic/rop/2016/3933/rop_453243.pdf.

21 E-Committee of the Supreme Court of India, *National Policy and Action Plan for Implementation of Information and Communication Technology in the Indian Judiciary*, 1 August 2005, accessed at https://cdnbbsr.s3waas.gov.in/s388ef51f0bf911e452e8dbb1d807a81ab/uploads/2020/05/2020053162.pdf.

22 Law Commission of India, *Arrears and Backlog: Creating Additional Judicial (Wo)manpower*, (245th Report, 2014) p.8.

23 Supreme Court of India, Centre for Planning and Research, *State of Judiciary: A Report on Infrastructure, Budgeting, Human Resources, and ICT*, November 2023, p. 82.

24 Computerisation of Courts, PIB, 8 August 2024, accessed at https://pib.gov.in/PressReleasePage.aspx?PRID=2042986.

7. How Many Judges Does India Need?

1 'An Overworked Chief Justice TS Thakur Breaks Down in Front of PM Modi', *The Times of India*, 24 April 2016, accessed at https://timesofindia.indiatimes.com/india/an-overworked-chief-justice-ts-thakur-breaks-down-in-front-of-pm-modi/articleshow/51964732.cms.

2 Current data on the sanctioned strength of the district judiciary can be accessed on the following link of the Department of Justice, Ministry of Law & Justice: https://dashboard.doj.gov.in/sanctiondata/sanctioned_posts. Of these, around 5,750 positions remain vacant but 2,229 of these vacancies are attributable to only three states: Uttar Pradesh, Bihar and Madhya Pradesh.

3 Law Commission of India, *Manpower Planning in Judiciary: A Blueprint* (120th Report 1987), p. 3.

4 Rajya Sabha, Q. No. 4046 asked by Bratin Sengupta to the Ministry

of Law, Justice & Company Affairs on the subject of 'Ratio/number of Judges' and answered on 23 April 2001.

5 Rajya Sabha, Q. No. 907 asked by Ghulam Nabi Azad to the Ministry of Law, Justice & Company Affairs on the subject of 'Number of Judges in Capital's Lower Courts' and answered on 28 November 2000. For data in the year 2024, visit the weblink contained in Supra note 2.

6 Shyamlal Yadav, 'What Is the Reason for the Large Number of Vacancies in the IAS?', *The Indian Express,* 25 March 2022, accessed at https://indianexpress.com/article/explained/explained-jitendra-singh-vacancies-in-the-ias-7835071/.

7 *Supra* n 3 (LCI; 1987) at p.3.

8 Ibid.

9 Affidavit of Marc S. Galanter, 5 December 1985, *In re Union Carbide Corporation Gas Leak Disaster at Bhopal, India.*

10 See, Sital Kalantry et. al., 'Litigation as a Measure of Well-Being', 62 *DePaul Law Review* (2013) p. 247. This paper convincingly makes the point that the most significant positive association was found between HDI (even when compared with GDP) and higher litigation rate.

11 Law Commission of India, *Reform of Judicial Administration,* Vol II (14th Report 1958) p. 159-160.

12 Justice Malimath et. al. *Report of the Arrears Committee,* 1989-1990, p. 137.

13 *All India Judges Association v. Union of India* AIR 2002 (4) SCC 247, accessed at https://indiankanoon.org/doc/125557979/.

14 SLP(Crl.) Nos. 1581-1598/2009 before the Supreme Court of India, accessed at https://indiankanoon.org/doc/50352079/.

15 *Imtiyaz Ahmad v. State of U.P.& Ors* 2012 (2) SCC 688 at para 61, accessed at https://indiankanoon.org/doc/50352079/.

16 Law Commission of India, *Arrears and Backlog: Creating Additional Judicial (Wo)manpower,* (245th Report 2014) p.8.

17 Ibid, p. 18.

18 Ibid, p. 24.

19 Supreme Court of India, National Court Management Systems (NCMS), *Policy & Action Plan released by Chief*

Justice of India (2012) at para 1.6, accessed at https://cdnbbsr.s3waas.gov.in/s3ec0490f1f4972d133619a60c30f3559e/uploads/2024/01/2024011772-1.pdf.

20 *Imtiyaz Ahmad v. State of UP,* Order dated 30.03.2016 in Criminal Appeal. No. 254-262/2012 before the Supreme Court of India.

21 Letter dated 1 April 2016 from Member Secretary, NCMS Committee to Joint Secretary, Department of Justice with annexure titled: 'Note for calculating required judge strength for subordinate courts for submission to the Hon'ble Supreme Court of India as per its directions to NCMS in *Imtiyaz Ahmad v. State of U.P. & Ors.'* (Criminal Appeal No. 254-262 of 2012) (On file with the authors).

22 Ibid at para 17.

23 Ibid at paras 10 & 11.

24 Ibid at paras 17-20.

25 *Imtiyaz Ahmad* v. *State of UP,* Order dated 2 January 2017 in Criminal Appeal. No. 254-262/2012 before the Supreme Court of India, accessed at https://indiankanoon.org/doc/44403361/.

26 Ibid at para 22.

27 Supreme Court of India, Centre for Planning and Research, *Subordinate Courts of India: A Report on Access to Justice* (2016) accessed at https://cdnbbsr.s3waas.gov.in/s3ec0490f1f4972d133619a60c30f3559e/uploads/2024/01/2024012553.pdf.

28 Alok Prasanna Kumar, 'How many judges does India really need?', *Mint,* 12 July 2016, accessed at https://www.livemint.com/Politics/3B97SMGhseobYhZ6qpAYoN/How-many-judges-does-India-really-need.html.

29 *Imtiyaz Ahmad v. State of UP,* Order dated 31 August 2017, in Crl.A. No. 254-262/2012 before the Supreme Court of India.

30 *Imtiyaz Ahmad v. State of UP,* Order dated 20 January 2020, Miscellaneous Application No. 2362-2370/2019 in Crl.A. No. 254-262/2012 before the Supreme Court of India; Office Report of the Assistant Registrar of the Supreme Court dated 20 November 2019 in the case of *Imtiyaz Ahmad v. State of UP* in Crl.A. No. 254-262/2012 before the Supreme Court of India.

31 *Imtiyaz Ahmad v. State of UP,* Order dated 7 July 2021, Miscellaneous

Application No. 2362-2370/2019 in Crl.A. No. 254-262/2012 before the Supreme Court of India.

32 Reply from Central Public Information Officer, Supreme Court of India, New Delhi under the RTI Act bearing Appl. No: 01-RTI/Copying/2022 dated 4 January 2022.

33 Supreme Court of India, Centre for Planning and Research, *State of the Judiciary*, (2023), p. 82 accessed at https://main.sci.gov.in/pdf/CRP/15122023_082223.pdf.

34 Ibid.

35 Ibid at p. 88.

36 Ibid at p. 90.

37 *Imtiyaz Ahmad v. State of UP*, Order dated 01.12.2021 in Miscellaneous Application No. 2362-2370/2019 in Crl.A. No. 254-262/2012 before the Supreme Court of India.

38 'The Need for New Judgeships in the Superior Courts: 2020 Update of the Judicial Needs Assessment', Report to the Legislature under Government Code Section 69614(C)(1) & (3), November 2020, accessed at https://www.courts.ca.gov/documents/2020_Update_of_the_Judicial_Needs_Assessment.pdf.

8. The Purse Strings

1 Khadija Khan, 'Justice system plagued by low budgets: India Justice Report 2022', *The Indian Express*, New Delhi, 6 April 2022, accessed at https://indianexpress.com/article/india/justice-system-plagued-by-low-budgets-india-justice-report-2022-8539575/.

2 Sumathi Chandrashekaran et. al., 'Building Better Courts: Surveying the Infrastructure of India's District Courts', Vidhi Centre of Legal Policy, August 2019, accessed at https://vidhilegalpolicy.in/wp-content/uploads/2019/08/National-report_single_Aug-1.pdf.

3 Abhimanyu Hazarika, 'Patna High Court to buy iPhone 13 Pro (256 GB) for all its judges', *Bar & Bench*, 22 June 2022, accessed at https://www.barandbench.com/news/patna-high-court-to-buy-iphone-13-pro-256-gb-for-all-its-judges-invites-bids.

4 Rajya Sabha, Unstarred Question No. 928 asked by Sanjay Kaka Patil & Ors to the Ministry of Law & Justice on the subject of 'Basic Facilities in Court Complexes' and answered on 8 December 2023.

5 Some special status states like the ones in the North-eastern region are expected to only share 10 per cent of the allocation.
6 Lok Sabha, Unstarred Question No. 317 asked by Kanumuru Raghu Ramakrishna Raju to the Ministry of Law & Justice on the subject of 'e-Courts project' and answered on 21 July 2023.
7 Lok Sabha, Unstarred Question No. 5641 asked by Sanjay Dina & Ors. to the Ministry of Law & Justice on the subject of 'Judicial Reforms' and answered on 29 April 2010.
8 For a good history of court fees in India, please see the following report: Law Commission of India, *Need to fix Maximum Chargeable Court-fees in Subordinate Civil Courts,* (189th Report 2009).
9 Law Commission of India, *Cost of Litigation*', (128th Report 1988), para 4.6.
10 'Indian Association of Lawyers demands rollback of court fees hike in Kerala', *The Hindu,* 18 June 2024, accessed at https://www.thehindu.com/news/national/kerala/indian-association-of-lawyers-demands-rollback-of-court-fees-hike-in-kerala/article68300427.ece.
11 Bhavya Sudhir, 'Beyond Revenue—Reimagining Court Fees as a Policy Tool for Judicial Administration', Daksh, 20 February 2024, accessed at https://www.dakshindia.org/beyond-revenue-court-fee-policy-tool/.
12 Ibid.
13 Schedule to the Insolvency and Bankruptcy (Application to Adjudicating Authority) Rules, 2016.
14 28 U.S.C. 1914—District Court Miscellaneous Fee Schedule, accessed at https://www.uscourts.gov/services-forms/fees/district-court-miscellaneous-fee-schedule.
15 *All India Judges Association v. Union of India* AIR 1993 SC 2493, accessed at https://indiankanoon.org/doc/1977799/; *All India Judges Association v. Union of India* AIR 2002 (4) SCC 247, accessed at https://indiankanoon.org/doc/125557979/; *All India Judges Association v. Union of India* 1998 (9) SCC 245, accessed at https://indiankanoon.org/doc/1957832/.
16 Justice M. Jagannadha Rao, *Report of the Task Force on Judicial Impact Assessment,* 2008, constituted by the Supreme Court in the *Salem Advocates Bar Association (II) v. Union of India* (2005) 6 SCC 344.

17 For a good discussion of the American position, please see Andrew W. Yates, 'Using Inherent Judicial Power in a State-Level Budget Dispute', Vol. 62, *Duke Law Journal* (2013) p. 1463.

18 *All India Judges Association v. Union of India* AIR 2002 (4) SCC 247, accessed at https://indiankanoon.org/doc/125557979/.

19 'HC wants recommendations on reducing court fee notified by December 22', *The Hindu,* 9 December 2016, accessed at https://www.thehindu.com/news/national/tamil-nadu/HC-wants-recommendations-on-reducing-court-fee-notified-by-December-22/article16780119.ece.

20 'High Court directs Delhi govt. to expedite financial sanction to implement hybrid hearing project', *The Indian Express,* 2 May 2024, accessed at https://indianexpress.com/article/cities/delhi/delhi-high-court-directs-delhi-govt-to-expedite-financial-sanction-hybrid-hearing-9301200/; *Anil Kumar Hajelay & Ors. v. Hon'ble High Court of Delhi* W.P.(C) No. 2018 of 2021 before the Delhi High Court, order dated 19 April 2024.

21 We calculated this amount per the capital outlay earmarked under the heads of 'Court Buildings' and 'Law & Judicial' in the Project-Wise Outlay for the year 2022-23 of the Government of Delhi, accessed at https://delhiplanning.delhi.gov.in/sites/default/files/Planning/generic_multiple_files/schemewise_budget_2023-24.pdf.

22 Government of India, Department of Justice, *Report of the Working Group for the Twelfth Five-Year Plan (2012-2017),* p. 14.

23 Niranjan Sahoo, 'Why the central scheme for judicial infrastructure needs and urgent overhaul?', ORF, 29 January 2022, accessed at https://www.orfonline.org/expert-speak/why-the-central-scheme-for-judicial-infrastructure-needs-an-urgent-overhaul.

24 Government of India, Department of Justice, Funds released under eCourts Project, accessed at https://dashboard.doj.gov.in/ecourts-projects-phaseII/funds.php.

25 Press Information Bureau, 'Computerisation of Courts', 8 August 2024, accessed at https://pib.gov.in/PressReleasePage.aspx?PRID=2042986.

26 Rajya Sabha, Question no. 4115 asked by Husain Dalwani on the subject of 'Low utilisation of budgetary allocation by states' and

answered on 7 April 2017.; Surya Prakash B.S., 'Budgeting for the Judiciary', *State of the Indian Judiciary,* Daksh (2016) p. 78, accessed at https://papers.ssrn.com/sol3/papers.cfm?abstract_id=3826289.

27 Arindam DasGupta, 'The 13th Finance Commission and Improving Fiscal Outcomes: An Assessment', *EPW,* Vol. XLV No. 48, 27 November 2010.

28 M. G. Rao, 'The 13th FC Report: Conundrum in Conditionalities', *EPW,* Vol. 45, No. 48, 27 November 2010.

29 Comptroller & Auditor General, *Audit Report (General & Social Sector)—Performance Audit of Modernisation of Judicial Infrastructure,* 31 March 2016, p. 25, accessed at https://cag.gov.in/uploads/download_audit_report/2017/Chapter_2_Performance_Audits_of_Report_No.3_of_2017_-_General_and_Social_Sector,_Government_of_Tamil_Nadu.pdf.

30 Comptroller & Auditor General, *Report of the Comptroller and Auditor General of India on General and Social Sector,* March 2016.

31 For a more detailed discussion on the CSS, please see Chitrakshi Jain et. al., 'Budgeting Better for Courts: An Evaluation of the Rs. 7,460 crores Released Under the Centrally Sponsored Scheme for Judicial Infrastructure', Vidhi Centre for Legal Policy, August 2019, accessed at https://vidhilegalpolicy.in/research/budgeting-better-for-courts-an-evaluation-of-the-rs-7460-crores-released-under-the-centrally-sponsored-scheme-for-judicial-infrastructure/.

32 Ibid, p.24-25.

33 Ibid.

34 Ibid, p.16

35 The portal which is called Nyaya-Vikas can be accessed here: https://bhuvan-nyayavikas.nrsc.gov.in/.

36 R. Balaji, 'CJI Ramana wishes for judicial financial autonomy', *The Telegraph,* 24 October 2021, accessed at https://www.telegraphindia.com/india/cji-ramana-wishes-for-judicial-financial-autonomy/cid/1835692.

37 Prashant Reddy T. and Chitrakshi Jain, 'India needs judicial reforms—but granting more powers to the chief justice won't solve anything', *Scroll,* 24 February 2022, accessed at https://scroll.in/article/1018077/india-needs-judicial-reforms-but-granting-more-powers-to-the-chief-justice-wont-solve-anything.

38 PTI, 'At joint conference, various CMs opposed national body to create judicial infra in states', *Economic Times,* 2 May 2022, accessed at https://economictimes.indiatimes.com/news/india/at-joint-conference-various-cms-opposed-national-body-to-create-judicial-infra-in-states/articleshow/91238163.cms?from=mdr.
39 Constitution of India, Articles 146 and 229.
40 Constituent Assembly Debates, Volume VIII, 27 May 1949, p. 388-392, accessed at https://eparlib.nic.in/bitstream/123456789/763269/1/cad_27-05-1949.pdf.
41 National Commission to Review the Working of the Constitution, *A Consultation Paper on the Financial Autonomy of the Indian Judiciary,* 2001, para 11.3, accessed at https://legalaffairs.gov.in/sites/default/files/Financial%20Autonomy%20of%20the%20Indian%20Judiciary.pdf.
42 Vaidehi Misra et. al., 'Sunshine in the Courts, Ranking the High Courts on their Compliance with the RTI Act', 2019, Vidhi Centre for Legal Policy, accessed at https://vidhilegalpolicy.in/research/sunshine-in-the-courts-ranking-the-high-courts-on-their-compliance-with-the-rti-act/.
43 Departmentally Related Parliamentary Standing Committee on Personnel, Public Grievances and Law and Justice, *Action Taken on One Hundred Sixteenth Report of the Committee on Demands for Grants (2022-23),* (123rd Report, 2022) p. 32, accessed at https://sansad.in/getFile/rsnew/Committee_site/Committee_File/ReportFile/18/171/123_2023_4_12.pdf?source=rajyasabha.
44 Reply from the Supreme Court of India under the RTI Act bearing No. Dy. No. 11266/RTI/22-23/SCI dated 17 March 2023.
45 Reply from the Office of the Director General of Audit (Central Expenditure) under the RTI Act bearing No.Admn.I/RTI/CJ/2023-24/2870 dated 13 November 2023.
46 Chitrakshi Jain et. al., 'A Call for Better Planning in the Judiciary', Vidhi Centre for Legal Policy, 2020, accessed at https://vidhilegalpolicy.in/wp-content/uploads/2020/06/BackToBasics_digital.pdf, p.19-20.
47 *Satara District Bar Association v. State of Maharashtra & The High Court of Bombay* W.P. No. 3879 of 2021 before the Bombay High Court, decided on 22 March 2022.

48 Manoj Mitta, 'Defiance and irregularities mark the life and personality of Justice V. Ramaswami' *India Today,* 15 June 1993, accessed at https://www.indiatoday.in/magazine/profile/story/19930615-defiance-and-irregularities-mark-the-life-and-personality-of-justice-v-ramaswami-811164-1993-06-14.

9. Reforming Court Bureaucracies

1 The indicative list of persons employed in district courts were found in a reply to an RTI application from the Bombay High Court, dated 27 February 2023, RIA/141/2023.

2 'Steno on leave, Judge types orders posts 'pain' online', *DT Next,* 21 November 2021, accessed at https://www.dtnext.in/city/2021/11/21/steno-on-leave-judge-types-orders-posts-pain-online; *Shri Ramesh Chander Goel v. Master Chirag Goel,* 2023/DHC/000491, accessed at https://indiankanoon.org/doc/18716048/; *Nijalingappa v. State of Karnataka,* Crl. Pet. No. 102239 of 2023 before the Karnataka High Court, 6 October 2023, accessed at https://indiankanoon.org/doc/25067228/.

3 Jharkhand High Court, Judicial Officers' Work Disposal (Gradings) Rules, 2015, accessed at https://cdnbbsr.s3waas.gov.in/s3ec0554ebdfbbfe6c31c39aaba9a1ee83/uploads/2023/12/2023121370.pdf.

4 A study on the Bengaluru courts showed that courts spend an average of 273 days at this stage for civil cases and 210 days for criminal cases. Vidhi Centre for Legal Policy, Daksh, 'Litigation Landscape of Bengaluru', 2019, accessed at https://dakshindia.org/wp-content/uploads/2019/08/litigation-landscape-bengaluru-rural-full-report-july-2019.pdf; Also, it is these apprehensions related to false reports of service that have ensured that in-person delivery survives as a method, although many High Courts have enacted rules that recognise service through other means, with proof of delivery safeguards.

5 Government of India, *Report of the Civil Justice Committee,* 1925, p. 3-4.

6 Supreme Court of India, Centre for Planning and Research, *State of the Judiciary: A report on infrastructure, budgeting, human resources*

and ICT, November 2023, Annexure K, p. 213, accessed at https://main.sci.gov.in/pdf/CRP/15122023_082223.pdf.

7 Ibid.

8 Reply from the Bombay High Court under the RTI Act bearing registration no: RIA/141/2023 and dated 27 February 2023.

9 Ministry of Finance, *Implementation of recommendation of Thirteenth Finance Commission—issue of utilisation of grant-in-aid for Improvement in Justice Delivery recommended by Thirteenth Finance Commission,* 20 September 2010, No. F 32(30) FCD/2010, accessed at https://dea.gov.in/sites/default/files/Guidelines%20for%20Improvement%20in%20Justice%20Delivery.pdf.

10 Thirteenth Finance Commission, 2010-2015, *Volume I: Report,* December 2009, p. 221-222, accessed at https://fincomindia.nic.in/asset/doc/commission-reports/13th-FC/english/13fcrengVol1.pdf.

11 Law Commission of India, 127th Report, *Resource Allocation for Infrastructural Services in Judicial Administration* (127th Report, 1988), p. 47 accessed at https://cdnbbsr.s3waas.gov.in/s3ca0daec69b5adc880fb464895726dbdf/uploads/2022/08/2022080875-1.pdf.

12 *Supra* n. 5, p. 145 (Civil Justice Committee; 1925).

13 Delhi District Courts Establishment (Appointment and Conditions of Service) Rules, 2012, accessed at https://cdnbbsr.s3waas.gov.in/s3ec0277ee3bc58ce560b86c2b59363281/documents/rules_and_regulations/DELHI_DISTRICT_COURTS_RULE_2012_1.pdf.

14 Geeta Oberoi, 'The Curious Case of Court Manager in India: From its Creation to its Desertion', 9(1) *International Journal for Court Administration* (2017), accessed at https://iacajournal.org/articles/245/files/submission/proof/245-1-857-1-10-20171225.pdf.

15 Shruthi Naik & Deepika Kinhal, 'Enabling Judicial Support Staff Key to Speed Up Justice', *Deccan Herald,* 12 August 2019, accessed at https://www.deccanherald.com/opinion/enabling-judicial-support-staff-key-to-speed-up-justice-753669.html; Chethan Kumar, 'With 16% vacancies, lower courts in Karnataka grapple with 20L+ pending cases', *The Times of India,* 12 August 2024, accessed at https://timesofindia.indiatimes.com/city/bengaluru/with-16-vacancies-

lower-courts-in-karnataka-grapple-with-20l-pending-cases/articleshow/112453717.cms; Rajya Sabha, Unstarred Question No. 416 asked by Dharmshila Gupta to the Ministry of Law & Justice on the subject of 'Shortage of Staff in Courts in Bihar' and answered on 25 July 2024.

16 High Courts at Gauhati, Bombay, Jammu and Kashmir, Gujarat, Meghalaya, Allahabad, Himachal Pradesh, Tripura recruit for all positions. *Supra* n. 6, p. 215 (*State of Judiciary*; 2023).

17 *Renu & Ors v. District and Sessions Judge, Tis Hazari*, CA 979 of 2014 before the Supreme Court of India decided on 12 February 2014 accessed at https://indiankanoon.org/doc/145930141/.

18 Anand Vardhan, 'The unchanging litany of woes against state public service commissions', *Newslaundry*, 14 May 2022, accessed at https://www.newslaundry.com/2022/05/14/the-unchanging-litany-of-woes-against-state-public-service-commissions.

19 High Court of Punjab and Haryana, Society for Centralized Recruitment of Staff in Subordinate Courts, accessed at https://sssc.gov.in/Guidelinesphc.aspx.

20 Pratik Datta et. al., 'How to Modernise the Working of Courts and Tribunals in India', 2019, NIPFP Working Paper Series, accessed at https://www.nipfp.org.in/media/medialibrary/2019/03/WP_2019_258.pdf.

21 Reply from the Supreme Court under RTI Act bearing registration no. DY. No.1728/RTI/23-24/SCI dated 26 September 2023.

22 National Court Management Systems of the Supreme Court of India, *Baseline Report on Human Resource Development Strategy* (2016) p. 26, accessed at https://main.sci.gov.in/pdf/NCMS/Human%20Resource%20Development%20Strategy.pdf.

23 United States Courts, About Federal Courts, accessed at https://www.uscourts.gov/about-federal-courts/judicial-administration.

24 Rajya Sabha, Departmentally Related Parliamentary Standing Committee on Personnel, Public Grievances and Law and Justice, *Demands for Grants (2018-19) Ministry of Law and Justice,* (96th Report, 2018) p. 52 [6.53] accessed at https://sansad.in/getFile/rsnew/Committee_site/Committee_File/ReportFile/18/104/96_2018_6_17.pdf?source=rajyasabha.

25 *Supra* n. 6, (*State of Judiciary*; 2023).

10. Redesigning the Judiciary

1 K. Rajagopal, 'Supreme Court proposes fast-track courts to clear dishonoured cheque cases', *The Hindu,* 4 March 2021, accessed at https://www.thehindu.com/news/national/supreme-court-proposes-fast-track-courts-to-clear-dishonoured-cheque-cases/article33991492.ece.

2 Reserve Bank of India, *Report of the Committee on Legal Aspects Relating to Operations of Banking and Financial System,* Bombay, 1992, p.9.

3 For a comprehensive history on the evolution of the Indian legal system, please refer to M. P. Jain, *Outlines of Indian Legal History,* N. M. Tripathi Pvt Ltd, 1952.

4 Ibid, p. 386-87.

5 B. Shiva Rao, *The Framing of India's Constitution: Select Documents,* Vol. II, Indian Institute of Public Administration, 1968, p. 447.

6 Ibid, p. 196.

7 Article 131A introduced by the 42nd Constitutional (Amendment) Act, 1976.

8 Article 32A introduced by the 42nd Constitutional (Amendment) Act, 1976.

9 Articles 323A & 323B of the Constitution.

10 Entry 11A of List III of the Seventh Schedule of the Constitution of India.

11 Rajeev Dhavan, *The Amendment: Conspiracy or Revolution?,* Wheeler Publishing, 1978.

12 'Enact law for additional courts to deal with pendency of cheque bounce cases: SC suggests Centre', *Economic Times,* 4 March 2021, accessed at https://economictimes.indiatimes.com/news/politics-and-nation/enact-law-for-additional-courts-to-deal-with-pendency-of-cheque-bounce-cases-sc-suggests-centre/articleshow/81333342.cms?from=mdr.

13 This data has been generated from the websites of the Lok Sabha and Rajya Sabha using specific keywords.

14 Sandeep Joshi, 'West U.P. lawyers may intensify stir', *The Hindu,* 10 January 2010, accessed at https://www.thehindu.com/news/national/other-states/west-up-lawyers-may-intensify-stir/article6773930.ece.

15 As explained in the 'Statement of Objects and Reasons' of the High Court of Kerala (Establishment of a Permanent Bench at Thiruvananthapuram) Bill, 2023, which is a private member bill moved by MP Shashi Tharoor.

16 Law Commission of India, *On the Proposal that High Courts Should Sit in Benches at Different Places in a State,* (4th Report 1956).

17 Ibid, para 5.

18 *Federation of Bar Associations in Karnataka v. Union of India* 2000 (6) SCC 715, accessed at https://indiankanoon.org/doc/1847945/.

19 Rajya Sabha Q. No. 2512 asked by Dr. Sasmit Patra to the Ministry of Law & Justice on the subject of 'Establishment of High Court Benches in the country' and answered on 10 August 2023, accessed at https://rsdebate.nic.in/bitstream/123456789/743092/1/PQ_260_10082023_U2512_p329_p331.pdf.

20 Lok Sabha Q. No. 2755 asked by Ramcharan Bohra and Shri Gopal Jee Thakur to the Ministry of Law & Justice on the subject of 'Setting up of benches of High Court' and answered on 10 July 2019, accessed at https://eparlib.nic.in/bitstream/123456789/952649/1/AU2755.pdf.

21 M. Govinda Rao and Nirvikar Singh, *The Political Economy of Federalism in India,* OUP, 2006, p. 41-61; online edition 2012 accessed at https://doi.org/10.1093/acprof:oso/9780195686937.003.0003.

11. Bringing Back Juries

1 *K. M. Nanavati v. State of Maharashtra* 1962 AIR (SC) 605.

2 James Jaffe, 'Not the Right People: Why Jury Trials were Abolished in India', *Socio-Legal Review,* 1 October 2020, accessed at https://www.sociolegalreview.com/post/not-the-right-people-why-jury-trials-were-abolished-in-india.

3 Ibid.

4 R. L. Lerner, *The Jury: A Very Short Introduction,* Oxford University Press, 2023, p. 46-48.

5 Ibid.

6 Sanja Kutnjak Ivković, and Valerie P. Hans, 'A Worldwide Perspective on Lay Participation', in *Juries, Lay Judges, and Mixed Courts: A Global Perspective,* edited by Sanja Kutnjak Ivković, Shari Seidman Diamond and others, Cambridge University Press, 2021, pp. 323–45.

7 Supra n. 4 (Lerner, 2023).

8 Ibid.

9 Jaihyun Park, 'The Korean Jury System: The First Decade' in *Juries, Lay Judges, and Mixed Courts: A Global Perspective*, edited by Sanja Kutnjak Ivković, Shari Seidman Diamond and others, Cambridge University Press, 2021 p. 88.

10 Supra n. 4, p. 51 (Lerner, 2023).

11 Thom Brooks, 'The right to trial by jury', in *The Right to a Fair Trial*, Routledge, 2017, pp. 83-98

12 Alexandra D. Lahav, 'The Jury and Participatory Democracy', 55 *William and Mary Law Review,* (2014) pp. 1029, 1036,

13 Ibid. 1035

14 See also, Valerie P Hans, and Jonathan D. Casper, 'Chapter 8: Trial by Jury, the Legitimacy of the Courts, and Crime Control', eds. Lawrence Friedman and George Fisher, *The Crime Conundrum*, Routledge, 2019, pp. 93-106.

15 Jennifer K. Robbennolt, 'Evaluating Juries by Comparison to Judges: A Benchmark for Judging?', 32(2) *Florida State University Law Review* (2005) pp. 469, 485–86; Harry Kalven, Jr., 'The Dignity of the Civil Jury', 1964, 50 *Virginia Law Review* (1964) pp.1055, 1066–67; Shari Seidman Diamond & Francis Doorley, 'What a (Very) Smart Trial Judge Knows About Juries', 64 *DePaul Law Review,* (2015) pp. 373, 374.

16 NYU Law News, 'Justice Sonia Sotomayer reflects on civil juries and is honored by Annual Survey of American Law', 12 February 2016, accessed at https://www.law.nyu.edu/news/Sonia-Sotomayor-Supreme-Court-Annual-Survey-American-Law-Civil-Jury-Project.

17 Kathleen M. O'Malley, 'Trial by Jury: Why it Works and Why it Matters', 68(4) *American University Law Review* (2019) p. 1095, accessed at https://digitalcommons.wcl.american.edu/cgi/viewcontent.cgi?article=2091&context=aulr.

18 Alexander Hamilton, Federalist no. 83, 558-74, accessed at https://press-pubs.uchicago.edu/founders/documents/amendVIIs12.html.

19 Supra n. 12, p. 1045 (Lahav; 2014).

20 Supra n. 4, pp. 127-128 (Lerner; 2023).

21 James M. Donovan, 'Magistrate and Juries in France', 22(3) *French Historical Studies* (1999), pp. 379-387.

22 Code of Criminal Procedure 1898 (CrPC 1898) ss 276, 319. The property and income requirement can be found in the rules laid down by the High Courts prescribing qualification criteria for selecting jurors. See Rules of the Calcutta High Court (Original Side), 1914, https://indiankanoon.org/doc/176072104/. Some historians have observed instances in Uttar Pradesh of women jurors. See also Kalyani Ramnath 'The Colonial Difference between Law and Fact: Notes on the Criminal Jury in India', 50(3) *The Indian Economic & Social History Review*, (2013) p. 357. https://doi.org/10.1177/0019464613494624.

23 Law Commission of India. *Reform of Judicial Administration,* (14th Report 1958).

24 CrPC 1861 s 329, accessed at https://lddashboard.legislative.gov.in/sites/default/files/legislative_references/1861.pdf.

25 Rules of the Calcutta High Court (Original Side), 1914, https://indiankanoon.org/doc/176072104/; Rules of the High Court if Judicature at Rajasthan, 1952, https://hcraj.nic.in/hcraj/Allfiles/RHCRules1952.pdf.

26 Code of Criminal Procedure, 1872 (CrPC 1872).

27 CrPC, 1872 s 263.

28 CrPC 1872, ss 305(3), 308.

29 Supra n. 4, p. 59 (Lerner; 2023).

30 The Commonwealth of India Bill (National Convention, India, 1925), accessed at https://www.constitutionofindia.net/historical-constitution/the-commonwealth-of-india-bill-national-convention-india-1925/.

31 CrPC 1861, s 324.

32 Government of India, *Civil Justice Committee Report,* (Central Publication Branch 1925), pp. 582-583.

33 Parliamentary Debates (House of the People), Vol III: No 18, 28 August 1953, 1803, 1837, accessed at https://eparlib.nic.in/bitstream/123456789/55657/1/lsd_01_04_28-08-1953.pdf

34 Ibid. pp. 1837-1838

35 Government of Uttar Pradesh, *Report of the Uttar Pradesh Judicial Reforms Committee,* (1952) p. 54, accessed at https://dspace.gipe.ac.in/xmlui/bitstream/handle/10973/51464/GIPE-071088.pdf?sequence=1&isAllowed=y.

36 Supra n. 2 (Jaffe; 2010).

37 Richard Vogler, 'The international development of the jury: The role of the British Empire', *Revue internationale de droit pénal,* Vol. 72(1), 525-550, (2001), accessed at https://doi.org/10.3917/ridp.721.0525.

38 Supra n. 23, p. 871 (LCI 14th Report; 1958).

39 Law Commission of India, *Report on Code of Criminal Procedure 1898,* (41st Report 1969).

40 Law Commission of India. *Reform of Judicial Administration,* (14th Report Vol. II 1958) pp. 878-882.

41 Catherine S. Meshievitz & Marc Galanter, 'In Search of Nyaya Panchayats: The Politics of a Moribund Institution' in Richard Abel (ed), *The Politics of Informal Justice: Comparative Studies,* New York, Academic Press, 1982, pp. 47-77; Upendra Baxi and Marc Galanter, 'Panchayati Justice: An Indian Experience in Legal Access', in M. Cappelletti and B. Garth, *Access to Justice & Emerging Issues & Perspectives,* Milan: Guiffre; Alpen aan den Rijn: Sijthoff & Noordhoff, 1979, p. 368-377.

42 Louis Dumont, *Homo Hierarchicus: The Caste System and its Implications,* University of Chicago Press, 1980; Robert S. Robins, 'India: Judicial Panchayats in Uttar Pradesh', 11(2) *The American Journal of Comparative Law* (1962) pp. 239–46.

43 Law Commission of India, *Gram Nyayalaya,* (114th Report 1986).

44 PRS India webpage on the Gram Nyayalayas Bill, 2007: https://prsindia.org/billtrack/the-gram-nyayalayas-bill-2007.

45 Ministry for Panchayati Raj, *The Report of the Committee on Nyaya Panchayats,* 2007.

46 Supra no. 41, p. 363 (Baxi & Galanter; 1979).

47 See, for example, Sanford C. Gordon, 'Elected v. Appointed judges', (2024) Democracy Reform Primer Series, accessed at https://effectivegov.uchicago.edu/primers/elected-vs-appointed-judges.

48 Akshaya Mukul, 'Law Ministry: Nyaya Panchayat Bill is Unconstitutional', *The Times of India,* 8 July 2007, accessed at https://timesofindia.indiatimes.com/india/law-ministry-nyaya-panchayat-bill-is-unconstitutional/articleshow/2185228.cms.

49 As discussed in Chapter 12 on procedure and evidentiary rules.

50 Pratiksha Baxi, Out of Place in an Indian Court: Notes on Researching Rape in a District Court in Gujarat (1996–8), In: Chua LJ, Massoud MF, eds. *Out of Place: Fieldwork and Positionality in Law and Society*, Cambridge Studies in Law and Society, Cambridge University Press; 2024, pp. 119-138.

51 Kiruba Munusamy, 'The nauseating nepotism and caste-based discrimination that exists in Indian judiciary', *The Print*, 11 April 2018, accessed at https://theprint.in/opinion/the-nepotism-and-caste-based-discrimination-that-exists-in-indian-judiciary/48542/.

12. Making Procedural and Evidentiary Rules Great Again

1 Upendra Baxi, *The Crisis of the Indian Legal System*, Vikas Publishing House, 1981, p. 41-43.

2 Justice Abdul Nazeer, Retired judge of the Supreme Court of India, 'Decolonisation of the Indian Legal System', Speech delivered at the National Council Meeting of the Akhil Bharatiya Adhivakta Parishad, Hyderabad, 26 December 2001, https://www.livelaw.in/pdf_upload/lectureofjusticesabdulnazeer-406739.pdf.

3 Law Commission of India, *Delays & Arrears in Trial Courts,* (77th Report 1978) para 3.1.

4 Ibid at para 3.4.

5 Government of Uttar Pradesh, *Report of the Uttar Pradesh Judicial Reforms Committee* 1950-51, Superintendent, Printing & Stationary, Uttar Pradesh, India, 1952, Vol. 1, p. 1.

6 Law Commission of India, *Reform of Judicial Administration,* (14th Report, 1958) p. 262.

7 Ibid, p. 263.

8 Reserve Bank of India, *Report of the Committee on Legal Aspects Relating to Operations of Banking and Financial System*, Bombay, 1992, para 2.2.

9 *S.P. Gupta v. President of India & Ors* [1982] 2 SCR 365, accessed at https://indiankanoon.org/doc/1294854/.

10 Harish V. Nair, 'High Court convicts 4 Mid-Day journalists of contempt of court', *Hindustan Times,* 12 September 2007, accessed at https://www.hindustantimes.com/delhi/high-court-convicts-4-mid-day-journalists-of-contempt-of-court/story-

s1XVfDDuvh5ga805zCtPQN.html; *Court on its motion v. M. K.Tayal & Ors.* before the Delhi High Court, decided on 11 September 2007, accessed at https://indiankanoon.org/doc/1710915/. (This judgment was over-ruled ten years later by the Supreme Court.)

11 1979 SCR (3) 532.

12 1984 SCR (2) 67.

13 Anuj Bhuwania, *Courting the People: Public Interest Litigation in Post Emergency India,* Cambridge University Press, 2016, p. 31.

14 The Recovery of Debts & Bankruptcy Act, 1993 (s. 22).

15 *Malay Kumar Ganguly v. Sukumar Mukherjee & Ors* 2009 (9) SCC 221, accessed at https://indiankanoon.org/doc/195460/; *Ethiopian Airlines v. Ganesh Narain Saboo* 2011 (8) SCC 539, accessed at https://indiankanoon.org/doc/33826647/.

16 Government of India, *Civil Justice Committee Report,* (Central Publication Branch 1925) p. 147.

17 Catherine S. Meshievitz and Marc Galanter, 'In Search of Nyaya Panchayats: The Politics of a Moribund Institution' in Richard Abel (ed), *The Politics of Informal Justice: Comparative Studies,* New York, Academic Press, 1982, 47, p. 65.

18 Ibid.

19 Upendra Baxi and Marc Galanter, 'Panchayati Justice: An Indian Experience in Legal Access', in M Cappelletti and B. Garth, *Access to Justice & Emerging Issues & Perspectives,* Milan: Guiffre; Alpen aan den Rijn: Sijthoff & Noordhoff, 1979, p. 368-377.

20 Law Commission of India, *Gram Nyayalayas,* (114th Report, 1986).

21 Ibid, para 6.10, p.34.

22 Bhadra Sinha, 'Why over 16,500 debt recovery cases are stuck in Delhi tribunals—poor infra, lack of staff', *The Print,* 27 December 2022, accessed at https://theprint.in/judiciary/why-over-16500-debt-recovery-cases-are-stuck-in-delhi-tribunals-poor-infra-lack-of-staff/1283406/.

23 'Top 5 tribunals in India have combined backlog of over 3.50 lakh cases, claims Law panel', *The Indian Express,* 29 October 2017, accessed at https://indianexpress.com/article/india/top-5-tribunals-in-india-have-combined-backlog-of-over-3-50-lakh-cases-claims-law-panel-4911883/.

24 'Parliament Panel Asks Central Tribunal To Decide Cases Pending For Over 10 Years', NDTV, 2 April 2023, accessed at https://www.ndtv.com/india-news/parliament-panel-asks-central-administrative-tribunal-to-decided-cases-pending-for-over-10-years-3913481.

25 Manish Raj, 'Forums delay justice, consumers sweat it out', *The Times of India,* 26 January 2014, accessed at https://timesofindia.indiatimes.com/india/forums-delay-justice-consumers-sweat-it-out/articleshow/29406867.cms.

26 National Green Tribunal Act, 2010 (s. 19).

27 *Kantha Vibhag Yuva Koli Samaj Parivartan Trust & Ors v. State of Gujarat & Ors* C.A.No. 1046 of 2019 before the Supreme Court of India, accessed at https://main.sci.gov.in/supremecourt/2019/51/51_2019_34_18_32866_Judgement_21-Jan-2022.pdf.

28 'Setting up Panel Doesn't Absolve Green Tribunal Of Its Duties: Supreme Court', NDTV, 7 September 2021, accessed at https://www.ndtv.com/india-news/constitution-of-committee-does-not-absolve-ngt-of-duty-to-adjudicate-matters-sc-2533117.

29 *Veena Gupta v. Central Pollution Control Board* C.A. No. 1865-1866 of 2022 before the Supreme Court of India, accessed at https://indiankanoon.org/doc/51597736/.

30 Supra n. 13, p. 85 (Bhuwania; 2016).

31 Ibid at p. 84.

32 Ibid at p. 56.

Epilogue: The Democratic Cost of Failing District Courts

1 Jeffrey Gettleman and Hari Kumar, 'After Horrific Rape in India Police Kill Four Suspects', *The New York Times,* 6 December 2019, accessed at https://www.nytimes.com/2019/12/06/world/asia/india-rape-murder-police.html.

2 Piyush Rai and Aakriti Handa, 'Asad Ahmed Case: 5 Encounters Daily in UP, 183 Accused Killed Since 2017', *The Quint,* 15 April 2023, accessed at https://www.thequint.com/news/crime/atiq-ahmed-son-asad-killed-encounter-uttar-pradesh-police-jhansi-umesh-pal-murder-prayagraj-yogi-adityanath-latest-news.

3 Saurav Das, 'Extrajudicial Killings May be Frequent in India's Most

Populous State', *New Lines Magazine*, 5 August 2024, accessed at https://newlinesmag.com/reportage/extrajudicial-killings-may-be-frequent-in-indias-most-populous-state/.

4 Madan B. Lokur, 'Delayed, Denied and Beyond Reach: A Disaster Called India's Justice Delivery System', *The Wire*, 10 August, 2024, accessed at https://thewire.in/law/delayed-denied-and-beyond-reach-a-disaster-called-indias-justice-delivery-system.

5 Reply from the Bombay High Court under the RTI Act bearing No. R.I.A./142/2023, dated 16 February 2023.

Acknowledgements

Writing books such as this one on contemporary policy issues facing India is very difficult in India due to the lack of institutional space or funding. We are thus very grateful for the generous, 'no-strings-attached' financial support provided to us by Dinesh Thakur, philanthropist and the brave whistleblower in the Ranbaxy case that exposed how India's largest pharmaceutical company was playing fast and loose with the quality of drugs that it was exporting to the United States. We are very grateful to Dinesh for his unwavering support.

We are also very grateful to our former colleagues at the Vidhi Centre for Legal Policy where both of us worked in the judicial reforms team, which, at the time, was very generously funded by the Tata Trusts. In specific, we would like to thank Tarika Jain (who also helped us with some specific sections of this book), Reshma Sekhar, Ameen Jauhar, Vaidehi Misra and Shreya Tripathy. We have fond memories of working with them to produce a series of reports on the workings of the district courts. In specific, Chapters 5 and 7 of this book draw upon the research that we conducted with them.

We would also like to thank Sidharth Chauhan, who teaches law at the National Law School of India University, Bengaluru. He is perhaps the only Indian academic to teach a course on the Indian legal system—his reading list for that course was the starting point of our research and helped shape our thinking on the issue. We are also grateful to Harsh Parashar, Sarim Naved and Hasit Seth, all of whom are practising lawyers, for sharing their insights on the workings of the district courts and brainstorming some of the ideas in this book. They do not necessarily agree with all the conclusions in this book. We are also very grateful to Rohit De, professor of history at Yale University, for taking out the time to answer several of our emails on issues pertaining to Indian legal history. We are especially grateful to Raeesa Vakil, a scholar of Indian constitutional law at the National University of Singapore, for reviewing and providing her valuable comments on some of the chapters in this book. Her encouraging feedback on those chapters gave us the confidence that we were on the right path.

We would like to thank Alok Prasanna Kumar, who, for the last decade, has been the most prolific commentator on the issue of judicial reforms in the mainstream Indian press. His writings have provided us with a launchpad for our own thinking on the subject.

While the High Courts in India have a deservedly poor reputation when it comes to transparency, there are some exceptions to the rule. We would like to thank the few Public Information Officers (PIOs) of the few High Courts who complied with the letter and spirit of the Right to Information Act while responding to our queries. Their replies to our queries for data have helped substantiate some of our arguments in this book. If only the remaining PIOs were as helpful, we would have had more data to substantiate our arguments.

Since neither of us authors had any institutional affiliations while writing this book, we had to depend on a variety of open-source databases for access to basic research materials. We are particularly grateful to Internet Archive for providing free access to old reports of the colonial government going back to the 19th century. We also relied extensively on Indian Kanoon and CaseMine, which are websites that provide open access to judgments delivered by Indian courts. Lastly, the superb online databases of the Lok Sabha and the Rajya Sabha, which have made historical parliamentary records easily accessible to everybody for no fee, made it possible for us to track information which otherwise would have been impossible to unearth.

Last, but not the least, we would like to thank the team at Simon & Schuster, especially its publishing director, Elizabeth Kuruvilla. It is not easy for writers like us, who write on contemporary policy challenges facing India, especially on a topic like judicial reforms, to get published. We are grateful to Simon & Schuster for publishing this book.

We would also like to thank Antra K. for designing the evocative cover page of this book.

—Prashant Reddy Thikkavarapu and Chitrakshi Jain

I would like to thank my parents, Sudhakar and Satya for all their support while I wrote this book. I moved back home with them in Hyderabad during this time and the comforts of home made it much easier to focus on writing this book. I am grateful to my parents for many things, including making sure I got the opportunities to pursue my interests even when the times were tough. I am especially grateful to them for teaching me the importance of thinking critically and being original in a country where rote learning is encouraged by the education system.

I would also like to thank Chitrakshi for readily agreeing to co-author this book when I first proposed the idea. She did much of the early spadework by filing RTI applications before we started the writing process. Co-authoring a book can get tricky when both authors have their own work schedules, are located in different cities and are coordinating over the phone, which is a medium of communication not conducive to non-verbal cues, such as an exasperated eyeroll. But co-authoring a book can also be a great learning experience, since the collaboration allows you to brainstorm ideas with another person on a subject of mutual interest, while also splitting the more mundane tasks. I could not have asked for a more enthusiastic co-author than Chitrakshi especially on a subject like reforming district courts, which is a topic that can bring out the cynic in the most optimistic of legal professionals and academics.

I am also very grateful to my brother, Vikas, and my niece, Ankita, a budding editor, for taking out the time to review multiple chapters of this book and provide their feedback on its readability, as non-lawyers. Their feedback was especially useful since we wanted the book to be accessible to readers outside the legal community. Ankita, who took the job especially seriously, gave me very helpful para-wise comments for each chapter—that was no mean task when my only offer of payment was a lunch.

My deep gratitude also to family and friends who have encouraged my attempts at writing books such as this one in their own ways, with small acts such as turning up at events for my earlier books or buying a copy of my book (despite having no interest in the subject) or, even better, gifting my books to others. I appreciate all of it and am thankful for their encouragement.

Last but not the least, I would also like to thank the unfailingly, courteous baristas who served me coffee every day at Third Wave cafes in Hyderabad, where I did most of my share of writing this book. It is surprisingly difficult to find a pleasant place, at a reasonable cost, to write a book, if you are not part of an academic institution. So, for the cost of two beverages a day, Third Wave has proven to be an oasis for my writing.

—P. R. T.

I would foremostly like to thank Prashant for asking me to co-write this book with him. At the time, he was very kindly vouching for the integrity and quality of my work to prospective employers and had sensed I was dissatisfied with the research I was staffed on. The book gave me an opportunity to think deeply about an unglamourous area of interest—reforming Indian district courts. Working with Prashant was also part of the offer and I took it up because it improves my own ways of thinking and writing. I do greatly admire his clarity of thought and his persistence to leave no tasks unfinished; both of these qualities stood well utilized and tested while writing this book.

I am indebted to my parents who educated me and gave me an upbringing that allowed me to think independently. They may have come to regret it over the years; I remain thankful nonetheless.

I also reluctantly thank my sister, Geetanjali, who is both a source of annoyance and warmth in my life. My gratitude also to my friends who travel with me and nourish my life with their companionship.

Lastly, I am thankful to my flatmates—my husband, Sumeysh, and my cat, Bum, who tolerate me at my worst and provide me with the affection and care I need to read, write and exist.

—C. J.

Index

V

W